ALWAYS THERE

ALWAYS THERE

Pamela Evans

headline

First published in 2002
by HEADLINE BOOK PUBLISHING

10 9 8 7 6 5 4 3 2 1

Cataloguing in Publication Data is available
from the British Library

ISBN 0 7472 7096 1

Typeset by
Letterpart Limited, Reigate, Surrey

Printed and bound in Great Britain by
Mackays of Chatham plc, Chatham, Kent

HEADLINE BOOK PUBLISHING
A division of Hodder Headline
338 Euston Road
LONDON NW1 3BH

www.headline.co.uk
www.hodderheadline.com

To Fred and the family, with love.

Chapter One

Undesirables were no rarity on the streets of Notting Hill Gate after dark in 1954, and Daisy Rivers ran into a crowd of them one night as she walked home from the station.

A gang of Teddy boys, gathered outside a late-night café, were amusing themselves by hurling abuse across the street to a group of West Indian youths, whose wide-brimmed fedoras were visible in the neon glare of the street lighting, as characteristic of them as the DA haircuts were of the Teds. The balmy summer night was fraught with obscenities.

'Excuse me, please,' requested Daisy, a petite woman of twenty-five, unfashionably dressed in a cotton dress that was thin and faded from the wear of many summers. 'Can I get by?'

The Teds, who were blocking the pavement and some of the road, ignored her.

'Excuse me,' she repeated more assertively, 'can I get through here . . . *please*?'

Heads turned towards her but none of the gang moved; they just eyed her with a kind of lazy disdain. The Teds around here had a proprietorial attitude towards the streets, almost to the point where the other residents felt they should ask their permission to use them. It was impossible for Daisy not to feel intimidated by these lads, whose drainpipe trousers, crepe-soled shoes and drape jackets were synonymous for many people with the coshes, razors and flick knives some of them were known to carry beneath their Edwardian finery, and which gave the entire youth cult a bad name. Not every boy who belonged to this minority group was a thug – some just liked the clothes – but rebellion against authority and antisocial behaviour were common among the big gangs.

Daisy daren't allow herself to be too unnerved by these or any other dodgy characters because her evening job as a waitress at a Bayswater hotel meant she had no choice but to be out at night on her own. She needed the money to support her two little daughters.

'So, you wanna get by, do yer . . .? Well, we're not sure about that, are we, lads?' one of the youths finally responded in a slow, mocking voice. He had a heavily greased quiff and a frightening earnestness about him.

1

In the luminous glow from the streetlamps Daisy could see the malevolence in his eyes; could feel it emanating from him, a tangible thing. The implied violence in his manner stirred a feeling of panic within her which wasn't entirely related to this situation, and her nerves jangled even more. Desperate to get home, she tried to break through the wall of aggression by pushing past into the road, only to have a youth with protruding teeth and elongated sideburns place himself deliberately in her way. He was wearing the uniform of his kind – a long jacket, plain white shirt with a bootlace tie, a silver chain jangling on his wrist.

It had been a long day and Daisy was tired. 'Oh, for goodness' sake, can't you stop behaving like morons just for long enough to let me get by?' she snapped.

'Ooh, hark at her,' sneered someone.

'Dunno who she thinks she is,' said another.

'Look,' she began through gritted teeth, 'you lot might have nothing better to do than roam the streets making a nuisance of yourselves but I've been working and I want to get home.'

'Don't waste your time on 'er,' one of the others suggested. 'Let 'er pass.'

Daisy had neither the time nor the money to look glamorous, as such, but she was easy on the eye with her big tawny eyes, dainty features and luxuriant light brown hair that fell loosely around her face when it wasn't tucked into her waitress's cap. Her looks didn't go unnoticed by the Teds.

'Fancy her, do yer?' taunted his mate, sizing Daisy up.

'I wouldn't say no,' came the boastful reply. 'She's not smart or nothin'. But she's not bad-looking, and older women are more experienced.' He paused, grinning. 'If you know what I mean.'

'Get out of my way,' demanded Daisy, trying to push past.

'Don't waste your energy trying to stop 'er,' said one of the gang. 'She ain't worth botherin' with. We've more important things to do.'

'Like stirring up trouble with the boys across the street, I suppose,' blurted out the indomitable Daisy.

'So what if we are? They shouldn't be here, stealing our homes and our jobs. They ought to go back to the jungle,' was the youth's ignorant reply.

'That's just the sort of stupid comment I'd expect from a bunch of goons like you,' Daisy said bravely. But she was frighteningly aware that the Teds weren't the only promoters of racial tension around here, which was growing along with the increasing number of immigrants. The Government didn't seem to do much to ease the inevitable culture clash, and the housing shortage didn't help.

'Nigger lover,' the ignorant one accused.

'Black man's trollop,' said another.

2

'Don't you dare talk to me like that,' Daisy objected.

'Why are you sticking up for 'em if you're not going with 'em?' the first one wanted to know.

'Because of something you wouldn't understand,' was her answer. 'It's called decency.'

One of their number stepped forward and stood so close to her she wanted to retch from a pungent mixture of nicotine breath and Brylcreem. 'We've had enough of you. We don't want black sympathisers polluting the air near us, so sling your hook before we catch something off you,' he said to a roar of support from the rest, and they all moved back to let her through, pushing and jeering.

Angry, but realising that further argument would serve no useful purpose and probably fire them up even more on the subject, she went on her way, eventually turning into Portobello Road. This narrow, winding thoroughfare – which was flanked by terraces of small shops and drew crowds to its famous market by day – seemed dismal and sinister at this hour, the heady sounds of jazz music and drunken laughter drifting from the basement windows of a drinking club. There were still some people about, despite the late hour: men talking and shouting outside a pub, some of them staggering; a noisy crowd coming out of a grill-room restaurant; a gathering of youths leaning against a wall and wolf-whistling at some girls, who shrieked expletives in return. It was no wonder this area had a bad reputation, Daisy thought, even more so since the Christie murders at Rillington Place had given it worldwide notoriety.

Turning into a side street, she headed past bomb sites, tumbledown crescents and cavities where the bulldozers had been. Despite the much-needed slum clearance programme in the area, more slums had been created than cleared as the bomb-damaged properties deteriorated further and the housing shortage continued despite some of the slum-dwellers being rehoused in the new towns and suburbs.

This was a contrasting corner of London where occasional gentrified areas thrived alongside poor but cosy neighbourhoods, the latter mostly tenanted by members of the indigenous population, where a sense of community and true neighbourliness still existed. Different again were the large, multi-tenanted houses that were filled with outsiders like Daisy, who lived there because they had nowhere else to go and the accommodation was cheap.

Benly Square came into this category. Huge terraced houses, split into bedsits and flatlets, stood around a small area of balding grassland scattered with broken milk bottles and household litter. Despite the general air of degradation, Daisy felt a warm feeling inside as she hurried up the crumbling steps of number twenty to the dilapidated front door with peeling paint and a rusty knocker.

This neighbourhood was a residential sewer and her tiny part of this

3

house just a couple of shabby furnished rooms in the attic. But they were her home, hers and her daughters'. Rented accommodation was extremely scarce in central London, and unfurnished rooms almost nonexistent so she was grateful to have a roof over her head. Anyway, living in an area like this did have its advantages: there was a kind of freedom here because no one asked you who you were or where you came from or where your children's father was. She could hardly bear to imagine the persecution she would have had to endure in a respectable leafy suburb.

Refusing to dwell on the fact that the new landlord was making the future at the house uncertain for all of his statutory tenants lately, she put her key in the lock, heaving a sigh of relief to be indoors. She made her way up the stairs, careful not to trip on the craters in the lino.

'I'll make us some cocoa, shall I, dear?' offered Nora Dove, Daisy's friend, neighbour and baby-sitter, a middle-aged spinster who lived in the attic rooms across the landing. She was a tall, angular woman with large hands and feet and a little round face that seemed out of proportion with the rest of her. Her poker-straight ginger hair was heavily peppered with grey and clipped to the side with kirby grips. Intelligent, vivid blue eyes beamed out from a sea of freckles, sometimes from behind the spectacles that she strung around her neck because she was always losing them.

'Yes, please,' approved Daisy, emerging from the adjoining bedroom where she'd been checking on her sleeping daughters. She and Nora usually had a companionable bedtime drink together when Daisy got home from work. It was almost a ritual.

'You look dead on your feet,' remarked the older woman, sniffing the milk bottle before pouring some of its contents into a saucepan and putting it on the gas to heat. She and Daisy were quite at home in each other's places and never stood on ceremony.

'We were busy at the hotel tonight so I do feel a bit whacked. But I shall sleep the sleep of the shattered and be fine in the morning,' she said, making light of her tiredness. 'You know me, I'm as strong as a horse.'

Nora nodded but they both knew that wasn't quite true. Daisy's strict upbringing in a Catholic orphanage had given her immense strength of character but her physical health wasn't so robust. Although she didn't make much of it, she was quite delicate and suffered dreadfully from bronchitis in the winter.

'Any problems with the girls while I was out?' Daisy enquired, taking a packet of digestive biscuits out of the cupboard and arranging some on a plate carefully. Poor living conditions hadn't robbed her of the will to maintain certain standards.

4

'None at all, dear. They're never any trouble to me, as you know.' Nora's beautiful diction was incongruous with her humble surroundings but natural to her, and her deep husky voice somehow reflected her warm personality even though it made her sound like a chain smoker. 'They love that Enid Blyton book I got from the library to read to them.'

'I guessed they would,' smiled Daisy.

'They were really tired tonight, though,' Nora went on. 'Neither of them could keep their eyes open beyond the first few pages.'

'That'll be the effect of the warm weather and the fresh air, I expect,' Daisy suggested. 'I took them to Avondale Park this afternoon as a change from playing in the street. At least it's grass under their feet. They certainly got rid of some of their excess energy.'

'They told me all about it,' said Nora, smiling at the memory. 'They had a whale of a time.'

'I try to take them to the park as often as I can in the summer.' The tiny backyard was full of potholes and smelly dustbins so she couldn't let her children play there. 'They're happy enough playing in the street with their skipping ropes and whips and tops but I don't want them to become complete street urchins like some of the poor little devils who play barefoot out there while their mums are in the pub. Once they start school it won't matter so much because they'll be out during the day.'

'Life will be easier for you altogether when they start school,' her friend suggested.

'Yeah, it will but I'm not wishing the time onwards because I enjoy having them at home so much.'

'Enjoy it while you can, dear, they'll grow up fast enough,' nodded Nora. 'Anyway, I'll take them over the park on Sunday for a breather while you're doing your lunchtime shift at the hotel, if the weather's fine.'

Daisy's heart warmed at Nora's endless supply of kindness, all the more genuine because she refused to take payment for looking after Shirley and Belinda, who were just coming up to five and four respectively. Because Daisy couldn't bear the idea of having them minded by a stranger, she worked weekday evenings, when Nora was around to look after them, and the lunchtime shift on Sundays because Nora was at home then too.

'That'll please them,' said Daisy, as the two women settled down with their cocoa in matching ancient and torn brown leatherette armchairs by the open sash window through which a light breeze was wafting, bringing with it foul fumes from the gasworks. 'What would we do without you?'

'You'd manage,' said Nora, settling back. 'But you won't have to because I'll be here for you for as long as you need me.'

While they were talking Daisy glanced idly round the room. Even the most ardently self-deluded couldn't call it smart. But with a little ingenuity and minimum expense, Daisy had managed to create an air of cosiness, despite the landlord's ugly furnishings and the smell of damp that lingered even in summer. New curtains with a bright contemporary pattern added colour to the room and a few cheap ornaments and vases gave it a homely touch. She had even, with the previous landlord's permission, repapered the walls during the six years she'd been here, and bought a second-hand wireless set, which sat on top of the sideboard, from the market.

The kitchen corner was small and basic, with a cooker, a table and a free-standing food cupboard. The cold water sink, which she shared with Nora, was on the landing. There was a leaky, smelly communal bathroom and lavatory for all the tenants on the ground floor.

'You're so good to us,' said Daisy.

'No more than you are to me,' Nora was quick to point out. 'What sort of a life would it be if we didn't help each other?'

'You always seem to be the one doing the helping, though,' observed Daisy, who was deeply indebted to this dear person, 'looking after the girls while I go out to work at night and giving me so much back-up support with them. I only wish there was more I could do for you.'

'You let me be part of your life and I don't need anything more,' Nora assured her. 'Besides, you've got the kiddies to bring up on your own, and I've only got myself to look out for. It's good for me to have someone else to think about. Anyway, I like to think I'm one of the family.'

'And you are.'

Daisy and Nora had become friends almost as soon as Daisy had moved in here. They were mutually supportive but the only practical way Daisy knew of to repay Nora, since she wouldn't take money, was to invite her to share meals with her and the girls on a regular basis and bring her a bottle of stout from the off-licence every so often.

'That means a lot to me,' said Nora.

Of a different generation, they were none the less two of a kind: both outcasts from society's norm, Daisy because she was an unmarried mother, Nora because she was a spinster. Nora, well-spoken and with such lovely manners, was an educated woman from a good family. Daisy had been told her friend's story and found it heartbreaking . . .

Having been an exceptionally bright pupil at school, Nora had gone on to train as a teacher. But while on the training course she'd fallen in love with a fellow student, a young man of a frail constitution. When she'd got pregnant, her outraged parents had banished her from the family in disgust but her lover had stood by her and promised to marry her. But the consumption that had taken so many lives back in the nineteen twenties had already got a hold on him and he'd become sick and died before the two had had a chance to marry.

The shock of his death had resulted in a miscarriage, the strain and grief eventually culminating in a nervous breakdown. Although she'd recovered, her loss of confidence was such that she didn't feel able to do anything other than menial kitchen work, which was why she now worked in a factory canteen instead of a library or a school, and lived in a shabby tenement house instead of a home of her own.

She found great pleasure in books, though. Daisy thought Nora must be one of the library's most regular borrowers, which accounted for her huge store of general knowledge. She was also an avid reader of newspapers so was always well informed about what was going on in the world. She was wise, sensitive and funny – some might say a little eccentric with her idealistic views – but Daisy admired her intelligence; it gave her such dignity.

Sadly, Nora was entirely alone in the world for there had never been a reconciliation with her family, or another man in her life. Once she'd reached an age to be labelled a spinster, men steered clear. Since Daisy had no family either, and had been motherless since she was five, they found strength and encouragement in each other. Nora was the most loving surrogate grannie her daughters could have wished for and the closest friend Daisy had ever had.

Now Daisy told Nora about the Teddy boys she had encountered on the way home.

'Young buggers. They're attention-seeking, that's all,' announced Nora. 'There was an article in the paper the other day about these Teddy boy gangs we've been seeing on the streets just lately. They're just working-class boys looking for some sort of an identity by wearing outrageous clothes and behaving badly.'

'Some of them can get quite violent, though,' declared Daisy, 'pursuing vandalism in the streets and dance halls. They smashed up a café the other week, according to the local paper.'

'Their violence is usually directed at other gangs, though, I think,' Nora pointed out in an effort to reassure Daisy. 'They might give you a lot of cheek but I don't think they'd actually harm you physically.'

'They were spoiling for a fight with the West Indian lads tonight,' Daisy told her.

'Because they're a rival group and the Teds see them as a threat,' surmised Nora. 'I don't think people like us are in any danger from them.'

'I don't either, but it doesn't feel like that when you come up against a crowd of them,' Daisy told her. 'I tried not to show it but they scared the pants off me.'

'Who wouldn't be scared?' Nora sympathised. 'Anyway, it's not nice for you to be out on the streets at that time of night on your own.'

'I don't have any choice, unless I put the girls into a nursery and go to work during the day,' Daisy reminded her. 'Working evenings suits me for the moment.'

Nora loved Daisy as her own, and her heart ached to see her struggling to raise her daughters with no contribution from their father, Nat Barker, who scrounged off her and used her. He hadn't actually deserted her when she fell pregnant but he hadn't helped her either. In Nora's opinion he was a thoroughly bad lot who didn't give a damn about Daisy or his beautiful daughters and didn't deserve her loyalty.

'Yes, I realise that, dear. So you'll just have to try not to let all this talk of Teddy boy violence in the papers frighten you on the way home. After all, we haven't yet reached a stage where a woman isn't safe to walk the streets at night, not even around here.'

Daisy cradled her cocoa mug in her hands, hesitant about her next words because she knew Nora didn't approve of the subject of her enquiry. 'Did anyone call while I was out?' she asked.

The other woman knew exactly who she meant but just said, 'No, dear. Nobody called.'

'Oh.' Her obvious disappointment twisted Nora's heart. 'I just thought Nat might have popped in to see the girls, if he happened to be passing. He knows I'd be at work so he wouldn't have called to see me.' She paused. 'Still, I suppose he guessed that the girls would be in bed.'

Nora believed that the main reason Nat Barker was likely to call on Daisy was to get his thieving hands on her pay packet. Either that or something of a carnal nature. It certainly wouldn't be out of genuine concern for her. Nora had been there to pick up the pieces on too many occasions to think well of him. He'd let Daisy down, broken promises and even stolen money from her purse. Her loveless childhood had made her strong and independent but it had also made her hungry for love, and she was a naturally warm and giving woman with a weak spot when it came to Nat.

'You're better off when he stays away,' she blurted out.

'Nat's all right,' defended Daisy, who had a tigerish need to stand by her man.

'He breaks your heart on a regular basis,' Nora couldn't help pointing out, though she did try not to make her feelings known too often because Daisy was so defensive of him. 'You should value yourself more than to let him go on doing it.'

'I never was attracted to gentlemanly types.' Daisy kept her tone light to avoid a serious argument. 'Anyway, he's the father of my kids, and we are sort of engaged. I know I don't have a ring but we do have an understanding.'

'If he had any sense of responsibility, you wouldn't have to go out waiting on tables at night to feed the girls because he'd be doing what he should and looking after you all,' was Nora's impulsive response.

In common with many women, marriage was the ultimate to Daisy. She didn't want a career or a good job or independence, just marriage to Nat and a family life for her children. 'He'll make an honest woman of me one of these days, you'll see,' she said.

The older woman frowned. Nat had been promising to do that ever since Nora had known Daisy. 'You're worth better than him,' she burst out. 'The best thing you can do is get rid of him.'

'If only it was that simple,' sighed Daisy, and the troubled expression in her eyes pierced Nora's heart. 'You're an intelligent woman, Nora. You were in love once. You must know that we don't have a choice in these things, and you can't stop loving someone just because they don't treat you right. Maybe it's the bad boy in him that attracts me to him – women have fallen for rogues since time began. I don't know why, but I do know that I can't change the way I feel about him.'

Nora regretted having let her affection for Daisy cause her to speak from the heart. It was bad enough falling for someone like Nat. Daisy didn't need to have it rubbed in. 'I shouldn't have spoken out like that. You've enough problems. You don't need me going on at you.'

'That's all right,' said Daisy with a shrug. 'I know it's because you care about me.'

Nora nodded.

'In romantic stories the orphan girl usually claws her way out of poverty and finds herself a rich husband and lives happily ever after,' Daisy went on. 'Unfortunately, it doesn't work like that in real life. I didn't plan to get involved with someone like Nat, a ducker and diver who's never had a proper job in his life and who ignores me and the girls for weeks at a time. But I have done, and that's all there is to it.' She paused, thinking back to the time when Nat had asked her to marry him and how wonderful and romantic that had been. After he'd persuaded her to sleep with him, however, he'd said the wedding would have to wait until he had enough money to give her the sort of wedding she deserved; then the delay had been because he didn't have a decent home to offer her. By the time she'd realised he was just making excuses she'd been too hopelessly besotted to end the relationship, and also pregnant with Shirley as a result of Daisy's idealistic Catholic views on contraception that she'd been later forced to revise for practical reasons after Belinda's birth. 'I have to go on believing that he'll marry me one day because I so much want us to be together.'

Lowering her eyes, Nora tightened her jaw with the effort of holding back. She'd already said too much on the subject. It was obvious to her that Nat Barker had no intention of marrying Daisy and she believed that the young woman knew that in her heart too. Nora

9

had seen her reviled and abused because of her status as an unmarried mother; she'd even been refused help with the pain during labour when she was having the girls because she wasn't married. Nat could have spared her all that but he'd chosen not to because he was too damned selfish.

Nora's dearest wish was to see Daisy married to a decent man who would treat her with the love and respect she deserved. But what chance did a single woman with two kids and a ruined reputation have of finding someone like that?

'I can't pretend to like Nat or think he's right for you, dear,' she said kindly. 'But if he really is the one you want, I hope it works out for you, and I'll try not to go on at you about him.'

'Thanks, Nora.'

'And on a lighter note,' said Nora, hoping to defuse the tension with a swift change of subject, 'are you coming down the Porto tomorrow?'

'You bet,' replied Daisy. They always went to Portobello market together on a Saturday afternoon.

Nora had a sudden idea to remove any lingering awkwardness between them. 'How about us having a ceremonial tearing up of ration books as we won't be needing them any more after today?' she suggested.

'What a smashing idea.'

Daisy went to the sideboard drawer to get hers while Nora popped across the landing for her own. Together they ripped the ration books into little pieces and threw them in the air to celebrate the end of all rationing after fourteen years, with meat the last thing to go. As the books turned to confetti, Daisy began to laugh, filling the room with the infectious giggle that was so much a part of her. They had come to the end of a punishing era and it felt so good they both went into paroxysms of laughter at the sheer joy of it.

The streetlights shining through the attic window was sufficient for Daisy to see to get undressed without switching on the bedroom light and possibly disturbing the girls. Slipping her nightdress over her head, she looked at them in the double bed they shared, two heads close together, brown hair spread over the pillow. They were very much alike to look at and had their mother's colouring as well as her eyes. Studying them now in repose, Daisy found their innocence and childish beauty bringing tears to her eyes. Her relationship with her children was the most important and sustaining thing in her life.

Daisy had had a sister once a long time ago; the age difference between them had been about the same as it was between her own daughters. Before the orphanage, they'd shared a bed too, just like Shirley and Belinda did now. She remembered less about her sister than the indescribable pain of losing her when she'd been taken away for adoption. Daisy had cried herself to sleep every night for ages after that. She still couldn't think of it without wanting to weep.

It was as though her sister had never existed after that. Daisy had been told by the nuns that she'd gone away to a new life, and was ordered to forget her. She'd done her best because the nuns were strict disciplinarians and she'd been terrified to defy them, even in thought. Looking back at her childhood from the perspective of a parent, she could see that some of the nuns' treatment of the children had been harsh to the point of cruelty, and their methods were not what she'd use on any child of hers. But although she'd never felt loved, and had truly hated some of the nuns at the time, she'd always felt secure in their care. As an adult, considering her upbringing she'd come to the conclusion that the nuns must have believed their rigid regime to be in the children's best interests. The kids had certainly known what to expect – even if it was a good hiding.

There had been happiness of a kind at the home too, a camaraderie with the other children which meant she'd never felt alone. She'd been bereft of this security and companionship when she left there at fifteen to make her own way in the world.

At some point she must have been told that her father had abandoned her and her sister because that's what she'd grown up to believe. You learned not to ask questions when you lived in an orphanage in the nineteen thirties and forties because it wasn't considered right to give a child personal information.

She'd often wondered what sort of a life her sister was having and longed to see her again. But since Daisy had left St Clare's she'd been too busy surviving from day to day to do anything about finding her. She'd had a variety of jobs: she'd worked in a factory, been a café counterhand, and had got into hotel waitressing after the girls were born.

The very last thing she'd planned was to bring up two children outside of marriage. But having got pregnant, her strict Catholic upbringing had ruled out an illegal abortion and she hadn't been able to bring herself to put her babies up for adoption, or to do what her father had done to her and her sister, just abandon them. She was very glad she hadn't been driven by desperation to take any of these steps because the girls were her *raison d'être*. Her religious faith had been a great strength and comfort to her through it all, in spite of the guilt that came with it.

Gently she covered them up, placed a kiss on each brow and got into the single bed beside them, saying a silent prayer for all the people she cared about, including one of the gentler nuns at St Clare's with whom Daisy had stayed in touch by letter.

In reflective mood as she closed her eyes, she found herself troubled again by the same uneasy feeling she'd had earlier that had

11

been triggered off by the Teddy boys' threatening attitude. Her eyes snapped open as she tried to banish tormenting thoughts. When she was feeling calmer, she turned over on to her side and curled up into her favourite sleeping position.

She was just dozing off when she was woken with a start by a loud din from downstairs: jazz music filling the house and booming voices, shrill laughter, drunken singing. The unmistakable sound of a riotous party.

'Oh, no, not again,' she groaned, because this sort of thing was getting to be a regular occurrence since the musicians had moved into the basement. Nobody minded a party but these shindigs didn't start until decent people had gone to bed and went on until all hours. It was generally believed among the statutory tenants here that the rowdy parties were being encouraged by the landlord as part of his plot to harass and drive them out so that he could relet the rooms at higher rents.

Judging by the fact that all complaints had fallen on deaf ears, the speculation would seem to be correct. Rent restrictions meant nothing to the unscrupulous man who had recently taken over the house. He knew his tenants weren't likely to report him because they were of the disadvantaged classes who felt powerless against the likes of him and his strong-arm tactics.

Rumour had it that he wanted to emulate other landlords in the area by removing white tenants so that he could exploit West Indian immigrants by charging them per head rather than for the room with as many as six to a room. The newcomers were particularly vulnerable because many property owners refused to rent to them. Some of the tenants here believed that the landlord also wanted to relet some of the rooms to prostitutes on a daily basis.

'Mummy,' murmured Shirley sleepily, 'what's happening? What's that noise?'

'It's all right, darling,' soothed Daisy, gently brushing the child's hair from her brow with her hand. 'It's only someone having a party. Go back to sleep, love, or you'll wake Belinda.'

In the attic, the noise from below wasn't as distressing as it would be for the tenants on the lower floors, and the children usually managed to sleep through most of it, albeit restlessly. Waiting until Shirley had gone back to sleep, Daisy went across the landing and tapped on Nora's door. She could hear people downstairs shouting at the basement tenants for the noise to stop and banging on the door of the offenders.

'Just popped across to see if you're OK with all the racket going on downstairs,' she said when Nora opened the door.

'I'm all right, dear,' Nora assured her. 'It's just a question of sticking our fingers in our ears and trying to sleep through it. As we know from past experience, if we try to make them stop they'll do it all the more. The tenants who are down there objecting ought to realise that by now.'

Daisy nodded in agreement. Previous confrontations with the basement tenants had resulted only in foul language and even louder music. 'I think I'd better pay our landlord a visit in the morning,' she decided. 'Something's got to be done about this. Can the girls come in with you while I'm out?'

'Course they can.' Nora looked worried. 'But you be careful. He's a nasty piece of work and can be dangerous to those who cross him, so I've heard. He isn't much of a muscleman himself but the blokes who work for him are real heavyweights.'

'Mm, I know,' said Daisy. 'But I can't just sit back and take it.'

'I'll come with you?' offered Nora.

'No. I'd rather you stayed here to look after the girls, if you don't mind.'

'Right you are, dear,' Nora agreed. 'Good luck. And mind how you go.'

'Don't worry about me,' said Daisy, moving back to her own door. 'I'll see you in the morning.'

Roland Ellwood lived in a ground-floor flat in a tenement house he owned a few minutes' walk from Benly Square. He didn't try to hide away from his tenants so Daisy didn't anticipate trouble in getting to see him. For the moment it suited him to be seen to be a caring landlord who was accessible to anyone with a problem, something she guessed would change as soon as he got rich enough to conceal himself in a mansion somewhere away from the area.

'So . . . what can I do for you?' he asked, showing her into a sitting room-cum-office where easy chairs were intermingled with a desk and a filing cabinet.

'It's about the people in the basement flat at number twenty Benly Square and the noise they make at nights with their parties,' she explained.

A small dapper man of about forty-five with heavily greased grey hair worn flat to his head and thin features, Ellwood was well turned out in a suit, but flashy with a bow tie and purple waistcoat. He leaned back in his chair, smoking a cigar and looking bored with Daisy's comments.

'People are entitled to let their hair down now and again, you know,' he pointed out.

'Of course they are. And nobody minds it now and again but this is a lot more often than that,' she told him. 'It's two or three times a week and it goes on for most of the night. The tenants on the lower floors are being driven mad.' She paused, giving him a knowing look.

13

'But you already know that, don't you?'

'It has been mentioned to me, yes,' he confirmed, his manner studiously congenial.

'Well, I'm mentioning it again.'

'With the idea that I'll have a few words with the offenders, I assume?'

'As long as you don't tell them to carry on with the good work,' she blurted out.

His dark, deep-set eyes hardened. 'What exactly are you implying?' he asked.

'I think you know.'

'Do I?' His gaze didn't falter.

'You're trying to drive us statutory tenants out so that you can let the flats at a higher rent and make a fortune,' she informed him briskly. 'Well, you won't get away with it as far as I'm concerned because I have a proper rent agreement from the previous owner and I'm staying put. So please get the noise at nights stopped. I've got two little girls and they need their sleep.'

Ellwood puffed on his cigar and exhaled a cloud of smoke. 'I'm not trying to drive you out but neither am I forcing you to stay,' he said after some consideration. 'Maybe you'd be happier living somewhere quieter.'

'And play right into your hands?' she replied, puffing her lips out in disgust. 'Not likely.'

His manner changed completely, the urbane attitude replaced by brutal honesty. 'You'd do well to realise, you stupid woman, that all my money is tied up in the houses I own and I've every right to get as much as I can in rent. I'm the one who has to pay for all the repairs and maintenance.'

'Repairs! Maintenance!' Daisy exploded. 'When do you ever do either? You've done nothing since you bought the house. The banisters are broken, the paint's peeling and the bathroom basin started leaking soon after you took over, and you've done nothing about any of it.'

'If you're so dissatisfied I'm sure you'd be better suited living somewhere else,' he suggested again.

'Oh, no. As I've just told you, you won't get rid of me that easily,' she made it clear. 'I'm not going anywhere.'

'In that case you'll have to put up with any . . .' he paused; she waited, 'with any little inconveniences that might arise, won't you?'

She knew he was threatening her. 'I'm not going to just sit back and take it, if that's what you think,' she declared.

Ellwood gave her a contemptuous look and dropped all pretence of civility. 'You're taking up space in my house that I could fill more profitably and, yes, I do want you out,' he informed her gruffly. 'People are crying out for accommodation in this area and I don't have any petty restrictions in my properties. I'm not prejudiced like some landlords around here. You won't see a "No Blacks, No Irish, No Dogs" sign on any of my houses.'

'I should think not,' said the outraged Daisy.

'There are plenty who aren't so easy-going as I am.' He paused, fixing her with a vicious look. 'I must be broad-minded. I even let unmarried mothers in,' he said pointedly.

She should have been immune to this sort of insult but it still hurt. She was suddenly painfully aware of what she had known all along: that he had all the power in this argument and she had none. But she wouldn't give in. 'You're all heart. You'll have me in tears in a minute,' she said sarcastically.

'The fact of the matter is, I want you and the rest of the statutory tenants out of my house,' he continued. 'And you'll go, I can promise you that. As you've told me, I can't throw you out because of your agreement but you'll go of your own accord, I can guarantee it. It might take a bit of time but you'll leave and be glad to.'

Put like that, it was frightening. 'This is harassment,' she retaliated. 'I've a good mind to report you.'

'Who to?' he challenged, his thin lips curling into a triumphant smile. 'The authorities won't be interested because this is private rented accommodation, not council housing. With the housing shortage in this area being so serious, I'm sure they've got better things to do with their time than bother about some moaning mother of two who got herself knocked up.' He paused for a moment, looking at her with malice. 'And not just once either, but twice, and probably doesn't even know who the father of her kids is.'

'That isn't true.' Daisy was shaking with rage now.

'There are no witnesses to this conversation so it would just be your word against mine, if you were foolish enough to go to the authorities,' Ellwood went on as though she hadn't spoken. 'And no one is going to take any notice of you. No one cares about scum like you and your kind – no-hopers who don't have two ha'pennies to rub together and no place in decent society.'

It was as much as Daisy could do to keep her hands off him but she managed to restrain herself, only because she didn't want to give him even more of an upper hand. 'You really are an evil little man,' she told him.

'If you say so,' he said indifferently. 'Though I see myself more as a good businessman. So why don't you go and get the local paper and see if you can find yourself somewhere else to live because you don't have a future in any of my houses.'

'You won't force me out.'

'Just watch me.' He drew on his cigar. 'In the meantime, I'd like you to leave. I'm a very busy man.' His tone was vicious. 'So get out.'

'I'll be glad to,' she said. 'Just being in the same room as you makes me want to throw up.'

And with that she hurried from the house. For all her ostensible courage, her legs felt like jelly and the stress had made her feel sick. Nora was right: he was a dangerous man. She wouldn't be beaten by him but his threats were scary, mostly because she had the girls to think of.

Unfortunately, she couldn't afford to pay more rent than she paid now, even if she could manage to find somewhere else to live, which was doubtful. But Roland Ellwood obviously intended to make life wretched for her and the others if they stayed on. Terrorising tenants was his speciality, so she'd heard. What made it even harder to take was knowing that some of what he said was true. People like her and Nora and the other tenants just didn't have a voice against someone like him.

All she could do was deal with whatever came as best as she could and not be driven out, she told herself, as she hurried through the grimy, run-down streets. There was always the faint hope that Nat would come to the rescue by keeping his long-term promise to marry her. But it was such a remote possibility, the thought didn't linger.

Shirley and Belinda were very taken with some glass beads on a stall in the Portobello market that afternoon. Amber and emerald winked in the sunlight among strings of simulated pearls and flashy cameo brooches.

'Ten bob,' announced the female stallholder, a bottle blonde with a shelf-like bosom and a multitude of chins.

'You do mean for two necklaces, don't you?' queried Daisy meaningfully.

'Don't try and rob me,' objected the woman. 'These are quality gear, the genuine article. Ten bob each.'

'Oh, do me a favour,' bartered Daisy. 'They're too expensive at half that price.'

'Daylight robbery,' put in Nora.

'OK, two for ten bob, one each for the little girls and that's my last offer,' said the woman.

'Five bob each for junk like that?' was Daisy's sparky response. 'A shilling is the most I'd pay.'

'Four bob each,' the woman offered.

'Three,' countered Daisy.

'Now you're just taking the mick.'

The stallholder was obviously not prepared to haggle further so Daisy and the others moved on. Her daughters looked somewhat downcast but not for long because they weren't used to expensive treats. Anyway, they still had the highlight of the week to look forward

16

.to – a visit to the sweet shop where they could choose what they wanted. The narrow street was heaving with noisy humanity and fringed by stalls displaying everything from cucumbers to Chippendale chairs.

Saturday was the big day here, especially recently since the antique trade had begun to arrive and the market was expanded by a few antique and junk stalls. Daisy and co. wandered from stall to stall, seeing silver trays and meat platters, antique clocks and Victorian china. Even rusty old lamps found a buyer here.

Being out among the crowds, with good-humoured bargaining all around her, cheered Daisy up after the traumatic meeting with Roland Ellwood. Nora had been a tower of strength too. Nothing was ever quite so bad when she'd talked to her about it.

Having rummaged through the entire stock at a second-hand clothes stall, they wandered on to the food barrows where Daisy bought fresh fruit and vegetables, giving the girls an apple each to eat right away.

'Wotcha, Daisy,' said a deep male voice, a hand simultaneously clamped on her shoulder. 'I guessed I'd find you around here somewhere.'

'Nat,' said Daisy, smiling at a stockily built man in a navy-blue pinstripe suit and a garish, multicoloured tie. Every inch a spiv, he had rich dark eyes, a dazzling smile and black hair with long sideburns. He wasn't handsome as such – his features were too uneven for that – but his rough charm was magnetic. 'We haven't seen you for ages.'

'Sorry about that, love, but I've been busy,' he said, spreading his hands apologetically.

'Doing what?' she enquired lightly.

With a nonchalant shrug, he cocked his head and told her uninformatively, 'Oh, a bit o' this, a bit o' that. You know me, I've always got something on the go.'

He dealt in anything with a potential market and carried out his business anywhere he could find customers: in pubs and clubs, even from a suitcase in the street.

'Surely you could have found the time to call round to see us?' she said in a tone of mild admonition.

'Don't give me a hard time,' he said with boyish persuasion.

'Well, you could have made an effort.'

'You know I'd have been round if I'd had the time,' he went on. 'Anyway, there's no point in my coming round in the evening, is there, as you're out working?'

'You could have popped in to see the girls.'

'OK, I should have but I didn't and I'm wrong and I'm sorry,' he reeled off. 'But don't have a go at me.'

Shirley had cuddled closer to her mother, Belinda was clutching Nora's hand. They were shy of their father, who rarely took any notice of them. When he came to the flat it was usually after they were in bed. Daisy drew comfort from the fact that he hadn't deserted her when she fell pregnant like many men would in that situation. But she wished most ardently that he would take more of a fatherly role, and constantly strived to encourage some sort of a rapport between him and his daughters, for their sake.

'Hey, you two,' she said, smiling down at them reassuringly, 'aren't you going to say hello to your dad?'

''Ello,' they chorused obediently, unusually subdued.

'Wotcha, girls,' Nat said awkwardly. He wasn't at ease with children; never knew what to say to them so said the first thing that came into his mind. 'How's school?'

'We don't go to school yet,' informed Shirley, staring at him accusingly. 'We can't start until we're five.'

'Whoops. Sorry.' He grinned, unbothered by the mistake. 'Trust me to get it wrong.'

Nora made a timely intervention. 'Come on, girls,' she said kindly. 'Let's walk on to the sweet shop while your mum and dad have a chat, and you can start choosing what you want. I know how long it takes you to make up your mind sometimes.'

'I'll meet you there in about ten minutes,' said Daisy, and they trotted off holding Nora's hand, two endearing little figures in summer frocks, each with light brown hair tied with a bow of blue ribbon on the side.

'I'll see to it that she doesn't keep you waiting, Nora,' Nat called after them.

'Sweet, aren't they?' she said to him, yearning for some sign of affection for them from him.

But all he said was, 'Yeah, they're nice kids, a real credit to you, Daisy.'

'Thanks.'

'So, how's it going?' he asked.

'I've had better days,' she told him.

'Why, what's happened?'

'I had a run-in with the landlord this morning.' She went on to tell him more about it.

'Blimey, that's a bit rough,' said Nat, who had furnished rooms in Paddington which he never offered to share with Daisy or invited her to visit. He said the place was barely big enough for one and was far too small to accommodate visitors.

'You can say that again.'

'There's a lot of that sort of thing going on around here.'

'Of course, if we were to get married,' Daisy began in a persuasive tone, 'that would solve my problem.'

She knew she was being pushy but Nat was the sort of man who

18

needed a shove to get him to make any sort of a commitment beyond the next half-hour. He wasn't the marrying kind but she had an unwavering belief that she was the only woman in his life and if he married anyone it would be her; she also believed that if she waited long enough it would happen.

In Daisy's opinion love wasn't about owning someone and she would never try to do that. But at the same time she had been involved with him since she was nineteen and felt she knew him well enough to exert a little gentle pressure from time to time.

'All in good time, babe,' he said predictably, putting his head to one side and tapping it. 'I've got it in mind. It's all up here.'

'Fibber,' she joshed, keeping the mood light because if she came on too strong he'd just find an excuse to leave.

'Don't be like that,' he coaxed, putting his hand on her arm. 'You know you're the only woman for me, and that I'll marry you, eventually.'

'I hope you manage it before the girls make grandparents of us,' she quipped.

'Oh, Daisy, you are a case,' he laughed.

'And you're a dead loss as a boyfriend.'

'You don't mean that.'

'I do,' she said, but there was a smile in her voice. 'I don't know what I see in you.'

'It must be my good looks.' He was teasing her.

'It certainly isn't your modesty.'

'Being humble never got anyone anywhere.'

'You might be right at that,' she agreed, becoming deadly serious as she remembered the meeting with the landlord.

Seeing the change in Daisy's expression and suspecting that things might begin to get heavy, Nat effected a swift change of subject. 'You and me ought to have a night out together soon, when you get an evening off. What do you say?'

She threw him a shrewd look. 'You wouldn't be trying to change the subject so that I won't mention the M word again, would you?' she suggested.

'As if I would . . .'

'You do it all the time.'

He made a face. 'You know how allergic I am to it.'

'Oh, Nat,' she rebuked.

'I thought you'd like a night out.'

'I would.'

'Well then, let's go out and enjoy ourselves,' he grinned. 'Plenty of time to talk marriage, later on.'

She should have been angry but suddenly it didn't matter because he gave her one of his most melting smiles and took her in his arms.

19

All she could think of was how good it felt to be close to him; even after all this time the magic was still there. As they stood there hugging each other with the crowds milling about all around them, she remembered why she had fallen in love with him all those years ago when they'd met in a café in Paddington where she'd been working. They'd had such fun in those early days. He could be loving and tender now too, when he was in the mood.

Nora only saw Nat's worst side, the side of him that caused him to let Daisy down and refuse to give her the respectability of marriage. She didn't see the tenderness he showed to her when they were on their own, or experience the sweet intensity of feeling that filled her whenever he was near. Daisy realised that a lot of women wouldn't put up with his offhand ways. The truth was she would sooner have him this way than not at all.

When, in the next instant, he tried to cadge money from her, she despaired of him. Her common sense told her she would be better off without him. But there was no logic to her feelings and she knew with absolute certainty that she could never give him up.

Chapter Two

Later that same day June Masters was dressed in a sun top and shorts, and sprawled out in a deck chair on the top-floor balcony of the Cliff Head Hotel on the outskirts of Torquay. The view of the bay was stunning from here. Elegant white hotels sat high above thickly wooded slopes that swept down to golden sands, the entire scene washed with early evening sunlight that turned the sea turquoise. The beaches and promenade were beginning to empty as holidaymakers headed back to hotels and guesthouses for their evening meals.

Glancing at her watch, June finished her tea and hurried inside to the flat, which was cool and luxuriously appointed, as might be expected of the private accommodation of the proprietors' son and his wife.

'Ah, there you are. I was just about to give you a call,' said her husband, Alan, appearing from the bedroom, fastening a black bow tie around the neck of a starched white shirt. 'Thought you might have forgotten the time.'

'No. I was just enjoying a few extra minutes in the sunshine. It's lovely out there,' she told him, taking her teacup to the kitchen, then joining him in the bedroom. 'But I'll start getting ready to go on duty now.'

Because they worked such late hours in the hotel, they needed to rest for an hour or two in the afternoons. He usually went to bed; she just sat on the balcony if the weather was nice, or relaxed in an armchair inside if it wasn't.

'Did you get some sleep?' she enquired.

'Yeah, I managed an hour and feel all the better for it,' he replied, slipping into a black tuxedo. 'I'll be glad later on as we're in for a busy night. There's nothing worse than feeling shattered on duty. I don't know how you keep going without a nap.'

'Plenty of staying power, I suppose,' she suggested. 'I never feel tired enough to sleep during the day.'

'You should come to bed with me,' he suggested waggishly. 'You'd sleep then . . . eventually.'

'Animal,' she accused jokingly.

'I try,' he laughed.

21

She smiled, slipping out of her clothes and into a housecoat ready for a bath. 'So . . . you reckon we're going to have a busy night, then?'

'Very,' he nodded, brushing his hair in front of the wardrobe mirror. 'Saturday nights in high season are hectic enough anyway, but it'll be especially mad tonight as we have a couple of parties of nonresidents booked into the restaurant as well. We're stretching our numbers to the limit.'

'But we'd be worried if we weren't rushed off our feet at the height of the season,' she commented.

'Exactly,' he agreed. 'It isn't good business practice to turn people away if we can possibly accommodate them.'

Alan was front-of-house manager in his parents' hotel and also a partner in the business. June worked in reception but would turn her hand to anything. Having worked here for nine years, she'd learned to be versatile.

But now Alan turned to her, looking magnificent, his brown curly hair brushed back from a tanned countenance blessed with shandy-coloured eyes and fine-cut features. At twenty-eight he was gorgeous and she was proud to be married to him, even after seven years together.

'I'll head off downstairs then.' His voice was deep and rich, a boarding school education having eliminated any tendency towards a Devonshire accent. 'I'll see you down there when you're ready.'

'You don't need to go on duty yet,' she pointed out, purely with his interests at heart. 'You could stay up here for another half-hour at least.'

'I'd sooner go down,' was his predictable response. 'You know me, I'm never happier than when I'm in the thick of it down in the hotel.'

'I just thought you could relax for a while longer, love, as it's going to be a long night.'

'As I'm ready I might as well go.'

She shrugged. 'If it's what you want,' she said amiably.

Alan had been brought up at the hotel and, apart from a spell in the army, had worked here since he left school. He was totally absorbed in the affairs of the Cliff Head, and dedicated to his job. Although it carried some weight in theory, he was very much subject to his parents, especially when it came to decisions. They lived off-site now but were still active in the running of the hotel, albeit that they worked fewer hours than they had in their younger days. They had a variety of duties behind the scenes, and June couldn't imagine them ever letting go of the reins, especially Alan's mother.

'See you later then,' he said, kissing her lightly on the cheek and striding purposefully from the room.

June had a quick bath and got dressed in a crisp white blouse and black skirt deemed suitable by Alan's mother for the receptionist of

22

this prestigious hotel, which was traditional and run on formal lines.

Applying her make-up at the dressing-table mirror, June saw an attractive face with fine bone structure, striking dark eyes and glossy black hair worn in a sleek shoulder-length bob, which was looked after regularly by one of the town's leading hairdressers.

She was well aware of the fact that she was extremely fortunate. At twenty-six she had more than most women could reasonably hope for: a husband she adored, a comfortable home, nice clothes and no shortage of money. People probably said she'd done very well for herself, and they would be right.

Following a miserable childhood she'd left home in a London suburb at fifteen, found cheap lodgings and worked in a factory until the war ended two years later. One day she'd spotted an advertisement in the *Evening News* which had changed her life. It was for a kitchen worker at a Torquay hotel. Attracted by the thought of living on the coast and the fact that accommodation was provided, she'd applied.

Determined to make something of herself, she'd worked hard in the kitchens here, while at the same time finding out everything she could about hotel administration so that when a vacancy for a receptionist had arisen, she'd got the job, assisted by the refined demeanour she'd had drummed into her as a child. Two years after her arrival here, when she was nineteen, she'd married the boss's son.

But now this woman of beauty and good fortune was suddenly overcome by the despair she'd been stifling all afternoon. She wept uncontrollably, rivers of mascara streaking her cheeks, make-up turning to blotches. She put her head on her hands on the dressing table and sobbed with the misery of knowing that she wasn't worthy of her husband's love.

Managing eventually to pull herself together, she washed her face and reapplied her make-up, combed her hair, straightened her clothes and left the flat, heading for the ground floor in the rattly old-fashioned lift.

To the casual observer she was a sophisticated and composed woman in control of her life. Because she was so skilled in projecting this image, nobody would suspect the depth of her emotional problems.

'If you'd just like to sign the register, I'll have someone take your luggage up to your room for you,' June said to a couple of late arrivals, handing them the key to their room across the reception desk. 'You're on the third floor but the lift is just down the passage on the left.' She paused, smiling from one to the other. 'May I take this opportunity to welcome you to the Cliff Head Hotel. All of us here wish you a very happy holiday and hope you'll enjoy your stay with us.'

'I'm sure we will,' said the man, glancing around. 'It seems very nice.'

'We think so,' said June truthfully.

Purpose-built as a hotel in the early part of the century, but tastefully modernised internally, the hotel was white-rendered, had balconies to all the front rooms and was set in extensive grounds. Here in the foyer, the walls were wood-panelled and a wide staircase rose to the gallery in a wealth of polished mahogany. On the ground floor there were various public rooms including a bar and restaurant that were open to nonresidents.

With expert timing, Alan appeared with the teenage boy they employed as a porter and general runaround. Alan introduced himself to the new arrivals and the boy led them to the lift, carrying their luggage.

'Are we expecting any more new arrivals tonight?' Alan enquired.

'No, they're the last,' June told him, glancing at the reservations book. 'A few are expected tomorrow but apart from them the guests for this week are all present and correct, and every room booked.'

'That's the way we like it, eh?' he smiled.

'It certainly is.'

It was turned ten o'clock and people were milling about in the foyer, some going out for after-dinner strolls, others asking at the desk for their keys so that they could turn in for the night. People tended to speak in hushed tones because this was a select hotel catering for a refined clientele. A mausoleum, June had been known to call it when she and Alan were alone. They both thought it needed an injection of new life and had discussed the possibility of making the place more child-friendly and attractive to families. They'd even talked about introducing some sort of evening entertainment such as weekly dances and cabaret nights. One of the lounges could easily be adapted to accommodate such functions.

But Alan's parents were fiercely opposed to any such changes, which they believed would lower the tone of the hotel. Apart from a period during the war, when it was requisitioned by the Government as a convalescent home for wounded soldiers, the hotel had been run on the same traditional lines for two generations. People came here for peace and tranquillity, was the Masters' argument. With characteristic hauteur they claimed that there were places like Butlins for people who needed entertainment and didn't mind dance music blaring out at all hours, or children shouting and screaming about the place.

June had no say in such matters, and it annoyed her that Alan had so little power. She wished he would be more assertive towards his parents, and told him so from time to time. But his easy-going nature and love of the hotel made him malleable.

Now a youngish man, with blond hair and blue eyes, and wearing a tuxedo, came up to the reception desk – Jack Saunders, the restaurant manager. 'Could you order a taxi, please, June?'

24

'Sure. Who's it for?'

'A Mr and Mrs Taylor from one of the nonresident parties.'

'Is the party breaking up already?' She was surprised. 'They looked in fine form and set to stay until we chuck them out when I passed the restaurant a little while ago.'

'The others in the party probably are,' he told her. 'But Mrs Taylor isn't feeling well so they're leaving early.'

'Oh dear,' she frowned. 'Nothing she's eaten, I hope.'

'In our restaurant, *never*,' Jack grinned. 'I suspect the answer lies in a few too many gins.'

June and Alan both chuckled. The same age as Alan, Jack was a pal of his, and June liked him too. Born and raised in London's East End, Jack had gone to Australia with his family in the post-war emigration craze. The rest of the family had settled there but Jack hadn't been happy so had come back to England after a couple of years. He'd gained hotel experience as a waiter, then head waiter in one of the big London hotels before coming to the Cliff Head three years ago.

'I'll do it right away,' said June, picking up the phone.

'Fancy a drink after work, you two?' Jack suggested. His voice was deep and husky with an attractive hint of his East End roots.

'Love to,' smiled June. They usually needed to wind down when they came off duty after a busy night or it was difficult to sleep.

'Suits me,' added Alan.

'I'll need to relax a bit after the night I'm having,' said Jack. 'What with Chef going into a mood and throwing his weight about, and a table for six being double-booked, I'll be glad when this shift is over.'

'Double-booked?' queried June in concern, putting the phone down for a moment.

'That's right,' he confirmed. 'Table number twenty. We had to set up another table sharpish since we couldn't turn the customers away as they'd made a booking, even though we were fully stretched. It's crowded in the restaurant, to say the very least.'

'Whoever took the first booking must have forgotten to write it down,' she said.

He shrugged. 'Exactly.'

A look passed between June and Jack. The culprit was probably Alan's mother, Irene, who liked to be seen front of house and sometimes covered in reception when June wasn't on duty if there was no other member of staff available. In her work behind the scenes Irene was reasonably competent, but efficiency took second place to vanity when she was out front. June's guess was that she'd been busy trying to impress someone in the foyer when the restaurant booking had come in, so had failed to enter it.

Jack was also thinking this but was far too diplomatic to say anything to Alan – partly because he was merely an employee, but

25

also because Alan was fond of his mother, who would rather die than admit to any sort of error.

'Not guilty.' June met her husband's questioning look. 'You know me better than that.'

'It must have been one of the staff then,' tutted Alan, becoming noticeably tense. 'People really should be more careful about that sort of thing.'

'No real harm done,' intervened Jack speedily. 'We soon got the problem sorted, and if Chef can't cope with a few extra covers at short notice he doesn't deserve to be in the job.'

'True,' agreed June.

Spotting the arrival of Irene and Gerald Masters, Jack prepared to make a hasty retreat, arranging to see Alan and June in the bar after work.

Alan greeted his parents in a jovial manner. 'Can't you two keep away from the place?' He was teasing them because they weren't on duty at night, on grounds of seniority. 'Talk about gluttons for punishment.'

'We're not here to work,' explained Gerald, who was quintessentially English, in a blazer and flannels and smoking a pipe. 'We've just called in for a nightcap.'

'Looking for some company, eh?' suggested Alan. His father was the gregarious type and liked to sit in the bar of an evening, chatting to the guests.

Alan's parents had used to live in the flat that June and Alan now occupied. These days Gerald and Irene had a house within walking distance and most nights they turned up here, probably because they'd always been too wrapped up in the hotel to have much of a social life outside of it, June guessed. She got on better with Gerald than his wife, but couldn't claim to be fond of either. He wasn't openly hostile towards her but neither did he go out of his way to make her feel like one of the family. He went along with the views of his wife because it was easier, she suspected, and Irene never left June in any doubt as to how disappointed she was in her son's choice of wife.

'That's right, son,' confirmed Gerald. 'It doesn't do any harm to be sociable to the guests . . . it creates goodwill.'

'I can't argue with that,' agreed Alan.

'Is everything all right here?' enquired Irene, a short, plump woman with cold grey eyes and honey-rinsed grey hair which was tightly permed and immaculate. She was wearing a royal-blue crepe-de-Chine cocktail dress with sequins around the neckline.

'Everything's fine,' her son assured her, 'apart from someone double-booking a table in the restaurant.'

Irene's brow furrowed. 'You ought to watch that, June,' she said, with her usual propensity to blame her daughter-in-law.

'It wasn't me,' denied June.

'You're our head receptionist,' Irene reminded her coolly. 'Bookings are your responsibility.'

'Not when I'm off duty.'

'You're not being fair, Mother,' Alan was swift to defend. 'If June says it wasn't her, then it wasn't. And she can't be held responsible for what other people do when she isn't on duty.'

'No, no, of course she can't,' conceded Irene quickly; she normally kept her hostility towards June out of her son's hearing and had slipped up on this occasion. 'It must have been one of the staff filling in on the desk. You need to deal with that, Alan. That sort of inefficiency is bad for business.'

'I'll look into it,' he told her.

Alan could hardly be unaware of the fact that his wife and mother didn't get on, given the tension that was always present between them. But he didn't know the extent of Irene's enmity towards June because she was so sly about it. June was only human and had mentioned some of what went on to Alan. But she wasn't heartless enough to shatter all his illusions about his mother by telling him everything.

'You've been on the desk a few times during the week, haven't you, Irene?' June didn't see why the older woman should get off scot-free when she was so eager to pass the buck.

Irene was full of affront. 'I hope you're not implying that I'm at fault,' she objected. 'I'm hardly likely to make such a careless mistake after all my experience in the hotel trade.'

'Anyone can make a mistake,' June pointed out. 'We're all only human.'

'I could run the reception desk in my sleep,' was her sharp answer to that.

A sudden flurry of guests needing attention ended any further discussion, and Irene and Gerald headed for the bar. People were checking breakfast times and ordering newspapers and early morning tea, asking for keys and making general enquiries.

Although June managed to conceal it, she was inwardly quivering. Irene usually managed to unnerve her, even after all these years. Her contempt was an ever-present force even when she was pretending to be friendly for Alan's benefit. From the instant he had shown a serious interest in June, Irene had systematically tried to break them up. It would have suited her if Alan had married Paula Bright, the daughter of one of the Masters' few friends, a couple who were Torquay hoteliers.

June had hoped that Irene's hate campaign would lessen once their marriage was an established fact. But, if anything, it had become more intense. When Alan was out of earshot, she didn't try to hide her venom and had told June often and in a variety of ways how she

27

wasn't good enough for Alan. June sometimes wondered how much more she could take, especially as she had reason to agree with her mother-in-law.

'Jack's a really good bloke, don't you think?' remarked Alan later that same night when he and June were getting ready for bed, having spent an enjoyable hour in the company of the restaurant manager.

'Yeah, he is good company,' she agreed. 'I enjoy his down-to-earth sense of humour.'

Alan tutted in an affectionate manner as he unbuttoned his shirt. 'Him and that damned motorbike of his,' he said, smiling. 'Talk about besotted.'

She laughed. 'I don't think any woman will ever come close to that thing in his priorities.'

Jack Saunders was a motorbike fanatic and devoted to the Harley-Davidson he'd bought second-hand and done up. It looked like new but he was always tinkering with it.

'It would have to be someone really special, that's for sure,' Alan agreed.

'He doesn't have any trouble getting women, though, does he?' June mentioned casually.

'He's a good-looking bloke, that's why,' said Alan. 'He's had a few girlfriends since he's been here.'

'Mm. There was that woman from Exeter he was going out with,' she remembered. 'I thought that might come to something but it went the same way as all the others.'

'I suppose he just hasn't met anyone he wants to settle down with yet,' observed Alan. 'He's happy as he is. What with the motorbike and his old cottage miles from anywhere, he's a one-off.'

'A good restaurant manager, though,' she pointed out. 'That's the main thing as far as we're concerned.'

'He's very good,' he agreed. 'He has a way with the guests, and he knows how to get the best out of the staff.' He paused thoughtfully, taking off his shirt. 'Yet I took a chance in giving him the job because he hadn't managed a restaurant, as such, before he came to work for us. It's just as well I interviewed him. I don't think Mum or Dad would have taken him on.'

'Which just goes to show what good judgement you have,' June praised him.

'A lucky guess more like it. I just knew he was right for the job, somehow.'

'You spotted something special in him,' she insisted, sitting on the edge of the bed in her slip to take off her stockings, 'which makes you a brilliant judge of character in my book.'

'Nice of you to say so.'

28

June was sitting with her back to Alan and she felt the bed shake as he got into it. She tensed as the moment she was dreading drew near. But for the time being he seemed content to chat about the hotel. 'It was a good night, wasn't it?' he said.

'It was busy, certainly,' she replied.

'Busy and good are the same thing to me,' he responded with enthusiasm. 'There's nothing like the feeling I get when we've got a full house. Even apart from the business side of it, it gives me a real buzz. When Mum and Dad retire and I'm running the place, I'll have this hotel humming with life. There'll be a feeling here . . . an atmosphere so cheerful and warm, people won't be able to wait to come back.'

'Why wait until they retire before doing it?'

'You know why, June,' he reminded her. 'They want things to stay as they are.'

'So . . . persuade them otherwise,' she challenged.

He paused before answering. 'My time will come,' he said in a tone of resignation.

Because she didn't want to pressurise him into something he didn't feel right about, she just said encouragingly, 'Yeah, course it will.'

She had often wondered if they should break away from his parents' business altogether, partly because she feared that Irene would eventually come between them, but mainly because she believed Alan needed to succeed at something in his own right, away from their control, to find true fulfilment. But she couldn't seriously expect him to leave this place. It was in his blood, was his birthright, and would be his eventually.

'Anyway,' he said, yawning and sliding his hand over her back, 'that's enough shop talk. Come to bed before I get too tired to make love to you.'

'I won't be a minute.' Maybe if he fell asleep she wouldn't have to tell him.

But no such luck. He sat up, caressing her shoulders. She moved away quickly and stood up, facing him.

'What's the matter?' He frowned at her.

'I can't.'

'Why not?'

She bit her lip, hating to utter the words she knew would distress him. 'I . . . I got my period this afternoon,' she explained through dry lips.

'Oh, oh, I see.' He rolled over and lay on his back, unable to hide his disappointment.

'I'm sorry there's not going to be a baby, Alan,' she told him miserably, slipping into her nightdress.

'Yeah, so am I.' He paused and she could feel tension draw tight

29

between them as he struggled to compose himself. 'But we mustn't lose heart. It'll happen one day.'

'I hope so,' she said with feeling. 'I really do.'

He lay still, staring at the ceiling for a while, then turned his head towards her. 'Look, June, I know how upset you must be feeling but you mustn't let it get to you,' he said.

'How can I not? I feel terrible, not only for myself but for you. I know how much you want kids.'

'We both do, don't we? But there's plenty of time.' She knew he was forcing himself to stay positive with great difficulty. 'We're still quite young. Maybe next month your period will oblige us and stay away.'

They'd been saying that for seven years and still a pregnancy eluded them. 'We'll just have to keep hoping,' she said.

'We will indeed.' He patted the bed beside him. 'Come on,' he urged her. 'I think we both need a cuddle.'

She slipped in beside him, only partly reassured to have him close to her. 'I feel as though I'm failing you, Alan,' she confessed.

'Don't be daft, of course you're not. It takes two to make a baby, remember.' He slipped his arm around her and she snuggled against him.

'I suppose so.'

'But for both our sakes, perhaps it's time we thought about getting some medical advice, as nothing seems to be happening in that direction,' he suggested. 'I was reading something about it the other day. Apparently, quite often just a minor adjustment is needed.'

June froze and he felt her trembling.

'Hey, why so tense?'

'It must be the thought of an operation,' she fibbed.

'Surgery probably won't even be necessary,' he was quick to reassure her. 'There might not be anything wrong at all. But if we see a doctor, at least we'll have more of an idea of what we're up against.'

'It's probably just a question of time,' she suggested, as though she really believed it. 'Unexplained infertility, they call it.'

'Exactly,' he agreed. 'But it won't do any harm to get some professional advice, will it?'

'It might be worth looking into . . . at some point,' she hedged.

'I think we should do it sooner rather than later. I know we're still young but we have been trying for quite a long time.'

'I'll think about it.'

'Promise?'

'I promise.'

'Good,' he said sleepily.

How hurt he would be to know what a fraud she was, she thought. She had no intention of going to see any doctor *ever* about her

30

inability to conceive because she knew exactly why it wasn't happening. But she couldn't tell him the reason. God, what a mess this was.

'Oh well, tomorrow's another day,' he yawned, kissing the top of her head. 'Good night, darling.'

'Good night, Alan.'

Just as she had settled to go to sleep the memory came, bringing her to with a start. She was trembling, her heart palpitating horribly. It always seemed to resurface when she was worried or upset about something and was always so vivid she could almost taste the fear as though it had happened yesterday instead of twenty years ago at least. Why it continued to bother her, she didn't know. But every so often back it came, unfaded by the passing of time.

Far too tense now to sleep, she slipped out of bed and went to the kitchen to make some tea, which she took into the living room, still feeling shaky. Her memory of her early childhood was somewhat sketchy, probably because she'd been told to forget everything before adoption. She knew she'd been six when she was adopted and that she hadn't been at the orphanage very long. She knew that her birth mother was dead and that she and her sister had been abandoned by their father. The rest was a mystery. She'd learned never to ask questions of her new parents, especially about her original background.

As always the flashback evoked memories of her sister, a small child with pigtails and a giggle, as far as she could remember. The pain of their parting had been awful. She'd never forgot it. She'd often thought about her and wondered how life had treated her, particularly as she'd grown into adulthood. She'd wanted to see her again but, having been brought up to believe that she must leave her alone to get on with her own life, she'd never made a move in that direction.

Drinking her tea, she came back to the present and her current problems, of which there seemed no way out. She couldn't give Alan the child he wanted, and didn't know for how much longer she could go on fooling him into believing that she could. If her reproductive apparatus was in good working order, it would have happened by now.

She finished her tea and went back to bed, careful not to disturb Alan. Listening to his even breathing beside her, she was imbued with love for him. There had been tension between them lately because she couldn't get pregnant. How long would it be before it destroyed their marriage altogether?

One afternoon a few weeks later, June found herself alone in the office with her mother-in-law, having gone there to collect some of the forms she used to make up the guests' bills. The office was behind the reception area and it was here that all the major hotel administration happened: the ordering of food and drink, the organisation of staff and wages, everything apart from the receptionist's work, which included hotel and restaurant bookings, making up guests' bills, answering the telephone and dealing with all enquiries.

It was a quiet time between lunch and tea. The guests were either out or resting. Gerald and Alan were taking a break and the secretary had gone to the kitchen to get some tea.

'Oh, hello, Irene,' said June. 'I didn't realise you were still here. I thought you'd have gone home by now.'

'I bet you did,' snapped Irene, who was seated at a desk, holding her spectacles between thumb and forefinger and idly swinging them to and fro. 'You wouldn't have come in if you'd known I was in here on my own.'

'Too true, I wouldn't.' June and Irene didn't pretend to like each other when they were alone. 'I'm not a masochist.'

'Sorry to disappoint you.'

June said nothing; just went to the store cupboard and took out a batch of the forms she needed. 'I'll take plenty of these,' she told her. 'I'm right out of them.'

'Fine.'

June walked to the door.

'While we're on our own,' began Irene, making June's heart sink because those words always heralded criticism of some sort, 'I'd like a word.'

June turned to face her, clutching the pile of forms. 'What about?'

'I'd like to know how much longer I'm going to have to wait for a grandchild.'

It wasn't the first time Irene had asked such an impertinent question but the subject was so raw and at the forefront of June's mind at the moment, it had more of an impact than usual. She turned scarlet, the forms slipping from her grasp and falling with a thud into an untidy heap on the floor. 'I think that's a personal matter between Alan and myself, don't you?' she replied, unable to conceal the quiver in her voice.

'Alan is our only child,' the other woman pointed out, her grey eyes resting coldly on June. 'Naturally Gerald and I are keen to have a grandchild. We want the family line to continue and not end with Alan. Surely you can understand that.'

'Of course.'

'As you know, this hotel has been in Gerald's family for a long time and we want to know that it will pass on through the generations after our time and Alan's,' she went on as though June had said nothing. 'And that can't happen if there are no succeeding generations, can it?'

'Obviously not.'

'Anyway, it's the natural thing to want grandchildren, and I don't want to be deprived of them or be too old to enjoy them if they do come along.'

'There's plenty of time,' June said steadily. 'Alan and I are both still in our twenties, and you're not exactly in your dotage.'

'Even so, you've been married long enough.' She was like a dog with a bone.

June felt her temper rising at this blatant intrusion of privacy. 'It's a personal matter,' she told her again. 'I can understand your wanting a grandchild but that doesn't give you the right to pry into our private life. Alan's a grown man now. He doesn't have to account to you and neither do I.'

'Maybe not. But Alan makes no secret of the fact that he wants a child,' Irene reminded her. 'You can't deny that.'

'I wouldn't dream of denying it,' June protested. 'All I can say is, that when we have any news on that subject, you and Gerald will be the first to know.'

'You've no reason to put it off,' the other woman persisted, as though trying to drive June into a corner. 'I mean, it isn't as though there's any shortage of money. You do well out of this business and could afford to move out of the flat and into accommodation more suited to a family.'

June went down on her haunches to gather the forms that were all over the floor. 'Drop the subject, for goodness' sake,' she said, standing up. 'It's none of your business.'

'I think it is,' the other woman disagreed. 'Alan is my son and when he isn't happy, I don't like it.'

Smarting from the impact of her words, June asked, 'What makes you think he isn't happy?'

'It's obvious. How can he be happy when he hasn't got the child he wants so badly?' she declared. 'He can't be properly fulfilled without that.'

June was so shocked to have her own fears spelled out so clearly, her head spun and she felt sick. She offloaded the forms on to the secretary's desk and held the edge for a moment to steady herself. But she was determined not to give Irene the satisfaction of knowing how rattled she was. 'He's contented enough as things are, with just the two of us,' she told her mother-in-law.

'He might pretend to be—'

'He isn't just pretending.'

'You don't believe that any more than I do.'

June was forced to stare at the floor so that Irene couldn't see the pain in her eyes.

'Is there a problem?' asked Irene, her eyes narrowing on June in a questioning manner. 'Is that it? Is all not well in that department?'

Choking back the tears, June was unable to answer and Irene took this to be a confirmation. 'Have you taken medical advice?' she enquired.

'No,' June managed to utter.

'Why not?'

'Because I've been hoping it would happen and there would be no need,' she said, and it wasn't a lie. 'Not that it's anything to do with you.'

'You can't leave something as important as that to chance,' Irene nagged.

'Give it a rest, Irene, please.'

'That's typical of you to let something as vital as that go on unchecked.'

June brushed a tired hand across her brow. 'How do you know what is typical of me?' she asked. 'You've never taken the trouble to get to know me.'

'You and I are poles apart so I couldn't see the point.'

'Do you hate me so much, you find it impossible to leave me alone?' June wanted to know.

'I don't hate you,' Irene corrected, 'I just don't think you're the right woman for my son.'

'I'd never have guessed,' June said with bitter irony. 'But apart from the fact that I'm not Paula Bright, what else have you got against me? I'm a good wife to him. I love him. He's my life and I'd do anything for him.'

'You hold him back,' Irene stated categorically. 'You always have done in other ways and now you're doing it in the worst way possible – by depriving him of a child.'

'I've never held Alan back,' June disagreed. 'If I've held anyone back, it's you and Gerald by getting in the way of your plans for him and Paula Bright, which would have made things nice and cosy, all good friends together.'

'And what's wrong with that?' Irene wanted to know. 'At least he'd have been with someone of his own type.'

'Instead of a jumped-up kitchen hand?'

'You said it,' returned Irene. 'If the cap fits . . .'

'You really are vicious.'

'I've never pretended to be a saint.'

'Except in front of Alan.'

Irene gave her a sharp look. 'Look, I'm just a mother who wants the best for her son. I've never made any secret of the fact that I wanted him to marry Paula,' she responded. 'Those two would have been perfect for each other.'

'Alan obviously didn't think so or he'd have married her.'

'And he would have done if you hadn't got your claws into him.'

'That just isn't true. I worked and lived at this hotel for a long time

34

before I married him, remember?' June pointed out. 'And I know that nothing was ever going to happen between him and Paula Bright. Not on his part, anyway. He never felt anything of a romantic nature for her.'

'Only because you stood in the way of it,' Irene persisted. 'Once you'd set your sights on him no one else stood a chance. You were absolutely determined to have him from the minute you set foot inside this hotel.'

June couldn't deny that she'd been smitten with him the moment she'd set eyes on him. She'd been seventeen, he nineteen, a soldier home on leave. The war was over but he'd still had some service left to do. She had wanted him desperately but she certainly hadn't entered into a callous campaign to get him in the way that Irene was suggesting. It had been a mutual thing. 'I fell for him at the start, I won't deny that,' she admitted. 'The feeling was reciprocated or we'd never have got together. Alan's very much his own man.' She paused before adding pointedly, 'Except, of course, in his dealings with you and Gerald.'

Irene chose to ignore this last remark. 'All men are susceptible to a flirtatious woman,' she declared, 'and Alan is no exception.'

'We fell in love. It wouldn't have gone beyond a flirtation if we hadn't.'

'Yes, well, that's all water under the bridge,' Irene said impatiently. 'As you did get your hooks into him, the least you can do is give him a child.' She hesitated for a moment, looking at June. 'If you have a medical problem, you must get it seen to without delay. You owe him that much.'

All the fight went out of June, just drained away with the awful truth of Irene's words. 'I'm fully aware of what I owe your son and I have his best interests at heart always, you have my word on that,' she said dully. 'I don't need you to tell me what I have to do.' She was ashen-faced and longing to get away from this woman's cruel tongue. 'Anyway, it's time I took a break from duty until this evening so I'll get some cover in reception and go upstairs to the flat for a couple of hours.'

And with that she left the office.

Alan was sitting in a deck chair on the balcony reading the *Hoteliers' Chronicle* when June got back to the flat.

'Not doing any serious sleeping this afternoon, then?' she said with false levity.

'I will have a snooze in a minute,' he told her. 'I was just glancing through this to keep up to date with what's going on in the trade.'

'We might as well make the most of the nice weather,' she remarked, sitting in the chair beside him and glancing out across the sunlit bay. 'It'll be winter soon enough.'

'You look as though you could do with some sun,' he mentioned, giving her a close look.

'Do I?'

'I'll say you do. You're very pale.' He looked concerned. 'You feeling all right?'

'I'm fine,' she assured him quickly, avoiding his eyes. 'I'll make a cup of tea and join you out here.'

'No tea for me, thanks. I'm going for a kip.' He put the magazine on the table and got up. 'See you later.'

'OK.'

She didn't bother to make tea for herself but sat alone on the balcony, browsing absently through the *Chronicle*. But thoughts of the encounter with Irene lingered, making concentration impossible. The advertisements were about all she could take in so she put the magazine down on the small table beside her and gave her thoughts full rein.

Alan was a good and loving husband. Irene was right when she said June owed it to him to give him the child he wanted. She had been nothing when she'd met him, just a seventeen-year-old kitchen worker who'd run away from home at fifteen. As his wife she'd enjoyed status and a good standard of living. All she'd had to give him in return was her love and loyalty. She didn't have Paula Bright's family back-ground or connections in the hotel trade. And now it seemed she didn't even have the capacity to fulfil that most basic of all human needs.

Even worse was the fact that she couldn't be honest with him about it. Although he was supportive and reassuring to her, the lack of a baby was beginning to put a strain on their relationship. She could feel tension simmering below the surface with ever increasing frequency. That would get worse as it became obvious that a pregnancy wasn't going to happen. Alan was much too good-natured to admit it, but a barren wife would become a burden to him eventually.

She couldn't allow that to happen. She loved him too much. So she must leave. Disappear from his life and give him the freedom to make a new start with someone who could make his life complete. She must do it in such a way that he wouldn't be able to talk her out of it. Irene's lethal tongue had accelerated this decision but it wasn't the cause. Sooner or later, June knew, she would have realised that this was the only solution.

Remembering something that had only half registered a few minutes ago, she reached across to the table and picked up the *Chronicle*, searching for an advertisement that had caught her eye and now seemed vital.

'Receptionist/bookings clerk wanted for busy London hotel. Marble

36

Arch area. Experience essential – accommodation available if required.'

There was a telephone number and a box number.

Hesitating for only a moment, she went inside and found a pencil with which she ringed the advert. Then she took the magazine and went to the telephone in the hall, closing the door carefully behind her.

Early the next morning while the hotel was still silent she slipped out of bed, packed a small bag, put an envelope containing a short letter on the kitchen table, planted a kiss on her sleeping husband's brow, took one last long look at him and stepped quietly from the room.

She left the Cliff Head and headed for the station to get an early train. There was hardly anyone about to see this sad figure walking through the streets carrying a holdall, tears streaming down her cheeks.

Later that morning, Alan stood with his finger on the doorbell of his parents' house near the seafront. When his mother came to the door, he stormed inside, waving a letter at her.

'What have you said to her?' he demanded. 'What have you done?'

'What have I said and done to whom, dear?' She was genuinely puzzled.

'To June, of course,' he blasted. 'She's gone. Left me. Just like that.'

Irene's eyes widened with surprise. 'Oh,' was all she could manage. She was careful to conceal her delight. 'How dreadful for you.'

'That must be the biggest understatement in the history of the world.' He was distraught. 'She wouldn't have just gone unless something had really upset her. So, Mother, I'll ask you again, what have you said to her?'

'Your wife's departure has nothing to do with me,' insisted Irene, secretly wondering if her conversation with June yesterday had had anything to do with it. 'Does she mention me in that letter you're flapping about?'

'No.'

'Why blame me then?'

'Because it's obvious that you don't like her.'

'I never have liked her but it doesn't follow that she left because of me,' she pointed out.

'What else could it be?'

'I've no idea,' she told him. 'What reason does she give in the letter?'

'She doesn't give one,' he explained distractedly. 'She just says she can't stay and it's better for us both if she goes, and I have to trust that she's made the right decision. No forwarding address or clue as to where she's going – nothing.'

'You're better off without her,' his mother couldn't help blurting out. 'I've always thought you were too good for her.'

They were ill-chosen words which served only to fuel his anger even more. 'You've never given her a chance or made any effort to like her,' he accused. 'I bet you've said things to her that I don't know about. It's sure to be something you've said that's finally driven her away. June wouldn't just go off and hurt me like this for no reason.'

Gerald appeared from another room and wanted to know what all the noise was about.

'His wife's gone,' Irene informed him. 'Walked out on him, just like that.'

'No!' gasped Gerald.

'Yes,' Irene confirmed triumphantly.

'I'm not letting her go,' mumbled Alan, holding his head in despair.

'She's already gone, son,' his father said gently.

'I'll find her,' Alan told them. 'I'm not leaving it at this. She loves me, I know that.'

'She's got a funny way of showing it,' was his mother's cynical reaction.

'Has she got another man, do you think?' suggested Gerald tactlessly.

'Definitely not,' was Alan's categorical reply. 'I would have known if anything like that had been going on. Anyway, she never goes anywhere to meet anyone. She could hardly have an affair when she's always at the hotel with me.'

'The best thing you can do is forget all about her, son,' his father advised.

'No!' roared Alan.

'You'll be a fool if you don't,' Gerald went on. 'Anyone who's capable of doing something like that isn't worth bothering with.'

'Your father's right.' Irene was in her element.

'She was never really one of us, anyway,' Gerald opined.

'Of course she was one of us,' Alan disagreed, his voice rising. 'She's my wife, which automatically makes her one of us, despite the fact that you two didn't accept her.'

'Yes, of course it does, dear,' conceded Irene, changing tack for fear of losing too much favour with her son. 'Your father and I are just upset on your behalf.'

'I've got to get her back but I don't know where to start looking.' He combed his hair back with his fingers in agitation. 'She could have gone anywhere.'

'Her mother's perhaps?' suggested Irene.

'She definitely wouldn't have gone there.' That much he did know. 'They don't get on. She hasn't lived at home since she was fifteen.'

'She'll have to let her mother know where she is at some point, though, won't she?' Irene pointed out, deeming it beneficial to her own relationship with her son to seem to be helpful and reassuring and not too damning about June at this point. 'She's still her daughter even if they hate the sight of each other. You can get her new address from her.'

'I can't because I don't have an address or phone number for her mother,' he muttered absently. 'All I know about her is that she lives in London somewhere. June has never said much about her family.'

'Oh, well,' sighed Irene. 'Perhaps June will get in touch with you to let you know where she is, eventually. As you said, she wouldn't just walk out for no reason at all. Perhaps it's just a temporary thing. She might have got into a mood about something and wants some extra attention.'

He shook his head. 'That's the last thing June would ever do. She isn't the type to seek attention.' He was adamant. 'No, she means it. She won't come back of her own accord, which is why I have to find her.'

'I don't see how you can, son, as you've got nothing to go on,' said his mother.

'Me neither,' added his father.

'Did she say anything at all or give any indication to either of you that she wasn't happy lately?' enquired Alan, looking from one of them to the other.

Irene wondered if it would be a good or bad move to mention the childlessness. She decided it wouldn't do any harm to remind him of his wife's flaws. 'I think perhaps she might have been fretting because a baby is a long time in coming,' she told him.

Alan scratched his head, pondering. 'Mm, there is that,' he said. 'I told her not to worry about it.'

'I said much the same thing,' lied Irene. 'These things happen in their own good time, that's what I told her.'

'She wouldn't have walked out on me just because of that, though, surely,' he said, becoming more frantic with every passing moment. 'There must be more to it than that. I have to find her; find out what all this is about.'

'Calm down,' advised his mother.

'How can I when I feel so powerless?' he snapped. 'How could she do this to me? How could she?'

'Come and sit down and have a cup of tea, dear,' suggested his mother. 'Have you had breakfast?'

'Breakfast!' he exploded. 'My world's just fallen apart and you ask me if I've had breakfast?'

'You must eat, son,' said Gerald.

'Of course you must.' Irene put her hand on Alan's arm. 'Just some tea and toast then.'

'No. I don't want any bloody toast, Mother, thank you very much,' he shouted at her. 'And will you please stop treating me like a five-year-old child?'

'Just trying to help.'

He sighed. 'I know you are and I'm sorry. I must go. There's no point in my staying here upsetting you.'

'I'd better come with you,' she said.

'Whatever for?' he thundered, misunderstanding her motive.

'To replace June in reception, of course,' she explained. 'Someone will have to do it until we get a new receptionist.'

'Oh, yes, of course,' he muttered. 'But that's the least of my worries at this precise moment. The way I feel, the hotel can grind to a halt for all I care.'

'That's an extremely selfish and irresponsible attitude,' admonished his father.

'I know it is,' Alan agreed, 'but I think I can be forgiven for a little selfishness when my wife's just left me. I'm hardly likely to be full of the joys of spring, am I?'

'No. But business must go on, whatever your personal problems,' preached his father.

'Yeah, yeah,' sighed Alan. 'I know all about that so you can spare me the lecture.'

But Gerald wasn't that easily silenced when it came to the subject of his hotel. 'The guests have paid good money to be well looked after and it's our job to see that they are, no matter what's going on in our personal lives,' he went on. 'They come to us to have a good holiday and if they don't have it, it must be through no fault of ours. A reputation can take years to build but it can be ruined much quicker.'

'Don't worry, I won't drive them all away with my bad temper. I'm too well trained for that,' Alan told him. 'To the guests, I'll be my charming self, as usual.'

'You can take the morning off if you don't feel up to it,' offered his father. 'Your mother and I will stand in for you.'

'No, no,' said Alan. 'As you say, the show must go on and I intend to see that it does.'

'That's the spirit,' approved Gerald.

'I'll be over in a few minutes,' Irene told him. 'I'll just wash the dishes and make myself look decent.'

'I'll come with her,' said Gerald.

Alan softened towards them. They meant well and it wasn't their fault that he hadn't been able to hang on to his wife. 'Thanks for the support,' he said.

'The least we can do,' said his mother.

Alan left and walked back to the Cliff Head. He couldn't ever remember feeling this desolate. There had been bad times when he'd been in action during the war, but at least he'd been able to fight back then. How could he fight back now when he didn't know what he was up against? Even worse was the thought that if he did find her, June might not want to come back. How could he reverse the process if she'd fallen out of love with him?

No, he couldn't accept that that's what had happened. He and June had had their ups and downs and things had been a bit strained between them lately because she couldn't get pregnant. But they still loved each other, despite everything. He was convinced of that. Why then had she left him?

His head was throbbing with tension as he made his way up the wide stone steps and into the hotel foyer.

Chapter Three

During a prolonged spell of wet weather in August that confined two lively little girls to two small rooms for longer than their ability to amuse themselves, Daisy saved the sanity of them all by teaching them how to play snap.

Being about right for their age group, the game quickly became a favourite, producing fun and sibling rivalry in equal measures. Shrieks of excitement and laughter were punctuated with howls of disagreement after simultaneous cries of 'snap'. They kept themselves amused for ages and Daisy congratulated herself on finding such a gem.

One rainy Saturday evening, when Daisy had a rare night off from waitressing, the girls persuaded her and Nora to join them in a game, and a companionable atmosphere settled over Daisy's flat as the four of them entered into this childish activity with gusto. To make her night off into a special occasion for them all, Daisy had bought crisps, pop, and a bottle of stout for Nora.

'Snap!' yelled Shirley, eyes gleaming victoriously.

'It was me, I said it first,' disputed Belinda heatedly.

'You did *not*, I did,' argued her sister.

'Liar,' came the vehement accusation.

'You're the liar,' Shirley returned hotly. 'Tell her, Mum. Go on, tell her.'

'That's quite enough squabbling, both of you,' admonished their mother. 'So pack it in.'

'It's her fault.' Belinda was very put out, her lips turned down at the corners and trembling slightly. 'She's cheating.'

'No she is *not*,' intervened the fair-minded Daisy. 'Shirley called snap first so don't spoil the game by being a bad sport.'

'She's the bad sport,' huffed Belinda, glaring at her sister. 'It's not fair.'

'Shirley was first to say it,' Daisy told her youngest daughter again and with emphasis.

'Your mother's right,' came back-up support from Nora.

'I said it first.' Belinda was really digging her heels in on this one.

But her mother could be equally as determined. 'I was listening carefully and I heard you both,' she said firmly to Belinda. 'She beat you to it by a fraction of a second but she *was* first. You'll probably do it next time, love.'

'I did it this time,' the child insisted, eyes brimming with angry tears at this conspiracy against her.

'Right, that's it.' Daisy decided it was time to get tough. 'You, Belinda, are behaving like a spoiled little brat and you'll go to bed if you don't give up . . . and you can stop smirking, Shirley, or you'll go with her. If the two of you can't play together without practically coming to blows, I shall confiscate the cards so that you can't play at all. I've never heard such a carry-on. You don't usually behave like this, do they, Nora?'

'Not normally, no,' supported the other woman, switching her gaze to the girls and adding, 'but you're like a couple of spiteful cats tonight.'

Belinda pouted a bit but finally decided to swallow her pride and they continued the game with noisy hilarity. Amid the gales of laughter there was an assertive knock at the door.

'You play my cards for me, Nora,' requested Daisy, smiling as she went to answer it. 'I won't be a minute.'

Opening the door to find herself confronted by two men she hadn't seen before, Daisy felt a chill settle over her at the air of menace about them. Tall and muscular, they both had their hair slicked back with grease and were wearing open-necked shirts with the sleeves rolled up to reveal big, solid arms. Each man was holding an Alsatian dog on a leash, one of which strained towards Daisy, barking and baring its teeth.

Its keeper pulled at the lead. 'Heel, boy,' he ordered gruffly, and the animal quietened down, though a growl continued to rumble in the back of its throat.

'Yes?' she said enquiringly, struggling to quell her rising panic.

'Rent,' was the brief reply.

'Oh? But it isn't due until Monday,' she explained. 'Someone usually comes to collect it on a Monday morning.'

'The boss wants it today,' she was informed by the man who seemed to be the spokesman.

As it happened she did have the rent money put aside so early payment wasn't a problem. But she was curious as to the reason for this premature demand. 'Does this mean you'll always be collecting on Saturdays in future?' she asked.

The man shrugged indifferently. 'Dunno,' he told her. 'We're just carrying out orders.'

She went inside to get the money from one of a series of empty jam jars in which she kept the cash for various bills, and handed it over with the rent book in which he entered the amount.

Giving her the book back, he spoke to her in a gruff monotone.

44

'We've got a message for you from the boss.'

'Oh?'

'Mr Ellwood said to tell you that he hopes your kids ain't afraid of dogs,' he informed her, looking towards the animals. 'He said to tell you that these two can get very vicious.'

'He ought to be ashamed of himself, threatening the safety of little children,' declared an outraged Nora, who had come up behind Daisy, leaving the girls sitting at the table waiting for the game to continue.

'Nothing to do with us, missus.' The second man spoke at last. 'We're just messengers.'

'You ought to be ashamed of yourselves too, working for a man like Ellwood,' Nora continued, 'someone who goes about threatening decent people with dangerous dogs.'

The man just shrugged.

While Nora went to her rooms to get her rent money, muttering furiously under her breath, Daisy stepped outside and pulled the door to behind her so that the children were out of earshot. 'You tell Mr Ellwood that if those dogs go anywhere near my children, I'll have him done for threatening behaviour.' The protective instinct towards her children was so strong as to make her fearless, despite her obvious vulnerability. 'I'll have the law on to him so fast he'll wonder what's hit him.'

The thug's manner was completely insouciant. 'We'll tell him,' he said lazily, and they turned and went towards Nora's front door, collected her rent, then made their way downstairs.

'That Ellwood is really stepping up his campaign to get us out, isn't he?' observed Nora, as the men's footsteps receded down the stairs. 'He's putting pressure on from all sides now.'

'Yeah, it's a real worry.'

Over the past month or so, since Daisy's confrontation with the landlord, the annoyance factor in the house had worsened. There were more frequent and louder all-night parties in the basement, radiograms playing at all hours and drunken brawls. Several of the other statutory tenants had left.

'Are we still agreed that we won't be moved, though?' asked Nora.

'I'm not prepared to be driven out of my home by a thug like Ellwood, are you?'

'Not likely,' Nora confirmed. 'The way I see it, it's a war of attrition. He'll try to wear us down and frighten us, but he wouldn't dare to cause us or the kids actual physical harm because then we really would have grounds to involve the law and he wouldn't want the police sniffing around.' She shook her head, puffing out her lips to emphasise the point. 'Oh, no. He's far too dodgy to let that happen.'

'Exactly,' agreed Daisy. 'So we have to stand firm and make sure that we keep that in mind when he makes things difficult for us. We mustn't be panicked into leaving and making ourselves homeless. It's a question of keeping our nerve no matter what he comes up with to scare us.'

'And in the meantime, we have a game of snap awaiting our attention.'

Daisy grinned. 'That's right. It'll take more than a couple of heavies and their snarling mutts to spoil our evening, eh, Nora?'

'Not half,' was her hearty agreement, and they went back inside together.

Within minutes the game was back underway, a warm, enveloping buzz of conversation and laughter filling the room as though they hadn't had visitors with a sinister message. Even the sound of the rain beating against the creaky old windows was barely noticeable alongside the merry din. But Daisy was far more worried than she was letting on. She could be brave when facing thugs, and positive in front of Nora and the children, but what chance did she and Nora really stand against someone like Roland Ellwood, who had money behind him and an army of strong men on his payroll? For how much longer could the women hold out against him if he was determined to get them out of here? And what lengths was he prepared to go to, to destat his property? Although she hated to admit it, the prospect of homelessness was beginning to loom with sickening intensity. If that were to happen and the authorities got to know about it, they would try to take the girls away from her.

She was recalled to the present by Belinda telling her it was her turn. 'If you don't pay attention, Mum, you'll have to stop playing because we don't want daydreamers in our game,' she said in an amusing parody of her mother.

'Don't push your luck, my girl.' But Daisy was smiling as she put her card down and shouted, 'Snap.'

Imbued by a strong feeling of wellbeing generated by the company, she felt cheered by a surge of new resolve. She had a huge incentive to fight back against the landlord: two little girls who were reliant on her to put a roof over their heads, and a neighbour she'd grown to love as a mother. They might all be society's cast-offs but they were a unit in themselves, a caring little sisterhood making the best of life at the bottom of the pile. This attic was cold, damp and hopelessly inadequate but it was their home and she was damned if she'd let a skunk like Roland Ellwood drive them out because of greed. If they ever did move from here it would be from choice and because they had somewhere better to go, she was determined about that.

It was raining heavily in Torquay that Saturday night, too.

'Bloody weather,' Alan complained to Jack Saunders, with whom

46

he was having a drink at the bar after work. 'It's more like November than August.'

'That's the British summer for you,' said Jack. 'Unreliable to say the least.'

'You must have been mad to leave all that lovely Australian sunshine behind to come back to our miserable weather,' commented Alan, who had been in the blackest of moods since June's departure a week ago.

'There's more to a place than good weather, mate,' he pointed out. 'It's a completely different way of life out there.'

'That's why people go abroad to live, surely.'

'And why some of them come back,' was Jack's answer to that. 'You've got to actually experience a country to know if you're going to take to it. Australia's a beautiful place with wonderful scenery and bags of opportunity – I can't speak highly enough of the country – but it just wasn't for me. It wasn't easy leaving my folks out there, but the longing to come home was just too strong in the end.'

'I suppose there was no point in your staying if you felt like that.' Alan sipped his beer, gloomily looking at the rain running down the windows. 'The way I feel at the moment I'd go there tomorrow if I could.'

'It isn't just the weather that's making you feel like that, though, is it?'

'No, of course not,' he confirmed. 'But the weather doesn't help when you're feeling down – not when you're running a seaside hotel, anyway.'

'Our line of business does make us more susceptible to the rain, I must admit,' agreed Jack.

'It isn't much fun for the guests when the weather does the dirty on them,' Alan went on. 'All year they look forward to a holiday by the sea and the last thing they want is to spend the whole time sitting about the hotel lounge playing cards and waiting for the rain to stop.'

'Still, at least we've had a television installed for them,' Jack reminded him. 'That helps to keep them entertained.'

Alan nodded. 'Mm. There is that. But people don't go on holiday to watch the telly. It's the kids I feel sorry for. I know we don't have many children staying at the Cliff Head but you see them trailing around the town with their mums and dads, hoping it will stop raining. All they want is for the sun to come out so they can go on the beach with their buckets and spades.'

'They're better off at home when it's like this.'

'They are,' agreed Alan. 'If I had my way I'd turn this place into a family hotel with an indoor pool and entertainment laid on for the bad weather.' He sighed resignedly. 'Still, I'm not likely to get my way about that, so there's no point my going on about it.'

'I gather from your mood that there's still no news of June, then,' Jack surmised.

'Not a word, mate,' Alan told him. 'What the hell possessed her to go off like that?'

'Don't ask me,' said Jack. 'I'm just a single bloke, and the last person to know what goes on in a woman's mind.'

Alan cast a studious eye over his handsome pal. 'You must know a thing or two about them, though,' he suggested. 'I mean, you're not exactly a novice in that direction, are you?'

'There have been women in my life, naturally,' Jack confirmed. 'I'm a normal, healthy twenty-eight-year-old.'

'But you haven't got married . . .'

'I've come close to it,' he confessed. 'But never actually did the deed.'

'Wouldn't you like someone to share your life with?' asked Alan, who'd loathed the single life this past week.

'Wouldn't we all? But not just anyone to save me from being alone,' he explained. 'I'm still soft enough to believe that there's someone specially for me out there somewhere. And if I meet her – wonderful. But until that happens my bachelor life suits me down to the ground. I've got my motorbike, my cottage and my freedom – that'll do me.'

'You can't seriously compare those things to a woman in your life?' said Alan.

'I'm not that weird,' Jack protested, 'but I'd never get married just because it's the thing to do. Anyway, I've got a bit set in my ways now. I come and go as I please. It would take someone really special to make me want to change my way of life.'

'Don't you get lonely living at the cottage on your own?' Alan asked. 'With it being a bit off the beaten track.'

Jack had an old stone cottage on the seashore at Gullscombe Bay, a small village a few miles outside Torquay. It was a beautiful spot but very remote, with a long sandy beach, rugged red cliffs and large expanses of open grassland.

'No, not at all,' he said without hesitation. 'I'm here at the hotel surrounded by people most of the time, anyway. And when I'm off duty I've got a friendly local pub where I can go at any time and find someone I know to talk to.' He shrugged. 'If I feel in need of something a bit more sophisticated, I just get on the bike and come in to town. It only takes about ten minutes. And Exeter's no distance on the bike if I fancy something livelier.'

'Sounds as though you've got yourself sorted.'

'I've no complaints.'

'Was it just the price that made you buy a place in such an out-of-the-way spot?' Alan enquired chattily.

'The fact that it was dirt cheap was the deciding factor, yeah,' he confirmed. 'But I've got to love it there and I wouldn't want to live anywhere else, especially now that I've renovated the cottage and got it how I want it. The location's great for me. I enjoy all that open space and rolling surf on my doorstep.' He grinned, raising his brows. 'And I don't live like a recluse. I do have the occasional female visitor.'

'Footloose and fancy-free, eh?' Alan was staring moodily into his beer glass.

'Exactly.'

'Technically that's what I am now, I suppose, now that my wife's left me,' Alan pondered. 'But I don't feel free. I just feel lonely and miserable.'

'Yeah, well, you're bound to feel like that at this early stage. Anyone would.' Jack was thoughtful. 'I still can't help thinking that there's more to June going off than you know about.'

'Another man is odds-on favourite among the staff, I bet,' assumed Alan. 'The gossips must be having a field day. It's wives who usually get deserted, not the other way round. She's made a right fool of me.'

'I expect there is gossip, but not in front of me,' Jack was quick to assure him. 'They wouldn't dare because they know we're friendly, and I would give them a mouthful. June was devoted to you, anyone could see that. And she certainly isn't the type to play around. You'd have spotted the signs if anything like that had been going on.'

'Yeah, I think so too – and being made a fool of is the least of my worries, to be honest.' He paused, looking at Jack in a questioning manner. 'You knew her quite well. Had she seemed to be worried or unhappy to you just lately?'

'No,' was Jack's considered reply. 'She didn't get on with your folks, that's common knowledge. But I don't think she'd have left over that at this stage because it's been going on for so long. You never know what someone's feeling inside, of course, but I got the impression she was used to the way things were between them and her, and didn't let it get her down.'

'It always seemed like that. And my mother swears blind she hadn't said anything to upset her.' Alan raised his eyes, tutting. 'God, I feel so powerless. If only I knew where she was.'

'You can't force her to come back, though.'

'No. But if I knew where she was, at least I could try to find out what it's all about.'

'Maybe she just needs some time on her own,' suggested Jack.

'Mm.' Alan pondered the idea. 'I've been assuming that she left on the spur of the moment, but when you think about it, she must have had somewhere to go. She wouldn't just walk out of here with nowhere to stay, would she? So she must have planned it.'

49

'Not necessarily,' Jack disagreed. 'If she'd gone to a relative she'd have felt she could just turn up without warning.'

'As far as I know she doesn't have any relatives apart from her mother,' Alan said. 'And she'd sooner sleep on a park bench than go to her.'

'Really?'

Alan nodded. 'That's the impression she gave me, anyway, though she never said what the trouble was. She never talked about her parents and I didn't press her to do so as it was obvious she didn't want to. I've never even met them. They didn't come to the wedding and she didn't want me to go with her to her father's funeral.'

Suddenly this seemed hugely significant to Alan. Surely it was unusual for a wife not to talk to her husband about her family background. Glancing back on their life together, in the light of what had now happened, he could see that there had always been an air of mystery about June.

'I can't imagine June doing anything underhand,' said Jack, 'so I don't think she would have planned it in advance.'

'No, I suppose not,' agreed Alan. 'But where the hell is she?'

'Search me, mate,' was all Jack could say. 'All you can do is hope for a lead.'

'One of those isn't going to drop into my lap, is it?'

'Something will turn up, eventually,' Jack suggested hopefully. 'And in the meantime, you'll just have to try and stop tearing your hair out and carry on as best as you can without her. You know where I am if you need a mate.'

'Thanks, Jack.'

It was well after hours. The bar was closed, the customers all departed and the bar staff gone off duty. Alan went behind the counter and got them each another drink – just a small glass of beer for Jack as he had to go home on the motorbike.

'Did you see that article in the *Hoteliers' Chronicle* about private bathrooms?' Jack asked, deliberately changing the subject to take Alan's mind off things.

'No, I only flicked through this month's issue,' Alan told him. 'Why? Is it interesting?'

'It's worth a look,' replied Jack. 'They reckon that en suite bathrooms will eventually become standard in all decent class hotels, rather than just a luxury that people pay extra for.'

'They must be talking a long time into the future then,' frowned Alan.

'They're not expecting it to happen tomorrow or next week,' Jack agreed. 'But whoever wrote the article seems to think that private facilities are going to be more in demand in the not-too-distant future. Some of the new hotels being built will have them to every room as a matter of course.'

50

'Seems a bit far-fetched to me,' said Alan.

'That's what I thought.'

'If it does happen, though, it'll create pressure for the rest of us to do the same or lose out to the opposition,' Alan observed darkly. 'And something like that is right out of our league here at the Cliff Head. It would cost an absolute fortune to get all our rooms upgraded.'

'Mm.'

'So whatever the trend is we'll have to manage with the few rooms with private bathrooms we already have,' Alan went on. 'It isn't as though we don't have hot and cold running water in every room.'

'They're taking the view that hotel proprietors will make the changes gradually over a long period, a room at a time,' Jack explained. 'Anyway, the article's worth a few minutes of your time. It might take your mind off your problems.'

'I'll have a look if the *Chronicle* hasn't been chucked out by mistake in all the upheaval of June going. I've been that distracted this week.'

'I've still got my copy if you can't find yours.' Jack finished his beer. 'Anyway, I must be off. If I have any more to drink I won't be in a fit state to go at all.'

'I'm a bad influence on you, keeping you out so late,' Alan apologised. 'I dread going to bed, that's why. Too many thoughts and too much emptiness upstairs in the flat.' He finished his drink and slipped off the bar stool with a purposeful air. 'But it has to be done and I must be man enough to do it. I mustn't keep you from your bed just because I don't want to face mine.'

'See you tomorrow.'

'Sure.'

Jack departed and Alan went behind the bar and rinsed their glasses. Then he turned off the lights and made his lonely way up to the flat in the lift.

The place felt like a morgue without her, Alan thought, as he stood in the living room staring out of the rain-soaked windows across the bay, the lights of Torquay hazed by the wet.

Still unable to face the prospect of the empty bed, he turned away from the window and rummaged through the untidy heap of newspapers and magazines on the coffee table until he found the *Hoteliers' Chronicle*. Settling into an armchair, he flicked through the pages until he found the article Jack had mentioned, which he read with interest.

The journalist predicted that hotels would thrive in the current affluent climate, which was expected to last for a while yet. People had more money to spend on leisure, which meant more of them could afford to go away on holiday, which in turn meant hoteliers would increase their profits, which would pay for them to improve their accommodation. The bit about the large increase in people taking their holidays abroad was rather worrying but the rest was fairly positive.

Alan leaned back in the chair, feeling slightly more relaxed for the diversion. He turned the pages in search of something to hold his attention until he was sleepy enough to face the lonely bedroom. Something caught his eye in the advertisement section. It wasn't the advertisement, as such, that interested him but the fact that it had a pencil ring around it. June was the only other person who would have looked at this copy of the *Chronicle* so she must have circled it. Why had she been interested in an advert?

When he read the advertisement – particularly the bit about accommodation being available – he understood why, and his heart leaped with new hope of finding her. There was no address and the name of the hotel wasn't given, but there was a phone number. It was a bit of a long shot but this just might be the lead he thought would never come. With optimism boosted considerably, he hurried to the telephone in the hall and asked the operator for a long-distance call to London.

'Central Hotel,' said a male voice he presumed to be that of the night porter.

'Sorry to bother you so late,' said Alan, pulses racing at this unexpected clue.

'No trouble at all, sir,' said the voice. 'That's what I'm here for.'

'The thing is,' began Alan, 'I have to meet someone at your hotel tomorrow and I'm not sure of your exact location. Can you help me with this, please?'

'Certainly, sir,' replied the man, and proceeded to give Alan the full address and directions to get there.

'Why did you do it, June?' Alan felt sad and puzzled rather than angry now that he'd actually found her. 'In heaven's name, why did you walk out on me?'

It was the evening of the next day and they were sitting drinking coffee in June's tiny room at the back of the hotel on the top floor. She'd moved in right away, having been given the job at the interview. She'd been very shaken on duty earlier when Alan had walked into reception with an overnight bag and booked a room for the night. When he'd explained how he'd tracked her down she'd cursed her carelessness. After she'd dealt with his booking, as though he was just any other guest, he'd asked for the chance to speak to her. She'd met him in the foyer when she came off duty and brought him up here because it was private.

'As I said in my letter, it's for the best.' She hadn't expected to have to confront him personally at this stage and was somewhat lost for words, as the truth wasn't an option. 'Believe me when I tell you that you're better off without me.'

52

'What's that supposed to mean?' he demanded, temper rising again. 'You're talking in riddles.'

'It hasn't been working for a while between us,' she stated categorically.

'That just isn't true.'

'You won't deny there's been tension between us lately,' she said.

'A little maybe, over this baby business,' he was forced to admit. 'But no marriage is a bed of roses all the time, and we shouldn't expect ours to be.'

'I realise that but—'

'Stop fobbing me off with excuses and tell me what's going on, June.' He was becoming aggressive now. 'I want to know why you walked out and I'm not leaving here until you tell me.'

She couldn't tell him the real reason without hurting him even more so she said rather feebly, 'I've never really fitted in at the Cliff Head.'

'You've always fitted in as far as I'm concerned. Surely that's what matters,' he was quick to point out. 'OK, so you never hit it off with my parents, but it's me you're married to, me you shared your life with, not them.' He fixed her with a stare. 'Anyway, if they were getting you down, you should have told me and I've have done something about it.' He paused again, squinting at her in a questioning manner. 'I don't believe that's why you left. We've been married for seven years and you've taken all that stuff with my parents in your stride. So let's have the real reason you walked out.'

His eyes were so full of hurt, she longed to hold him in her arms and soothe it away. But to do so would give him false hope because there was no possibility of her going back to him. She hadn't left on a whim. The decision to go had been a sudden one but she'd always known deep in her heart that she should never have married him.

Because she couldn't be honest with him, she just said, 'It wasn't any one thing—'

'It's got something to do with your not getting pregnant, hasn't it?' he guessed.

She reeled from his words but managed to answer in an even tone. 'No,' she lied to avoid any possibility of persuasion or suggestion of medical advice.

'I want a child. I'd be lying if I said otherwise,' he admitted. 'But if it isn't meant to be, I'll have to cope with that and so will you. But we will face it together. There's no point in your running away from it, June.'

'I'm sorry, Alan, but I'm not coming back.' She knew she must be strong, for his sake. 'I know it was a terrible thing for me to walk out without any warning. But I knew you'd try and stop me if I told you, and I really did have to go.'

He ran a critical eye around the room, which was sparsely furnished and so small as to be more of a cupboard than a room. There were no facilities beyond a bed, a wardrobe and the chairs they were sitting on. She had to go down the corridor to the bathroom, staff kitchen and sitting room.

'Look what you've come down to,' he told her. 'This is little more than a rabbit hutch.' He went to the window and stared out at the dreary view of the windows of buildings opposite and a yard far below. 'You must really be desperate to get away from me to have given up a comfortable home with a seaview for a miserable little gaff like this.' He turned to look into her face. 'We had a good life, didn't we? What more did you want from me?'

'Nothing at all, Alan,' she assured him. 'My leaving had nothing to do with any fault in you, or the way we lived.'

'All right, so we had to work bloody hard in the season,' he went on, as though trying to make sense of it. 'But things are not so bad in the winter. I was even going to suggest that we think about going abroad for a holiday this winter. Somewhere warm. I thought you'd like that.'

'I would, of course—' she began.

'Our future is assured, June,' he continued as though she hadn't spoken, too distressed for rational conversation. 'The Cliff Head will be ours one day.'

'Yours,' she corrected.

'Same thing. What's mine is yours.'

'It's irrelevant anyway because I'm not coming back.'

'I can't understand it.' He looked bewildered. 'Instead of staying to work with me and reap the rewards of our hard work, you choose to turn your back on it all, for this.'

'It's a job and a roof over my head,' she pointed out dully. 'It'll do for now.'

'But you don't need to make do in a place like this.' He spread his hands expressively. 'Your home is with me at the Cliff Head.'

'Not any more, Alan,' she said sadly.

He was silent for a while. Then: 'In all the years we've been together, I've never thought of you as a selfish person.' His voice was distorted with anguish and frustration. 'But that's the only conclusion I can come to now. You're being downright selfish, June. Have you any idea what you're doing to me?'

'Of course I have.' She was struggling not to break down.

'So why put me through it, then?'

'It's something I have to do, Alan.' She was very subdued. 'I really am very sorry.'

'You're *sorry*? You walk out on me after seven years and all you can say is sorry?'

She bit her lip. 'It's awful, I know.'

'That's an understatement, if ever I heard one.' Really distressed

54

now, he paced around the small room, head down, hands in pockets. 'OK, you say you weren't discontented with the way we lived. You say it isn't my parents who have driven you out and it isn't our apparent lack of ability to procreate. So the only explanation left is that you don't love me any more.'

'Leave it, Alan—'

'So tell me, when exactly did you fall out of love with me?'

She winced. Nothing could be further from the truth, but if his believing that would help him to accept the fact that she wasn't going back to Devon with him and that he must make a life without her, she would go along with it. 'It was a gradual thing,' she lied, staring at the floor.

'So . . . you don't even fancy me now, then?'

She forced herself to look up and face the torture in his eyes. 'I'm so sorry,' she said.

'Did I suddenly become repulsive to you? Did you have to shut your eyes and think of other things or pretend that I was someone else?' He wasn't going to let this go. 'Is that how it was?'

'Alan, stop it.'

'I want to know.'

'I don't know exactly,' she said through dry lips. 'I didn't keep a record of my emotions.'

He grabbed her by the arms. 'Of course you don't know because it isn't true.' He was shouting now. 'I refuse to believe that you don't love me or fancy me. I just won't have it.'

'Go home, Alan,' she urged him, exhausted by the trauma. 'It's busy at this time of the year at the Cliff Head. You'll have made things very awkward for the others by rushing off and leaving them to it.'

'They'll just have to manage without me,' he said. 'This is more important.'

'Nothing you say will make me change my mind.' She was adamant. 'So there's no point in continuing with this conversation. All you're doing is upsetting us both.'

'Oh, so it's all my fault, is it?'

'Of course not.'

He moved forward and took her face in his hands, forcing her to look at him. 'Look me in the eyes and tell me you don't love me. Go on, say it.'

She tried to avoid his probing gaze but failed completely. The depth and richness of his eyes drew her to him, making tears swell beneath her lids.

'Go on,' he ordered. 'Let me hear you say it.'

'All right.' She took a deep breath and forced the words out. 'I don't love you, Alan. And I'm not coming back to Devon with you – *not ever.*'

He stared at her in silence, then: 'I still don't believe that you don't love me,' he challenged her.

'You might not want to believe it, Alan,' she told him. 'But it's true.'

He looked so utterly stricken, for a moment she thought she was going to weaken and pour her heart out to him. She had to restrain herself physically from abandoning this whole thing and taking him in her arms. But she was saved from temptation when he flew into a sudden rage, fuelled by his powerlessness over the situation.

'You selfish cow,' he said with vehemence. 'My mother was right all the time. You're not worth bothering about.'

'I wondered how long it would be before she came into it,' June blurted out.

'Any woman who can do what you've done to me can't be worth bothering with,' he ground out. 'I don't need my mother to tell me that.'

'You're right. I'm not going to argue with you about it,' she told him wearily. 'So go home to Torquay and forget about me. You can divorce me if you wish. I won't put up any opposition.'

'You speak about divorce as though it's of no more importance than what's on at the cinema,' he exploded.

'I didn't mean to give that impression.'

'I don't believe I'm hearing any of this.' He shook his head. 'I really thought I knew you. I thought we were soul mates.'

'We were for a while,' she said. 'Everything has its time, and the time for us has gone.'

'I thought you women were red hot about remembering your marriage vows but you seem to have forgotten yours completely,' he said bitterly. 'Marriage doesn't have its time. It's a forever thing . . . in good times and bad.'

'Things aren't always that neat and tidy.'

'Apparently not. After all we've been to each other, I thought I knew you,' he said through tight lips, as though she hadn't spoken. 'But you're like a stranger now.'

'No one ever really knows anyone else, Alan,' June pointed out. 'We're all on our own when it comes down to it.'

'I can do without the psychology, thank you very much.' His voice was tight with controlled rage. 'I'm just an ordinary bloke who thought he had a decent marriage. I don't need a lecture on the deeper side of human nature.'

'This isn't getting us anywhere so I think you'd better leave.' She stood up. 'If I were you, I'd get some sleep and take an early train back to Torquay in the morning.'

'I will, don't worry.' His attitude was harsh now, with a new edge of determination as he accepted the fact that she wasn't going to change her mind. 'But I can tell you one thing: you'll be sorry you did this, *very sorry.*'

He couldn't know how bitterly she regretted it already. 'Perhaps,' she sighed.

'No perhaps about it.' He was hitting out and saying things he didn't mean in the heat of the moment. 'Even if you don't miss me personally, when the novelty of freedom wears off and you're stuck in this miserable hole with no home comforts, you'll realise what you've turned your back on.'

She nodded.

'You could have had it all, June – a good life with a secure future – and you've just thrown it all away.'

'Which proves how serious I am about not coming back.' Her mouth was so parched she could hardly speak. 'No one chooses to live in accommodation like this.'

'If I'd treated you badly, what you've done would be justifiable.' It was as though he was thinking aloud. 'But I've never been unfaithful, never laid a finger on you.'

'I've told you that none of this is your fault.'

'Right, that's enough begging and pleading,' he said, his tone ice-hard. 'You've just blown your last chance with me. I wouldn't have you back now if you got down on your knees and begged me.'

She didn't say anything.

'So don't come crawling back when you've had enough of being on your own because my door will be closed to you,' he roared. 'Understand?'

Still she didn't put up a fight or try to explain the real reason for her behaviour. There was no point as she had no defence she could tell him about. There hadn't been a word of truth in what she'd said. Her brutal callousness was the best thing for him in the long term and she must stand by her decision. 'I understand,' she said in a subdued tone.

'What shall I do with your stuff?' he asked bitterly. 'You only took the basic essentials.'

'Perhaps you could give it to a charity, or if that's too much bother just throw it out,' she suggested sadly.

He gave her a long hard look, the fury in his eyes softening momentarily into a look of pleading. She almost weakened but managed to stand firm.

Without another word, he marched to the door and opened it, turning towards her. 'I hope you rot in hell,' he said, and left, slamming the door behind him.

She couldn't move; just stood where she was, frozen to the spot. She had experienced terrible things in her life, things most people couldn't even imagine: indescribable pain and humiliation almost beyond human endurance. But she couldn't remember ever feeling this desolate before.

Forcing her limbs to work, she walked slowly over to the bed in the corner and lay face down, burying her head in the pillow, unable even to relieve herself in tears. She thought this must surely be her darkest moment.

Chapter Four

It was a big day in the Rivers household because Shirley was starting school. Despite her mother's most ardent reassurance, the little girl was beset with doubts about the 'new adventure' on account of something she'd heard from an authority on the subject, a seasoned schoolgirl of several months' standing whom she played with in the street.

'She said the teachers are all horrid old witches who shout at you and make you stand in the corner if you do anything wrong,' she said while Daisy was brushing her daughter's hair and putting an Alice band on it.

'The teachers aren't all horrid old witches at all,' Daisy assured her. 'They're good people who'll teach you to do lots of new things.'

'They're horrid.' Shirley was convinced. 'Jane said if you're really bad you get the cane, though I think that mostly happens to the boys.'

'Whoever's been filling your head with these stories obviously doesn't behave herself.' Daisy chose her words carefully, wanting to be honest without frightening her. 'If you're naughty, of course the teacher will get cross with you, the same as I do. But I'm sure you won't give her any cause. And as for getting the cane, well, that's very unlikely.'

'I wish I didn't have to go, Mum.'

'I know, love. But once you get there with all the other children, you'll be fine, I promise,' Daisy told her, swallowing a lump in her throat. 'I'll be at the school gate waiting for you when you come out and you'll be dying to tell me about all the new things you've been doing.'

A cheery rat-a-tat at the door announced the arrival of Nora, who had called in on her way to work to wish Shirley luck. 'My word, someone looks smart this morning,' she complimented, admiring Shirley's navy-blue gymslip and white blouse, both bought second-hand and made to look new by Daisy.

Shirley managed a stiff little smile but her lips were dry and her eyes like saucers in a face that was pale with nervous apprehension. 'Thank you,' she said politely.

'She's got navy-blue knickers on,' divulged Belinda, triumphant to be the bearer of such privileged information.

'She would do now that she's going to school,' was Nora's reaction. 'All schoolgirls wear those.'

'I want a pair, Mum.' Belinda didn't like to be left out.

'When you go to school you'll have them whether you like it or not,' she was told by her mother. 'This time next year you'll both be wearing navy-blue drawers.'

'A year's a long time, isn't it?' said the wistful Belinda.

'It'll come round before you know it . . . much too quickly for me,' remarked Daisy, managing to sound chirpy though there was a certain poignancy in the air, today being the end of an era as well as a new beginning. 'You're both growing up so fast I'm losing my babies.'

'Well, I'm off to work then,' announced Nora. 'See you later. Have a good day, Sherl. Ta-ta all.'

'Ta-ta,' they chorused.

Daisy and Belinda walked to the school with Shirley, who carried a navy-blue shoe bag containing a pair of plimsolls, as instructed on the school list Daisy had received in advance. It was a crisp autumn morning with the promise of sunshine, though a smoky mist currently shrouded the dusty streets. There was a steady procession of children trekking towards the school, the new ones staying close to their mothers, the old hands making their own way, scuffing and pushing and showing off.

As it was Shirley's first day, Daisy was allowed inside the school to deliver her into the care of the reception teacher, a painful business for both mother and daughter. After a last brave hug, Daisy left feeling heartless. Knowing that to send a child forth was just one of life's brutal necessities didn't make her feel any the less emotional about it. Daisy hoped most fervently that the day would be kind to her first-born.

'Well, Belinda love, it's just you and me today,' she remarked, as they headed home hand in hand. When there was no reply she looked down to see that the small child was crying silently. 'Aah, what's the matter?'

'I want Shirley,' she sobbed, huge tears meandering down her cheeks.

'She's only gone to school, darling,' Daisy pointed out. 'She'll be back this afternoon.'

But the child wasn't soothed. 'I want Shirley, I want my sister,' she wailed.

The look of sheer misery on her face triggered off a memory with such painful clarity that Daisy felt winded by it. More than twenty years ago she'd said the same thing about her own sister and received a good hiding for daring to mention her. 'She'll be home before you know it,' she said kindly, wiping her daughter's eyes with a rag hanky

60

and giving her a cuddle. 'It'll soon be time for us to come back to the school to meet her.'

Belinda seemed pacified with this and Daisy thanked God she could give her that reassurance. She herself hadn't been blessed in that way. In retrospect she could see that she'd never felt complete after losing her sister, and resolved there and then that her own daughters wouldn't be put through the misery of being parted, not while she had breath in her body. Perhaps in these enlightened times more thought was given to the agony of splitting up siblings. But no one had considered it important back in the 1930s. Feed them, keep them clean and teach them right from wrong, that had been the maxim for children in care. Their emotional wellbeing hadn't entered into the equation.

'How long till she comes home?' enquired Belinda, her voice still wobbling slightly.

'A few hours, that's all,' replied Daisy. 'She's gone to school – not emigrated.'

'Hours means ages,' she sighed.

'How about us doing something nice to make it go quicker for you?' suggested Daisy in a positive manner. 'We could go to the swings later on and have a sticky bun in a café afterwards. Would you like that?'

'Ooh, yes, please, Mum.'

The bond between siblings was a curious one, thought Daisy, because within minutes of Shirley being home from school she and Belinda would probably be scrapping like street dogs. Yet, such was the complexity of human nature, they hated to be apart. She wondered how she would have got on with her sister in adulthood had they stayed together. Would they have remained close or drifted apart? That was something she would never know.

Just when Daisy had given Nat up as a complete dead loss, he would do something to redeem himself.

This happened one evening in November. After not showing his face for a couple of weeks, he turned up at Daisy's place on her Saturday night off, gave her some money towards the bills, brought sweets for the girls and offered to take Daisy to the pictures. Nora was enlisted as baby-sitter, and the couple went to see *Young at Heart* with Doris Day and Frank Sinatra. All of this and chocolates too, a half-pound box no less, and he also took her for a couple of drinks at the pub afterwards.

She guessed he'd done some lucrative business deal but she knew better than to quiz him about it, and just accepted the treat graciously.

'This is lovely,' she said, sipping a gin and orange at a table in the crowded pub. 'Us having a night out together. We should do it more often.'

Reluctant as ever to commit himself to anything beyond the current moment, Nat said, 'Yeah, it would be nice but it isn't that easy, is it? Because of the girls.'

'Nora is always willing to sit with them if we want to go out on my night off,' Daisy pointed out, her joy at this rare attention from him giving her an added radiance, eyes shining, cheeks glowing prettily against her bright red coat. 'We could take the girls out sometimes too. During the day on a Saturday, for instance . . . to the park or the river.'

'Mm.'

'Don't overdo the enthusiasm.'

'You know me,' he reminded her. 'I'm not at my best with kids. I never know what to say to them.'

'These aren't just any kids, they're your daughters,' Daisy was quick to point out. 'You'd know what to say to them if you would only take the trouble to spend time with them and get to know them. They're growing faster than weeds. Surely you don't want to turn around one day to find that they're adults and you're a stranger to them.'

'Of course I don't.' He wasn't really bothered and didn't want to talk about his responsibilities when he'd gone out to enjoy himself for the evening. 'I suppose I've just never got round to spending time with them.'

'You are their father, Nat,' she said. 'You really should make the effort.'

'Yeah, yeah. Don't spoil a good night out by giving me a load of grief,' he protested. 'I'll try to be better in the future.'

'I've heard that before.'

'I mean it this time.'

'I wish I could believe that.'

He reached for her hand across the table. 'I know I'm a bit unreliable sometimes but you mean the world to me,' he said, his mood becoming tender.

'You don't love me enough to marry me, though.' She had seized the opportunity to make a point but was doing so in an affectionate manner.

'I will, one day.'

'I've waited so long, I'm beginning to lose hope.'

'It'll happen, Daisy,' he said softly, 'I promise.'

In this mood he was irresistible, and the common sense she usually had in such abundance just vanished. She could have wept with love for him. 'I believe you, thousands wouldn't,' she said lightly.

They had another drink, then walked home hand in hand. It felt utterly perfect and Daisy was content. At the bottom of the attic stairs, he commented on the fact that the whole area was in darkness as it had been the last time he was here. 'It's about time this light was fixed, isn't it?' he observed. 'Someone could fall and hurt themselves.'

'You don't have to tell me how dangerous it is,' she said. 'We have to use candles to go up and down stairs at night, and to use the sink on the landing. It's a damned nuisance, especially when one of the kids wants to go to the bathroom in the night.'

'I take it it doesn't just need a new bulb then?'

'If it was as simple as that we'd have seen to it by now,' she pointed out. 'It's a job for an electrician and the landlord's responsibility. He's supposed to be dealing with it but we're not holding our breath.'

'He can't be bothered, I suppose.'

'There's more to it than that,' she informed him. 'It's all part of his plan to get us out of here. When something needs fixing in the house, he leaves it in the hope that the inconvenience will drive us out. Some of the other long-term tenants have left. But Nora and I won't budge.'

'Wouldn't it be easier to just leave?' he suggested.

'Where would I find a place at a price I can afford?' she asked, reminded again of his lack of interest in her problems.

'It would be difficult, I suppose . . .'

'Anyway, it's downright wicked what Ellwood is doing – trying to drive decent people out of their homes,' Daisy continued. 'And you never know what stunt he's going to pull next. What with getting people to keep us awake at night with loud music and parties, employing gangster types to collect the rent in a menacing manner, and withdrawing any sort of maintenance, I don't know where it will all end.'

There was a silence, then he said worriedly, 'You know that I'm not in a position to offer you and the girls a home with me at the moment, don't you, Daisy? I would if I could but I just don't have the room.'

She was used to the fact that he shirked involvement. But for some reason it touched a raw nerve and something rose in her, something so strong it pushed aside her devotion to him so that she was able to take a clear, realistic look at the situation. Not only did he refuse to offer her and the girls a home or financial support, he didn't give them any practical help either. He never offered to speak to the landlord on her behalf, or to have a few words with the offending neighbours in the hope of making them more considerate. His children could fall down the stairs and break their necks without a light to see by and his only contribution was a feeble remark about the light needing fixing. Where were his paternal instincts? Where was his sense of duty towards her? Absolutely nonexistent.

Tears swelled beneath her lids and she admonished herself for being so soft. After all, it was a long time since she'd been under any illusions about Nat. If he'd had a responsible bone in his body she'd have spotted it by now. She'd always accepted him as he was, with all his faults. But tonight, for some reason, his attitude stuck in her craw.

'I'd have to be really thick not to realise that, Nat,' she snapped. 'So you can stop panicking. The last thing I would ever do is ask you for help.'

She couldn't see his face in the dark but guessed his expression would be one of relief. He didn't even bother to make a token protest and they made their way up the darkened stairs slowly and carefully, in silence.

Because Nat had no sense of diplomacy, he made the reason for the evening's generosity glaringly obvious as soon as Nora had gone and he and Daisy were alone. He slipped his arms around her as she waited for the kettle to boil for coffee.

'Don't, Nat,' she said, pushing him away.

'Why not?'

'Because I don't want you to.'

'The girls are asleep and the bedroom door's closed,' he pointed out, insistently putting his arms around her again. 'So we've got this room to ourselves.'

'No.' Her tone was more assertive.

'Oh, I get it. It's the time of the month.'

'No, it isn't that.'

'What then?'

'I just don't want to,' she informed him briskly, pouring water on to the bottled coffee essence in the cups.

Nat wasn't easily deterred when it came to pleasures of the flesh. He grabbed her by the arms roughly and pulled her round to face him. 'Come on, Daisy. Don't mess me about,' he said in a threatening manner.

She was sickened by him; even more by herself for allowing him to use her and take her for granted for so long. She'd cheapened herself because of her feelings for him and she felt dirty and stupid suddenly. 'I'm not messing you about,' she told him. 'I'm just being truthful. I don't want to do it and that's that.'

'There's a name for women who lead men on,' he declared.

'I haven't led you on.'

'Oh, not much,' he said vehemently. 'You were all over me when we were out, while I was spending money on you. Now you don't want to know.'

She was deeply hurt but her spirit remained intact. 'It was a trip to the local cinema, for heaven's sake, not a weekend at the Ritz,' she reminded him. 'And now I'm expected to show you how grateful I am.'

'There's no need to make it sound as though I'm committing some sort of a crime in expecting it,' he admonished sulkily. 'That's how these things work. I haven't noticed you putting up any objections before.'

'Maybe I'm beginning to wake up and see things in a different light,' she told him. 'After all this time I can see that the only thing that stops my relationship with you being prostitution is the fact that I do it for nothing.'

'There's no need to be vulgar, Daisy,' he rebuked primly. 'It doesn't suit you.'

'The truth can be crude.'

'Well, that's gratitude for you.' He was outraged. 'I took you out, gave you a good time, I even bought you chocolates—'

'And a couple of drinks at the pub and my cinema ticket. And you gave me money towards the bills.' She was furious now. 'As I'm not prepared to pay you in kind perhaps you'd like me to give you the money back. I'll have to repay what you've already spent on a weekly basis.' She paused for a moment, then added with emphasis, 'Unlike you, I don't have any spare cash to hand.'

'You can mock,' he chided her. 'But it all added up to quite a bit in the end.'

She marched across to the sideboard and took her purse out of her handbag. Dragging out the ten-shilling note he'd given her, she thrust it towards him. 'Here, have it back,' she demanded.

'Don't be like that.'

'You might as well take it 'cause you'll get no other form of payment from me.' She waved the note at him. 'Go on, take it. You know you want to.'

Surely even Nat wouldn't sink that low, she thought, but he said, 'All right, I will,' and snatched the money from her.

'You disgust me.' Her voice was dull with disappointment now. 'Get out.'

He walked to the door, paused for a moment, then turned and came back to her. Handing the money to her, he said in a conciliatory manner, 'Daisy, love, this is silly and beginning to get out of hand. Don't let's part on bad terms.'

'Just go.'

'You and me have been together a long time and we've always managed to patch things up before.'

'Only because I'm soft.' She didn't take the money.

'That's one of the things I love most about you,' he told her, his manner blatantly persuasive now. 'The fact that you're so warm and loving.'

'I'm also a fool,' she said coldly.

His limited patience soon ran out. 'Oh, I'm not staying here with you in this mood. I came here for pleasure not punishment,' he said irritably, walking to the door, stuffing the money into his pocket. 'I'll see you around.'

The door closed behind him and Daisy heard him cursing as he fumbled his way down the stairs in the dark. She felt battered and broken inside. How can he still have such power to hurt me? she wondered, sitting in the chair with a cup of coffee. After all these years and my knowing him for what he is?

With the same certainty that she knew he would be back, she knew she would forgive him. It was no life, being in a perpetual sulk with someone you cared about. At times she wished she'd never set eyes on him but mostly she didn't regret falling in love with him. How could she when he had given her the girls who were so obviously meant to be? Anyway, it wasn't as if he was wicked. He was just extremely immature and selfish. You had to make the most of what life sent you and Nat was part of her package.

As basic and poky as it was, the 'miserable little gaff' that Alan had been so derisive about did actually begin to feel like home to June that autumn. It was a far cry from the comfortable accommodation she'd been used to, but it was surprising how quickly she adapted to it. There was a certain comfort in being one of a number in the staff quarters, all people who for one reason or another had nowhere else to live.

There were foreign waiters, and waitresses and chamber maids from all over the UK. As they shared a sitting room and kitchen, naturally camaraderie evolved. There was always company on hand if June wanted it. Obviously she couldn't stay here for ever but it suited her in the short term.

She didn't hear from Alan again, but adjusting to life without him didn't seem any easier for that. Her salvation was the job, which was far more demanding than her position at the Cliff Head had been. The atmosphere here was totally different: much busier and less personal. The well-to-do guests in this central London hotel wanted efficiency and privacy rather than personal conversation. The phone rang constantly and there were always people milling about in the foyer, many of them from abroad.

The human touch was something she missed but she enjoyed the challenge of the work, which was never less than absorbing. No matter how desperate she was feeling about the state of her personal life, while she was actually on duty, she was forced to put it to the back of her mind.

At night it tormented her, though. On her own in her lonely room she longed for Alan and wondered how he was.

Day followed day, though, and life went on. Somehow June was managing without him, albeit that she seemed merely to be skimming over the surface of everyday life.

One afternoon in early November two policemen walked into the hotel reception while she was on duty and said they were looking for Mrs June Masters.

Instantly alarmed at the thought that something must have happened to Alan, June's hand flew to her throat. 'I'm June Masters,' she said with a pounding heart. 'Has something happened to my husband?'

'Not as far as we know,' replied one of the officers, adding quickly, 'But we would like a word. Can someone take over from you here for a few minutes?'

Before June had a chance to arrange cover on the desk, the front-of-house manager bustled on to the scene and whisked her and her visitors out of sight into a small office behind reception. Policemen at the hotel were not good for business.

'So, what's all this about?' she asked through dry lips as soon as they were alone.

'You are the daughter of Margaret Grey?' The policeman needed it confirmed.

'That's right,' she said with a nod. 'Is my mother ill?'

'She's had an accident, I'm afraid,' he explained in an even tone. 'She was knocked down by a car in Hounslow High Street earlier this afternoon.'

'Is she . . . is she badly hurt?'

The man hesitated, his mouth tightening slightly. 'I'm sorry to have to tell you that she died in the ambulance on the way to the hospital,' he informed her gravely.

'Oh . . .'

'The person your mother was with at the time of the accident told us she had a daughter and we tracked you down through an address book in her handbag,' he explained.

'I see.'

'I'm afraid we'll have to ask you, as her next of kin, to make a formal identification,' one of the officers told her. 'But there's no hurry. You've time for a cup of tea to steady your nerves first.'

'I'm all right,' she said, though she was breathless with shock. 'I'll just go and tell my boss what's happened, then I'll come with you.'

'If you're sure you're feeling up to it . . .?' he said kindly.

'I'm sure.'

June thought the policemen might be shocked to know that her prevailing emotion was one of relief that nothing bad had happened to Alan.

The death of her adopted mother barely touched her at the time. There had been no love lost between them anyway, but the all-consuming pain of missing Alan meant that everything else paled into insignificance. June even arranged the funeral and endured it without much emotion.

It was only when she was at the house in Hounslow where she'd grown up, sorting through her mother's things and getting the property she'd inherited, as next of kin, ready for sale that memories of the past began to flood in. Sitting at the bureau in the living room one morning, going through some family papers, she discovered a photograph of herself with her adopted parents that caused tears to flow. Not with sadness because they were both now dead but because of the agony of her life with them.

In the photograph, the three of them were in the garden of this house, standing under the lilac tree, June between the two grown-ups. Anyone else would see a picture of family contentment. But the mere sight of her father sent shivers up her spine. She still couldn't bear to look at him, and he'd been dead for four years.

Both parents had died relatively young – in their fifties – thus disproving the theory that only the good did that. It would have been hypocritical of her to pretend grief at the passing of either. It was hard to grieve for anyone you'd feared and hated. Adulthood and distance hadn't warmed her to them on her rare duty visits.

She tore the photograph up and let it flutter into the wastepaper bin. There were others that received the same treatment. She didn't want anything left to remind her of them. There were various family documents: her father's army discharge papers, her parents' marriage certificate.

Coming across a large fat brown envelope, June opened it curiously, her heart turning somersaults as she realised it was the official correspondence between her parents and the adoption authorities.

It was a weird feeling to see details of yourself in black and white; strange and rather frightening to be confronted with your background after a lifetime of ignorance. Her hand trembled as she fingered a letter, words and sentences leaping out at her.

Regarding your application to adopt legally June Rivers, currently in care at St Clare's Home for Destitute Children in Hammersmith, we feel it necessary to point out that the case of the Rivers sisters is a particularly tragic one. June may be mentally disturbed after such a sudden loss of parents and family life. It is deemed to be in the children's interest for them to remain unaware of the shocking circumstances that resulted in their being taken into the care of the authorities.

We also believe it important to June's future stability for her to be encouraged to forget her previous background, including her sister, as this may impede her progress in adapting to a new and stable family life again.

As June read other correspondence and newspaper cuttings which gave her the basic details of what the 'shocking circumstances' actually were, she shook violently from head to toe, bile rising in her throat and sending her scurrying to the bathroom. Now at last she

68

knew why she and her sister had been abandoned, but the reason was so dreadful she wished she'd never found out. She could understand the authorities' logic in not telling two little girls about their original background. Knowing something that horrifying at such a young age could have damaged them for life.

But June did know now. And she couldn't erase the knowledge or leave it at that. She had to learn the full story. Washing her hands and face, she went back to the living room. Jotting down a few dates, she got her coat and hurried to the nearest library.

Finding 1934 in the book of old copies of a national newspaper in the reference section of the library, June began to turn the pages. The story of her early background unfolded. It was like reading cheap horror fiction but it had all actually happened. When she saw the name Morris Dodd in print, she knew with sickening certainty why she'd been haunted by the memory of him for all these years. Her heart pounded at the huge significance it now had.

There was one thing she now had to do urgently. She had to find her sister, Daisy. This filled her with excitement, then despair at the impossibility of the task. Twenty years was a long time – she could be anywhere. She might not even have survived the war. St Clare's was June's only lead. It was a long shot after all these years but they just might have some idea of where she was.

'Please, God, let her still be alive,' she prayed silently as she left the library and headed for the tube station, en route for Hammersmith.

Later that same day June walked through the squalid backstreets of Notting Hill, past windows boarded up, stucco rotting on the front of terraces, fumes from the local factories mingling with the stench from wasteland used as an open rubbish dump.

It was a cold and misty November day but small children played in the street despite the weather, women stood at front doors gossiping, a crowd of young West Indian men stood on the corner engaged in conversation.

Although June's circumstances had taken a dive when she'd left Alan, the area in which she now lived was, none the less, a world apart from this, yet less than two miles away. She couldn't help but be shocked by the deprivation of the neighbourhood and was ashamed of her disgust.

She found the address in Benly Square the nuns had given her and knocked on the front door, which swung open at her touch because the lock was broken. Finding herself in a hallway that was foul with the smell of damp and stale cooking, she didn't know what to do next. The address just said number twenty Benly Square; there was nothing about a flat number.

A woman came out of one of the rooms and walked towards the front door dressed in a brown mac and carrying a shopping bag. Her eyes rose at the sight of June's smart grey suit and high-heeled court shoes.

'You looking for someone?' she asked without much interest.

June nodded. 'Daisy,' she said. 'Daisy Rivers she was. She might not be using that name now.'

'Up in the attic,' the woman informed her, and left the house.

June made her way up the creaking stairs, becoming increasingly horrified at the conditions. At the top of the attic stairs, she was greeted by a middle-aged woman with wild ginger hair and enquiring blue eyes. 'Can I help you?' she asked in a cultured voice that didn't match the ambience.

'I'm looking for Daisy,' June explained.

'She's gone to meet her little girl from school,' Nora explained pleasantly. 'She's taken her other daughter with her so there's no one in her flat at the moment.'

'Do you think she'll be long?'

'She should be back at any minute.'

'Thank you.'

'You're welcome to come and have a cup of tea in my place while you're waiting,' Nora offered, curious as to who June was but courteous enough not to enquire. 'Daisy and I are very good friends.' She gave her a wide grin. 'Well, we're more like family, really. I know she'd want me to make you welcome.'

'It's very kind of you to offer but I think I'll wait outside as she'll only be a minute,' June said, first because she was feeling emotional about the imminent reunion and needed to be on her own, and secondly because the oppressive atmosphere inside this building was making her nauseous and she was desperate for some fresh air.

'As you wish, dear,' said Nora.

'See you later then,' said June, and made her way down the broken stairs.

Relieved to be outside, despite the cold grimy atmosphere, she took a deep breath to prepare herself for the meeting. Suddenly the sound of laughter filled the air, and looking down the street she saw a small woman in a red coat – with several inches of grey skirt showing beneath it – coming towards her holding the hands of two little girls, one of them dressed in a navy-blue school raincoat. They stopped for a moment, listening to the girl in the raincoat, then there were gales of laughter.

Obviously it wasn't possible to recognise the adult from the child she remembered but she knew instinctively that the woman was Daisy, and the thing that struck June was the closeness of the trio, obviously happy to be together. On jelly legs, her heart thudding madly, June walked towards them.

Shirley was regaling her mother and sister with the story of one boy, Paul, in her class who had taken his pet mouse to school in his pocket and how it had escaped and everyone had screamed and stood on their desks, even the teacher. Daisy and Belinda had thought this hilarious.

'What happened to the mouse?'

'Paul found it and the caretaker looked after it until it was time to go home and Paul took it with him,' Shirley explained. 'Miss was very cross with him for bringing it to school and scaring everybody.'

'I expect she was,' said Daisy, imagining the teacher's embarrassment if Shirley's version of her behaviour hadn't been exaggerated.

'What's for tea, Mum?' asked Belinda.

'Fish paste sandwiches and toasted buns.'

'Toasted buns, yippee,' cried Shirley.

Immersed in her children, Daisy hadn't paid any attention to someone approaching but looked up now to see an extremely smart woman in a fitted suit and high-heeled shoes. She's out of place around here, Daisy thought, and hoped she hadn't come from the landlord with some message of doom.

'Daisy?'

'That's me,' she replied, noticing how strikingly attractive the woman was, with fine features and sleek, dark hair. 'What can I do for you?'

The woman seemed upset about something, too upset to answer; there were tears running down her cheeks.

'Shirley, love, give the lady your hanky,' said Daisy, because Shirley was the only one who had a proper handkerchief for school; the others had rag ones.

Shirley handed her the handkerchief, which seemed to make her cry even more.

'Oh, my Lord, you are in a state,' was Daisy's kind response; she was too concerned about the woman to ask how she knew her name. 'Can I help in any way?'

June stared at her.

'Whatever it is that's troubling you, you'll feel better for a cup of tea and a sit-down,' said Daisy warmly. 'You don't want to be out on the street when you're so upset, love. We only live a few doors down. So come in and have a cup of tea with us.'

'Oh, Daisy, don't you see,' said the woman, 'I'm not crying because I'm sad.'

'I dread to think what you'd be like if you were then,' quipped Daisy. 'The whole of London would be under water.'

'Daisy,' the other woman began in muffled tones, 'do you remember that you once had a sister?'

71

'Course I remember,' Daisy told her. 'I'm not likely to forget a thing like that.'

The woman stared at her meaningfully.

Daisy gulped, her eyes narrowing on her in a questioning manner. 'You?' she gasped.

'That's right. I'm June,' she informed her thickly. 'I'm your sister.'

'You never are,' said Daisy, staring at her in disbelief, trying to recognise something about her and remembering only that the child in her memory had had dark hair.

'I am.'

'But how—'

'I'll tell you everything all in good time,' said June. 'But for now, let me give you a hug.'

Now Daisy was weeping unashamedly. After all these years she'd come face to face with her own flesh and blood. The little girls looked on in bewilderment as the two women clutched each other, wailing loudly.

'Are we going in for tea soon?' asked Shirley at last, bringing an air of normality to the proceedings. 'It's cold out here and I'm starving.'

'Yes, love, we're going indoors for tea now.' She looked at June. 'You will join us, won't you?'

'Love to.' The terrible miasma inside the house was forgotten in the joy of the moment.

'This is your Auntie June, girls,' said Daisy, sniffing into the handkerchief.

'What, a *real* auntie?' queried Shirley. 'Not a pretend one like Nora is our pretend grannie?'

'No, this is your real auntie,' Daisy confirmed.

'Cor,' approved Shirley.

'Smashing,' added Belinda.

It was strange, thought June, an hour or so later, how the pungent hallway and landings of the dilapidated building ceased to exist once you were inside Daisy's flat, the gas fire spreading a glow over the shabby room, the curtains drawn against the murky weather outside and the crumbling window sills.

Nora went to the bakers to get more buns, which were toasted with a fork on the gas fire, and they all sat around the table having tea and talking, the sweet scent of cinnamon from the buns filling the air.

Daisy had insisted that Nora stay. 'She's like a mum to me,' she'd explained to June, 'and I wouldn't want her to miss out on a special occasion like this.'

'Of course not,' June had approved.

The two sisters had exchanged basics about themselves, their jobs, their personal circumstances. June knew Daisy was an unmarried mum. June mentioned that she'd recently separated from her husband and touched on her life as a hotelier's wife but offered no details about the cause of the separation. They both agreed how fortunate it was that Daisy had kept in touch with St Clare's, who'd been able to direct June straight to her. They both had so much to say, though Daisy did mention that she had to keep her eye on the time because she was on duty this evening. June said she was having a couple of days off to sort out her late mother's affairs.

'But tell me, June,' said Daisy, when everyone had finished eating, 'why come looking for me now, after all this time?'

'I've always wanted to, of course—'

'I know that,' cut in Daisy, because they had already discussed how their upbringing had deterred them from looking for each other, 'but what actually drove you to do something about it at this particular time?'

June bit her lip, looking uncomfortable. 'It's a bit delicate, actually,' she told her.

'Come on, girls,' said Nora, taking the hint. 'Let's go and have a game of snap in my place while your mother and her sister have a chat.'

They went without argument because snap was still a big favourite with them.

'So, what is it you have to tell me that isn't suitable for little ears?' asked Daisy.

June moistened her lips. 'I've had to go through my adopted mother's papers following her death,' she explained, 'and I've found out how we came to be in St Clare's.'

'We already know,' Daisy pointed out. 'Our mother died and our father abandoned us.'

'Yes. Basically that's true,' June confirmed, 'but there was much more to it than that.'

Daisy waited for her to go on.

After taking a deep breath to try to calm herself, June asked, 'Do you remember a man called Morris Dodd?'

'Mr Dodd,' she responded, looking startled. 'Yeah, I remember him all right.'

'You remember that night he threatened us, don't you?' June guessed. 'I can tell from the look on your face.'

'It's haunted me on and off all through my life,' Daisy confided, eyes glazed as she recalled the incident. 'You and I were in bed when we heard shouting downstairs.'

'And we crept halfway down, scared to go further because we were

73

supposed to be asleep and would have got told off if Mum had found out.'

'Mr Dodd was in the hall on his way to the front door,' Daisy continued.

'And he grabbed us and shook us and told us to go back to bed and if we ever told anyone he'd been at our house that night, he'd come after us and do something so terrible we'd wish we were dead.'

'I was so scared I nearly wet myself,' remembered Daisy. 'I still go cold when I think about it.'

'Me too,' said June. 'I can still see those eyes, glaring at us, his face close to mine. Ugh.'

'The memory of it has kept me awake many a night and I don't know what it means,' confessed Daisy.

'Neither did I until today,' June told her. 'Now I know why he was so rough with us that night.'

'And?'

She took another deep breath before uttering her next words. 'Our mother didn't die of natural causes,' she said through dry lips. 'She was murdered.'

Daisy turned pale; she was too shocked to speak.

'It gets worse,' June warned her. 'Our father was convicted of the murder. That's why we were abandoned.'

'Our father a murderer?' Daisy couldn't believe it.

'He was found guilty, yes.'

'Was he . . . was he hanged?'

'No, it wasn't considered to be premeditated so the sentence was commuted to life imprisonment,' she explained. 'You'll have to come with me to the library to read the newspaper reports of the trial to get the full story. But I don't think our father did it. Morris Dodd was our mother's lover, apparently, and I think he killed her.'

'Why do you think that?'

'Because our father claimed throughout the trial that he was innocent and Dodd killed her. Dodd denied being at our house on the night of the murder, which I reckon is the same night he scared the living daylights out of us, as we ended up in St Clare's soon after,' said June. 'That's why he was so keen to keep us quiet.'

'Ooh, June, I think you're right.'

'According to the reports, no one saw him arrive or leave the house and his wife claimed that he was with her on the night of the murder,' June went on to say. 'But we both know that he was there at the house, don't we?'

'Yeah.'

'And we are the only people alive, apart from our father and the Dodds, who know that he was lying,' June continued. 'I don't know if

74

our father is still alive. But I do know that you and I are the only people who can clear his name.'

'Oh, June,' gasped Daisy.

'Big responsibility, isn't it?'

'Huge,' agreed her sister.

Chapter Five

'Mother murdered while babes sleep' was just one of the gruesome headlines that confronted the sisters at Kensington reference library the next day when they scoured the old newspapers for reports of the trial in 1934 of Lionel Rivers for the murder of his wife, Rose.

'It simply beggars belief that such a thing could have happened in the house while we were actually in it without us knowing about it,' Daisy said to June as they comforted themselves with a steaming espresso in one of the new-style coffee bars that had opened recently in Kensington High Street. As today was Saturday, Daisy had been able to leave the girls with Nora in whom she'd confided. 'Our mother strangled to death, our father sent to prison and we knew nothing about any of it until now. It's incredible.'

'Spooky,' was June's opinion. 'I can understand why we weren't told, though, can't you?'

Daisy sipped her coffee, pondering on this for a moment. 'Having to cope with the ghastly truth at that age wouldn't exactly have helped us through life.'

'Quite. I suppose we were considered too young to be questioned by the police about whether we saw or heard anything too,' suggested June, 'especially as we were assumed to have slept through the whole thing.'

'We must have been whisked away into care as soon as the police came on the scene, to protect us from the horror of it all,' Daisy surmised.

'I expect that's the sort of thing that would happen in a case like that but I don't remember anything about that part of it.'

'Me neither.'

'Do you think we were from a Catholic family, as we were sent to St Clare's?' wondered June.

'That doesn't necessarily follow,' Daisy replied. 'It could just have been that they happened to have room for us there. There were lots of children in care then. Homes got overcrowded.'

'Mm, there is that.'

A thoughtful silence descended.

'Just think of the difference it would have made to our father's case if we'd told someone we'd seen Morris Dodd at the house that night,' mused Daisy.

'I've been agonising over that too.' June shook her head, sighing. 'But we weren't to know that, as we had no idea what had happened.'

'We probably wouldn't have realised the significance if we had known, being so little. We'd have been too terrified to open our mouths, anyway, after that roughing up from Mr Dodd,' was Daisy's opinion. 'At that age you just do what you're told.'

'Especially in those days,' added June. 'Children were very much seen and not heard then.'

'Still are in a lot of families,' Daisy mentioned chattily. 'But not in mine. My daughters have plenty to say for themselves and I wouldn't have it any other way. I'd hate them to have a childhood as strict and loveless as mine was.'

'They're lovely kids,' June smiled. 'You're very lucky to have them.'

Lucky wasn't a word much used to describe Daisy, whose circumstances meant she was either perceived as a cheap little tart or a husbandless no-hoper burdened by a couple of bastards. 'Yes, I am,' she agreed wholeheartedly, 'and every day I thank God for them. They're everything to me.'

'And you are to them,' June told her. 'It shines bright from all of you. Nora as well.'

Daisy smiled, and June couldn't remember having met anyone who exuded such warmth before. So, which of the two of them had fared better from life, she found herself wondering: a child 'favoured' by adoption, who'd grown up in a comfortable home to have good manners and refined speech, and now had a broken marriage, an inability to have children and no real friends because her childhood had robbed her of the capacity for friendship? Or Daisy, an orphanage girl struggling to raise two children on her own in poor accommodation and living from hand to mouth, but having the unqualified love of her daughters, the affection of a close woman friend and a generous heart towards everyone? The question answered itself.

'Yeah, we're a close little band, and Nora's like one of the family.' Daisy sensed a profound sadness in June that her general air of confidence couldn't hide. Presumably her broken marriage was the cause. It must be heartbreaking to have had something as precious as that and lost it, she thought, her mind drifting to her own long-standing desire for marriage to Nat, with whom she'd made her peace last week as predicted. 'She's the nearest thing I have to a mum – one that I can remember, anyway. My memories of our real mother are quite vague.'

'Mine too. Which is only natural as we lost her so young,' said June.

'And when you think about it, she must have been a bit preoccupied at the end of her life too, as she was having an affair with Morris Dodd,' Daisy pointed out, her thoughts returning to the findings in the library. 'I wonder what she did with us while she was with him.'

'Perhaps we were at school or something,' suggested June. 'It said in the paper that Morris Dodd was some sort of a sales rep. Those people can be flexible during the working day as they're out and about, so he could have seen her then, while our father was out at work.'

'The mind boggles,' said Daisy. 'An adulterous mother doesn't exactly match the cosy maternal figure I imagined her to be all these years.'

June gave an understanding nod. 'Morris Dodd was a family friend, apparently, which is how she knew him and why we remembered him being familiar to us.'

'So, let's run through it,' began Daisy, wanting to summarise the whole dreadful business. 'According to our father's evidence, Mother ended the affair but Morris Dodd is the sort of man who likes to get his own way so he went round to the house with the idea of persuading her to reconsider her decision.'

'He just burst in there apparently, and the whole thing got out of hand,' June continued. 'He confronted her in front of Dad and when she wouldn't agree to leave him, Dodd lost his temper and started knocking her about, which accounts for the shouting we heard from upstairs. Dad tried to fight him off and was knocked unconscious. When he came to, Dodd had gone and Mother was dead, strangled. Dodd must have been running from the scene of the crime when he saw us.'

'It sends shivers right through me,' said Daisy, sucking in her breath and wriggling her shoulders, 'to think what was going on downstairs while we were in bed.'

'It must have been all over by the time we crept down the stairs, though,' June speculated.

'Though Dodd tells a different story.'

June nodded. 'He denied being at the house at all that night and his alibi is watertight because his wife swore under oath that he was at home with her,' she went on. 'Because no one could prove otherwise, his version of events was believed and it was assumed that Dad was lying to save his own skin.'

'Of course, we can't be absolutely certain that the night Morris Dodd terrorised us was the night of the murder because we were just children and it was a long time ago.' June wanted to be realistic.

'I'm sure in my own mind, though,' Daisy responded thoughtfully. 'I remember that nothing was ever the same again after that.'

'No it wasn't.' June paused, sipping her coffee. 'Not that anyone in authority will believe us. Two women suddenly claiming to remember

79

something they saw over twenty years ago when they were children won't carry any weight at all. We won't stand a chance of getting the case reopened on that alone.'

'There is one other person besides us and our father who knows that Dodd was lying in court.'

'His wife.'

'Exactly.'

'She's not likely to admit to perjury, though, is she?' June pointed out.

'Not without a very strong incentive,' Daisy was forced to agree. 'But she's the only person who can back up our story so we have to try to find her and see if she can't somehow be persuaded to co-operate. Don't ask me how because I haven't a clue at this stage. But I do know we must at least try to clear our father's name, however hopeless it seems.'

'You won't get any objections from me,' June assured her. 'But before we do anything about that side of it there's something more important we must do.'

'Find out if our father is still alive and, if so, where he is, then arrange to pay him a visit,' guessed Daisy.

'You've got it,' confirmed June. 'I've no idea how to set about it, though. Have you?'

'Not really. But I should think the police station would be a good starting point,' suggested Daisy. 'They'll know what the procedure is for finding out which prison someone is in.'

Because both sisters had jobs and Daisy also had the children to consider, they couldn't just drop everything and devote all their time to their father's plight, as much as they both wanted to. But they both gave the matter a great deal of thought and did what they could within the parameters of their other commitments.

June had access to the telephone books at work and planned to make a list of all the Dodds in the London area. As personal calls from work were prohibited she intended to use a call box to contact them.

Her first task, however, was a visit to the police station where she was informed that information about relatives in custody could be obtained from the Home Office, who would issue a visiting order only if the prisoner agreed to it. They gave her the address and she got a detailed letter in the post immediately.

Meanwhile, Daisy was keeping busy. In the hope of moving things forward with regard to finding the Dodds, she approached the Salvation Army, having heard that they offered a service for tracing missing people. But the job was too big for them because she had no information beyond what she'd read in the paper: that the Dodds had once lived in Wembley, where the crime had taken place. The

Salvation Army officer suggested that she contact them again if she could get more details for them to work with. It was a huge disappointment.

The keenly awaited news from the Home Office was better. After opening the envelope with a great deal of trepidation, June learned that Lionel Rivers was indeed still alive and had agreed to see his daughters.

So it was that one bitterly cold afternoon in December, June and Daisy travelled together to Wormwood Scrubs.

Daisy's desire to see her father was strong, but she felt somewhat tremulous and her stomach churned horribly on the bus to the prison.

'Weird, isn't it,' she remarked to June, to take her mind off the imminent meeting which could turn out to be an ordeal, 'us being together like this? It seems unreal.'

'It is peculiar,' agreed her sister. 'The last thing I expected to be doing was going to see a father I've not seen for over twenty years – in prison.'

'I meant more in terms of us getting back together after all these years,' Daisy amended.

'Oh, I see. Yes, it does seem too good to be true.'

'You haven't said much about your childhood,' commented Daisy.

'Haven't I?' June was deliberately vague.

'I imagine from the way you've turned out, being so smart and well spoken and everything, that it was a damned sight better than mine.'

'I doubt it,' she surprised Daisy by saying.

'Oh? But you were one of the chosen few who got out of St Clare's and into a proper home,' Daisy reminded her.

'There's more to a happy life than a comfortable house, Daisy,' June pointed out.

'I realise that but—'

'Let's not talk about me,' she cut in quickly. 'Tell me about yourself.'

'There's nothing much to say really,' Daisy told her. 'I stayed at St Clare's until I was fifteen.'

'It must have been hard, having to stay there for such a long time,' sympathised June. 'I remember what tartars some of the nuns were.'

'They were strict, yeah. But they had to be with all those kids to look after,' said Daisy. 'Without discipline we'd have run wild. I've a lot to thank them for. They gave me a decent upbringing and I'm grateful for that.'

'Did you stay with Catholicism after you left there?' June enquired with interest.

She nodded. 'Did you?'

'No. My adopted parents had once been practising Catholics, which

81

was why they went to St Clare's looking for a child to adopt, but they lapsed and I didn't take it up.'

'My faith is important to me. I really need it,' Daisy went on. 'I don't know how I'd have managed without it through the bad times. When all else failed, I still had that.'

'It must be nice to have something like that to turn to.'

'It is a comfort.' Again Daisy perceived deep unhappiness in her sister but didn't pry as June had made it obvious that she'd said as much as she was going to about her past life. It was still early days in their new relationship. Daisy hoped that at some point in the future June might trust her enough to confide.

'Can you remember what our father looked like?' asked June chattily.

'I've been thinking, and all I can remember about him is that he was a big man with dark hair.'

'I remember him being big too,' said June, 'He had a loud voice and a booming laugh too.'

'Oh, yeah,' smiled Daisy. 'Now you come to mention it, I remember that too.'

Far from being large and dark, Lionel Rivers was short and stockily built, with a bald head and wispy white tufts at the side of his heavily lined countenance. He didn't have a loud voice either but was quietly spoken with sad brown eyes and a look of defeat about him. He didn't look as though he'd laughed in years, in a booming way or otherwise – which was hardly surprising considering what he'd been through, Daisy thought. He couldn't be more than about fifty but he looked like an old man.

Dressed in prison uniform of a drab grey woollen jacket and trousers with a whitish flannel shirt, he observed them with an air of bewilderment across a table in the visitors' room. 'I couldn't believe it when they told me my daughters wanted to see me,' he said, his voice shaking with emotion. 'I'm sorry to have to admit this but you're so different to how I remember you, I'm not sure which is which.'

'I'm Daisy.'

'And I'm June.'

The silence was piercing; there was so much to say but no one knew where to start. He stared from one to the other, as though searching their faces for some sign of recognition.

'It doesn't half feel queer to be looking at the two of you as women,' he said at last. 'You've always been nippers in my memory, you see.' He shook his head slowly. 'Too many years have passed since I saw you.' He sounded so sad, Daisy thought he was about to burst into tears, which made her wonder if this visit was such a good idea after all.

'I've got two little girls of my own now,' Daisy told him, struggling with her own turmoil.

'Grandchildren.' His face worked.

'That's right.'

He didn't say anything; was obviously trying to compose himself. 'That's lovely,' he uttered eventually. 'I've often thought about the two of you, wondered how you were getting on. But I never thought I'd see either of you again.'

'If we'd known what had happened, we'd have been here long before this,' Daisy was keen for him to know.

'How did you find out where I was?' he asked. 'You were supposed never to know.'

'It's a long story,' June told him. 'Too long to go into in one visiting session. The important thing is, we know why you're here and why we were taken into care.'

His eyes widened. 'Oh, I see.' He swallowed hard. 'At the time you thought I'd abandoned you, didn't you?' he muttered thickly. 'Just dumped you because I didn't want to keep you?'

They both nodded.

'It broke my heart, having you think that I would do a thing like that. But it was considered best for you to grow up believing that, rather than know the truth. There were no relatives willing to take you in, you see,' he explained. 'And I was ordered not to try and contact you or to find out where you were.' He emitted a dry, humourless laugh. 'I'd have had a job, being locked up in here.'

'We've worked all of that out for ourselves,' Daisy said gently.

'You must have been very hurt at the time, though.'

'I was,' said June.

Daisy nodded, biting back the tears. 'But that's all in the past,' she said in a positive tone. 'Now we're in the picture. We've read the reports of the murder trial in the old newspapers in the library.'

'You bothered to do that?' He sounded astonished, his face lighting up.

'It was the only way we could find out more about it,' explained June.

Lionel put his hand to his head. 'You poor things.' He looked distressed. 'It must have been a shock to read such things about your parents.'

'It was,' they confessed in unison.

'For what it's worth, I didn't kill your mother,' he said, his tired brown eyes brimming with tears.

'We know that.' June was unsure how to address him. 'Lionel' didn't seem appropriate and 'Dad' was still a label she associated with a man she'd hated.

'We know it was Morris Dodd,' added Daisy.

His eyes bulged. 'How could you possibly know that?'

Between them they told him.

'Well, stone me,' was his amazed reaction.

'We want to try to clear your name and get you out of here,' Daisy informed him.

His face worked with emotion, muscles tightening, mouth twitching slightly. 'It's very kind of you to want to do that for me, but, being realistic, you'll be wasting your time after all these years.' He shook his head sagely. 'We'll never get the case reopened now. You can only get an appeal if there's new evidence. They won't consider your childhood memories to be evidence.' He cleared his throat. 'They'll say you just imagined it unless you have proof to back it up.' He rummaged in his pocket, produced a rag handkerchief and blew his nose. 'Anyway, you've got your own lives to lead. Don't waste your time on my account.'

'June and I have discussed it at length and we know they won't take our word for it,' Daisy made clear. 'We also realise that Dodd won't admit the truth. But we're thinking in terms of trying to get the truth out of his wife, somehow. We know for a fact that she lied under oath.'

'She'd never admit it,' he stated categorically.

'We think it's unlikely too, but we want to try and find the Dodds anyway,' June was firm on this point, 'see if we can't persuade her to do the right thing.'

'Look, I'm really touched that you want to do this for me but there's no need,' he tried to convince them. 'You know that I didn't murder your mother and that I didn't just abandon you because I didn't want you, and that's enough for me.' He shrugged. 'I've been here so long I'm resigned to prison life. It's all I know after all this time.'

'But you're locked up for something you didn't do,' emphasised Daisy. 'Justice must be done.'

'Fine words, love, but I don't want you getting mixed up with the likes of Morris Dodd,' he told them. 'Your mother lost her life because of his vile temper so I think you should steer well clear of him. I've found you again after all these years and that's all that matters to me.'

The two women exchanged glances. This was what the justice system had done to him. It had beaten the spirit out of him and killed his appetite for normal life.

'You can't just give in,' Daisy admonished.

'It took a while but I eventually accepted my fate because I had no choice,' he explained. 'I couldn't fight back because I had no ammunition with which to do so. No one was interested in the truth. To you that might seem pathetic – to me it's plain common sense.'

'But you've got us on your side now,' Daisy encouraged.

'You can't possibly know what that means to me.' His voice was muffled by stifled tears. 'But I don't want you getting into trouble on my behalf. Come and see me every now and again when you can manage it. That'll do for me.'

'We'll be the judge of that.' Daisy fell silent, a question burning inside her. 'Do you mind if I ask you something, though it might be painful for you?'

'Fire away,' he urged her. 'I'm long past secrets.'

She chewed her bottom lip; this was a delicate matter. 'Why did our mother have an affair?' she blurted out, adding quickly, 'Sorry, I realise the subject might hurt.'

'It does, of course, though time in here has toughened me up,' he told her. 'I must stress that your mother wasn't in the habit of taking lovers. She was the last person on earth you'd expect to get involved in that sort of thing. She'd always been a good wife and mother, the homely type.'

'Having an affair with a married man isn't a very homely thing to do,' June couldn't help mentioning. 'Especially when you've a couple of young kids to look after.'

'I can't argue with you about that,' Lionel agreed dully.

'Why do you think she did it?' wondered June. 'If she cared so much about her family?'

'Morris Dodd was a charmer in those days and he turned her head,' he told them. 'I was a gardener working for the parks department of the council, always in overalls; he was a rep for a firm of stationers, earning good money; he had nice clothes and plenty of chat. He had a reputation with women – knew how to make them feel good. I got to know him in our local pub and he and his wife became family friends – well, more just acquaintances really. They weren't our usual type but he was good company in small doses. From the way he used to talk to the men in the pub I knew he didn't have much in the way of morals but that was his business. I never dreamed he would go after my wife.'

'How did you find out about the affair?' asked Daisy.

'Your mother told me,' he explained. 'Said she'd come to her senses and couldn't carry on deceiving me any longer. She said she had ended the affair with him and begged me to forgive her and give her another chance. I don't think she ever loved him. She was infatuated for a while, that's all. Anyway, I agreed to try and forgive her, for the sake of the family. And because I still loved her, despite what she'd done.' He sighed. 'What happened after that is history, as they say.'

June cleared her throat; Daisy blew her nose. They were both struggling not to break down.

Lionel stared mistily into space. 'Life was so good before she got involved with that bugger. Everything changed so suddenly I was in a state of shock for months.' He gave them a wry look. 'Now I can hardly believe I ever had any other life but this.'

'It's so sad,' murmured June almost to herself.

'Don't feel sorry for me,' he was quick to protest. 'I'm all right, honestly. I'm in good health and that's worth a lot. You mustn't worry about me.'

'Easier said than done.' Daisy paused thoughtfully. 'Do you have any idea how we might find the Dodds?'

'I've told you I don't want you getting involved with them,' he reminded her. 'He's a nasty piece of work.'

'There are two of us so we'll be quite safe,' Daisy assured him. 'If he bumped us off he'd be signing his own death warrant. He wouldn't get away with it a second time.'

'The fact of the matter is, we've decided to try to find Mr and Mrs Dodd with or without your co-operation,' June added in a tone that didn't invite argument. 'So if you've any ideas, you'll save us time by sharing them with us.'

'All right,' Lionel conceded with an eloquent sigh. 'They used to live near us in Wembley, but it's most unlikely that they'd still be there now. They wouldn't have stayed there after all the scandal, not with his affair being splashed all over the papers in connection with the murder. His wife wouldn't have stood for that.'

'No, probably not,' agreed June.

'They could be anywhere now,' he went on. 'They could have moved away from London altogether.'

'But if we had their last address it would be a start,' Daisy pointed out. 'I doubt if they'll be there now but someone in the neighbourhood might have stayed in touch with them or have some sort of a clue as to where they went. So can you remember the address?'

'That's one I'll never forget,' he told them. 'It's number three Laverstock Avenue, Wembley.'

Daisy repeated it. 'That's an easy one to remember,' she remarked. 'You be careful.'

'Don't worry,' she told him kindly. 'We won't put ourselves at risk.'

'I'll make sure of that,' June further assured him.

'I'll have to take your word on that.' He looked from one to the other. 'Anyway, that's enough about the Dodds. I want to know all about you. You've grown up into such fine women, just like your mother.'

They both shot him a look.

'She *was* basically a good woman, no matter what you may be thinking about her,' he told them. 'She was human, she made a mistake.'

Daisy couldn't help thinking about the high cost of that mistake, to them all.

'Yes, well, I think we'll have to leave the catching up until next time,' mentioned June, glancing towards the warder, who was looking at his watch. 'It's time we were going.'

'You'll be coming again then?' Lionel suggested hopefully.

'Try keeping us away,' said Daisy.

'Thank you.' His humility tore at their hearts.

As they watched him being led away, they held their tears in check. Once outside the prison, they broke down and sobbed in each other's arms.

The warders on duty near Lionel's cell heard the sound of muffled weeping despite his attempts to conceal it for fear of seeming weak. Prison life had hardened him. There had been so much pain he'd grown several skins. Over the years he'd lost all purpose in life; had just let day follow day in a state of indifference. Not feeble, just resigned. But seeing his daughters again had inspired him with new life and purpose; had given him a reason to live.

Naturally in the past there had been times when he'd imagined what it would be like to walk along the street again, a free man, despite the stoicism he'd needed to carry him through. He was a realist, however, and knew that freedom wasn't something he was likely to taste again, despite his daughters' best endeavours. But even if he ended his days in custody he would die a happy man having seen them again and knowing that they knew the truth about him. His tears were a glorious outpouring of joy.

'Well, I think the whole thing is downright ridiculous,' disapproved Nat one evening a week or two later. 'I don't think you should waste another minute looking for these Dodd characters. You'll never find them after all this time, not in a million years.'

It was Daisy's night off so she and June had taken the opportunity to go to Laverstock Avenue, where they had drawn a complete blank.

'Be fair, Nat,' she said in a tone of mild admonition. 'The Wembley address was just a starting point. We didn't really expect to find them there. That would have been too easy.'

'But you've just said that you knocked on every door in the streets around there and no one knew where they'd gone to. So use your loaf and give up before you waste any more time on a wild-goose chase.' Because Nat was the man in her life Daisy had confided in him about the extraordinary revelations regarding her background. 'And even if you were to find them, what good would it do? I mean, this Dodd bloke isn't likely to confess to a murder, is he?'

'We're prepared for that,' Daisy told him.

'What's the point of chasing after him then?' Nat wanted to know, his voice rising.

'Don't shout, you'll wake the children,' Daisy rebuked. 'And to answer your question, the point of chasing the Dodds is because our father is in prison for something he didn't do. He's our *father, our own flesh and blood.* We can't just let him rot in prison when he's innocent without lifting a finger to help him. We have to take some sort of action.'

'I don't see why,' scoffed Nat. 'So what if he is your own flesh and blood? You haven't seen him for over twenty years. He can't possibly mean anything to you. The man's a stranger.'

'Of course he is, and he will be until we get to know him,' admitted Daisy. 'But he's been wrongfully imprisoned and we are the only people apart from him and the Dodds who know that. How can we live with ourselves if we don't do something for him? I admit it's going to be like looking for a needle in a haystack, but I'm not prepared to give up.'

'Personally,' intervened Nora, 'I think it's one of the saddest stories I've ever heard, even apart from the fact that he's the girls' father. That poor man locked up for all those years for something he didn't do – it's only natural they would want to do something to help him, even if it's only to tell that Morris Dodd that they're on to him, that he hasn't quite got away with it after all.'

Nat gave her a withering look. He thought Nora was an interfering old bag. She had far too much to say on the subject of his treatment of Daisy, and ought to learn to mind her own business. 'They were little kids when the murder happened, for God's sake,' he pointed out scathingly. 'Daisy was five years old. How can she possibly remember something that happened as far back as that?'

'I can remember my first day at school,' claimed Nora.

'Rubbish,' dismissed Nat.

'I know what I remember,' retorted Nora.

'No one can remember that far back,' argued Nat. 'Daisy probably imagined seeing the geezer at the house that night.'

'You're wrong about that,' June was quick to amend, 'because I saw him too and we can't both have imagined it. And before you say that I put ideas into her head, I didn't. She remembered it without any help from me.'

This sister of Daisy's had a bit too much to say for herself as well, Nat thought gloomily. This wasn't the first time she'd tried to put him in his place. Left alone, Daisy was as sweet as a nut. He could twist her around his little finger. But having the influence of opinionated types like Nora and June around made things more difficult for him.

'All right, so you both think you remember it, but I still think you're on a hiding to nothing in trying to clear your father's name,' he persisted.

'We know it won't be easy,' admitted Daisy. 'But we're going to give it our best shot.'

'Why are you so dead set against it anyway?' Nora wanted to know.

'It isn't as if she's asking you to help. I can't see why it matters to you one way or the other.'

'It matters to me, *my dear*,' he said with seething impatience and strong emphasis to indicate the opposite to endearment, 'because I care what happens to Daisy and I don't want her getting mixed up in something that's out of her league.'

'Cut out the squabbling, for goodness' sake,' rebuked Daisy, 'and let's see if we can't come up with something constructive between us.'

'As I've already said, I'll look in the phone book at work,' said June, 'and phone any Dodds in the London area from a call box. They have all the phone books in the library for a more thorough search, though as we haven't a clue which area they're in, that could take for ever.'

'The same thing applies to the electoral roll at the library and town hall,' Nora put in thoughtfully. 'As you don't know where they're living you'd need two lifetimes to get through the job.'

Daisy thought about this. 'I don't think they would have moved away from London, you know,' she observed. 'A different neighbourhood – yeah, definitely. But they're Londoners and the place would be in their bones, especially as they could escape from the scandal just by moving across town. A few miles up the road and you're a stranger in this city of ours. You don't need to move away from the capital to make a new start.'

'I still don't think the electoral register would be a good idea, though,' said Nora after more consideration. 'London's a densely populated place. Without knowing the actual borough, it just wouldn't be viable.'

Daisy and June nodded in agreement.

'You wouldn't believe it could be this difficult to find someone, would you?' mentioned Daisy.

'If it were easy, people wouldn't manage to stay missing and detective agencies wouldn't thrive,' Nora pointed out.

'True. Anyway, June's idea of going through the phone books is a good one,' said Daisy.

'We're frantically busy at work in the run-up to Christmas but I'm not going to let that stop me,' said June determinedly.

'I've got to work more shifts because of all the Christmas functions too,' Daisy informed them. 'I'm glad of the additional hours because of the extra dosh, but I'm going to find the time to go back to Wembley in daytime and ask around in the local shops. Someone might know something.'

'Good thinking,' approved June.

'I should forget about it altogether if I were you,' muttered Nat sulkily.

'I'm not going to do that, Nat,' asserted Daisy. 'So you may as well stop being such a doom merchant.'

'Suit yourself,' was his sharp retort. 'Frankly, I'm bored stiff with the whole flaming subject.' He threw a glare in June's direction, then looked back at Daisy. 'You've thought about nothing else but your father since your sister turned up.'

'Nat,' rebuked Daisy, flushing with embarrassment. 'Don't be so rude.'

'I'm only saying what's true,' he insisted. 'And as you obviously prefer your sister's company to mine, I might as well go down the pub.'

'Don't be like that.' Daisy looked worried now; she was only prepared to go so far in defiance of him.

'Don't leave on my account,' June told him frostily. 'It's time I was off anyway.'

'Me too,' said Nora.

And they both made hasty departures, leaving Daisy and Nat to sort out their differences in private.

'I wish you would try to be a bit nicer to my sister.' Daisy and Nat were sitting on the sofa.

'She's a stuck-up cow with her la-di-la voice and her posh clothes,' was his opinion.

'I think she speaks lovely. I could listen to her talk for hours,' Daisy said. 'Anyway, she has to be well presented in her job at a West End hotel.'

'She isn't my sort of person at all.'

'Maybe not, but she is my sister and therefore part of me,' Daisy reminded him. 'And as you're part of my life too, it would make things easier for me if you could make some sort of an effort to get along with her.'

'You haven't been the same person since she arrived on the scene,' he complained. 'You've changed.'

'Have I . . . really?'

'That's what I said.'

'It isn't intentional but I suppose June coming back into my life is bound to have an effect,' she reasoned. 'I've never had anyone of my own before.'

'You've got me.'

Even Daisy, with her huge capacity for self-delusion where Nat was concerned, could see what a gross distortion of the facts that was. She hadn't 'got him', as he put it. She never had. He appeared without prior notice at odd times and was never there when she needed him. She'd never met any of his relatives because he didn't go in for all that 'family stuff'. But there was no point in her complaining about it because he would never change. She either gave him up or accepted him as he was.

'My relationship with June is very important to me,' she said, 'but it

90

hasn't affected my feelings for you.'

'Ooh, not much,' he disagreed. 'It's June this, June that, my father this, my father that.'

'Surely you're not jealous.'

'Do me a favour . . .'

'Be pleased for me then.'

'I am, of course,' he said rather unconvincingly. 'It's just that with your sister and Nora being around so much I never get a chance to be on my own with you.'

Privacy had never been readily available to them, given the size of the flat and the fact that the girls were always around. 'Yeah, I can see your point about that,' Daisy agreed. 'But as I never know when you're going to turn up I can't keep people away on the off chance that you'll pay me a visit, can I?'

'I suppose not.' There were no promises of reliability in the future. That wasn't his way.

'You can't complain if other people are here then, can you?' she said.

'Oh, stop yapping, woman,' he said, putting his arm around her, 'and give us a kiss.'

This wasn't a problem for her because she was still attracted to him, however deeply in the doghouse he was. But something was missing lately; she was becoming increasingly conscious of a change in her attitude towards him, a need to draw back. Maybe having relatives thrust upon her suddenly had altered her. But it wasn't just that. June and her father had given Daisy's life a new meaning certainly, but subtle changes in her feelings towards Nat had begun before they'd appeared. She was irritated with him more often now, less willing to be a doormat.

But then he whispered the magic words into her ear, 'I love you, Daisy,' and she could forget all her complicated emotions and succumb to the sheer pleasure of him.

'And I love you too,' she sighed.

June sat on the tube back to Marble Arch thinking about Nat and his appalling behaviour towards Daisy, and pondering on the power of human emotions that allowed people to make such fools of themselves. An intelligent and spirited woman like Daisy would never put up with that sort of treatment were she not besotted.

Having seen the way Nat behaved towards her sister had made June reappraise Alan's virtues. He'd been no saint but he'd always treated her with respect and listened to her opinions. Whereas Nat behaved as though Daisy was some half-wit who existed purely for his convenience.

His abysmal manners obviously embarrassed her and you could tell she was hurt by his lack of interest in the girls. But still the relationship continued. Complicated things, love affairs. However crazy or unbalanced they might seem to those on the outside, only the participants knew about the indefinable ingredient that held it together.

There was one thing that June did know for sure, though. However much she might feel compelled to voice her opinion of Nat to Daisy, to do so would almost certainly damage her new adult relationship with Daisy, who would take the side of the man she loved against a sister she hardly knew. So June would hold her tongue rather than jeopardise something of such value to her, especially while it was still embryonic and delicate.

Her thoughts drifted back to Alan. She was still thinking about him as she emerged into the street, the Christmas lights shining brightly along Oxford Street, a cheering spectacle of colour and festivity which eliminated the winter gloom and made her want to cry with the pain of missing Alan. Her first Christmas without him was going to be hardly bearable, she thought, heading off down a side street to the Central Hotel in the cold December night.

Chapter Six

The next morning while June was on duty, a tall, thin man of about fifty emerged scowling from the lift, marched across to the reception desk and fixed her with a stony stare. 'I want to see the manager,' he demanded, obviously simmering with umbrage.

To save the unnecessary use of management time, receptionists here were encouraged to deal with complaints in the first instance, referring them to a higher level only if their own efforts at conciliation failed.

'Certainly, sir,' she said with immaculate manners. 'Is there a problem?'

'Ooh, not so you'd notice,' was his ironic reply.

'Perhaps you'd like to tell me about it.'

'I'm suffering from exhaustion with every possibility of pneumonia developing,' he explained through clenched teeth, pale face set in a grim expression; his short brown hair was worn in a traditional style with a side parting and greased flat to his head, making him look even sterner. 'And the appalling standards in this hotel are to blame.' His eyes rolled heavenwards in tandem with a supercilious sigh. 'Quite frankly I'd be better off sleeping in a shop doorway, and since you charge the earth for a room here, that's nothing short of a disgrace.'

'I'm so sorry to hear you're not enjoying your stay with us,' June said in the courteous, noncommittal tone she was trained to adopt in such a situation. 'Would you like to tell me what in particular hasn't pleased you?'

'Nothing has pleased me,' he informed her brusquely. 'This place is a joke.'

Needing to get to the crux of the matter, she asked, 'Is there something wrong with your room, sir?'

'You'd be nearer the mark to ask if there's anything right with it,' he barked at her. 'I was kept awake all night by the noise. I haven't had a wink of sleep.'

'Ah, I see.' She gave a sympathetic tut. 'People come up to town for Christmas functions at this time of the year and book in here overnight. I'm afraid the festive spirit makes some of our guests a little boisterous when they come back to the hotel.'

'It wasn't the other guests who disturbed me.'

'Really?'

'No. It was the traffic.' He became incandescent with rage as he thought back on it. 'Roaring past my window all night long. I've never heard such a racket.'

'The traffic noise can be disturbing if you're not used to it,' June agreed in an understanding manner. 'Unfortunately – with the best will in the world – we can't do anything about that as the hotel is situated in London's West End. Traffic noise is par for the course around here.'

'All night?'

'It does ease off in the small hours, naturally, but it doesn't usually stop altogether.'

'Nobody told me that when I booked.'

'They must have assumed you would guess,' she suggested politely, 'this being the capital city.'

His eyes bulged at this implied criticism and June had to think fast to head off an explosion. 'What's your room number, sir?' she enquired.

'Ninety-two.'

She gave him a knowing nod. 'Now I understand. That room is on the corner of the hotel directly above the traffic lights,' she explained. 'Vehicles stop outside with their engines throbbing, then roar away when the lights change. I know what it's like because I live here at the hotel and my room is on the same corner but much higher up. The noise used to be a problem for me when I first moved in. But it doesn't bother me now that I'm used to it.'

'I'm booked in here for three more nights and I can assure you that I have no intention of getting used to it,' the man made clear with seething irritation.

'Of course not, and we wouldn't expect you to.' June was a very fair-minded woman and could usually see the customer's point of view. But she knew instinctively that this man was the type to find fault with the service at Buckingham Palace were he ever invited as a guest. She took a deep breath, keeping a grip on her professionalism. 'Would you like me to see if we have a vacant room in another part of the hotel, further away from that junction?'

'There's no point,' he snapped. 'Because the noise isn't the only thing that's wrong.'

Here comes the cause of his possible pneumonia, she thought, but said, 'Could you tell me what else is troubling you, sir, so that we can put it right? Our guests' comfort is everything to us here at the Central Hotel. If you're not happy, we're concerned.'

'My room is freezing,' he informed her. 'I've been chilled to the bone all night.'

This puzzled her because the heating in this hotel was excellent and she hadn't been notified of any problem in the boiler room. 'Oh? Is the radiator not working?'

'I wouldn't be complaining if it was, would I?' was his abrupt reply. 'It's stone-cold.'

'That's strange.' At this crucial moment in customer relations, the telephone rang. 'Please excuse me for a moment,' she said.

He frowned in reply.

'Central Hotel. Good morning,' she said in her best business voice. 'Can I help you?'

The operator's voice crackled down the line informing her of a long-distance call from Torquay. With heart pounding, June told her to put it through.

'Hello, June.'

'Alan.' She quivered from top to toe. 'How are you?'

'I'm all right. Yourself?'

'I'm fine.'

'I'll come straight to the point as I'm calling long distance,' he began.

'Look, Alan, I can't talk—'

'The fact is, June,' he went on as though her interruption hadn't registered, 'I'm calling you on impulse because I still miss you and I just can't bear the thought of Christmas without you.'

'Oh,' was the best she could manage. With the furious guest focusing her with a disapproving stare, this wasn't the time for a personal conversation.

'So, I was wondering if you might consider coming down to Torquay for the holiday,' Alan continued. 'So that we can talk things over.'

'No, Alan, that isn't a good idea.' It was a wonder to June that she didn't wither and turn to dust under the lethal glare of the disgruntled guest. It was her job to pacify him and the need to do so grew more urgent by the second. If he reported her to the management for taking a personal call when she was supposed to be giving him her undivided attention, she could lose her job, which would render her homeless as well as unemployed. 'I really can't talk now, I'm sorry,' she said *sotto voce*.

'Oh. Oh, I see.' He sounded hurt; obviously thought she was just putting him off. Although Alan was familiar with how things were on the working side of a hotel reception desk, the Cliff Head reception was a playground compared to this one, and he couldn't possibly imagine how ill-timed his call was.

'I'm on duty, Alan.' She spoke in a whisper. It wasn't possible for her to explain to him that she had every hotelier's nightmare giving her the look of death, without the man hearing her. 'It's difficult right now.'

'Oh, don't worry about me,' said the man with seething sarcasm. 'I'm only a paying guest. I should hate to interfere with your private life.'

She put her hand over the mouthpiece and looked at him anxiously. 'Sorry about this, sir. I'll be with you in a second,' she assured him.

'Don't bother to find me another room,' he roared, almost beside himself with rage now. 'I'll check out of this dump and find somewhere else to stay as the receptionist here is too busy with a personal call to attend to me. I want my money back for last night, though. I'm not paying for a room in which it's impossible to sleep.' He puffed out his lips. 'Not likely.'

A demand for a refund as well as a customer complaint about the conduct of the duty receptionist would almost certainly result in dismissal. 'I have to go now, Alan,' June said quickly, and replaced the receiver without waiting for his reaction.

She was trembling from the effect of contact with Alan as she turned her attention back to the man, though she concealed it well. 'I really am very sorry about that, sir,' she apologised again.

He gave her a curt nod.

Being accustomed to dealing with the public at large, June was a consummate professional and could turn on the charm when necessary. She gave him one of her most melting smiles and behaved as though his threats to leave hadn't happened. 'Now, about the radiator in your room. It's cold, you say?'

'That's right.'

'And it's definitely turned on?'

He gave her a pitying look. 'Of course it is,' he said in a superior manner.

'That's really odd,' she said in a confiding manner, 'because the heating seems to be working well enough in the rest of the hotel.' She paused, choosing her words carefully. 'I wonder if perhaps the previous occupant of your room preferred a cool temperature and turned the radiator off.'

'How could they have done when the heating is controlled from a central point by your people?' he blasted.

'You're quite right, of course,' she conceded gracefully. 'The heating is controlled from a central point by us. But each radiator is also self-regulating and can be individually operated as long as the system is turned on, which it is in the winter.'

'Oh.'

At least he had the grace to look sheepish so she decided to help him out. 'Some of the older central heating systems don't have that individual facility,' she pointed out, 'but ours has been recently modernised.'

'I know how central heating works.' He obviously hadn't realised but would sooner die than lose face by admitting it. 'Obviously I checked to see if the radiator was turned on. And I can assure you that it was, and it was cold.'

'Yes, I understand,' she said, managing to sound convincing. 'I'll have one of our maintenance men go up to take a look.'

'Thank you.' He was noticeably more subdued.

A swift look at the hotel booking plan revealed a room vacant in a different part of the hotel. 'As luck would have it, we've had a cancellation so I can have you moved to a quieter room if you wish, though we can't erase the noise of the traffic altogether any more than any other hotel in central London can.'

He appeared to be pondering the question.

Winning him over had become a challenge to June now. 'Or, if you'd rather, I'll ring through for the manager to come and see you if you still wish to make a formal complaint and continue with your plans to check out.' She gave him a look of concern. 'But to make sure you're not left without a bed for the night, I can ring a few hotels to find out if they have any vacancies. Most London hotels are fully booked in the run-up to Christmas with so many people coming up to town for shopping.'

The extent of her helpfulness took the sting out of his argument. Much to her relief her ploy worked. 'No, no,' he said. 'If you get me moved to a different room for tonight, I'll give it a try.' He gave her a stern look. 'But if I have so much as a hint of cause for complaint, you'll be hearing from me again.'

I bet we will, she thought, but said sweetly, 'I'll have someone move your things.'

Clearly impressed by the lengths she was prepared to go to in his interests, he became much more amenable. 'That's very nice of you,' he said. 'Thank you.'

'A pleasure,' she assured him. 'No trouble at all.' She smiled at him and decided she might as well grovel some more in the interests of customer relations. 'Might I suggest that while we're organising your move, you make yourself comfortable in the lounge and I'll have some coffee and biscuits brought to you.'

'That would be lovely.' He was smiling now and looked almost human. There was even some colour in his cheeks.

'I'll arrange everything and coffee will be along in a minute,' she said.

He nodded, then walked away towards the lounge with an air of triumph, obviously congratulating himself on winning all this attention.

But as far as June was concerned, she was the victor in this battle. Sighing with relief, she rang through to the kitchen to order his coffee.

★ ★ ★

As soon as she came off duty June went to the telephone box around the corner armed with coins, and put in a long-distance call to Torquay. Christmas with Alan was out of the question but she didn't want him to think she'd snubbed him. The mere thought of hurting him in that way upset her.

'Cliff Head Hotel, can I help you?'

Much to her annoyance June realised the voice belonged to her mother-in-law.

'Hello, Irene,' she said nervously. 'This is June.'

There was a brief silence while she digested the information. 'My God, you've got a nerve, ringing up here after what you've done to my son,' was her acerbic reaction.

'Is Alan there, please?' June wasn't prepared to waste time in conversation with Irene, since the call was costing a fortune and the money running out fast.

'No, he isn't.'

'Could you put me through to the flat then, please?'

'He isn't there either.'

'Oh. So he isn't in the hotel at all?'

'That's right. He's out on business.'

'Do you know when he'll be back?'

'No.'

'Look, I really need to speak to him urgently,' June continued, daunted but not deterred by the resistance Irene was giving her. 'He rang me earlier and I couldn't speak to him because I was on duty. It's a very busy hotel where I work and I need to explain that to him.'

'You can't if he isn't here, can you?' said the other woman unhelpfully.

'Will you tell him I called then, please?' June requested.

'Yes, I'll do that.'

'Can you explain to him why I wasn't able to speak to him?' June asked, feeling desperate now. 'I was dealing with a difficult customer when his call came through and I couldn't pay attention to him. You know how it is in a hotel reception.'

'I'll tell him.'

'Thank you . . .' The pips interrupted the conversation and the line went dead.

Her first instinct was to call again later and try to speak to Alan personally, but a call box wasn't really suitable for something of such a sensitive nature with the money running out with the speed of light. The message she'd left for him would be enough to convince him she hadn't just been putting him off.

Just as Irene was replacing the receiver after the call from June, Alan walked into reception from the restaurant where he'd been discussing something with Jack about the large private function they had booked for this evening. Despite what she'd said to June, his mother had been fully aware of his whereabouts.

Passing the desk on his way to the office, he noticed that she looked cross. 'What's up, Mother?' he asked. 'You're looking a bit rattled.'

'I'm all right,' she said innocently.

'You could turn milk sour all the way to Exeter with that face,' he teased her. 'Has someone on the phone upset you?'

'No,' she denied swiftly. 'It was someone making a restaurant booking for next week. Just a routine call.'

He gave her a shrewd look. 'You've definitely got the look of battle about you, as though you've just been putting someone in their place.' He wasn't as cheerful as he sounded after the disappointing call he'd made to June earlier, and was just putting on a front. 'Are you sure you haven't just had a complaint?'

'What, against the Cliff Head Hotel?' She made a joke of it. 'Never let it be said.'

'Spoken like a true professional,' he approved, moving away. 'If you need me I'll be in the office.'

'All right, son.'

She had no intention of telling him about June's call. It would only unsettle him. He needed to get that dreadful woman out of his system so that he could get on with his life. And the sooner he forgot about her the better.

'I've rung all the Dodds I could find in the phone book but none of them has a Morris in the family, not even a distant relative,' June informed her sister.

'And I've had no luck in the shops around Wembley,' said Daisy, looking disappointed. 'Still, we didn't expect it to be easy, did we? We'll just have to keep trying.'

It was Sunday morning at Daisy's place. She and the girls hadn't long been back from Mass and she was peeling a pile of sprouts to go with the piece of scrag end of lamb she was cooking for lunch with roast potatoes. Shirley and Belinda were in Nora's flat, making paper chains with her.

'It's all we can do,' June agreed. 'But I thought I'd better pop over and let you know how I'd got on, even though it's a negative result.'

'I appreciate that,' Daisy said. 'It's a pity we don't have a phone we can use to save you coming over every time there's a message.'

'It's no trouble,' June assured her. 'It's only three stops on the tube.'

'Would you like to join us for lunch?' invited Daisy impulsively. 'I can easily do a few more spuds. Nora will be coming in. We always have Sunday lunch together if I'm not out working. Otherwise she gives the girls theirs.'

'I'd love to but I'm on duty at half-past twelve,' June told her.

'Another time then perhaps,' suggested Daisy.

'Thanks. I'd like that.' June paused thoughtfully. 'How come you're not working today?'

'I am. We're having a very early lunch and I'm going in to work as soon as I've eaten mine,' she explained. 'At the hotel where I work they don't start serving lunches until half-past twelve and I don't think they're likely to complain if I'm a bit late getting in today as I've agreed to stay on to serve afternoon teas and dinner tonight. As I'll be out all day until after the girls go to bed, I want to have lunch with them before I go.'

June nodded.

'I try to spend as much time as I possibly can with them, especially at this time of the year. But it's never enough.'

'Are you working over Christmas?' June enquired.

'No fear,' Daisy said. 'You?'

'No.'

'Are you doing anything exciting on Christmas Day?' Daisy asked casually.

'I've nothing planned,' June informed her gloomily. 'I suppose there might be a few of us in the staff quarters with nothing on, so maybe we'll get together for Christmas dinner. No one's said anything about it, though.'

Seeing the sadness in her sister's eyes, Daisy realised that Christmas would be difficult for her, having recently parted from her husband. She cast her eye around the room. 'This isn't exactly the Ritz,' she pointed out unnecessarily, 'but we usually manage to enjoy ourselves in our own simple way at Christmas. You're very welcome to join us.'

June was more touched than Daisy could possibly know. 'I'd really love that, Daisy, but—'

'Don't feel you have to say yes,' she cut in defensively. 'I realise it isn't what you're used to.'

'I live in a basic little room in staff accommodation, for heaven's sake,' her sister reminded her, tutting to emphasise the point.

'Now you do, yes, but you have been used to better things,' Daisy went on.

'Yes, I have,' June wasn't ashamed to admit. 'But that isn't the reason I hesitated before accepting your invitation. I didn't say yes because I don't want to spoil Christmas for Nat. I'm not exactly his favourite person, am I?'

'Nat won't be here,' Daisy was quick to inform her. 'We never see him over Christmas. He goes to relatives in the East End somewhere. Some sort of a family commitment, apparently. I don't know the details.'

'And you and the girls don't go with him, not even for part of the time?' June was incredulous at this further evidence of the man's cavalier attitude.

'Nat isn't the type to take his girlfriend home to meet the family,' Daisy explained. 'That isn't his style.'

A stab of rage towards Nat whipped through June. Surely Daisy and the girls should have first call on his time at Christmas. But if her sister was upset she wasn't showing it. Probably so used to his shabby treatment as to have become immune, June guessed. 'In that case I'd love to join you,' she smiled. 'But only on the condition that I pay my share.'

'You won't get any argument from me about that,' Daisy told her with a wry grin. 'Christmas is an expensive business when you've got two kids with high expectations in the Santa department.'

'That's settled then.'

'Lovely.'

Warmth towards Daisy swept over June, making her eyes feel hot and moist. 'I haven't been looking forward to Christmas one little bit this year, but you've just taken the dread out of it for me,' she said with feeling. 'And I thank you for that with all my heart.'

Daisy smiled, her cheeks flushed with pleasure. But she wasn't given to extravagant displays of sentimentality so she just said, 'We'll be delighted to have you. The more the merrier.'

Lionel Rivers lay on his bunk reading the letter for the umpteenth time, staring at the words and drinking in the joy of them. A letter in itself was a huge event for him. One like this was enough to make him shout with the pleasure of it.

It was from a friend of his daughters', someone called Nora Dove. She hoped he didn't mind her writing to him but Daisy and June had told her his story and she was so moved by it she wanted to write to offer her support and friendship. She went on to explain that she was of his generation rather than his daughters' and thought he might appreciate having someone of his own age to communicate with. She was keen to make the point that he mustn't feel under any obligation to correspond with her if he'd rather not.

She mentioned his daughters' determination to try to clear his name, adding that it might take a long time. He must take comfort in the fact that they would do everything in their power to see that justice was done. They were fine young women and he could be proud to be their father.

The letter was warm and chatty, and contained several amusing anecdotes about his granddaughters, and how they and Daisy meant so much to Nora. The letter didn't spare him the grim realities of life outside altogether. She mentioned a ruthless landlord and the possibility of herself and Daisy losing their home.

'You reading that letter again?' asked Lionel's cell mate from the bunk below.'

'That's right.'

'Blimey, you must know it off by heart now,' the other man joshed. 'I haven't had a word out of you for hours and it'll be lights out soon.'

'Mm.'

'It must be from a woman to keep you that interested,' the other man went on to say.

'It's from a friend and the fact that she happens to be a woman is irrelevant,' explained Lionel. His words had a strange ring to them because it had been so long since he'd called anyone a friend. He couldn't wait to reply to her.

'There's no need to look quite so fed up, Alan,' admonished Paula Bright, a smart woman in her late twenties with short fashionably cut red hair and sparkling blue eyes. 'I realise that our parents' Christmas get-together isn't the most exciting event on your social calendar but it isn't that bad.'

'Sorry,' he apologised. 'Am I being very rude?'

'I wouldn't go so far as to say that,' she said. 'But you're not exactly lively company.'

'It's nothing personal,' he smiled, making an effort. 'I'm just not feeling very sociable this evening. But that's no excuse for bad manners.'

'Don't worry about it.' She seemed very relaxed on the subject. 'I realise that you only came to this little soirée because your parents would have given you a whole lot of grief if you hadn't.'

He gave her a knowing look. 'You too?' he said.

'Surely you don't think I enjoyed being thrown together with you at every possible opportunity when we were growing up in the hope that someday the two of us would make a go of it, do you?' she asked candidly.

'I'd never really thought about it from your point of view,' he was forced to admit.

'Too busy trying to protect yourself, I expect,' she chuckled.

'Something like that.'

'In actual fact I was about as interested in you romantically as you were in me,' she informed him. 'It was a relief to me when you got married.' She raised her eyes, tutting. 'Of course, now that you've split up with your wife, the folks will probably start to get ideas again. But you can relax in the knowledge that they're wasting their time as far as I'm concerned.'

'Oh.'

She cupped her hand behind her ear as though listening to something in the distance. 'Is that the shattering of an ego I can hear?' she chuckled.

'Just a little bruised perhaps,' he smiled, finding her candour rather entertaining.

'You men want it both ways,' she opined. 'You can't bear the idea of a woman not being interested in you even if that woman is the last person on earth you want to be with.'

'I don't think that's a gender thing,' he said. 'It's just a quirk of human nature.'

She shrugged. 'Maybe,' she conceded.

'I'm glad we've got things clear between us at last, anyway.'

'Me too.'

It was the evening of the day before Christmas Eve and he and Paula were sitting chatting at a table in the Cliff Head bar. She had come over with her parents for a seasonal drink with the Masters and other friends of her and Alan's parents. The older generation were standing in a group talking nearby. Alan and Paula had drifted into conversation as a matter of course.

'I should have thought that being sociable was second nature to you, as a hotelier, whether you're in the mood or not,' she remarked, sipping her gin and tonic, blue eyes peering at him over the rim of the glass. 'It's all in a day's work to us.'

'That's true . . . up to a point.'

'But the sparkling conversation doesn't happen instinctively for a friend of the family who isn't going to pay the going rate for a room?' she suggested with a knowing twinkle in her eye. 'Am I right?'

'It isn't a conscious thing on my part but there might be something in what you say,' he returned, Paula's light-hearted manner cheering him up. 'As you say, being sociable is an automatic thing in our business.'

'Dare I ask what's made you so gloomy?' she enquired casually.

The breakdown of his marriage was the answer to that but he wasn't going to bare his soul to Paula about the fact that his wife couldn't even spare the time to talk to him on the phone or return his call. After the painful rejection she'd given him at the hotel in London, it had taken a lot of courage to call her and suggest they spend Christmas together. And she wouldn't even consider it; just put the phone down on him. Ever since then he'd been struggling to accept the truth – that it was over between them and there was no point in his trying to get her back.

He thought back to happier times. They had both been so full of hope and harmony when they'd got married. And the sad thing was he'd never noticed it slip away; still couldn't fully accept that it had. But for some reason best known to herself, June didn't want him in her life. She seemed so cold and distant now. Not the woman he had fallen in love with at all.

But now Paula was saying, 'Talk to yourself, why don't you, Paula? It seems as though that's the only way you're going to get any answers.'

'Sorry.' Alan gave her a wry grin. 'I was miles away.'

'Problems of a personal nature rather than business, I suspect,' she speculated.

He gave her his full attention. 'You're very astute.'

'Difficult guests and hotel disasters don't carry the same look of pain somehow,' she said lightly. 'I know about these things; I'm in the same line of business, remember.'

'Yes, of course.'

Her expression became more serious. 'I was sorry to hear that you and your wife had parted,' she told him. 'Even though it's probably turned our folks into dedicated matchmakers again, now that you're back in circulation. You and your wife seemed good together whenever I saw you. From what I knew of June, she seemed nice.'

'I always thought so.'

'You're speaking in the past tense, I notice,' Paula pointed out. 'And that seems a bit harsh. Just because it didn't work out for the two of you, that doesn't mean she's a lesser person than you thought she was.'

'I know that,' he corrected. 'I meant more that I feel I couldn't have ever really known her. I mean, before this happened I would have staked my life on her loyalty, on her staying with me until we were a couple of old codgers. But to just walk out like that with no warning . . .' He sighed, shaking his head. 'It still shocks me to think about it.'

'She must have had a very good reason,' was Paula's opinion. 'Or thought she had.'

Deciding he'd already said too much, he called a halt. Despite what she'd done, it seemed disloyal to June to discuss their problems with a relative stranger.

'Yeah, I expect you're right.' He looked at her and saw shining blue eyes, a flawless skin suffused with cleverly applied make-up. A fitted black suit sat well on her trim figure. She wasn't a stunning beauty but she was attractive and sexy. 'But that's quite enough about me. Let's talk about you now. Is there anyone serious in your life?'

'I'm not about to get married, if that's what you mean,' she told him.

'I'm surprised you're not married already.'

'Most people are,' she told him. 'A man can stay single beyond the age of about twenty-five and everyone assumes he's enjoying life as a bachelor too much to want to settle down. A woman does it and they think there must be something wrong with her because she can't get a man. It never occurs to anyone that she might actually enjoy the single life.'

'I thought most women wanted to get married,' Alan said. 'Thought it was the natural thing, all part of the nesting instinct.'

'It is,' she agreed. 'Finding a husband and settling down to have babies is the life plan of the average 1950s woman. I suppose that was all I wanted too up until I was about twenty. But when it didn't happen, I got to thinking that being single wasn't so bad after all, especially as I got more involved in the management of the hotel. I'd like to meet Mr Right, of course, but if it isn't meant to be I can live with it. I realise that I'm some sort of a freak because I didn't rush up the aisle at the first opportunity.'

'I'm sure there was no lack of offers.'

'I've had a few.'

'You just didn't fancy them?'

'I've had my moments,' she said with a wicked grin. 'But that doesn't mean I was ready to give up my independence and settle down just because it's the done thing. I haven't yet met anyone I'd want to give up my single status for, even if that does mean people will soon start calling me an old maid. Anyway, apart from anything else, I have to make sure it's me they want and not the hotel. Like you, Alan, I'm an only child. My parents' hotel is worth a lot of money and will be mine one day. That factor alone makes me attractive in some men's eyes.'

'You're attractive anyway,' he told her, and meant it. 'Regardless of your material assets.'

'Thank you.' She smiled, seeming pleased.

'It was never that I didn't find you attractive.' It suddenly seemed important that she knew that. 'It was just the minute I clapped eyes on June there was no one else for me.'

'Explanations aren't necessary,' Paula assured him breezily. 'As I've said, it was a mutual thing.'

'You're doing terrible things to my ego again,' he teased her.

She laughed. 'Your sense of humour didn't die altogether when June left then,' she remarked.

'Apparently not, I'm surprised to discover.'

'I suppose one of the reasons our folks were so keen for us to get together was because we each had our own assets,' she said thoughtfully. 'So they could be sure that if it did happen it wouldn't be for material gain on either side.'

'Mm.' Alan's thoughts turned to less personal matters. 'But tell me, do you still close your hotel over Christmas?'

'That's right.'

'Same here. But I'd like to throw open the doors and make a big

105

thing of it. Do a special Christmas programme.'

'Would you get any takers, though,' she wondered, 'Christmas being a home and family time?'

'I think we might. A lot of people would probably welcome the chance to escape from all the domestic slavery that goes on at Christmas.'

'Why don't you give it a try then?'

'Mum and Dad won't hear of it,' he explained. 'They want things to stay exactly as they have always been at the Cliff Head.' He paused, looking at her. 'I expect you have the same trouble with your folks, don't you?'

'Not at all,' she surprised him by saying. 'My parents are leaving things to me increasingly. They're content to take a back seat and let me shoulder the responsibility, glad to have some time to themselves.'

'So, you have a real say in what goes on, then?' he said thoughtfully.

'More than that, I practically run the place nowadays – with a good team of staff, of course,' she replied.

'I didn't realise your parents had retired.'

'They haven't – officially. They're still working but they've handed a lot of the responsibility over to me. They trust me to keep the place flourishing and they seem to like my new ideas. They've worked hard all their lives. Now they're only too pleased to take things a bit easier.'

'Lucky you.'

'I've no complaints.'

'I'd like to turn this place into a family hotel,' Alan said, looking around the room at the dark furnishings and décor, a few tasteful Christmas decorations dotted about, a sprig of holly here, a touch of tinsel there. 'I think we should be more child-friendly and liven the place up with entertainment and so on – something for the whole family to enjoy on holiday.'

She made a face. 'I can't see Irene and Gerald going for that one. The Cliff Head has always been a quiet, select hotel.'

'I wasn't thinking of turning it into a glorified holiday camp,' was his answer to that. 'I just want to give it some new life. It's too staid, too old-fashioned.'

'With all due respect to your parents, I agree with you. A few changes can only be a good thing,' Paula enthused. 'All of us in the hotel trade are going to have to look to our laurels over the next few years.'

'Because of the competition from holiday camps, you mean?'

'Yes, holiday camps are a worry.'

'But Butlins wouldn't appeal to the sort of people who like a hotel holiday,' Alan pointed out.

'I wouldn't bank on that,' Paula warned. 'People can easily get converted. They try a holiday camp once to see what it's like and want to go back the next year. Anyway, I think we have a much more powerful opponent looming.'

'Oh?'

'Holidays abroad.'

'Surely not.' He was sceptical. 'Only a tiny proportion of the population can afford to go abroad.'

'At the moment, yes,' she agreed. 'But foreign package holidays are getting more popular all the time. People aren't afraid of a foreign holiday if everything is organised for them and they have the security of the tour company behind them.'

'But package holidays abroad are still very much in their infancy,' he debated. 'They are only within the reach of a fraction of the market.'

'At the moment you're absolutely right,' Paula nodded. 'But they'll be a force to be reckoned with in the future if things go on as they are and the economy continues to improve. You must have read all the talk about it in the trade press.'

'I have, but I didn't think there was an immediate threat.'

'There isn't but, at the same time, we can't just sit back and expect things to stay the same for ever.' She was very confident. 'We're living in an age of prosperity and we have to bear in mind the fact that foreign holidays will get cheaper as the demand for them grows.'

'There is that.'

'Ask yourself, Alan, if you had a choice between a holiday in Spain with guaranteed sunshine, cheap drinks and entertainment laid on, or a fortnight in Torquay in a hotel with no entertainment and the possibility of tramping about the town all day in the rain, which would you choose?'

'Mm, I see your point,' he was forced to concede. 'So are you planning on doing anything about it at your place?'

'We certainly are,' she informed him brightly. 'For starters we're going to be installing an indoor swimming pool.'

'Wow!'

'That will be only our first move,' Paula explained. 'We are intending to make other improvements too, gradually. We're planning on having a games room and dancing in the dining room a couple of times a week.'

'You've really done your thinking,' he approved.

'You have to think ahead if you're to survive in business these days.' She looked at him thoughtfully. 'Is that the sort of thing you'd like to do in your dream hotel?'

'That would be a part of it,' he replied. 'And those sorts of improvements would have to be made, of course. But my dream is more to create a feeling, an atmosphere.'

'The facilities would have to come first, though.'

'Of course. But then I'd want to build something over and above that. Something that can be created only by a human touch. A welcome so warm people would want to book ahead for the following year.'

'Well, you've certainly got the enthusiasm,' she told him. 'And that's the sort of attitude that breeds success. I think you should persuade your parents to let you go ahead with it. You seem to know exactly what you want, so talk to them about it again, sell them the idea.'

How many times had June told him the same thing? How many times had he tried to get his parents to listen to his ideas? Paula was a similar age to him and she was practically running the Brights' family-owned hotel. Discontent flashed through him. It really was time he was given some credibility around here. He would talk to them, make a stand. Be determined.

'You're absolutely right,' he said, her optimism filling him with fresh hope. 'I'll raise the subject again as soon as I see the opportunity.'

'Good for you,' she said. 'I wish you luck.'

'Thanks.'

This was the first time he'd had a proper conversation with her and he was beginning to enjoy himself. At least it had taken his mind off his problems. Now that he knew her better, he liked Paula and was enjoying her company. They had plenty in common and she talked a lot of sense.

'You must let me know the outcome,' she suggested casually. 'I'd be interested to hear how you get on.'

'Yeah, I'll do that.' He gave her an uncertain smile. 'Perhaps we could meet up for a drink sometime – just for a chat.'

'I'd like that.'

'I'll give you a ring to get something arranged then, sometime in the new year,' he told her.

'I'll look forward to it.'

'In the meantime, can I get you a drink?'

'That would be lovely,' she smiled. 'I'd like a gin and tonic, please.'

'A pleasure.'

As he walked towards the bar, he was aware of approving glances being cast in his direction from his parents. With June out of the way, their hopes for Paula and himself had been given a new lease of life. Fortunately, now that he and Paula understood each other, there wasn't a problem.

Chapter Seven

'It's your go, Auntie June.' Shirley passed her aunt the little plastic cup containing the dice; they were playing a game of snakes and ladders.

There were shrieks of triumphant laughter from her opponents when she landed on a snake and had to move her counter down the board. 'Oh, not again,' she wailed, entering into the spirit of rivalry with a good heart. 'I think you lot have fixed the dice to go against me.'

'Now, now,' joshed Nora. 'Don't let's have any bad sportsmanship.'

'Bad sports aren't allowed in our house, Mum says, even if they are grown-ups,' Belinda told her solemnly. 'So you'd better watch out, Auntie.'

'Ooh, hark who's talking,' retaliated June, winking at the others. 'Who was it who got a fit of the sulks when she didn't win at ludo earlier on?'

'Now then, kiddies, and that includes you, June,' began Daisy, who was so glad she'd invited her sister; she was such good fun, and wonderful with the children, 'can we have a bit less mucking about and more concentration, please? There's a serious game in progress here.'

'Yes, ma'am,' said June, making the children laugh with her mock salute.

It was the evening of Christmas Day and they'd decided on a board game in the hope of quietening the mood before the girls' bedtime, after the excitement of the day. But June could see no sign of a slow-down; they were still as lively as a couple of puppies.

Her gaze wandered idly around the room, which was suggestive of a grotto with its dazzling festive décor. A Christmas tree glowed in the window, the ceiling was a mass of home-made paper chains and lanterns, while a plethora of cardboard Santas, snowmen and reindeers beamed from various points.

Garish and tasteless was how Alan's parents would describe it, she thought wryly. And yes, perhaps it was a bit excessive. It was also a triumph of the human spirit, in June's opinion. Scraping the money together from her meagre resources, Daisy had transformed this tatty room in a seedy tenement house into a seasonal wonder for two little girls. No child could have had a Christmas richer in goodwill. And by working all hours Daisy had ensured they didn't go short of presents either.

Never mind the fetid hallway and dangerously dark landing and stairs – inside this room the heart and spirit were so uplifted, it was all that seemed to matter.

Alan hadn't been far from June's thoughts all day and the festive season emphasised the sadness of her fractured life. But being here with this little family had eased her path through what could otherwise have been an unbearable time. In concentrating on making the occasion a happy one for the children, she'd cast out her own problems; had even managed to experience moments of genuine pleasure since she arrived last night, having come on the tube before public transport had stopped for the holiday. Nora had put her up on a camp bed in her flat as Daisy was pushed for space.

The girls had been beside themselves this morning, feverishly unwrapping parcels, then rummaging in their stockings to find an apple and orange, little packages of sweets, a comb, new hair ribbons and a few cheap sundries. The only expensive items were the roller skates that Daisy had been saving for all year. These had already made their debut on the street, the aspiring skaters clinging for dear life to walls, lampposts and each other. June had given them satin pyjama cases, on which their names were embroidered, complete with new pyjamas. She'd given Daisy a talcum and soap set, and a book of Betjeman poems for Nora because she knew he was a favourite of hers. She herself had received apple blossom bath cubes from Daisy and a letter-writing set from Nora.

But now the game was coming to an end and the children's reserves of energy were finally running out. Bedtime didn't bring forth its usual crop of protests tonight, though, because of the lure of the new pyjamas.

'They're absolutely whacked,' said Daisy when the three women were settled with glasses of port from the bottle June had brought with her, Daisy and Nora on the sofa, June in the armchair. 'It's been quite a day for them.'

'For me too,' added June. 'It's lovely having children around at Christmas; makes such a difference.'

Daisy gave her a questioning grin. 'You managed to survive their high spirits without losing your sanity then,' she remarked light-heartedly. 'Their boisterousness can be a bit much if you're not used to it.'

'It didn't worry me.' It was true to say that the girls' exuberance didn't bother June but she didn't feel entirely at ease with them either. Suddenly finding herself with two lively nieces was something of a challenge to someone with no experience of children, and she wasn't yet confident in her new role. Some aunts would probably consider their function to be that of an authority figure, an issuer of discipline and back-up support to the children's mother. But June, in the ardent pursuit of their love and friendship, saw herself more as a purveyor of fun and pleasure. She had to admit, though, that the playful persona she thought would appeal to their age group and win her popularity had proved difficult to sustain over a long period.

'They've worn me out today, I know that much,' Nora confessed wearily. 'I'll be asleep as soon as my head touches the pillow tonight.'

'Me too,' said Daisy, covering a yawn with her hand. 'The little perishers had us up so early this morning, it's no wonder we're exhausted.'

'Anyway.' June raised her glass. 'How about a toast? To absent friends.'

'Absent friends,' they chanted.

'Wouldn't it be great if Dad was able to spend Christmas with us next year?' said June.

'Mm,' agreed Daisy. 'I think having us visit him just before the holiday will have helped him through Christmas this year. From what he's said, visitors have been nonexistent until now, except perhaps for official prison visitors.'

'His friends have probably shunned him, thinking he was a murderer,' suggested June.

'Yeah. He's got himself a pen pal now, though, hasn't he, Nora?' smiled Daisy, turning towards her friend. 'He was tickled pink with your letter.'

'It was kind of you, Nora,' approved June.

'I probably got as much pleasure from writing it as he did receiving it.' She was quite frank about it. 'I've always enjoyed letter-writing so I was glad of an excuse to put pen to paper.'

'It was appreciated, anyway,' said June. 'And while we're on the subject of appreciation, I want to thank you both for helping me through my first Christmas without Alan. You've made me feel so welcome here, it's made all the difference.' She lifted her glass. 'To many more Christmases together.'

'I'll drink to that,' cheered Daisy, swigging her port, cheeks suffused from the alcohol and the heat from the gas fire. 'Though God knows where we'll be next year.'

Nora nodded sagely. 'Don't let's think about that, dear, not on Christmas Day,' she said.

June had gathered from what had been said that they were having trouble with their landlord but she didn't know how serious the situation actually was. 'Are things bad enough for you to move out, then?' she enquired.

Daisy sighed. 'It's getting to be that way. It depends how much

111

more we can take of our landlord's devious tactics.'

'Didn't you say something about being determined to stand firm against him?' June queried.

'That's the plan, but we have to be realistic about it. It's all very well standing up for your rights, and we'll do that for as long as we can, but I have the kids to think of,' Daisy pointed out. 'If things get any worse we might be forced to leave here but don't ask me where we'll go because I haven't got a clue, with the housing shortage being so bad in London.'

'A hundred thousand houses were destroyed completely in London during the war, and another million were war-damaged,' Nora explained. 'That's why people like Roland Ellwood are so powerful.'

'But the war has been over for nearly ten years,' June objected. 'Surely new houses have been built.'

'Plenty of them – out in the suburbs and new towns,' Daisy told her. 'But around here the crisis is as bad as ever.'

'What about council housing?' asked June.

'Don't make me laugh,' was Daisy's quick reply. 'I've been on the waiting list for years.'

'This borough has the lowest level of council housing in London,' added the knowledgeable Nora.

'I see . . .' said June.

Daisy went on to tell her sister about the way some landlords were exploiting the West Indian immigrants by charging per head. 'Six to a room and sleeping in shifts. The property owners are making a fortune and the immigrants are so grateful to have a roof over their heads they pay up and think the landlords are wonderful.'

'There must be someone you can complain to about the situation,' was June's outraged reaction.

Daisy shook her head. 'There isn't, believe me. We've been down that road and it leads nowhere. The authorities have got so many homeless people to deal with, they just haven't the time to bother about the conditions people *with* homes are living under. Anyway, this place is better than some of the others. You should see the squalor some people have to live in around here – rat-infested places with no facilities and barely any sanitation.'

'Having no light on the stairs and landing is bad enough, though,' said June. 'Especially with two children needing to go up and down after dark.'

'Ellwood's probably hoping one of us will fall down the stairs and hurt ourselves; not seriously – just enough to unnerve us into moving out,' Daisy suggested. 'He's got a mind like a cash register. All he can see is the money he could make from the rooms if we weren't here.'

'I didn't realise that things were so bad,' June confessed.

'I don't suppose people outside the area do realise what it's like.

Why should they?' Daisy shrugged. 'You've got to live here to know what's going on.' She gave June a shrewd look. 'And of course you were sheltered from inner city problems when you were living in Torquay.'

'You're not kidding,' she swiftly agreed. 'I'm beginning to understand just how easy I had it down in Devon.'

'If we had anywhere else to go we'd have been out of here long ago,' Daisy went on to say. 'Wouldn't we, Nora?'

'Not half.'

'Enough about that,' Daisy said hastily. 'It's Christmas night and not a time to be moaning and groaning. So let's talk about something else.'

But June had lapsed into thought, plans of her own coming into focus suddenly and forming an idea that would benefit them all. 'I've just realised that I can help,' she said after a while, her voice rising with excitement.

They both gave her a questioning look.

'Don't say you're thinking of trying to fix us up in the staff accommodation at the hotel where you work,' grinned Daisy, making a joke of it to lift the gloom that had crept into the atmosphere. 'Somehow I don't think the management would be too keen on that idea.'

'Don't be daft. I'm going to be moving out of staff accommodation myself soon anyway,' June explained with growing enthusiasm. 'And when I do, I can solve your problem too, make things better for us all.'

'How?' Daisy wanted to know.

'Well, my mother's little house in Hounslow came to me automatically when she died and I put it up for sale straight away because I didn't want to live in it. I've found a buyer and am just waiting for the sale to be finalised. With the money I get for it I'm going to buy somewhere else.'

'And invite us over to give us a break from this dump?' surmised Daisy.

'No. I was thinking more in terms of you all moving in with me.' Seeing the question in Nora's eyes, she added quickly, 'You too, Nora.'

'Ooh, I like the sound of that,' beamed the older woman. 'What a smashing idea.'

But Daisy reacted differently and her fierce opposition was completely unexpected to both June and Nora. Her eyes blazed, her lips tightened and an angry flush stained her cheeks. 'I might not have much but I'm not a charity case yet,' she said coldly.

An abrasive silence fell over the room.

'No one is suggesting that you are,' June said at last. 'And I'm not offering charity.'

'Sounds remarkably like it to me,' snapped Daisy.

'You must have misunderstood me, then,' June was quick to point out. 'Because with the best will in the world, I'm not in a position to offer charity to anyone. I don't have any money.'

'Oh, not much,' uttered Daisy with uncharacteristic scorn. 'You've enough to buy a house and you say you've no dough. You're living in a different world.'

'Look – the only reason I can buy a house is because my adopted parents' place came to me as their next of kin,' she explained. 'I'm not saying that I'm not lucky to have it because I know that I am – *very lucky*. But it's a one-off and certainly doesn't mean I have money, as such. By the time I've paid for somewhere to live I'll be skint again, and I'll find it difficult to afford the costs of running a house on my own because I'm not on a high salary. I work in a West End hotel, yes, but I am only a receptionist. I probably don't earn much more than either of you.'

'You don't know what hardship is,' accused Daisy with unusual hostility. 'You've had it good for most of your life. Adopted by people who were well off enough to own a house, got yourself a rich husband with a part-share in some posh hotel.'

June wasn't prepared to supply her with details about her past so she just said, 'But I left all that behind me and I'm in the same boat as you are now, except that I don't have any children to support. I'm a single woman looking out for myself, just like you are. We're two of a kind.'

'Don't make me laugh,' came Daisy's cynical response. 'You'll never be the same kind as me, not with the start in life that you've had.'

'Look, Daisy, I can't help the way it worked out for us when we were children,' June reminded her. 'I didn't have any say in what happened any more than you did, and you know that in your heart.' She moved on swiftly, rather than dwell on those unhappy times. 'Anyway, when I suggested that you all move in with me, I was thinking in terms of us sharing the house, rather than my just letting you some rooms.'

'Sounds good to me,' approved Nora.

'We'd still be your lodgers.' Daisy looked extremely doubtful.

'Technically, I suppose you would be my lodgers. But what I have in mind would be more of a house-sharing arrangement, all of us on an equal footing,' June told her. 'I thought we could live like a family and split all the costs three ways: coal, gas and electric, the rates, all the running costs of the house plus any decorating and maintenance bills. It would be a joint enterprise. We'd each do our share of the chores.'

'What about rent?' asked Daisy.

'I haven't got round to thinking about that yet. But obviously if I

114

can pay for the house outright from the sale of the other one, and you're paying your share of everything else I won't need to charge rent—' she began.

'Forget it,' cut in Daisy rudely.

'Daisy,' rebuked Nora, frowning at her.

But Daisy was at the mercy of new emotions which she could neither understand nor control, and she was deaf to Nora's protests. Her voice was shaking as she spoke. 'I'm prepared to accept any sort of a hand-out for the sake of my kids, and I'll grovel with the best of 'em for their benefit. But I won't take charity from my sister.' She shook her head in despair. 'I just can't do it.'

'It isn't charity, I've told you,' insisted June, distressed by this turn of events. 'You'd be the ones being charitable because you'd be doing me a favour if you move in with me. I don't want to live in a house on my own.'

'Oh, for goodness' sake,' Daisy sneered. 'Do you think I'm thick or something? You must do if you reckon I'd swallow that load of old rubbish.'

'If it would make you feel better, pay me some rent then.' June was at a loss to know what to say.

'Now you really are being patronising,' retorted Daisy through tight lips.

June was perplexed. What had seemed like a fantastic idea just a few minutes ago had turned into an explosive situation she couldn't handle. Whatever she said would be misunderstood by Daisy in this mood. 'I'm sorry you feel like that about it. I really didn't mean to upset you.'

'For heaven's sake, Daisy,' said Nora in a firm tone, 'June isn't trying to belittle you in any way. She's come up with a scheme to help us all, herself included.'

'Nora's right.' June was glad of the support. 'The idea popped into my mind just now and seemed like a practical solution for us all. You have problems with your landlord and I can't afford to rattle around in a house in my own. So the sensible thing is for us all to move in together. Even apart from the financial side, I don't fancy the idea of living by myself. It isn't as though I've got any friends in London. Sharing might be fun and it would give you and me a chance to get to know each other again after all these years.' She gave Daisy a look of defiance. 'And yes, I did think it would make things better for you. There wouldn't be any point in my asking you to move in with me otherwise, would there?'

Daisy shrugged, feigning indifference.

'You can't deny that it will be easier for you than staying on here, worried to death the whole time about what the landlord will do next,' June continued.

'Course it will be better,' confirmed Nora. 'And if you weren't so stubborn, you'd see that, Daisy.'

'I don't know yet what sort of a place I can get with the money from the sale,' June continued. 'I didn't get a fortune for my mother's house because it's out of town and anything in central London will be a lot more expensive so it won't be anything too grand. If you did decide to come in on it with me, we might have to settle for something that needs doing up to get enough room for us all at the price I can afford. But you'd certainly have more space and freedom than you have here, especially if I can get something with a little garden for the girls to play in.'

'I'm not so dim that I can't tell whether someone's being big-hearted or big-headed, you know,' expressed Daisy.

June felt as though she'd been physically slapped. 'I didn't mean to be either of those things,' she tried to make her sister understand. 'It was a spur-of-the-moment idea which would benefit me as much as you.'

Daisy pondered on this. 'Mm, maybe it would but I can't do it,' she told her.

Nora couldn't believe she was hearing this. Daisy must be having some sort of a brainstorm to behave in this way because she was usually so sensitive to other people's feelings and completely unashamed of her impecunious state. It was obvious how hurt poor June was and it was unlike Daisy to be cruel to anyone. The two of them were so different, Nora observed, Daisy so open-hearted and straightforward, June more secretive and withdrawn but equally as vulnerable, somehow. They needed each other and it tore at Nora's heart to see their new-found relationship foundering before it had got past the first post. Deciding, however, that this was a family matter and it was time she made a diplomatic exit, she said, 'Well, I'll leave you two to fight it out.'

'Don't go,' urged Daisy, feeling guilty for spoiling the evening for them all.

'It's time I was in bed anyway,' said Nora, affecting a yawn as she stood up. 'It's been a long day.'

'I'll come with you.' June got up and looked down at Daisy, who was sitting on the sofa looking forlorn. 'Thanks for a lovely day. It's been really great.' She paused, fiddling with her fingernails nervously. 'Look, forget the idea of us all moving in together. I should never have suggested it. The last thing I wanted to do was upset you, especially at Christmas.'

'Don't worry about it.' Daisy was very subdued.

Tension drew tight in the air. Nora could almost taste the bitterness between the sisters. Although she wanted to put her arms around them both and guide them out of this impasse, she knew she mustn't

116

interfere. This was something they had to work out for themselves. 'G'night, love,' she said to Daisy. 'See you in the morning.'

''Night, Daisy,' added June.

''Night, both.'

As the door closed behind them, Daisy sat motionless on the sofa, feeling terrible. Looking around her, she noticed how the Christmas decorations had an irrelevant look about them now somehow. The happy day had ended on a sour note. She tried to comfort herself with the thought that it hadn't been spoiled for the children. But it didn't help.

Lying in the bed next to her sleeping daughters, listening to the now familiar sound of music and laughter from a party in the lower regions of the house, Daisy felt physically ill with remorse as she replayed the altercation in her mind and recalled how hateful she had been to June.

What made it even worse was the fact that she could see how stupid she'd been to react so negatively to the idea of them all moving in together when it was the perfect solution. Why was it so easy for her to give yet so hard for her to take? If anyone knew about Christian charity, Daisy did, after the upbringing she'd had. She knew all about kindness and generosity, and give and take. It wasn't as though she hadn't been on the receiving end of kindness before. She'd had it in abundance from Nora. So why did it stick in her throat when it came from June?

Sibling rivalry and pride, she was ashamed to admit. But looking at the matter logically, June really did stand to gain as much as Daisy and the others from such an arrangement. It hadn't been an act of charity but an opportunity for them all. Company for June and the chance of a decent home for her and the girls and Nora. God knows, they needed it. And what had she done? Thrown it back in her sister's face, and deprived her children of a better standard of living because she was too proud to accept something in the spirit with which it was given.

She was furious with herself, and sad. Nat came into her mind for some reason and she felt a pang. Trust him not to be around when she needed him. June was right when she said they were both in the same boat. Neither had a man to love and comfort her. Nat loved her in his way – if she didn't believe that she'd have given up on him long ago – but, although it hurt to admit it, he was only a part-time lover.

But she and June did have each other. Fate had brought them together again and their relationship could become special, given time. Why throw the chance of that away just because of sisterly competition?

117

Weary of tossing and turning, she got up and went in the other room and curled up in the armchair with her dressing gown over her, waiting for the agonising night to end so that she could put things right.

The girls slept in the next morning after the late night. As soon as Daisy heard signs of life from across the landing, she went and tapped on Nora's door.

June opened the door in her dressing gown, looking tired and pale and extremely wary of her sister.

'You don't look as though you've had any more sleep than I have,' Daisy observed.

'I've had better nights,' was June's cool response.

Daisy bit her lip; she was full of contrition. 'Look, I'm really sorry about last night,' she said. 'I said some horrid things.'

'You're entitled to your opinion,' June told her frostily. 'I told you to forget it.'

'I know you did but I don't want to forget it.' She made a face. 'Help me out here, June. I'm trying to put things right.'

'Why the change of heart?'

'I was stupid. I don't know what got into me.' She looked at her persuasively. 'I'm sorry. And I'd really like us all to move in together. It's a brilliant idea.'

June was so thrilled she didn't bear a grudge. 'If you're sure, then that's what we'll do,' she smiled.

'As long as you let me pay my way,' Daisy made it clear in a warning tone.

'I won't have any choice about that.' June's tone was just as firm. 'As I've already said, I can't afford to keep you and the kids as well as myself. I'm only a hotel receptionist.'

'I'll have to make sure you're not out of pocket then, won't I?' said Daisy, satisfied now on this point.

'We'll work out the details when we've found somewhere. I haven't even started looking for a place yet.' She paused. 'Perhaps we could do that together, all of us.'

'That would be smashing,' enthused Daisy.

With the release of tension, they both got a fit of the giggles, hugging each other and hovering between laughter and tears.

'What's going on out here?' came Nora's throaty tones as she scuttled on to the scene in her dressing gown and slippers. 'What's all the noise about?'

Daisy grabbed hold of her and swung her round. 'We're getting out of here,' she said excitedly, linking arms with her and dancing round, lifting her knees in the air. 'We're all going to be living together . . . so what do you think of that?'

'Thank God you've come to your senses,' was Nora's enthusiastic reaction. 'It's the best bit of news I've heard in a very long time.'

In the same way as June found salvation over Christmas in Daisy and the girls and Nora, Alan found comfort in Jack Saunders' company and large quantities of alcohol drunk together in a matey fashion on Christmas Eve after work. On Christmas Day he went to his parents' house where everything was pin neat and traditional, with turkey and stuffing and perfect mince pies.

The business being a family one, shop talk was never taboo, even at Christmas. So as they lingered at the table over lunch, Alan decided to take the opportunity to raise the subject that had been on his mind ever since he'd discussed it with Paula.

'I really believe it's time for some changes at the Cliff Head,' he said in conclusion, having outlined his ideas.

'But you already know what we think about turning our hotel into a bear garden,' said Gerald.

'Bear garden, my foot. It would be a bit livelier, that's all,' corrected Alan, managing to stay calm. 'There would be no lowering of standards.'

'It's Christmas,' interrupted Irene, staidly clad in a navy-blue twinset, her hair welded into place with setting lotion. 'Not a time to talk business.'

'It's the very best time to do it,' Alan disagreed. 'We can talk without being interrupted.'

'We've been through all this before, son,' pointed out his father smugly, cheeks flushed from his pre-prandial tipple. 'And your mother and I have agreed that it wouldn't be wise to introduce the changes you're proposing to the Cliff Head.'

'Why doesn't that surprise me?' Alan said cuttingly.

'Don't be facetious, dear,' requested his mother primly.

Alan looked from one to the other. 'I know you don't, personally, want to consider my ideas but give me one good solid reason why some changes wouldn't be wise from a business point of view.'

'You know why.' His father was impatient now. 'Because we are a refined hotel catering for people who want peace and quiet. We'd lose all our customers if we changed our policy.'

'We'd gain more than we'd lose.' Alan was adamant about this. 'There's a gap in the market for a family hotel. There aren't enough of them around.'

'Maybe not,' said his mother, helping herself to more Christmas pudding. 'But we are not going to add to their numbers.'

'Hear! Hear!' Gerald supported.

'So, you won't even think about it then?' said Alan, looking from one to the other.

'We already have done and the answer is no,' confirmed his father dismissively. 'So let's forget it and talk about our plans for the coming season.'

'I thought I was supposed to be a partner in the business,' Alan reminded them.

'And you are, dear,' his mother assured him. 'That isn't in question.'

'I'm questioning it.' He was really fired up now. 'I might as well be a chamber maid for all the say I get in the running of the hotel. My ideas are never even given any consideration, just dismissed out of hand.'

'That isn't fair,' his father argued. 'It's just this one thing we can't agree on.'

'No, Dad, it's everything.'

'Rubbish!'

Alan thought his father probably believed his own words so it was useless to argue the toss over that one. But he wasn't ready to give up on the main point. 'Why exactly are you so much against the ideas I've just outlined anyway?' he asked, getting heated. 'I know you're keen on all things traditional but there must be more to it than that.'

'It's Christmas, Alan,' his mother reminded him again. 'I don't want any arguments.'

'I have no intention of having an argument,' he assured her. 'I just want a straight answer to my question.'

'All right, I'll give it to you straight,' said his father, leaning back slightly in his chair and regarding his son with an air of complacency. 'Even apart from believing that a family hotel isn't right for the Cliff Head, I don't actually *want* to run the sort of place you have in mind. I would hate it.'

'Me too,' added Irene.

'But you're a sociable sort of a chap,' Alan pointed out, looking at his father. 'I should have thought you'd enjoy working in a livelier environment.'

'I might be sociable but I'm very selective about the company I keep and I'm quite happy with the way things are,' he stated. 'I don't want our refined cocktail bar to become like the public bar of some backstreet pub.'

Alan gave a dry laugh. 'You'd vet the guests before you took their booking if you could afford to turn people away, wouldn't you?' he said bitterly.

'I certainly would.' Gerald wasn't ashamed of his snobbery. 'I don't want riffraff in my hotel, neither do I want snotty-nosed kids making a racket about the place.'

'You're quite right, dear,' agreed Irene.

'It may be a very good idea in principle and right for other hoteliers, but it would never work for us,' boomed Gerald. 'So accept it once and for all, boy, and let's hear no more about it.'

In a defining moment Alan finally did exactly that: he faced up to the truth. Not only would they never agree to make the changes he wanted, it would be a disaster if they did. Anything outside of the hushed atmosphere they were used to would be anathema to them so their presence would not be conducive to the atmosphere Alan had in mind.

He'd clung to the idea because he was a man with a dream, but it was *his* dream not theirs. If he wanted a different kind of hotel he would have to do it without them. And as that was completely out of the question, he had no choice but to put it out of his mind and satisfy himself with the Cliff Head as it was, and likely to stay – in his parents' lifetime, anyway. There was certainly no point in trying to persuade them into changes that were wrong for them.

'Yes, Dad,' he said with a sigh of resignation. 'I'll do that.'

'Thank God we've got through to you at last about this,' said his father.

His mother looked relieved. 'Mince pies anyone?' she offered, smiling.

The two men answered rather absently in the affirmative and she scuttled off to the kitchen to get them. 'While we're on the subject of business,' Gerald began, 'there's a hotel and catering exhibition at Earls Court in March. I've had some literature in about it. Wondered if you fancied going.'

'I suppose it might be quite interesting.' Alan was too disappointed about the other thing to show much enthusiasm.

'It'll be worth a visit, certainly. It's always a good idea to keep up to date with what's going on in the trade.' He gave his son a wry grin. 'As long as you don't come back with more ideas for this wretched family-style hotel you're so keen on.'

Alan ignored his attempt at humour. 'Aren't you going then?' he asked.

'No. I don't fancy the London crowds,' his father explained. 'I thought you might like to go instead. Stay overnight. Give yourself a break. There won't be a problem with your getting away at that time of the year.'

'I'll think about it.'

Suddenly Alan felt about six years old. Then it had been sweets and toys, now it was a trip to London to keep his parents in his favour. Did they really not know how transparent these attempts to placate him were?

Something significant happened to him at that moment. He realised with blinding clarity what he'd known for years and not allowed himself to fully admit: he needed to find his own way, to fail or succeed for himself, away from his parents. But he was trapped. Even

121

apart from the hideous personal complications of breaking away, he had very little in the way of material assets outside the Cliff Head.

'Here we are,' said Irene, bustling back into the room with a plate of mince pies. 'Nice and warm, straight from the oven. When we've had these we'll go in the other room and listen to the Queen's speech.'

'Lovely, dear,' enthused Gerald, helping himself to one and munching into it.

'Come on, Alan, tuck in,' urged his mother.

'I don't think I can manage one after all,' said Alan, feeling suffocated.

'Don't be silly, dear,' she admonished as though Alan was an infant. 'Of course you can manage one.'

He was so angry he wanted to slap her. 'I think I'm old enough to judge my own appetite, thank you, Mother,' he snapped.

She shot him a look. 'Don't you dare raise your voice to me,' she warned. 'A lot of hard work has gone into making Christmas a happy time for us all.'

Her rebuke produced the desired effect and filled him with compunction. 'Sorry,' he said, taking a mince pie and forcing himself to eat it, just to keep the peace. But he longed for some breathing space from a relationship that was becoming unbearably claustrophobic.

'You're getting to be good at this, aren't you?' Jack Saunders complimented Alan when the latter beat him at a game of darts in the Gullscombe Arms on the evening of Boxing Day. 'You'd better watch yourself, mate. They'll try to rope you into the darts team if you carry on like this.'

'Fancy another game?' suggested Alan.

'You can't get enough of it now,' grinned Jack. 'But let's take a break and have another game later; leave the board free for someone else to have a go.' He paused, looking at him. 'It's my shout, as you won, so what's it to be?'

'A pint, please.'

'Coming up.'

The Gullscombe Arms was an old-world tavern in the picturesque village of Gullscombe Bay. The pub was at the centre of village life and was warm and cosy, with oak beams, fishing nets on the walls and log fires. It was Jack's local and he knew everyone by name. It wasn't too crowded tonight as some of the locals were at Boxing Day parties so the two men were able to find a table near the fire where logs were crackling.

'My folks would have a fit if they knew that I was drinking pints and getting to be red hot at the dart board,' Alan remarked, taking the top off his pint. 'Gin and tonics at the golf club are more the sort of thing they have in mind for me. And for you too, if it comes down to it, you being their restaurant manager.'

'Yeah, well, I think it's my right to do what I feel comfortable with when I'm off duty, as long as it doesn't hurt anyone and is legal,' observed Jack. 'Same applies to you, in my opinion. If you enjoy a pint and a game of darts, you're perfectly entitled to have one, regardless of the social implications.'

'You're right, of course.' He made a face. 'But I must admit I find it easier not to mention these things to the folks. It causes too much trouble. They're good people and have done their best for me but our ideas and opinions don't often seem to coincide these days.'

'You'd be a bit odd if they did,' was Jack's opinion. 'Every generation has its own ideas. Anyway, we're all individuals – free-thinkers, thank God.' He cast his eye around the pub. 'There's nothing nicer to me than a game of darts and a sociable pint in a pub where everyone knows my name. And if anyone objects to that, that's their problem.'

'It's different for you,' Alan pointed out. 'You're a free agent with no one to answer to.'

'So are you now that you've split up with June.'

Alan's features tightened at the mention of it but he just said, 'I do have my parents to answer to, you know.'

'Only to a certain extent,' Jack told him. 'You're a grown man, a responsible adult.'

'Because I work with them I'm still under their control,' Alan explained.

'Then you shouldn't be, not at your age,' Jack disapproved.

'It's just the way things are.'

'You can't spend your whole life doing what they want, if it isn't what you want,' Jack went on. 'I'd still be in Australia if I'd done that.'

'It took courage to come back.'

'Don't talk daft,' laughed the modest Jack. 'Where's the bottle in getting on a ship and coming home?'

'You cut your family ties and came back on your own, to start again from scratch with no back-up,' Alan reminded him. 'That seems quite a brave thing to me.'

'My mother would probably call it selfish, going off and leaving the family like that.' He smiled with fond memories. 'Mum's a good sort, though. She wished me well and said I must do what I felt was right for me. It was traumatic for us all. I mean, Australia is the other side of the world, not near enough to go for a holiday – not unless you've got plenty of dough, anyway. But I was convinced that I had to make the move back to England while I was still young. I didn't want to go against my instincts and stay there just because it was easier, then be full of regrets on my sixty-fifth birthday because I'd been trapped by family ties.'

'I'm up to my neck in family ties at the moment.' Alan went on to tell his friend about his ideas and the frustrations he was having at the Cliff Head.

'Strike out on your own, mate,' was Jack's immediate reaction, 'if you're feeling that fed up.'

'Easier said than done,' Alan pointed out. 'Even apart from the emotional element – and make no mistake about it, my parents would be devastated if I left the partnership – what would I do if I did leave? Get a job as a hotel manager working for someone else? I don't think so.'

'You want a family hotel, so go out there and get one,' Jack suggested.

'What with? I've got a bit saved but not enough to buy a hotel, nowhere near.'

'You could raise the dough if you sold your share in the business,' advised Jack.

'If I ever were to leave, I'd give them my share, not sell it,' Alan said. 'But I couldn't walk out on them. It would break my mother's heart.'

'She's probably tougher than you think.'

'Even so . . .'

'Parents want the best for their offspring; it goes with the job, apparently, or that's how it's supposed to work. So once they got used to the idea, they'd want you to do what you know is right for you.' Knowing Alan's parents, and judging them to be extremely self-centred, Jack had grave doubts about this but kept them to himself because Alan needed encouragement to break away and live his own life. 'I'm sure they wouldn't want to hold you back once they realised how much you want to do it.'

'But how would they manage without me?'

'By employing somebody to do the job that you do, of course,' Jack replied. 'No one's indispensable.'

'I couldn't do it to them,' Alan insisted. 'They'd be absolutely devastated.'

Jack shrugged. 'So what are you going to do then? Wait until they retire or die, then do what you want with the Cliff Head? And in the meantime get increasingly frustrated and miserable? You'll grow into a crusty old sod if you don't get your life sorted out.'

'I don't have a choice.'

'You're an unattached man, Alan,' Jack reminded him firmly. 'Of course you have a choice.'

'You make it seem so simple.'

'I'm not saying it will be easy but it certainly isn't impossible, and if you stay as you are, you'll never know if you could have made it on your own. This idea of yours isn't going to go away. You're stuck with it. And taking over the Cliff Head when your folks retire won't be the same thing as making a success of something in your own right, not the same thing at all.'

'I can't just disregard obligations.'

'Look, it's natural to grow up and make your own way in the world – we all do it,' Jack reminded Alan. 'You went into the family business instead. I'm not saying there's anything wrong with that. It works very well for some people, but obviously not you, or we wouldn't be having this conversation. So, take the plunge and do something about it.'

'Everything you say is true but I couldn't desert Mum and Dad,' Alan said. 'It would be too cruel.'

Jack tutted. For years he'd watched Alan be browbeaten by the people he was so loyal to, and thought he deserved better. 'Your parents aren't disabled or even very old,' he said gently. 'They'll be fine.'

'It was different for you when you made the break,' said Alan. 'You weren't locked into a family business.'

'I was part of a family, though,' Jack was keen to point out. 'Even now, I still miss them all – Mum and Dad, my sister and brother. How do you think it feels, knowing that they're so far away and I probably won't ever see them again?'

'I didn't realise,' Alan confessed. 'You always seem so cheerful and in control.'

'That sort of thing stays inside. I made my choice and I have to get on with things. No point in going about with a long face and making other people miserable. I like my life here and you can't have everything, can you? Not many people get that.'

'Exactly,' agreed Alan. 'And I have so much more than most. A partnership in a thriving business and financial security if I stay with it.'

'None of it's worth a light if you're permanently frustrated, though, is it?'

'I'm not so sure.'

'If you don't break away and become your own man, you'll never have peace of mind,' Jack lectured.

Alan shrugged. 'Maybe not. But it's just something I'll have to live with.'

'It's your choice, but I reckon you'll live to regret it.'

'All right, Jack, you've made your point,' said Alan firmly. 'Now let's change the subject before we come to blows over it.'

'Suits me,' agreed Jack with a shrug.

'How do you fancy coming with me to London in March?' asked Alan. 'All expenses paid by the Cliff Head.'

Jack's eyes lit with interest. 'I wouldn't say no. Why, what's on?'

Alan told him about the exhibition. 'I'd be glad of the company,' he explained. 'And it'll be of interest to us both as it's our line of business. I'll arrange for you to have the time off. They can manage without you in the restaurant for a couple of days.'

'I'm game,' enthused Jack.

'Good. I'll book us some accommodation when things open up again after the holiday. In the meantime, let's have another drink. A pint for you?'

Jack nodded. 'I'll come to the bar with you,' he grinned. 'The new barmaid's quite tasty.'

Standing at the bar counter waiting to be served while Jack chatted to the barmaid, Alan reflected on the conversation they had just had. Jack talked a lot of sense and made a change of course seem so straightforward, whereas to Alan it was impossible.

June came into his mind and he knew instinctively that she would agree with Jack. He also knew that he could never make that break. The emotional ties were just too strong.

Chapter Eight

'Did you have a good Christmas, Nat?' Daisy enquired sociably.

'Yeah. It was all right,' he told her with an air of disinterest. 'How about you?'

'I had a lovely time.' Enthusiasm radiated from her. 'It was really smashing this year. One of the best Christmases I've ever had, I think.'

'Why?' His dark eyes rested on her with lurking disapproval as he took a slow, contemplative drag on his cigarette. The knowledge that Daisy was capable of having a good time without him was unsettling because it challenged his power over her. 'What did you do that made it better than usual?'

'Nothing different. Just stayed at home and did all the normal festive things with the girls and Nora,' she told him. 'But June was with us and that made it sort of special, somehow. She's ever such good company and the kids have taken to her in a big way. Having a real auntie is still a novelty to them, and she seems very fond of them.'

It was evening, a couple of days after Christmas. The girls were in bed, and Daisy and Nat were ensconced on the sofa. Daisy was enjoying the fact that she didn't have to go back to work until tomorrow night.

He laughed drily. 'Must have been a barrel-load of laughs with that stuck-up cow under your feet all over the holiday,' he said sarcastically.

'I wish you wouldn't say such horrible things about her,' she frowned. 'You know how it upsets me. June's great. You haven't given her a chance.'

'Why should I make an effort with someone who thinks she's a cut above the rest of us?'

'She doesn't think that,' defended Daisy heatedly. 'Just because she's got a touch of class you've branded her a snob and she isn't like that at all. Far from it.'

'You're so taken with the idea of having a posh sister, you can't see what she's really like,' he said calumniously.

'That just isn't true,' she denied, her voice rising. 'You know very well that I'm the last person on earth to be impressed by someone because they're posh.' She was reminded of the altercation she'd had with June on Christmas night, which proved her point.

Even Nat could see that his accusation didn't carry any weight. 'Yeah, I s'pose so,' he muttered grudgingly.

'Anyway, I'm not going to argue with you over it.' A gleam came into her eyes and she smiled. 'Because I've got something far more exciting to tell you.'

He exhaled a cloud of smoke, looking at her thoughtfully. 'You're like a dog with two tails tonight.'

'And with very good reason.' She told him she would soon be having a change of address and gave him the details. 'Isn't it wonderful?' she enthused. 'At last I can get the girls out of this stinking hovel, get us all away from the landlord and his vile threats.'

'Where exactly will you be moving to?' Nat showed not a grain of enthusiasm.

'Not sure yet,' she told him excitedly. 'It depends where we find a house that's big enough for us all and within June's price range. We won't be moving far, though, because we all need to stay within easy reach of our jobs.'

'What's all this "we" business?' he queried disagreeably. 'It'll be your sister's house. You won't get a say in its location, or anything else for that matter.'

'We will,' she corrected. 'She wants it to be a joint venture and we're all going to have a say in everything. She's quite definite about that.'

'Use the brains you were born with, Daisy,' he warned nastily. 'You and Nora will just be lodgers.'

'No we won't.'

'Of course you will,' he insisted. 'You'll be subject to all sorts of petty rules and regulations like they are in boarding houses where the landlady lives in the house.'

'It won't be like that at all because we're going to live together as a family, on equal terms.'

'Equal terms, my arse.'

'Don't be so cynical.'

'Surely you don't really believe you're going to be equal with June?'

'Yes, I do, as it happens.'

'It'll be her house, for God's sake,' he blasted. 'Of course she's going to rule the roost.'

'The house will be hers, and she'll have the responsibility for it, obviously. But it won't be like you're suggesting.'

'Give me strength,' he sighed emphatically. 'I really don't think you should do this. It'll be a disaster.'

Naturally she was disappointed by his reaction. 'I don't know why you're getting so het up about it,' she said.

'Because you're being so blind,' he ranted on. 'Three women and two kids sharing the same house – you'll be at each other's throats in no time. And then where will you be? You'll have burned your boats with this place.'

'I certainly won't lose any sleep over that.'

'At least here you have a degree of privacy,' Nat pointed out. 'You've got your own cooking facilities and that. All right, so the landlord is a bit of a bugger but at least he doesn't live in the house, checking up on everything you do.'

'And neither will June.' Daisy was beginning to get exasperated now. 'The three of us have discussed it thoroughly and agreed that if this thing is to work we must respect each other's privacy. The girls will probably have to share a bedroom as they do now. But we're hoping that the rest of us will have our own rooms where we can go when we want to be on our own.'

'You'll have to share the kitchen and bathroom, though . . .'

'And the living room, and sitting room if there is one,' she added with an air of defiance.

'You're asking for trouble if you go ahead with this move.' He shook his head. 'I'm telling you.'

'Why do you want to spoil it for me?' Daisy asked. 'This chance means a lot to me.'

'I'm just trying to save you from yourself,' he insisted. 'It's no good shutting your eyes to the actual reality of something like this.'

'My eyes are wide open,' she assured him. 'And I know it's going to be good.'

'Oh, well, it's your funeral,' he said in a doom-laden voice.

'Yes, it is.' She stood firm.

'Anyway, I thought you were planning to stay on here to prove that the landlord can't drive you out.'

'We're not being driven out,' she reminded him. 'We're moving out of our own accord to somewhere better, so it's not my loss.'

'Even so . . .'

'I'd be mad to turn this opportunity down,' she said with a sigh of irritation. 'It'll be so much better for the girls, especially if we can get a place with a little garden.'

'That sister of yours will have a field day, lording it over you and Nora.'

'There won't be anything like that.' Having cleared the air about this on Christmas night, she could be confident. 'I've told you, we're going to live as a family.'

'Family be buggered,' Nat scorned. 'It'll be one big battleground once the novelty wears off.'

She was hurt by his attitude but determined not to let him bully her into changing her mind. 'Whatever happens it's got to be better than this,' she said, waving her hand towards the room. 'And let's face it, Nat, I'm not going to get the chance of family life with the father of my children, am I? So I might as well go for the next best thing.'

'How many more times must I tell you, we'll get married eventually.' He was impatient now. 'We're all right as we are for the moment.'

'Of course we're not all right,' she disagreed. 'The situation is ridiculous.'

'Don't start—'

'I'm not starting anything; just defending myself against your unreasonable disapproval of my plans to move in with June,' she declared. 'I don't ask much from life – you know that. As long as my girls are happy, then so am I. But I'm only human and I want a decent life for them, for all of us.' She paused. 'Nothing too flash. Just somewhere reasonable to live without the constant threat of eviction.'

'I'll give you that.'

'If I wait for you to face up to your responsibilities, I'll be an old woman.'

'You're nagging again.'

'Do the right thing and I won't have to.'

'Yeah, yeah, I will.'

'And while I'm waiting for you to grow up, it's up to me to look out for myself and get the best I can for our daughters.'

'You won't find the best with your sister,' was his gruff prediction. 'I can promise you that.'

'I can't see why you're so much against it because it won't affect you, except, of course, that you'll see more of June.' She paused, her eyes narrowing in thought. 'That's it, isn't it? You'll feel uncomfortable visiting me in her house.'

'I'm not scared of her,' he objected heatedly. 'I won't like that aspect of it because I can't stand the woman, but that isn't why I think it's wrong for you. I think you're doing the wrong thing because it'll be like living in lodgings and too restricting.'

'And I'm not restricted now?'

Nat glanced around the room. 'Not as much as you will be playing happy families with your sister. Anyway, living with relatives never works out, it's a well-known fact; there are always petty squabbles.'

'Having relatives to squabble with is a first for me so I'll have to learn as I go along,' she told him. 'I'm looking forward to it, whatever you say.'

'I'm only thinking of you, Daisy.' Not true. His comments were entirely selfish. He could hardly bear to imagine what it would be like when he went to see Daisy with that high-and-mighty sister of hers hovering in the background just waiting to find fault. It was bad enough having Nora bend his ear at the slightest opportunity. With two of them on his back about the way he treated Daisy, it was going to be hellish, especially as the house would be June's. 'As I've told you before, that sister of yours has changed you. She's a bad influence, first of all filling your head with rubbish about trying to clear your ol' man's name – now this.'

'Clearing my father's name is *not* rubbish,' Daisy was quick to amend. 'We're serious about it.'

'You've got your head in the clouds if you think you can beat the system and get him out of prison.'

'I don't agree with you.' She wouldn't be put off. 'If we get new evidence, we can appeal and he'll be released once the truth comes out. He needs help, and June and I are all he's got. If we can find Morris Dodd and his wife we'll—'

'You're as powerless as your ol' man is, can't you see that?' he interrupted rudely. 'You don't stand a cat's chance in hell of finding them.'

Daisy couldn't deny that there was some truth in what he said. 'I know it seems hopeless but we're not going to give up,' she said. 'So you might as well face up to it and stop being such a doom merchant.'

He shrugged, stubbing out his cigarette in a saucer. 'All right, have it your own way,' he told her.

Daisy was still worried to death about her father and wouldn't rest until justice was done. But things had come to a halt for the moment. How did you find someone after more than twenty years when you had no idea where to start looking? Even a seasoned detective would be at a loss with nothing to go on at all. There was a way, she was convinced of that; something they'd yet to think of. 'I admit we're at a dead end at the moment,' she confessed. 'But we'll think of a way, given time. And it'll be easier once June and I are living in the same house because we'll have more of a chance to discuss it, to pool our ideas and work out what to do next.'

'I still say that sister of yours is bad news.' Nat just wouldn't give up. 'She unsettles you, gets you fired up about things.'

'I do have a mind of my own,' Daisy reminded him.

'I know you do. But she's the type who can manipulate anyone,' he stated categorically. 'You hardly know her, even though she's your sister.'

'That's one thing you are right about,' she conceded. 'And what better way to rectify that than to share a house with her. There'll be times when we don't see eye to eye, of course. But I'm optimistic, and if it doesn't work out . . . well, I'll just have to cross that bridge when I come to it.' She took his arm impulsively, her mood softening as she looked into his eyes. 'Be pleased for me, eh? It would mean so much to me.'

Noticing how pretty she looked, her eyes sparkling with enthusi-asm, her luxuriant hair shining in the light, his heart melted. He wasn't

131

a romantic man and never thought in terms of 'love' as such, but he did feel something for her and still fancied her, even after all these years.

'OK, babe,' he said with a sigh of resignation. 'If it's what you really want I'll try not to spoil it for you.'

'Thanks, Nat.'

'And while we've got a bit of privacy we might as well make the most of it,' he suggested. 'There'll be precious little of it when you move house.'

'There will if I have my own bedroom,' Daisy pointed out with a giggle. 'We can shut ourselves away in there.'

'Not if the Gestapo have anything to do with it,' he said with a wry look. 'I'll be lucky if I'm allowed inside the house at all, let alone into your bedroom, with that pair of prison warders living there with you.'

'Whereas if we were to get married, we could move into a place of our own and have as much privacy as we want.' Her tone was light. She wasn't being serious; not this time.

'Yeah, yeah, I know,' he murmured into her hair. 'We're a pair, you and me. You know we'll do that, all in good time.' He paused, turning her face to his. 'Don't you?'

And because Daisy wanted to believe him she said, 'Yeah, course I do.'

The area north of Holland Park Avenue up as far as the Harrow Road – which was regarded loosely these days as Notting Hill but more usually known to its residents as North Kensington – was still riddled with building sites in the winter of 1955, as the slum clearance programme continued. Plans for major improvements and a massive road-widening scheme at Notting Hill Gate were heavily rumoured.

But at the moment, in stark contrast to its affluent neighbour Holland Park, the Notting Hill area in the majority was poor, over-crowded and grimy, with pockets of bohemia adding life and colour in some parts. Even before the Caribbeans had arrived there had been a multiethnic mix of Eastern European, Russian-Polish Jewish, Cypriots and so on. But the area was becoming increasingly cosmopolitan as ever larger numbers of West Indians continued to move in. Integration into the white community was still very poor.

House buying was a completely new experience for Daisy and she was surprised at the difficulty in finding somewhere suitable. There were properties for sale, of course, but many were big, brooding terraces, more suitable as letting houses than for single-family occu-pancy. Either that or they were in a state of neglect and needing major structural work, so couldn't be considered.

As conditions continued to deteriorate for Daisy and co. at Benly

Square – a leaking sink on the landing, a faulty lavatory cistern and broken bathroom window now adding to the other miseries they had to endure – they were increasingly anxious to find a place with all possible speed.

Then one cold Sunday morning in January, with watery sunlight beaming through the clouds intermittently, they discovered number seventeen Larby Gardens, a terraced house on the hinterland of Notting Hill in the direction of Shepherd's Bush.

'So, what do you think?' asked June as they studied the house from the outside.

'Needs a lick of paint,' observed Daisy in a gross understatement because the paint had peeled down to the bare wood in places around the windows.

'A good few gallons, I'd say,' added Nora.

'It's structurally sound, according to the agent,' June told them, 'though I'd have to get a survey done, of course.'

'Looks a bit run down,' Daisy felt obliged to point out, still rather in awe of this entire venture.

'Anything we can afford with enough bedrooms for us all isn't going to be in top-class condition,' June told them. 'We'll have to allow enough cash for furniture and decorating, remember. This is central London. It might be a run-down neighbourhood but it's still close to the West End, walking distance of Marble Arch in comfortable shoes. We can't afford to be too choosy, not unless we move further out, which none of us wants because of our work.'

'It's your money that's being spent, June,' Daisy reminded her. 'It has to be your decision.'

'Exactly,' agreed Nora.

'You know that isn't the way I want it to be.' June was adamant. 'We agreed that the choice of house would be something we were all happy with. And I really do want your honest opinion.'

Daisy looked down the street, which was a cul-de-sac full of ragged children playing and women gossiping on their doorsteps. It wasn't salubrious by any means but some of the homes showed signs of pride unknown in Benly Square. A few of the houses here even looked as though they'd been recently painted and had net curtains several shades lighter than the decaying grey lace that hung in the windows around there. Larby Gardens was only about ten minutes' walk from where they lived now, and undeniably shabby, but there was a friendly feel about it somehow, a sense of hope and possibility. 'I think it's got definite potential,' she stated.

'I like it around here,' said Shirley, looking enviously at a group of scruffy children playing marbles in the gutter nearby.

'So do I,' put in Belinda.

'We'd better go and see what it's like inside, then, hadn't we?'

133

smiled June, the agent having given them the key as the property was empty.

Watched by a crowd of curious children who had no inhibitions about asking if Daisy's girls would be joining them as playmates, June unlocked the front door and they all trooped into a dusty hallway.

'Very promising,' was Daisy's instinctive verdict as they clattered through the empty rooms, their footsteps echoing on the bare floorboards, the air thick and musty from being closed up. 'It needs plenty of work but I think we could make this into a home. There's a nice feel about it somehow.'

'Not a bad size either,' added Nora.

As was so often the case with old terraced houses, this one was bigger than it appeared from the outside. There were four rooms upstairs and a hideous bathroom with a stained bath, and a sink that was coming away from the wall. Downstairs there were two reception rooms and an old-fashioned kitchen with a small lobby that led into the back garden. Through the window they could see that the latter was pocket-sized, and beyond the high wall at the bottom, a factory chimney towered over everything. But the house did have a garden. As tiny and overgrown as it was, it was somewhere for the children to play outside in safety.

'Cor, a garden,' shrieked Shirley in delight, as June opened the back door. 'Ooh, can we live here, please? Please, Auntie June, please say that we can.'

The three women exchanged glances.

'You two go outside and have a look while we talk about it,' she requested of them.

The little girls bounded through the door; they were well wrapped up in red coats with red and white pixie hoods that matched their gloves, and which Nora had knitted for them.

'So, what's it to be?' asked June, looking at Daisy and Nora. 'Do I go ahead and make an offer?'

Daisy cast her eye around the ancient, browning wallpaper, a flash of sunlight through the window emphasising the stains, the cracked square sink and worn-out wooden draining board. 'I feel as though I want to open all the windows and let some fresh air in,' she said excitedly. 'And tear all that awful wallpaper off and paint the walls in lovely light colours.' She paused, looking at her sister. 'But yes, I think it's right for us.'

'Hear, hear,' added Nora.

'Well, I hope you two are handy with wallpaper scrapers and paintbrushes,' grinned June, 'because you'll need to be if we take this place on. It would cost a fortune to have a professional in to do all the decorating.'

'I'm game,' smiled Daisy.

'Me too,' said Nora.

'Looks like we've found our new address then, doesn't it?' said June, looking pleased.

Daisy giggled. 'Larby Gardens, here we come,' she said, making a pattern with her finger on the dusty window.

'Cor, am I glad to take the weight off my feet,' said Jack when he and Alan finally managed to find a table to sit down to lunch on pie and chips in the cafeteria at Earls Court. 'It's a smashing exhibition but more exhausting than a week's work.'

'It's all the pushing and shoving to get through the crowds,' Alan commented, glancing around. The place was heaving; the queue at the self-service counter was snaking around the cafeteria and people were milling about with trays, trying to find somewhere to sit with their food.

'I'm enjoying it, though,' Jack remarked, shaking the ketchup bottle. 'It's really interesting.'

'It is,' nodded Alan, sprinkling salt on his chips. 'But I think we've seen enough now, having been here all day yesterday as well as this morning.'

'Which leaves us with the rest of the afternoon free,' Jack pointed out, 'as we're not going back until tomorrow.'

'That's right.'

Pouring a dollop of ketchup on to the side of his plate, Jack said conversationally, 'I think the thing that's impressed me most here is the hotel kitchen equipment.'

'Mm.'

'Mind you, it needs to be special at the price they're asking,' he chatted on. 'The trouble with exhibitions is that they make you want everything on show.' He concentrated on his food for a few moments. 'Still, I suppose that's the whole point.'

Alan nodded but he wasn't really listening. He was tormented by the fact that he was in London and so was June. He wanted to see her *so* much. The change of address card she'd sent him recently was in his wallet and filling him with temptation. But it would be pointless to visit her. Why should he chase after a woman who didn't want him?

'What about that cocktail bar they had on display?' Jack continued to enthuse. 'Wasn't that something? Too much of a contemporary look for the Cliff Head, of course, but very smart with all that mirror glass and Formica . . . Alan, are you listening to me?'

His friend started slightly. 'No, I wasn't. Sorry.'

'At least you're honest,' was Jack's breezy reply. 'So what's making you so preoccupied?' He squinted at Alan knowingly. 'As if I didn't know.'

'It's being in the same town as her,' he admitted with a wry look.

'Naturally, she's on my mind. She is my wife, after all.'

'We're free this afternoon if you want to pay her a visit,' suggested Jack, who still thought Alan and June were made for each other.

'She'll probably be out at work.'

Jack shrugged. 'If she is, we'll go and see her there. You know where she works, don't you?'

'Yeah, but it might make it awkward for her,' said Alan, whose common sense was fighting with his desire to see her. 'Anyway, what would be the point? She's made it clear that it's over between us.'

'No harm in calling in for old times' sake, is there?' said Jack. 'As we're in London with time to spare, I'll go with you to make it seem more casual.'

'No. I'd better stay away.'

'It's up to you,' Jack told him with a sage look. 'But I think you'll regret it if you go back without even seeing her.'

Was it worth giving it one more try? Alan wondered. In his heart he knew he'd never forgive himself if he went back to Devon without making a final attempt. But this was her last chance. If she turned him down again this time, he would *never, ever* approach her again. And that was definite.

'You're right,' he said, his voice rising excitedly. 'I'll get a London A to Z and work out exactly where she lives when we've finished here.'

Daisy was listening to *Woman's Hour* as she worked with the scraper on the living-room walls. I'll have bigger muscles than Tarzan's by the time we've got rid of this horrible wallpaper, she thought, standing halfway up the ladder, rubbing her aching arm. But it'll be worth it in the end.

It was a March afternoon and a blustery wind whistled through the house, rattling the windows and seeming to send the dark clouds scuttling across the metal-grey skies. Daisy was alone in the house. June was out at work, Shirley was at school. It was Nora's day off and she'd taken Belinda to the park so that Daisy could get on with the decorating. Daisy had teased her; said she herself had drawn the short straw. There had been plenty of laughter since they'd moved in here together.

Having given the walls a thorough soaking, Daisy got busy with the scraper, tearing off a sizeable strip and being rewarded with a moment of satisfaction. It was more than a month since they'd moved in and, by pulling together, had made good progress with the decorating, spurred on by a mutual desire to get the place into some sort of shape. There was still chaos on a grand scale in this room, though, with tattered curtains inherited from the previous owners, a carpet of newspaper on the bare boards, partly stripped walls and only deck chairs to sit on. When the work was finished, June was going to buy furniture and they were all very excited about that.

While she worked, Daisy listened with interest to a debate on the programme. Two women were getting quite heated about women's role in contemporary Britain. One of the debaters was a feminist whose views seemed extremely daring in that they challenged the accepted view that a woman's place was indisputably at home. The feminist speaker believed passionately that women were conditioned to enjoy a form of dedicated slavery, and that they shouldn't be made to feel guilty if they didn't enjoy being tied to the house, looking after children all day. If a woman preferred to go out to work, it didn't mean that she was flawed as a mother or loved her children less. Her opposer was rattled by this and quoted from a recent bestselling book by some doctor, who was also an expert in child care, and stated in print that the mothers of young children were not free to earn.

'Some of us don't have any choice, mate,' Daisy muttered under her breath. 'And you can't make me feel any more guilty than I already do for going out to work and leaving my girls.' As usual unmarried mothers weren't mentioned in the discussion. Daisy had accepted long ago that women in her position didn't exist except to be quoted as a bad example. She was enjoying the discussion, though. It was rather refreshing to hear a different point of view.

Pushing her hair back from her brow, she looked at the clock on the mantelpiece and wondered if she could afford the time to stop for a tea break. In the end she decided to carry on working because Nora and Belinda would be back at any minute and it would soon be time to break off to collect Shirley from school anyway. Most of the local children walked to school together but Daisy wasn't ready to let her go on her own just yet.

No sooner had she denied herself a rest than there was a knock at the front door so she had to stop work anyway. Opening the door she found herself confronted by two smartly dressed men in suits and dark overcoats. Immediately her guard was up. A well-dressed man around here was either a rent man, an insurance man or a doctor; definitely officialdom of some sort.

'Yes?' she said nervously, unable to see beyond the smart clothes and their implication.

'Is June Masters in, please?' asked one of them, a youngish, good-looking man with brown curly hair and a worried expression in his eyes.

Daisy looked at him warily and didn't reply. Good suits spelled trouble.

'Well?' he continued, looking questioningly at Daisy. 'Is she here or not?'

'Who wants to know?'

137

'I asked the question first.'

Years of being in thrall to rent collectors had made her ultra-sensitive about them. 'If you've come for the rent, you've come to the wrong house, mate,' she blurted out. 'We don't pay rent here. My sister owns this house.'

His face worked with astonishment and he looked very tense. 'Really?' he said.

Daisy was still afraid to admit to anything. She stared at him, pulling the door to in front of her as though to stop them entering.

'We're not gangsters about to force our way in, you know,' she was informed by the other man. 'So you're quite safe.'

'Perhaps I'd better explain,' said the first man. 'June sent me a card with her new address on it. We're in London on business and decided to call on the off chance that she might be in.'

The tone of the conversation now indicated that they weren't officials of any sort so Daisy relaxed a little. 'You know my sister well then?' she said enquiringly.

'I ought to,' he said with a half-smile. 'I'm her husband.'

'Oh, oh, I see.' He was the last person she expected it to be because he lived so far away.

He thrust his hand forward. 'Alan's the name,' he announced in a friendly manner.

'I'm Daisy,' she said, shaking his hand.

'Pleased to meet you.'

He being a relation altered things considerably. Her instinct was to invite them in and make them welcome. But would June want her estranged husband in her home? Daisy didn't know how civilised the break-up had been. If it had been a bitter parting, June wasn't going to thank Daisy for making him welcome here. 'As you've probably gathered, she's not at home at the moment,' she informed them. 'She's out at work.'

'What time are you expecting her back?'

'About five thirty.'

Alan looked at his watch. 'We'll come back later then, shall we?' he said.

'I suppose that would be best.' Daisy felt awkward. It seemed so rude not to ask them in.

'We're in London for a hotelier's exhibition,' he chose to explain. 'But we're going back to Devon first thing in the morning. It would be nice to see June before we go back, just to say hello. It didn't seem right to be so near and not call in.'

It went against the grain with Daisy to turn someone away without so much as a cup of tea on a winter's afternoon. But her name would be mud with June if she didn't want him encouraged to stay around. On the other hand, her sister had sent him her new address so she must have wanted him to know where she was, and he was going to come back later, anyway.

She was still debating the issue when Alan's companion made a timely intervention. 'We could murder a cuppa tea,' he said, winking at her. 'There's a bitter wind blowing out here and walking around the exhibition has done terrible things to our feet.'

Alan tutted and looked at him with mock disapproval, then turned back to Daisy. 'This is a friend of mine, Jack Saunders,' he informed her. 'He's a bit of a big mouth, I'm afraid.'

'So I gather.'

'We could freeze to death while you two stand there beating about the bush,' said Jack, and Daisy noticed his strong London accent. 'The two of you are sort of related and the two of us are dying for a cup of tea and a sit-down. Makes sense to put the two things together.'

Focusing her gaze on him, Daisy saw a pair of laughing blue eyes beaming at her from a fine countenance topped by short blond hair being blown flat to his head by the wind. Smiling almost despite herself, she succumbed to impulse, opened the door and invited them inside.

'Excuse the state of the place,' she said, leading them into the living room, waving her hand towards the patchy walls and indicating that they make themselves comfortable in the deck chairs that were near the fire, which she stirred into life with the poker. 'As you can see, we're in the middle of doing it up.'

They nodded politely. Daisy took their coats and hung them up in the hall on the hooks that had been left by the previous occupants.

'I didn't know that June had a sister,' Alan informed her when she came back into the room.

She explained briefly about their recent reunion. 'It's a long story,' she concluded. 'I'm sure June will give you all the details.'

He nodded. 'Is it just the two of you living here?' he enquired with interest.

Daisy explained the setup.

'Cosy,' remarked Alan.

'It is, very,' said Daisy, saddened by the bitter edge to his tone; the sorrow that was very often visible in June's eyes she could now see reflected in his.

She went to the kitchen to make tea and when she came back into the room with a tray of tea and biscuits, Jack did most of the talking. Alan just added the odd polite comment. Daisy felt sorry for him. He seemed preoccupied and had a bewildered look about him; had obviously known nothing about how June had become a home owner.

'Terrible job, that, isn't it,' remarked Jack, looking at the walls, 'stripping off wallpaper?'

'Sounds as though you're speaking from experience,' Daisy replied,

139

sitting in another deck chair with a cup of tea and a biscuit.

'From more experience than I care to think about,' he said lightly. 'I bought an old cottage and spent what seemed like the whole of the first year getting all the old wallpaper off.'

'I hope it was worth it and you've got it as you want it now,' she said chattily.

'More or less,' he replied. 'There's always something else you want to do, though. By the time you get to the end of it, the beginning needs doing again.'

'Don't say that.' She made a face. 'We've only just started on this place and I feel as though I've had enough already.'

'I know the feeling.'

'We all have jobs so can only work on it at odd times,' she told him.

'I did mine that way too.'

'I shouldn't be taking this break now, to tell you the truth,' she confided. 'I wouldn't have stopped work if you hadn't arrived.'

'I bet you're glad we turned up then,' he joked.

'Ooh, yeah,' she admitted with a grin. 'Any excuse to put that damned stripper down.' She sipped her tea. 'I would have to be stopping soon anyway, though, because it's nearly time I went to collect my daughter from school.'

'You have a daughter?' he said with the note of surprise the absence of a wedding ring evoked in people.

'I have two daughters.' The sound of voices at the back door indicated the arrival of Nora and Belinda. 'One of them has just come in now.'

Belinda, a dainty, talkative child with her mother's smiling eyes, came into the room like a great bolt of energy and immediately launched into an enthusiastic account of the trip to the park and how she'd been on the swings and they'd seen some flowers which Nora had said were crocuses. Daisy gave her a hug and listened with interest, making introductions and explaining that the men were waiting for Auntie June.

They all had more tea and Daisy said she had to go and collect Shirley from school. The men talked about leaving and coming back later, whereupon Nora took it upon herself to say that they were very welcome to stay, rather than roam the streets in the cold, until June got home.

Jack astonished them all by saying, 'It's nice of you to offer but if we stay we make ourselves useful, right? So have you got another one of those wallpaper strippers?'

When Daisy left, both men had their jackets off and sleeves rolled up and were working with the strippers on the walls. When she got back from school with Shirley, the wall she'd been working on was bare of wallpaper and they were making inroads into another, ably

140

assisted by Belinda, who was collecting the strippings into a bucket and keeping up a constant flow of chatter. Daisy was infused with the warmth of the atmosphere as soon as she entered the room.

'Wow. You haven't half shifted.' She was impressed.

'We don't hang about,' grinned Jack. 'Anyway, there are two of us at it.'

'You must be supermen to have done all that in such a short time,' she teased them lightly.

'I'm the superman,' claimed Jack, making the little girls laugh by pulling a face at Alan, 'because I've had plenty of practice. Whereas my mate here doesn't have to do his own dirty work so is a bit of an amateur.'

Alan took it all in good part, even though he still seemed worried, obviously anxious about the meeting with June. 'Honestly, you'd think he had a degree in interior decorating to hear him talk,' was his jokey response. 'Just because he bought a ruin of a cottage and made it habitable.'

'What's a cottage?' Shirley wanted to know.

'A small house, love,' her mother explained.

'Like the ones in storybooks that are always in the country?' she said. 'Is yours in the country?'

'Mine's even better than that,' Jack told her. 'It's by the seaside.'

'Seaside, like Southend?' said Belinda.

'That's right,' said Jack.

'Do you make sandcastles?' she wanted to know.

'I'm a bit old to want to do that sort of thing myself,' he told her. 'But it's a good sandy beach and children do make them.'

'Ooh . . .' Belinda was breathless with awe.

'Sounds lovely, and I bet you've made your cottage a lot more than just habitable,' said Daisy, because Jack Saunders had the air of someone who would make a thoroughly good job of anything he took on.

'I suppose I might manage to admit to it being comfortable,' amended Alan, teasing his pal.

'You're just jealous,' joshed Jack.

'Jealous because I don't live miles from anywhere?' he returned. 'Don't kid yourself.'

'Anyway, do we have another volunteer?' asked Jack, smiling at Shirley.

'I don't mind,' said Shirley, giving him a shy look. 'But only if you'll tell us more about your cottage at the seaside.'

'It's a deal,' he agreed. 'You help your sister pick up the paper and I'll keep talking.'

'OK. I'll just go and get changed,' she said, immediately at ease with him.

'You've both done wonders in this room,' praised Nora, who had

141

fallen under the spell of these two amiable young men.

'You certainly have,' grinned Daisy. 'You can keep it up for as long as you like.'

'Are you going to get another paint stripper and give a hand?' asked Jack.

'Afraid not,' she told him. 'I have to get ready for work in a minute.'

'Work?' he said with interest.

She told him what she did and explained that she was given a free meal at the hotel when she was on duty so wouldn't be staying for supper with the others.

'I hope you two boys will stay for a bite to eat with us, though,' Nora said. 'It's nothing special but there's plenty if you'd like to join us.'

'Please stay,' chorused the little girls.

'You'll have to ask the boss about that,' Jack told her, grinning towards Alan.

'Do stay,' Shirley urged Alan, adding as an extra incentive, 'We'll show you our bedroom, if you like.'

'It's been done up and it's very pretty,' Belinda put in. 'Mummy and Auntie June and Nora painted it and put wallpaper up for us. It's got toys on it.'

'In that case, how can we say no?' said Alan.

'Hurray!' shrieked the girls, who, like their mother, were very sociable.

'You seem to have made a hit,' remarked Daisy, looking from one of the men to the other.

'If only it was that easy with bigger girls,' was Jack's light-hearted response.

'I can't believe that you'd have any trouble,' said Daisy.

'He doesn't,' Alan informed her. 'So don't listen to him. He's just trying it on.'

Daisy was amused by their banter. They were all laughing when June walked in, smiling, her face instinctively lighting up when she saw Alan, then becoming grim when the reality of the situation registered fully.

'What are you doing here?' she demanded coldly.

The laughter ended abruptly and tension crackled in the air as the couple stared at each other in stony silence.

Chapter Nine

Daisy's journey to and from work took a bit longer from Larby Gardens because she had further to walk from the station. But the extra travelling time was the last thing on her mind that night on her way home on the tube. She was lost in thought, reliving that terrible moment when June had walked in and sent the atmosphere in the house plummeting to freezing point.

Even the children had been subdued, though not for long, thanks to Jack's entertaining company. After June and Alan had made a silent departure to her room, leaving a resounding hush behind them, Jack had carried on stripping the wallpaper, chatting to the girls as though nothing untoward was happening.

Heaven knows what had happened since then. Daisy had gone to work soon after, leaving the girls in Nora's care, assisted by Jack, who was regaling them with tales of life at the seaside.

Running over June's arrival again, Daisy recalled her initial joy at seeing Alan. She'd simply lit up at the sight of him. Daisy wondered what the problem could possibly be because the couple obviously adored each other. Whatever it was it must be serious because June didn't seem like the sort of person to walk out on someone on a whim.

Her thoughts turned to Jack with whom Daisy had struck an instant rapport. He'd made a big impression on her with his casual charm and sense of humour. His blond good looks hadn't gone unnoticed either. Oh well, they'll both be gone when I get home, she thought. June would surely have sorted things out one way or the other by now.

She was jolted out of her thoughts when someone approached her in the station foyer. 'Hello, Daisy,' he greeted her.

'Jack?' She smiled broadly, pleased but astonished to see him. 'What are you doing here?'

'That's the second time today I've heard that question,' he said with a wry grin. 'Fortunately, this time it wasn't said with quite the same venom.'

She made a face. 'Wasn't it awful?' she said, tutting. 'June was really fierce, wasn't she?'

'Enough to frighten the pants off Alan.'

'What happened after I left?' she asked, pulling her coat collar up against the strong wind as they made their way out of the station into the street.

'They stayed upstairs until supper.'

'And then . . .?'

'They came down and we all ate a meal together.'

'In agonising silence, I suppose.'

'They weren't exactly laughing and joking but they did make an effort at polite conversation so it wasn't too bad,' he told her. 'And the rest of us did enough talking to cover the tension. The kids kept things moving along. With them around there weren't any awkward silences.'

Daisy smiled affectionately at the thought of them. 'Just as well they aren't any good at keeping quiet, in this particular instance then,' she remarked.

'Absolutely.'

'So, what's happening with June and Alan?' she asked.

'They went back upstairs to June's room after the meal and were still there when I came out,' he told her. 'I called up the stairs to them to tell them where I was going and Alan shouted down in reply. So they haven't murdered each other. That's all I know.'

'What are you doing here anyway?' she asked again. 'I thought you'd be back at your hotel by now, going to bed at a decent hour as you're going back to Devon in the morning.'

'That was the original intention. But I couldn't very well drag Alan away while he was in the middle of an emotional crisis, could I? And poor Nora looked so whacked, I told her to go to bed and not worry about staying up to entertain me,' he explained. 'I thought I might as well come and walk you home, to save sitting around at your place on my own. Nora gave me all the gen so that I knew where to meet you.'

'It's very kind of you,' Daisy said as they left the station lights behind and began to stride out against the wind, passing a staggering drunk, a tramp in a shop doorway and a crowd of Teddy boys hanging around on a street corner.

'It wasn't kindness that inspired me to come,' he confessed.

'No? What then?'

'I enjoyed your company so much earlier, I wanted some more of it.'

'At least you're honest,' she approved. 'And I'm flattered.'

They walked on in comfortable silence for a while, then: 'I shouldn't really say this but I'm going to stick my neck out and say it anyway,' he began hesitantly. 'Is it a good idea for you to be out on the streets on your own at this time of night with so many dodgy characters about?'

'No choice, I'm afraid,' she informed him chirpily. 'Anyway, I'm used to it so it doesn't worry me.'

'Wouldn't a daytime job be better for you?'

144

Daisy explained her situation and her reasons for working unsociable hours.

'Where's the kids' father?' Jack asked.

'He's around and we're still together,' she said, adding in the defensive way that had become almost second nature to her, 'We'll be getting married, eventually.'

'Doesn't he worry about you being out on your own at night in such a dangerous part of London?' he queried. 'I know I would if you were my girlfriend.'

'I don't think Nat ever gives it a thought, to be perfectly honest,' she replied. 'We're Londoners; urban life is what we know. Anyway, it isn't as dangerous as it might seem to an outsider. It can't be because I always get home safe and sound.'

'I'm not a complete outsider, you know,' he pointed out. 'I haven't always lived out in the sticks in deepest Devon. I'm originally from Hackney.'

Which explained the accent, she noted, but said, 'You've lived away for quite a while, though, haven't you? So you've probably got a bit out of touch with the way things are here.'

'Are you suggesting that I've become a bit of a yokel?' he grinned, teasing her.

'I wasn't, actually.' She paused, giggling. 'But I think you might look rather fetching in a smock.'

'Cheeky,' he admonished good-humouredly. 'We don't all have straw in our hair down there, you know.'

'And it isn't all pimps and prostitutes up here,' she countered quickly.

'I suppose I asked for that,' he laughed. 'But seriously, though, you must admit that this part of London does have a reputation for being a bit rough.'

'Things go on around here, so I've heard. But they don't affect me or my children,' Daisy said. 'I just get on with my life and let other people get on with theirs. Being out on my own at night isn't a problem.'

'As you say, I'm probably out of touch with how things are here now that I'm a country boy,' he conceded.

She nodded. 'You really like it down there then?'

'Love it.'

'Is it living by the sea that appeals to you in particular?'

'I enjoy having the ocean on my doorstep, yeah, sure. But I like the general feeling of space I get from living on the seashore,' Jack explained. 'I spent some time in Australia. I think that gave me a taste for the outdoors.'

'You wouldn't come back to London to live then?'

'It would have to be something really special to make me do that,'

145

he told her. 'My folks are all settled in Australia so I don't have any family ties here now. I'm still a London boy at heart and I don't suppose I'll ever lose that. But I've got used to the slower pace of life down there. Clean air, not so much traffic. And the countryside is beautiful.'

'It sounds wonderful.'

'It is,' he confirmed. 'And my cottage is in a fantastic location.' He paused, turning to her with a wry look. 'Sorry, I'm probably being boring. I'm afraid I get a bit carried away with enthusiasm for the place.'

'You're not being at all boring.' She couldn't believe he would ever be that. 'But I must admit, I can't imagine you living miles from anywhere. You're far too sociable.'

'I'm no hermit, believe me,' he quickly put her right. 'I'm out at work a lot of the time and it's only ten minutes into town on my motorbike.'

'A motorbike eh?'

'My pride and joy.'

'What is it with men and motorbikes?'

'The speed, the freedom . . .'

'The wind in your hair?'

'Yeah, that too,' he laughed.

'You're building up a picture of a fabulous way of life.'

'It'll do for me.'

They moved on to other things. She told him about her job and asked about his. He told her a bit about the Cliff Head and his position there.

'And you are best mates with Alan, despite the fact that his parents own the hotel?' she remarked. 'Some people might be put off by that.'

'The fact that he's the boss doesn't interfere with our friendship at all,' Jack told her. 'He doesn't pull rank on me when we're off duty or ram his position down my throat, that's why. We wouldn't be mates at all if he did and he knows it. We hit it off from the start. We're the same age and have similar views about things. It was only natural we should get pally.'

'You seem to know June quite well too.'

'Not as well as I know him but I was friendly with them as a couple before she did her disappearing act,' he explained. 'He turned to me then. The poor bloke was beside himself.'

'What happened to split them up?'

'No idea. And from what he's said, I don't think Alan knows either. She just went, out of the blue, leaving him completely shattered.' He paused thoughtfully. 'But you're her sister – hasn't she talked to you about it?'

'Hardly at all. She said that her husband was the son of a hotelier in

Torquay and she left him but she's never said why, and she makes it clear she doesn't want to talk about it.'

'It's all very odd.'

'Mm.'

'Naturally there's been gossip,' he mentioned. 'Some people think his parents drove her out. But I think there's more to it than that. She's too strong-minded to be driven out of anywhere, and she's certainly a match for them.'

'She didn't get on with them, then?'

'They didn't get on with her, to be more precise, especially his mother. She gave June a really hard time. I've watched her in action. I've seen her put June through it over the years.'

'Didn't Alan stick up for her?'

'He did if he caught his mother at it,' he told her. 'But she was as nice as pie to June when he was around. Far too clever to let him get wind of what was really happening. June must have told him about it, I suppose, but maybe she didn't tell him just how bad it was. June's always struck me as a caring sort of a woman, despite what she's done to Alan. Maybe she didn't want to come between mother and son.'

'You could be right.'

'Anyway, I still don't think that was why she left,' Jack went on to say. 'But I'm convinced she must have had a very good reason to walk out like that. I worked with them for a long time. I've seen how they were together. She always seemed loyal and absolutely devoted to him. But you're her sister, you know what she's like.'

'I don't actually.' Daisy briefly explained the unusual situation with June and herself. 'I'm still getting to know her. She seems very deep; keeps things close to her chest.'

'Mm, you're probably right. Anyway, I hope they can patch their marriage up,' he said. 'They were a great team and Alan hasn't been the same man since she went.'

'Perhaps they're getting back together as we speak,' she suggested.

'If talking has anything to do with it, they will be,' he grinned. 'They've been at it long enough. He'll have to call it a day soon so that we can go back to the hotel to bed.'

'You're not staying at the hotel where June works, I take it, or she wouldn't have been so surprised to see you.'

'Alan didn't want to crowd her,' explained Jack. 'We only came to the house on the spur of the moment.'

'He seems very genuine to me.'

'He is.'

They'd reached the house and he stopped outside and turned to her, the wind blowing his hair about. 'In case Alan's ready to leave and drags me off in a hurry and I don't get a chance to mention it,' he began, smiling uncertainly, 'I just want to say how much I've enjoyed meeting you.'

'The same goes for me too.' She shivered against the wind that was whipping around the buildings and sweeping litter along the pavement. 'It's been lovely.'

'And those daughters of yours are a couple of smashers,' he continued.

'Thank you.' She smiled broadly. Compliments about her children always pleased her.

'I wish you all the best for the future.'

'The same to you,' Daisy responded, noticing that his mood had become formal but oddly intimate somehow. 'When London seems especially hectic and the tube impossibly crowded, I'll think of you with envy in your cottage by the sea.'

'Anyway,' he said with a note of finality, thrusting his hand towards her. 'It's been a pleasure.'

'Likewise,' she said, shaking a hand that felt firm and strong.

'Come on then, let's go and see if those two have made any progress towards a reunion,' he said, and they walked up to the front door together.

'If you didn't want me to find you, why send me your change of address?' Alan wanted to know.

'How many more times must I tell you,' replied June impatiently. 'It was in case of an emergency. I just didn't feel able to move house without letting you know my address.'

'If you really wanted it to be over between us, you would have moved without giving me a second thought.'

'I was just being responsible. You could have had an accident or been seriously ill and needed to contact me,' she went on to explain. 'Or you could have wanted to file for divorce. There are any number of reasons why you needed to know where I was. It just didn't seem right not to tell you.'

'You didn't find it necessary when you left,' he reminded her. 'I had to use my own methods to track you down and only did so then because of luck.'

She lowered her eyes in shame. 'I know. That was really bad of me,' she admitted. 'I would have let you know eventually. You beat me to it, that's all.'

'Let's put all that behind us and you come home, June,' he begged for the umpteenth time.

'Alan, we've been going over this for hours and I've told you I'm not coming back,' she insisted. 'I can't. My life is here in London now.'

'The reason we've been going over it for hours is because we both

148

want the same thing – to be back together. But you won't admit it for some reason best known to yourself.'

They were in her bedroom, not yet refurbished, the walls suffused with wallpaper darkened with age, the floorboards bare. He was sitting in a wicker chair near the sash window. They'd been talking for a long time but not only about their marriage. There had been a mutual exchange of news. She'd told him about the bizarre circumstances that had led to the reunion with Daisy, and their hopes to clear their father's name. She'd explained how she came to buy this house. He'd given her an update about things at the Cliff Head.

'Apart from anything else,' she said now, 'I need to be in London with Daisy to do what we can for our father.'

'So stay here for a while longer, and then come back,' Alan suggested. 'If I knew you were coming back eventually, I could live with that.'

'I'm not coming back, Alan,' she repeated. 'Not ever. So you must try to accept it.' She had to force the words out. 'When I made the decision to leave you, it was for good.'

His expression was grim. He stared at her, then looked down at his hands as though pondering. When he spoke again, his tone was sad but positive. 'OK, I'll do what you want and go away and get on with my life without you. I won't come after you again. But don't expect me to believe that it's what you really want because I know that it isn't.' He raised his eyes to meet hers and added vehemently, 'I'll never believe that. Not ever.'

'That's up to you.'

The silence was painfully tense until Alan changed the subject completely. 'About this business of your father – I admire you for being willing to have a go and I don't want to put you off, but I think you should prepare yourself for disappointment. It all seems a bit pie-in-the-sky to me.'

'It is, extremely,' June agreed. 'We've got nothing to go on at all. But because Daisy and I know that he's innocent we have the motivation to keep trying. It could take years to find these people, and we might never do it but we can't give up. Can you understand that?'

'Yes, I think so. Just be careful.'

She nodded. His mood was now one of dull resignation and she guessed that he had, at last, accepted their separation as permanent. He was finished with shouting and pleading. He was going to make the best of his life without her. It broke her heart.

Noises from downstairs drifted up.

'Sounds as though the others are back,' Alan said, standing up with a purposeful air and a heartbreaking show of dignity. 'So I'd better be on my way.'

'Yes.'

'It isn't fair to keep Jack hanging about any longer,' he said lamely, in an effort to delay the inevitable.

'No it isn't.' She swallowed hard. 'Could you make my apologies to him for me, please?' Dangerously close to tears, she could barely trust herself to speak. 'I'd rather not go down and see him off. I'm sure he won't mind.'

'Of course he won't,' he said coolly, and left the room quietly while June remained where she was, sitting stiffly on the edge of the bed.

'No luck with June then?' observed Jack as he and Alan headed for the station.

'Does it look like it?'

'All right, no need to bite my head off, mate,' Jack retaliated. 'Just making conversation.'

'Save your breath,' was Alan's sharp response. 'I'm not in the mood for a chat.'

'Suits me fine,' said Jack, who knew Alan far too well to be offended.

'Good.'

Jack was concerned about his friend, of course, and hated to see him miserable. But thoughts of someone else were filling his mind as they walked through the dingy streets of Notting Hill, occasionally splashed with neon and the sound of jazz music drifting from some basement.

Daisy had made a huge impression on him and his heart lifted at the memory of her: her beaming smile, the things she'd said, the way she was with her children. She wasn't smart or glamorous but she was so richly endowed with warmth and vitality, a natural beauty radiated from her. Her sex appeal was magnetic, all the more so because it was completely uncontrived.

He longed to see her again but knew such feelings were pointless. Apart from the obvious geographical problem, she was still involved with the children's father, and therefore not available. She was as good as married, and married women were off limits as far as he was concerned. It was a pity, though, because he'd really taken a shine to her.

He was recalled to the present by Alan. 'Sorry I've been such a pain, snapping your head off and keeping you waiting all that time at June's place.'

'No problem,' Jack was able to assure him honestly. If Alan hadn't decided to call on June, Jack would never have met Daisy. He'd probably never see her again but he felt richer for having briefly made her acquaintance.

Daisy was having much the same thoughts about him as she heated milk for cocoa in the kitchen. Meeting Jack had been a real tonic. He'd made her feel light-hearted and vibrant, somehow. It was a pity she wouldn't be seeing him again because he was such a smashing bloke. Ah well, ships that pass in the night, she thought wistfully. She'd not thought it possible to be so profoundly affected by a complete stranger. She barely knew him but he'd felt special to her. Her feelings for him weren't entirely platonic either, she admitted, grinning to herself. She'd been involved with Nat for so long she'd forgotten how exhilarating it was to fancy someone new.

Her mind drifted on to the other events of the evening and she was sad as she remembered Alan coming downstairs looking gloomy but proud, and leaving the house with Jack so quietly. He and June had obviously not managed to work things out.

The house felt achingly silent now. Usually at this time when she got back from work, she, June and Nora would have a cup of cocoa together and a chat before they went to bed. Nora had obviously been exhausted by the tension of it all but was probably lying awake worrying about it. June definitely wouldn't be asleep after such a trauma.

Suddenly decisive, Daisy heated more milk and made three mugs of cocoa, put them on a tray and carried it upstairs. Pausing outside June's room, she could just hear the low sound of stifled sobbing. June was obviously struggling very hard not to be heard. They had a strict house rule here: the privacy of someone's bedroom was sacrosanct. This was where you went when you wanted to be left alone and everyone respected that. If Daisy went in, she would be intruding. But her heart ached for her sister and she wanted to help. Surely it was permissible to bend the rules under the circumstances.

Holding the tray with one hand with her arm supporting it, she tapped tentatively on the door.

No reply.

She knocked again. 'I've brought you some cocoa, June,' she called.

All was silent.

'Can I come in?'

As the request was ignored and the crying continued, Daisy dispensed with house rules altogether and followed her instincts, turning the door handle and looking cautiously into the room. Her sister was lying face down on the bed, her body heaving.

'Oh, June, love.' Putting the tray on the dressing table, Daisy went over to the bed and sat down, putting a comforting arm around her sister's shoulders. 'You and Alan weren't able to sort things out then?'

'No, and we never will. We can't ever get back together, and I've told him that,' she spluttered. 'He shouldn't have come here. All he's done is upset us both.'

'Perhaps you shouldn't have let him know where you are if you feel

151

that strongly about it,' was Daisy's cautious suggestion.

June turned over and sat up, mopping her face with a handkerchief. 'I couldn't just cut myself off from him altogether. It wouldn't have been fair,' she said, her voice muffled with tears. 'He needed to know my address, even if only because he wants to start divorce proceedings.'

'There is that, I suppose,' Daisy agreed.

'Sorry you've all been made to feel awkward in the house,' she apologised, sniffing into her hanky. 'And about my imitation of Niagara Falls.'

'Don't be silly,' Daisy assured her. 'I was out at work so I wasn't affected. And everyone's entitled to a good old weep now and again. I'm your sister. I want to be here for you.'

'And I'm your friend and the same goes for me,' added Nora, entering the room. 'The last thing I want to do is intrude but I heard you crying and I heard Daisy come in.' She paused, looking at June. 'I want to help, June.' She picked up the tray and offered the cocoa mugs to them.

June seemed to recover and managed a watery smile after moistening her mouth with the hot, sweet liquid. 'That means a lot to me,' she told them, her eyes glistening with fresh tears. 'I've never had any real friends before.'

'I am surprised,' expressed Daisy. 'You being so confident and everything.'

'That doesn't necessarily bring friends.' She didn't enlighten them as to the reason for her friendless state. She hated to talk about it, and, besides, she didn't want to burden them with her past. 'None that I was close to, anyway. I suppose Alan was the best friend I ever had. And even then there was always . . .' her voice tailed off.

'Always what?' urged Daisy.

'Nothing.'

'As Alan obviously means so much to you, and vice versa, is there no chance of your getting back together?' asked Daisy with feeling. 'It seems such a terrible waste. Anyone can see the two of you still love each other.'

'Love isn't always enough,' said June thickly.

'Surely it's the main ingredient, though,' suggested Daisy hopefully. 'If you've got that, the rest can be sorted out. Or am I just being naïve?'

'You are rather,' muttered June.

'You might feel better if you talk about it, dear,' suggested Nora kindly. 'A trouble shared and all that. It goes without saying that nothing you say will go any further.'

'There's nothing to say, honestly,' she insisted, composing herself suddenly, as though fearing they might persuade her to say something she would later regret. 'It's over between Alan and me, and that's that.'

Daisy knew that June's demons, whatever they were, had not been exorcised by her leaving Alan. She was still a very tormented woman. 'Well, you obviously know your own mind. And being completely selfish, we'd have missed you like mad if you'd gone back to Devon,' she said in an effort to lift the atmosphere as June obviously didn't want to confide.

'By the way,' began June, taking this opportunity to make something clear, 'if anything ever happened and I did have to sell up and go away for any reason at all, I would make sure you weren't left without a home.' She paused and added most emphatically, 'You have my word on that.'

'That's nice of you,' said Daisy.

'Yes,' added Nora.

'So, having cleared that up, let's talk about something more cheerful,' June suggested, trying without success to convince them that she was feeling better.

'One good thing has come out of today,' Daisy grinned, determined to cheer them all up.

They both looked at her enquiringly.

'All the old wallpaper has been stripped off in the living room, thanks to our visitors.'

'It is true what they say about an ill wind then,' said Nora with a chuckle.

Even June attempted a smile at Daisy's down-to-earth way of getting things back to normal.

As the air warmed and softened to spring and then summer, the occupants of number seventeen Larby Gardens lived in harmony together. Rooms turned from dingy and old-fashioned to fresh and contemporary as the decorating progressed. Furniture was bought, carpets laid and homeliness added with pictures, ornaments and lamps.

June paid for all of this from the money she'd put by from the sale of her mother's house, but everything else was shared: the chores, the bills, the decisions. Meals were eaten together whenever possible against a clamour of conversation, with the children making their contributions. Late-night cocoa continued to be a regular habit. Naturally there were differences of opinion but generally speaking they got on well.

But the long-term co-existence of human beings was rarely that simple, and Daisy's first falling-out with her sister was over Nat, and was very painful for them both.

'I don't know why you put up with it,' June blurted out one night when he'd not been near for a fortnight, then turned up just before bedtime, expecting Daisy to make supper for him, and had gone off in a huff when she'd refused. 'It's disgusting the way he treats you. Ignoring your existence for weeks on end, then turning up just when he feels like it. He's got a flaming cheek.'

Daisy wasn't easily offended and could take any amount of criticism about herself, but when it came to Nat, her defence mechanism went into top gear. 'My relationship with Nat is my business,' she told June sharply.

Having managed to restrain herself from saying too much about Nat's offhand behaviour towards her sister for all these months, now that she had spoken out, June couldn't stop.

'I'm only thinking of you,' she went on. 'That man has no right to treat you the way he does. You shouldn't stand for it.'

'It's got nothing to do with you.'

'It's pathetic, the way you let him get away with it,' June ranted on with her sister's interests at heart. 'You're not soft or stupid, so why keep him in your life when he obviously doesn't have a serious thought in his head as regards his intentions towards you? Why don't you just tell him to get lost?'

Daisy was furious. 'I don't have to explain myself to you,' she retaliated, her cheeks almost matching her red dressing gown. 'I don't tell you how to run your life so don't try and tell me how to run mine.'

'Girls, girls,' intervened Nora worriedly. They were in the living room, ready to go to bed, and until a few moments ago the atmosphere between them had been as jovial as ever. 'Calm down, both of you, before you say something you'll really regret.'

'You agree with me, surely?' said June, turning to Nora for support. 'You must be able to see how that dreadful man is using her.'

Indeed she could and had said so many times. But now wasn't the time to take sides. 'My opinion doesn't come into it.' She was treading warily. 'As Daisy says, it's her business. Only she knows how she feels about Nat. I think the two of you should agree to differ on this one.'

But June was too fired up in her sister's defence to stop now. 'You're an attractive and intelligent woman, Daisy. You can do a lot better than Nat Barker,' she went on. 'You're much too good for him.'

'Like you're too good for Alan. Is that what you do, June – judge people; give them points out of ten for good behaviour and character?' retorted Daisy, who wasn't normally sarcastic or cynical; this issue was beyond the intellect and was rooted entirely in the emotions. Words were flowing out of her mouth, almost as though someone else was saying them. 'Is that why you left him, because he didn't measure up to your high standards?'

'My marriage to Alan has nothing to do with this,' she declared hotly.

'Oh, no, when it comes to your private life, you don't want it mentioned, do you? You clam up completely and no one's allowed to say a word. Yet you think you have the right to lecture me.' Daisy glared at her across the hearth. 'You are in no position to comment on my relationship with Nat since you couldn't even keep your own marriage together.'

'That has nothing to do with this issue,' June insisted. 'I can't stand by and see Nat treat you so badly.'

'How dare you preach to me?' said Daisy through clenched teeth. 'Nat is the man I chose, the man I fell in love with. Whether I stay with him or not is my decision, *not yours*. It's nothing to do with you so keep your big nose out of my business.'

'You must be able to see—'

'I do have eyes in my head and a brain,' Daisy roared. 'Of course I can see that he isn't perfect, and that he pushes his luck with me something rotten. What do you think I am? Some sort of halfwit?'

'Haven't I just said the opposite to that?' June replied angrily. 'It's because I know that you're an intelligent woman and worth better, I think you should get rid of him.'

'And as I've just said, what I choose to do about Nat is my business and nobody else's, certainly not yours,' Daisy told her. 'People are people, a mixture of everything, and we all have some good and bad in us. Not only the decent, well-behaved ones are lovable, you know.'

'Now you're suggesting that *I'm* a halfwit.'

'If the cap fits . . .'

June didn't reply to this, just looked at Daisy in outrage, cheeks scarlet in her otherwise pale countenance.

'To hear you talk anyone would think you were an expert on men,' Daisy ranted.

'I've never claimed that.'

'You couldn't very well, could you? Because you wouldn't have a leg to stand on.' Daisy was out of control, driven on by her protective instincts towards Nat and her right to live her life in the way she chose. 'And even if you did have a more impressive track record in that direction, you'd still have no right to tell me what to do. I know you own this house and I'm just a lodger but that doesn't mean you can interfere in my life.'

June was further enraged by this suggestion. 'This has nothing to do with the house,' she denied hotly. 'I've told you that I never think of you and Nora as lodgers. This is a personal thing.'

Daisy stood up, her voice shaking with emotion. 'Be that as it may, Nat is the man I love and the father of my children, so I would thank you to respect that fact in future. Whatever he does, however badly he behaves, it has *nothing whatsoever* to do with you. Is that clear? It's my life, so just leave me alone to get on with it in the way that I choose.'

And with that she rushed from the room.

Ashen-faced and shaky, June looked at Nora contritely. 'I don't know what came over me,' she said, biting her lip. 'It all just came pouring out.'

'Nat has the same effect on me and I've had plenty of words with Daisy about him in the past,' Nora told her. 'But I try to keep shtoom now because she's very sensitive about it and won't hear a word against him.' She sighed. 'And what she says is quite true, of course. It isn't any of our business. Daisy's no fool. She knows in her heart that Nat is no good for her but she loves him. And us being critical doesn't help because she knows she can never give him up. He can twist her around his little finger.'

'It makes me so mad.'

'Me too, but it'll never change. It's been going on too long. So we might as well accept it and keep our opinions to ourselves.'

June looked worried. 'I don't know what to do, Nora,' she confessed, raking her hair with her fingers anxiously and biting her lip. 'The last thing I want is to be at war with Daisy.'

'Give her a few minutes to calm down, then go up and see her,' suggested Nora.

'Yes, I think I shall have to,' agreed June. 'Because I can't leave it like this.'

Daisy was sitting up in bed looking at a magazine when June made a cautious entry, having tapped on the door first.

'If you've come to say more horrible things about Nat, then you're wasting your time because I don't want to hear them so I won't listen,' she said, holding the magazine open and keeping her eyes fixed on it.

'I've come to apologise actually,' June said sheepishly.

'Oh.' Now Daisy put the magazine down and looked at her sister, waiting for her to go on.

'I shouldn't have said those things,' June admitted ruefully. 'I really am very sorry.'

'You're right, you shouldn't have said all that stuff,' Daisy responded coolly.

'You said some pretty rotten things to me too, you know,' June pointed out.

'Only after serious provocation.'

'I suppose you're right.'

'You shouldn't have got me fired up like that,' Daisy told her, her tone becoming warmer. 'You can't expect to say things like that to someone about their man and not expect them to retaliate.'

'In future then the least said the soonest mended when it comes to Nat,' suggested June.

'I think we need more than just that to keep the peace between us

156

on the subject,' Daisy informed her.

'Meaning . . .?'

'Whether you like it or not, Nat is the man in my life,' she began, 'and he comes to this house as a guest of mine.'

June waited.

'So I'd appreciate it if you could treat him with courtesy, in the same way as I do when your friends come to the house,' Daisy requested.

'I'm always polite to him.'

Daisy gave a dry laugh. 'In an arctic sort of way,' she pointed out. 'You could make him feel welcome when he's here, rather than painfully uncomfortable.'

'Point taken.'

'Good.'

'I'm sorry about just now, Daisy, I really am,' said June, keen to make amends. 'I went too far.'

'Yes, you did, and I hope you truly realise that.'

'I do.' June paused. 'And I really don't think of you and Nora as lodgers. I think of us all as friends sharing a house.'

Daisy was ashamed now. 'Yeah, I know you do,' she sighed. 'I was angry . . . I said things I didn't mean.'

'We both did.'

'Except for the things you said about Nat.' Daisy gave her sister a questioning look. 'You did mean those, didn't you?'

'I'm sorry, Daisy.' June made a face. 'There's no point in my lying about it. But I will make an effort to make him feel more welcome here.'

'Thanks. Live and let live, eh?'

June nodded. 'Friends again?' she asked hopefully.

'Yeah, course we are,' said Daisy, sitting up and giving her sister a hug. 'It'll take more than a man to split us up.'

But June sensed that this was a fragile peace that needed looking after. She knew she must tread carefully on the subject of Nat or risk losing Daisy.

And Daisy knew that Nat would remain a sore point between them even if he wasn't mentioned. The fact that June was absolutely right in everything she said about him didn't make any difference. He was Daisy's man and she would defend him against anyone.

Chapter Ten

On duty one evening in late July, Daisy served roast beef to the wrong table, knocked a jug of water over on another and got more coffee in the saucers than the cups when pouring. When she compounded the whole shoddy performance by dropping a pile of dirty plates on to the hotel kitchen floor, sending broken china and food leftovers flying everywhere, the head waiter suggested, quite forcibly, that she go home as she obviously wasn't fit for work.

'Anyone can see that you're ill.' He was a small immaculate man of Italian extraction, with dark hair greased close to his head and a neat moustache. He'd lived in London for most of his life and spoke perfect English.

'I'm all right, honestly, and I'm sorry I've been so careless.' She was afraid for her job. 'I'll be more careful from now on so it won't happen again.'

'It certainly won't happen again tonight because you're going off duty right now,' he announced, far more concerned about the smooth running of the hotel restaurant than a sick member of staff. A complaint about the service would mean a reprimand for him from the manager. 'You shouldn't have come in to work if you weren't feeling well.'

'I didn't want to let you down,' she said weakly. 'Anyway, I need the money.'

'You're not doing yourself or us any favours by being here,' he insisted in a firm but not wholly unkind manner. 'It's no wonder you dropped the plates – you're shivering too much to hang on to anything.'

'I can't afford to take time off work. You know I have two kids to feed,' she reminded him.

'You'll just have to manage with sick pay from the State because you're certainly no good to us around here,' he insisted. 'You should be at home in bed.'

'I'll be all right, really—'

'Go home before you pass out, girl.' He was ordering her to go now.

Although she protested some more, Daisy knew he was right because she did feel terrible. In the staff room, changing out of her black and white uniform, her teeth were chattering and she was covered in goose pimples but her skin was hot and painful. Every bit of her hurt, and when she took off her black cap, with its starched white trim, it felt as though she was making a flesh wound on her scalp. She hadn't felt well for the last couple of days, ever since she'd got drenched in a heavy summer shower while out shopping at Portobello market and her clothes had dried on her. She seemed to be more susceptible to chills than most people; she always had been and put it down to her weak chest.

But now she headed for the tube and home, feeling worse by the second.

'Into bed with you,' Nora said when Daisy stumbled into the house, feeling faint.

'We'll bring you up a hot drink and some aspirin in a minute,' said June.

'The girls—' Daisy began.

'The girls are fast asleep,' Nora assured her. 'So go to bed before we have to pick you up off the floor.'

'Come on,' urged June, taking her sister's arm gently. 'Let me help you into bed.'

'There's no need for all this fuss,' she insisted. 'I'll be fine after a good night's sleep.'

But sleep wasn't for Daisy that night. As her condition worsened, she thrashed about in the sheets, shivering but soaked in sweat, her chest hurting, head aching, breathing painful. Nora and June were so alarmed the next morning, neither of them went to work. June rushed out to the phone box and called the doctor, who diagnosed pneumonia.

At the sight of an ambulance, a crowd gathered to watch the barely conscious Daisy being carried out of the house on a stretcher. June went with her in the ambulance and Nora stayed with the girls, who were pale with fright and staying very close to her. She put a comforting arm firmly round each one.

'I don't want Mummy to go away,' said Shirley tearfully, as the ambulance doors were closed.

'Nor do I,' added Belinda shakily, huge tears rolling down her cheeks.

'You want her to get better, though, don't you?'

They nodded.

'That's why she has to go to the hospital for a little while,' Nora explained. 'So that the doctors can make her better. I know that you two are going to be very brave.'

'I don't like it when Mummy's ill,' said Shirley. 'It makes me feel funny inside.'

'It makes me scared,' Belinda whispered.

'There, there, you two. She'll be back home before you know it,'

160

said Nora, saying a silent prayer and trying not to show the little girls how worried she was.

Over the next day or so, Daisy wasn't aware of very much at all. Drifting in and out of consciousness, she realised in a vague sort of way that she was in hospital but was too ill to take notice or ask questions. But when the drugs started to work and her confusion began to clear a little, the first thing she said was, 'My children – where are they?'

'Your daughters are at home with your sister,' the nurse assured her calmly.

'But she has to go to work.'

'She's taken compassionate leave to look after them, apparently,' explained the nurse, a middle-aged woman of large proportions, with a nice smile and a kindly manner.

'My eldest is on school holidays,' muttered Daisy worriedly. 'The two of them together are quite a handful. My sister isn't used to coping with them on her own.'

'I'm sure she'll manage.' The nurse was very soothing. 'They're only children, not wild animals. And your friend helps out when she gets home from work, I believe.' At Daisy's querying look, she went on, 'We had a chat when they came to see you and they told me all about it. You were asleep. They asked me to give you their love when you were awake and taking notice.'

Daisy tried to sit up but fell back weakly against the pillows. 'I'm needed at home,' she said anxiously. 'I've got to get out of here.'

'You'll go when the doctor says you're ready.' The nurse was kind but firm. 'And that won't be for a while yet. You'll soon know how weak you are if you try to get out of that bed, my dear. So stop fretting.'

And Daisy felt too frail to argue.

'Will you eat your lunch, please, girls?' requested June of her nieces as they all sat at the kitchen table.

'No.' The gleam of rebellion was strong in Shirley's eyes.

'We don't like sausages,' added Belinda.

'Yes, you do,' June disagreed patiently. 'They're one of your favourites.'

'We only like them when Mummy's here,' said Shirley in truculent mood.

'We don't like *your* sausages,' added Belinda, fixing June with a hostile stare. 'We only like Mummy's; we're not eating your mouldy old sausages.'

'We want our mum,' announced Shirley, her little mouth set determinedly. 'We don't like you.'

'We hate you,' supported Belinda.

'You're horrible,' Shirley declared.

'Yeah,' was Belinda's contribution.

June guessed that part of the reason for their appalling behaviour was that they were missing their mother and taking it out on her. But she sensed also that they were testing her – and winning hands down at the moment, she was forced to admit. They were at an age of physical perfection, smooth-skinned and unblemished. She ached with love for them. They were so alike to look at, with the same shiny brown hair and their mother's beautiful tawny eyes, though theirs were currently simmering with resentment.

Although she was ostensibly calm, June was actually in despair, her nerves shattered by the monsters her nieces had become since she'd been in charge. It seemed feeble for a grown woman to have to admit but, without actual maternal experience, she felt vulnerable to the point of being almost afraid of these small children. Ridiculous, she knew, but she just didn't have Daisy's natural armoury which would enable her to be in a position of control with the girls. This whole miserable experience was particularly upsetting because until June had become a temporary substitute for Daisy, she'd prided herself on the rapport she was beginning to have with them. Maybe she'd never felt completely at ease but after her initial confusion as to her function, she'd settled into the role of indulgent aunt, giving them presents, attention and fun, and it had seemed to work very well.

Until these past few days, when they'd given her hell, arguing the toss about every single thing, from the food she gave them to having a bath and what clothes they would wear. At first she'd treated them with the gentle touch, sensitive to the fact that they were missing their mother. When they'd responded to this with mutiny, she'd tried being firm, but their enmity had continued. Yet Nora had no trouble with them at all. June couldn't bear to imagine what a battle there would be at bedtime if Nora wasn't at home then to give her some support.

She and Nora had agreed that June should be the one to take time off work to look after them as she was allowed some compassionate leave with pay – only for a limited period but long enough for Daisy to get back on her feet, she hoped. The important thing was that Daisy was over the worst and expecting to be discharged from hospital in a few days.

June was disappointed in herself for failing so miserably as Daisy's stand-in. She wanted so much to make the children feel secure and loved in her care. Not having any children of her own, from the minute she'd first set eyes on them she'd wanted to play a special part in their lives. It was Daisy's job to administer discipline, her own to supply pleasure. And what was her peculiar reward? Anarchy.

Working at the hotel was a holiday compared to looking after two

162

stroppy kids. She'd sooner be dealing with tedious, unreasonable hotel guests than these two little horrors. They knew they had the upper hand and she didn't seem able to turn things around.

'OK, so you don't like me,' she said now in response to their hurtful utterings. 'Well, I don't like you very much at the moment either. But we're stuck with each other until your mother is better so let's try and get along, shall we?'

They stared at her in stony silence.

'All right, I'll do a deal with you.' Daisy would be appalled at such blatant bribery but she wasn't here, and June was desperate. 'You eat your lunch and I'll buy you some sweets when we go out to the shops. How about that?' She gave them a smile, forcing her tone to be softly persuasive, despite her sorely tried patience. 'And we could take a picnic to the park later on too, if you're good girls and eat your lunch. Would you like that?'

Shirley gave June a defiant look and pushed her plate away so violently it shot across the table. She then got up and ran towards the kitchen door. Belinda followed.

At that moment something snapped inside June. After days of torture from these horrors, she had finally had enough. Acting on instinct, she fled to the door and stood in front of it facing them, barring their way. 'Oh, no,' she told them with an air of grim command. 'You're not going anywhere. You're going to sit back at the table.' She paused, staring at them. '*Now.*'

Pale with shock at the dramatic change in their pushover aunt's manner, they did as she said without a word of argument, their sullenness now tinged with awe.

'Right,' June began, looking down at them from a standing position with her arms folded. She wasn't shouting; her manner of quiet assertiveness was far more effective. 'I've had it up to here with you two these past few days. You've been rude, disobedient and downright horrid and I'm not going to put up with any more of it, do you understand?'

Four tawny eyes rested on her; two little pink mouths began to tremble.

'I've taken the trouble to cook sausages and beans for your lunch because I know that you like them,' she went on. 'I could have given you something you don't like, like mince or liver. But, fool that I am, I made your favourite, which you now choose to say you don't like. All right, if you don't want what I've given you, don't eat it but you'll get nothing else. When you're hungry enough you'll eat what I put in front of you even if it's just a bit of dry bread; that's how nature works, you see. Meanwhile, there'll be no sweets, no park, no treats at all until you have both said sorry to me for your disgusting behaviour and promised to stop all this silly nonsense.'

They said nothing. Just sat close together, holding hands, staring at her, their eyes like great brown saucers against their sudden pallor.

'You might as well do as I ask because I'm going to make you sit there until you're ready to apologise to me for being nasty little brats your mother would be ashamed of,' she told them. 'I know that you're upset because your mum isn't around and you want to make me suffer for it.' She drew in her breath and turned up the volume. 'I've made allowances for all of that but now I have had enough.'

They sat there without moving. Neither said a word. The appearance of tears in their eyes twisted June's heart and she wanted to hug them better. But that must wait until later. All would be lost if she showed signs of weakening now. She could see that she'd been wrong to think she could be just their pal, someone who could be relied on for fun and pleasure. They were small children who looked to adults for authority. She could be their friend, yes, but they needed to know who was boss. Discipline gave them guidelines and made them feel secure, however bitter the pill was to swallow. Better she destroy any bond she might have with them and start again from scratch by taking a hard line than let them run rings around her. If she gave in now, they would lose all respect for her.

'So, what's it to be?'

Silence.

'I've got all the time in the world,' she told them, looking at her watch. 'I've taken days off work to look after you so I can wait here all afternoon if necessary.'

She wasn't as confident as she sounded. She was a novice when it came to child psychology. Heaven only knew what her next move would be if this didn't work. With her heart in her mouth, she sat down at the table and waited.

Shirley was the first to crumble. The trembling lip began to wobble and she bowed her head and wept silently, followed soon after by her sister, who wailed loudly.

'You won't get round me that way,' said June, suspecting that they would because her heart was breaking for them. 'You can cry all you like but you're not leaving here until I've heard you both say sorry.'

She was surprised to observe that even at this tender age, pride was a problem. 'Sorry,' mumbled Shirley at last, head down, words barely audible.

'What was that, Shirley?' asked June. 'I didn't hear what you said.'

'Sorry.' Slowly she looked up at June, who watched all the defiance slip away, leaving the child looking forlorn but relieved. June had to bite back her own tears. 'I'm sorry I've been naughty, Auntie June. I'll be good now, I promise.'

'I'm sorry too, Auntie June,' echoed Belinda.

'That's better.' Swallowing hard, June opened her arms to them.

'Come here, come on, both of you,' she said thickly.

They both climbed on to her lap and cuddled into her, their lithe little bodies trembling. She held them close for a long time, knowing instinctively that the three of them had passed some sort of a watershed.

'Can we have our sausages and beans now please, Auntie June?' requested Shirley.

'Course you can, darling,' she said to them. 'But they'll be cold by now. I'll warm them up for you.'

'Thank you, Auntie June,' said Belinda.

'It's a pleasure.' Such was the strength of her love for her nieces at that particular moment, she knew she would brave fire and flood for them if ever it was necessary. These past few days had taught her that motherhood was not always a picnic but it had not lessened her longing for children of her own.

That evening they all went to the hospital to see Daisy. A maximum of two visitors at the bedside was the usual rule but the understanding sister turned a blind eye so that they could have a few minutes all together.

'How are you feeling, dear?' asked Nora.

'Fine,' said Daisy, who still looked ghastly. She was paper-white and skinny, with dark circles under her eyes and a general look of frailty about her.

'When are you coming home, Mum?' Belinda was eager to know.

'Very soon, I hope,' sighed Daisy wistfully. 'I miss you all so much. They're ever so good to me in here and everything, but I'm fed up with being stuck in hospital. I'll recover quicker at home.'

'It isn't wise to rush things, though,' warned Nora. 'You'll end up back in here if you do that.'

'We have to be realistic, Nora,' was Daisy's answer to that. 'I've got the girls to think about. June can't have time off work to look after them for too long.'

'But I can do it for a bit longer,' June assured her.

'And if she can't, I will,' Nora offered. 'We'll manage between us somehow. The important thing is for you to get well.'

'Even when you do come home, you'll have to take it easy for a while, I should think,' suggested June. 'You're not going to be able to get back to normal right away.'

'Don't you start,' Daisy responded in jovial admonition. 'I've had enough of that from the doctors. They've really been giving me earache about how I mustn't overdo things when they discharge me from here. I know they mean well but they don't have a clue about what life is like for someone like me – well, they wouldn't, would they, being professionals with healthy salaries and sick pay when

165

they're ill?' She paused and brushed a tired hand across her brow. 'All I hear from them is, "You need to go away on holiday and get some sea air and plenty of rest and good food to build yourself up." I mean, I ask you. How can I do any of those things? I need to get back to work as soon as possible and start earning again.'

'You won't be able to go back to work for a while, surely?' June was worried by her attitude.

'Let's just say that I won't be sitting about the house for any longer than I absolutely have to. But let's wait and see how I feel.' Daisy smiled at them all. 'That's quite enough about me. How are you all getting on?'

'We're missing you like mad, of course, and we can't wait for you to come home,' Nora told her. 'But everything's under control at the house and running smoothly.'

Daisy looked at her daughters, who were sitting either side of the bed, each holding one of her hands. She then fixed her gaze on June. 'How have they been behaving?' she asked lightly. 'Not giving you any trouble, I hope?'

A look passed between June and the children. She perceived a moment of apprehension as they wondered if she was going to spill the beans.

'No trouble at all,' she said to Daisy, then looked towards the children. 'We're getting along just fine, aren't we, girls?'

'Yes, Auntie June,' they chorused, looking relieved and beaming broadly at June and then their mother.

June smiled too. She wasn't naïve enough to expect it to be all plain sailing between herself and her nieces because human relations were never that easy, but she did feel a definite bond with them now. Something had happened this afternoon that would live on into the future; she could sense it and it warmed her heart.

But now another visitor arrived for Daisy and her face lit up with joy.

'Nat,' she said, beaming at him. 'How lovely to see you. It's good of you to come.'

Seeing this as their cue to make a diplomatic exit, June and Nora said their goodbyes and left with the children.

Daisy was shocked at the extent of her weakness when she got home from the hospital. Being in such a feeble state made her angry with herself. She'd expected to be back at work in a few days but she hardly had the strength to get out of bed, let alone go to work. It was as much as she could do to look after the girls and she didn't feel as though she was doing that properly.

Feeling this fragile wasn't like Daisy at all. She was a fighter; she had inner strengths and, no stranger to bad health, she usually

166

managed to carry on however ill she felt. If she did have to take to her bed, it was never for long.

But this was different. It wasn't the illness itself but the aftermath, and she didn't seem to get any stronger despite all the beef tea and egg custards she was consuming to build herself up. Being at the mercy of extreme physical limitations made her low in spirits too. She just didn't seem able to cope with anything. Everything was too much effort; even taking care of her beloved daughters seemed beyond her. She was literally dragging herself around, even though she insisted that June go back to work.

'I don't think I'd better leave you. You're in no fit state to cope on your own just yet,' was June's reaction to that.

'For goodness' sake, June,' Daisy responded sharply, 'you've been absolutely brilliant and I'm really grateful to you for looking after the girls for me, but I'm back home now and I'm not an invalid.'

'But—'

'Look, June, the best thing for me is to get back into the swing of things.' She was trying to convince herself as much as June. 'I'll never get my strength back by taking it easy. The sooner we return to normal around here the better for us all. I want to go to work again in a day or two.'

But after almost passing out on Saturday when they were all out shopping in Portobello market, Daisy knew she must accept that recovery was going to take longer than she'd expected, and be patient.

'I know you like to be some sort of a superwoman but even you can't beat nature, Daisy,' said Nora that night after the girls had gone to bed. 'You simply have to let it take its course.'

'I know. But it's dragging on and I feel such a burden to the rest of you,' confided Daisy, tears running down her cheeks and making her feel worse because crying seemed like weakness.

'You're not being, so you can put that out of your mind,' June assured her.

'You've both been wonderful,' Daisy told them. 'But I'm not pulling my weight around here.'

'You've not heard us complaining, have you?' June was keen to point out. 'You've been ill and you need time to recover. So stop being so impatient.'

However, Daisy wouldn't be fully assured. 'I appreciate your support. But not only do I need to get back to work of an evening, I need to be more energetic during the day too. It's the school holidays. Belinda starts school in September and I want to take the girls out and about a bit before then.' She looked at Nora. 'We always go to Southend for the day around this time.'

'And we will do when you're feeling up to it.'

'It's no fun for them having me sitting about with hardly the strength to tie their hair ribbons for them, is it?' Daisy went on. 'I feel like a complete dead loss.'

'Oh, for goodness' sake,' rebuked Nora, 'you've only been home from hospital a few days. Nature will take longer to heal you if you fight it and go against how you feel.' She sighed, giving a worried tut. 'I know it isn't possible to have one, but the doctors were right when they said you need a holiday. It wouldn't do the girls any harm either, after all the disruption they've had. You and the girls need to get right away from here for a couple of weeks.'

'There are lots of things the girls and I need, Nora,' Daisy told her. 'But we're not going to get them so there's no point in thinking about them, is there?'

'I suppose not,' agreed Nora.

June had gone quiet, mulling something over. The next morning when she went out to get a Sunday paper, she then went to a telephone box and made a long-distance call.

Alan and Jack were having a drink together at the Cliff Head bar that Sunday night after work. The bar was closed and they had the place to themselves. They chatted about business for a while, moving on to some basic male observations about Marilyn Monroe, whose new film, *The Seven Year Itch*, had just come out. They enjoyed a spot of light-hearted crudity on the subject of sex, like most men when they were in all-male company.

'Talking of women,' said Alan, becoming more serious, 'I had a phone call from June this morning.'

'That sounds promising,' responded Jack.

'No. My relationship with her is well and truly over,' Alan said with a wry look. 'Her call had nothing to do with her and me.'

'What did she want then?'

'A favour,' he explained. 'She wants me to try and find some holiday accommodation for her sister, Daisy, and the little girls, for a couple of weeks.'

'Really?'

'Mm. Daisy's been ill, apparently.'

'Oh dear.' Jack was immediately concerned. 'Nothing serious, I hope.'

'Serious enough to put her in hospital. She's had pneumonia.'

Jack frowned. 'God, poor Daisy. How is she now?'

'She's at home, but very weak and run-down, apparently,' Alan informed him. 'So June's trying to arrange a holiday for her and the girls, to try to get her back on her feet.'

'We're fully booked here at this time of the year, I suppose,' Jack surmised.

Alan nodded. 'June said the Cliff Head wouldn't be suitable for

168

them anyway,' he said. 'It's too quiet, too expensive and too restricting for the children. I agree with her about that. I mean, we don't actually ban children but we don't make them particularly welcome either.'

'What sort of place is Daisy looking for?' Jack enquired, his interest growing.

'Daisy isn't looking for anything,' Alan explained. 'In fact, she knows nothing about it yet. June wants to get everything arranged before she tells her so that she'll feel she can't refuse, if it's all booked up. Daisy can't afford a holiday so June is footing the bill. But Daisy is funny about that sort of thing, apparently. She's very proud and won't accept charity.'

'What a kind thing for June to do,' commented Jack.

'I thought so too.'

'Any luck with the accommodation?'

'None at all, so far. I've been on the phone to quite a few places, but it being the height of the season, all the hotels are booked up, which is why June's turned to me. She wants to get something organised double sharp because she and Nora are afraid that Daisy will go back to work before she's properly recovered and suffer a relapse. I've still got a few more places I can try. June's going to ring me tomorrow to find out if I've had any luck.'

'You need look no further,' announced Jack with a broad smile. 'Daisy and the girls can stay at my cottage.'

Alan gave him a questioning look.

'They'll all have to share my spare room and I'll have to get a couple of camp beds for the girls,' Jack went on enthusiastically, 'but I'd love to have them.'

Stroking his chin thoughtfully, Alan said, 'It's very good of you to offer, mate, but I'm not sure if that's the sort of thing June has in mind. I think she was thinking more in terms of a B. and B. on the seafront.'

'My place is on the seafront.'

'Here in Torquay, close to all the amenities, I mean,' Alan clarified. 'June wants me to keep an eye on them and make sure they're all right while they're here, with Daisy having been so ill. June can't go away with them because she can't get the time off work.'

'I'll look after them if they stay with me,' offered Jack. 'And you won't get a healthier place than Gullscombe Bay.'

'You seem very keen,' was Alan's shrewd observation.

Actually Jack couldn't believe his luck in being given a chance to see Daisy again, and he wasn't going to let the opportunity pass him by. 'Just trying to help, mate.'

'That's why you look as though you've just come into money, is it?' his friend joshed.

'All right, I admit it. I did take a fancy to Daisy when we were in

London,' Jack confessed. 'But there would be no funny business if she stayed with me, I can promise you that. I genuinely want to help and I can't think of a better place to convalesce than Gullscombe Bay. Ideal for the kids too, with the safe beach being so close to the cottage.'

'But you'd be at work a lot of the time and they'd be stuck out there on their own, miles from everything,' Alan objected. 'Daisy is a town girl; she might feel too isolated.'

'Obviously I'd have to have some time off to look after them and entertain them,' Jack pointed out with a grin. 'But I've got some holidays owing to me.'

'At the height of our busy season, you must be joking.' Alan didn't look pleased.

'I've got a good deputy,' Jack reminded him. 'And I wouldn't take all that much time off – just a few evenings, and the odd day or two. I'm at home for part of the day anyway so they wouldn't be too lonely.'

'I'm relieved to hear you're not planning on deserting us for the whole two weeks,' said Alan ruefully. 'But I'm beginning to wish I'd never mentioned it.'

'I don't believe that,' challenged Jack. 'You'd do anything to please June.'

'Once that might have been true, but not now,' Alan said. 'But I'll pass on your invitation to her when she rings me tomorrow, see what she thinks about it.'

'I'll look forward to hearing her reaction,' beamed Jack.

A few days later, over breakfast, Daisy read a letter that had come for her in the post. She smiled, then frowned, then glared at her sister and said, 'You've been meddling, haven't you?'

'Meddling?'

'Don't try and tell me that this letter from Jack Saunders, inviting me and the kids for a holiday at his cottage, isn't your doing because I won't believe you.'

'I had nothing to do with that,' June denied truthfully.

'How did Jack know that I'd been ill then, if you didn't tell him?' Daisy wanted to know.

June bit her lip and held up her hands in a gesture of surrender. 'All right, I admit it. I got on the phone to Alan and asked him to find some accommodation for you. And before you go up in the air about it, I didn't tell you because I knew you would squash the whole idea even though it will be so good for you,' she explained. 'Anyway, Jack got to hear about it and offered for you to stay at his cottage. I really didn't have anything to do with that part of it. But knowing what your reaction would be to anyone doing anything for you at all, I asked Alan to ask Jack to write to you and invite you properly. Apparently

170

he's dead keen for you and the girls to go. He's crazy about where he lives and wants to show it off.'

'You had no right to do this, June,' rebuked Daisy.

'She was only thinking of you, love,' intervened Nora, while the two little girls ate their cornflakes, listening.

'What am I, some hard-up half-wit who isn't capable of organising her own life, or something?' erupted Daisy, tears swelling beneath her lids. She was touched by June's attempts to help and that made her feel worse because she didn't have the means to accept and she felt so damned helpless. This weakness was making her spiteful to people who didn't deserve it and she hated herself but couldn't stop. 'I've had pneumonia, I haven't lost the use of my brain.'

'Look, I think you need a holiday, so I tried to organise one for you and I can pay the costs out of the money I had left over between selling my mother's house and buying this one,' June spelled out for her. 'I acted on impulse and Alan seemed the obvious person to approach as he's in a position to find out about seaside accommodation. Is that such a crime?'

At the word 'seaside' the children's interest was aroused.

'The seaside,' said Shirley excitedly. 'Are we going to Southend for the day?'

'The seaside, goodee,' enthused Belinda. 'Can we have a bucket and spade?'

Seeing those young eyes shining with hope, Daisy was filled with shame. She was spoiling everything for them as well as June because of her stupid pride. What right did she have to deprive them of a holiday, and June the pleasure of giving? June wanted to help her because she was her sister. If the situation was reversed she would want to do the same thing for her.

She remembered how upset she'd been initially when June had offered them a home. She'd grown closer to her since then; knew her well enough to recognise this for what it was – a kind gesture with no ulterior motive.

'Better than a day at Southend,' Daisy informed them with a tearful smile. 'Much, much better. Two whole weeks at the seaside in Devon thanks to your lovely Auntie June.'

Forgetting the table manners Daisy had been at pains to teach them since they were old enough to understand such things, they slipped off their chairs and tore around the kitchen, then up and down the hall, shrieking with delight. 'We're going to the seaside, the seaside, the seaside!'

'Sorry about just now, June,' said Daisy. 'I was an idiot. I think I must be touchy because I'm feeling so low physically. I didn't mean to be horrible.' She put her hand on her sister's arm. 'It's ever so good of you to do this for us and I really do appreciate it.'

'It's a pleasure,' beamed June, getting up and hugging her.

'Why are Mummy and Auntie June crying, Nora?' asked Shirley, looking worried.

'Because they're happy,' Nora explained.

'That's all right then,' said Shirley, looking happy too.

Predictably, the one person who wasn't happy about the forthcoming holiday was Nat.

'You're going to Devon to stay with some bloke,' he disapproved sternly, that same evening. 'Daisy, how could you?'

They were on the sofa in the living room; smart and comfy now, it had been refurbished with bright contemporary wallpaper and a red carpet. The girls were in bed. June was washing her hair and Nora was in her room writing a letter.

'It isn't how you're making it sound,' she told him, having already given him full details of the holiday and how it had come about. 'Jack's offered to put the girls and me up, that's all. It's perfectly innocent.'

'You might be gullible enough to believe that, but I'm certainly not,' he barked.

'So, without knowing anything about him, you've got him down as a rapist, have you?'

'I didn't say that.'

'You're questioning my morals then?'

'No. I'm just saying that he's a man and he'll make the most of having you in the house.'

'And you think I'm daft enough to fall into his arms?'

'No. I'm just pointing out what could happen.'

'That is sick,' objected Daisy. 'You shouldn't judge other people by your own standards.'

'You're trying to tell me that you're going to be sharing a house with an unattached man for two weeks and nothing like that will happen?' he said cynically.

'Yes, I am telling you exactly that,' she said with emphasis. 'What do you take me for? A tramp? Such a thing hadn't even occurred to me.'

'Then it should have,' he warned her. 'You know nothing about the man. You don't know what he's capable of.'

'He seemed thoroughly decent to me on the one occasion that I met him.' She didn't add that she'd liked Jack a lot and knew somehow that he was to be trusted, because Nat would deliberately misunderstand her feelings. 'Anyway, June knows him quite well and she wouldn't have me stay with someone who isn't trustworthy. He'll be out at work a lot of the time anyway, apparently, and he's giving us the complete run of his house while he's out. Frankly, I think it's very kind of him.'

'Huh.'

'You're jealous, aren't you?' Daisy accused. 'That's what this is all about.'

'Well, how would you feel if I told you I was going away for a fortnight with a woman?' Nat challenged her.

'I wouldn't like it at all,' she admitted. 'But I'm not going away with a man. I'm simply using his house.' She sighed. 'Look, I've been ill and I've been advised to take a holiday by the doctors. Thanks to my sister's generosity and the kindness of one of her husband's friends, the girls and I can have one.'

'I don't think you should go.'

'Don't you want me to get better?'

'You'll get better if you stay here, eventually,' he said. 'Nature will take its course wherever you are.'

Daisy was very tired suddenly. 'You're probably right and the last thing I want to do is upset you, Nat,' she told him wearily. 'But I've been given this opportunity and I feel I must take it.'

'Even though I don't want you to.'

'If you won't change your mind, yes. I'm feeling so rotten I have to do something about it. Let's face it, I'm not much use to anyone as I am now, especially our little girls, the poor lambs. First I give them a scare when I'm carted off to hospital, then I'm like a wet weekend when I come home. I owe it to them to try and speed up my recovery. I've been so bad-tempered with them lately. Anyway, even apart from all of that, a holiday at the seaside will be really smashing for them. Surely you want something nice for your daughters.'

As mean and self-centred as Nat was, he wasn't entirely without feelings, and the sight of Daisy looking so pale and pinched touched something inside him. 'Yeah, course I do,' he said with a change of attitude.

'Really?'

'Yeah. You go and enjoy yourself.'

'Thanks, Nat,' she beamed.

He reached into his pocket and took out some notes. 'Here's some spending money for you, an' all,' he said, handing her a few pound notes. 'And I want you to come back with some colour in your cheeks, do you understand?'

'Oh, Nat, are you sure about this?' she queried, looking at the money.

Giving her one of his most dazzling smiles, he said, 'Go on. Take it before I change my mind.'

'You're all right, Nat Barker, do you know that?' she told him, slipping her arms around him.

'Glad you think so,' he muttered, looking bewildered. He was astonished by his own impulsive generosity, and was wondering what had come over him.

'You never cease to surprise me,' she told him. 'It's no wonder I still love you, even after all these years.'

'I make it my policy not to be too predictable,' he said, back on form with the chat. 'You might start to take me for granted if I did that.'

'Never.'

'And I intend to make sure it stays that way.'

'If this is how you're going to do it, you won't hear me complaining.'

Daisy had decided to go to Devon whatever Nat thought about it because she knew it was the right thing for everyone at the house. But having his blessing meant that she could go away with an easy mind and enter into the spirit of the holiday with the same enthusiasm as her excited daughters.

Chapter Eleven

The road from Torquay to Gullscombe Bay wound through lush green countryside, the soft undulating hills a patchwork of thickly wooded slopes and rich expanses of grassland. There were picturesque villages with cob-walled, thatched cottages, and stone-built bridges over clear streams. When the road became coastal – high above sea level – tantalising glimpses of the sea could be caught through the trees. Daisy had never seen anything like it before, and the girls were breathless with awe, shrieking with delight at every new view of the ocean.

'I thought they couldn't get any more excited than they were when June and Nora saw us off on the train,' Daisy confided to Jack, who had met them at Torquay station and was driving them to his cottage in a black Ford Anglia, she in the front with him, the girls in the back, 'but I was wrong because they've reached such a pitch now, I think they might explode.'

'There's nothing quite like the enthusiasm of childhood, is there?' he smiled.

'I'm not so sure about that because I'm nearly as bad as they are,' she admitted. 'None of us has been further than Southend until now, so this is all quite stunning for us.'

'You wait till you see Gullscombe Bay,' he said, sounding as thrilled to be showing them the area as they were to see it. 'We'll be there in a minute. It seems to be taking for ever because I'm used to whizzing to and fro on my motorbike.'

Daisy turned to observe his clean-cut profile, a summer tan making him look even more wholesome than she remembered, especially with the white sports shirt he was wearing with lightweight fawn slacks. 'You have a car as well as a motorbike then?'

'No. This little motor belongs to a pal of mine. He's given me the use of it while you're here,' Jack explained, deeming it wise to alter the facts slightly so as not to mention that he had actually hired the car from a friend who had a car-hire firm, and paid the going rate for it because he wanted Daisy and the girls to travel in comfort while they were on holiday. He'd been warned by Alan, who'd been briefed by June, to be extremely cautious about anything with so much as a hint of charity.

'That's very nice of him but won't he be needing it himself?' she enquired.

'No. He has another vehicle he can use.' At least that was no lie.

'Two cars. Wow.' She was impressed. 'I can see that the scenery around here isn't the only thing that's different from what I'm used to. I don't know anyone with one car, let alone two.'

Jack didn't reply to that; just concentrated on the road. 'We're about to turn into Gullscombe Bay now.' His voice rose with enthusiasm. 'It's just round the bend.'

They turned a corner and began to descend a steep hill. Daisy gasped at the sight ahead of them. Golden sands fringed the sea round a bay flanked by red cliffs, the turquoise ocean shimmering in the afternoon sun and dotted with little white sailing boats. At the foot of the hill there were huge expanses of meadow edged with sand dunes leading to the beach. A little further on they came to Gullscombe Bay village, a pretty gathering of whitewashed thatched houses with a pub, a general stores with a Post Office sign, and a church, all set around a village green.

Driving down a narrow track towards the seashore, Jack turned off the road and pulled up outside a cottage, the like of which Daisy had seen before only in picture books.

'Well, what do you think?' asked Jack proudly as she and the girls got out of the car and stared at the little whitewashed house with a blue door, a thatched roof and 'Seagull Cottage' written in bold letters on a sign on the front wall above a dazzling abundance of hollyhocks and wallflowers.

'It's beautiful, *really beautiful*,' breathed Daisy, turning to her wide-eyed daughters. 'Isn't it, girls?'

They nodded vigorously.

'Before we go inside, I want to show you what it's like out the back.' He looked at Daisy excitedly and grinned at the girls. 'Come on, follow your Uncle Jack.'

He led them through a blue wooded door at the side of the property into a garden with rolling lawns, bordered by trees and shrubs between which the sea could be seen. Going out of a gate at the bottom, they came to wide steps sloping down gently to a sandy beach, the cries of the gulls rising above the whisper of the sea at low tide.

'Cor,' gasped Shirley.

'The sea is in the back garden,' said Belinda in wonder.

'Not quite,' said Jack proudly. 'But almost.'

'So what do you think of that, eh, girls?' asked Daisy. 'Are we lucky to be here, or what?'

'Ooh, yeah,' enthused Shirley.

'Very lucky,' added her sister.

176

'It's safe for bathing,' Jack told Daisy. 'There aren't any strong currents in the shallow waters so you can let them paddle without any worries.'

Belinda was jumping up and down now with excitement. 'Can we go in the water? Can we, please, Mum? Can we?'

'When we've got our stuff out of the car and got changed, we'll go and dip our toes in,' promised Daisy.

'I expect you'd like something to eat too,' suggested Jack. 'I don't suppose you've had any lunch.'

'We haven't but I'm not expecting you to feed us,' Daisy was quick to point out. She thought he was doing quite enough by letting them stay and she wasn't prepared to impose further on his good nature. 'I saw a shop in the village. I can pop over there and get us something.'

'Don't be so silly.' He was outraged at the suggestion. 'I've got plenty of food in.'

Realising that to insist would be bad manners, she said graciously, 'Thank you. You're very kind.'

Inside the cottage there were wooden beams against buttercup-yellow walls in a living room with soft squashy sofas and French doors leading to the garden. Up a rickety wooden staircase, Jack showed them into a pretty room with low ceilings, a sea view and three beds, two of which were camp beds.

'I'm sorry you have to share,' he apologised, guessing it would embarrass Daisy if he were to give her his room and sleep on the sofa himself, as willing as he was to do this. 'I only have the one spare bedroom.'

'Don't apologise, for goodness' sake,' Daisy urged him. 'We're very grateful to be able to stay here. You've done us proud and I really do appreciate it.'

'It gives me a chance to show off my cottage,' he said lightly, and stepped towards the door. 'I'll leave you to sort yourselves out then. The bathroom is just along the landing and when you come downstairs I'll show you where everything else is.'

She smiled in thanks and told him they'd join him down there in a few minutes.

There were only two room downstairs – the kitchen and the living room – but both were of a reasonable size. The kitchen was quarry-tiled and oak-beamed, with a long farmhouse-style table. Jack made a pot of tea for Daisy and gave the girls a real treat: chilled lemonade with ice cubes from his fridge.

'I have to go to work now,' he explained to Daisy, 'but there's plenty of food so help yourselves to anything you fancy. There's fresh bread in the bread bin – and stuff to go with it in the fridge – ham, cheese, corned beef pie and so on. The larder's quite well stocked as well.'

177

'Sounds as though you've been having a busy time at the shops,' she said.

'Well, you do when you've got guests coming to stay, don't you?'

Having guests to stay didn't feature in Daisy's life but she just said, 'Yeah, I suppose so.' She hadn't expected this sort of hospitality and found herself in an awkward position. She didn't want to offend Jack but neither did she want to sponge on him. 'Look, Jack. It's very kind of you to put us up, but as I said just now, I don't expect you to feed us as well. So, let me give you some money.'

'Right. Since you've brought the subject up, we might as well get it sorted out here and now so that we both know where we are,' he said, his expression becoming grave. 'And this is how it will work. I want you to treat this place as your home for the next two weeks. That means having anything you want to eat and drink. But you are my guests so I want no talk of money.'

She bit her lip. 'Well, if you're sure . . .'

'I am, so let's hear no more about it,' he told her firmly. 'I won't be here all of the time because of work commitments but I've arranged to take some time off later on, to show you around the area.' He paused, spreading his hands, his blue eyes resting on Daisy. 'Please, please, make yourselves at home.' He winked at her. 'If you look in the ice-making compartment of the fridge you'll find something the kids might enjoy later on. I've arranged to get off early tonight so I'll be back about eight and I'll bring something from the hotel kitchen for our evening meal. OK?'

Without causing offence there wasn't much else Daisy could say except, 'Thank you so much.'

'Thanks aren't necessary because it's my pleasure.' He paused thoughtfully. 'My work number is on the pad by the telephone on the living-room windowsill. Any problem, or anything you want to know, give me a call.'

'Will do,' she said, and he left by the kitchen door.

Pressured by the girls for an immediate investigation of the ice box, they found a block of strawberry and vanilla ice cream which Shirley and Belinda were told they couldn't have until after they'd eaten some lunch. Daisy was just setting out some crusty bread and butter with fresh cheese and thick slices of ham and luscious tomatoes when Jack came back and popped his head around the door. 'I forgot to tell you that there are some deck chairs in the shed.' He grinned at the girls. 'There's a couple of buckets and spades in there too.'

The girls beamed. 'Bucket and spades . . . for us?' said Shirley. One treat after another – she could hardly believe it.

'Well, I didn't buy them for your mother,' he grinned. 'I think the deck chair is more up her alley.'

Daisy laughed, realising it was the first time she'd done so properly since her illness. 'Oh, Jack, this is so kind of you.' She turned to the girls. 'What do you say to Uncle Jack?'

'Thank you very much, Uncle Jack,' they chorused with delight.

'You're welcome,' he said, and left.

A few minutes later they heard his motorbike roar away. Daisy had to admit to being glad of this time to themselves to get used to the place. Although she felt very much at ease with Jack, he was little more than a stranger and she might have felt a bit awkward with him hovering over them so soon after their arrival.

What a kind and generous man he was. And with such a lovely home. His standard of living and the fact that he had modern refinements only dreamed of by Daisy – such as a fridge, a telephone, and a small television set in the corner of the living room – reminded her that he was in a management position and was therefore in a different league to her as a waitress. He was a smashing bloke, though, with no airs and graces.

Roaring through the lanes on his Harley-Davidson, the high speed causing an invigorating rush of cold air on his face around his goggles, Jack was thinking of Daisy and hoping he'd done the right thing in leaving her and the girls on their own so soon after they'd arrived.

Some people might think it was rather a rude thing to do but he'd given the matter some thought and decided to make himself scarce with the idea that she might feel more relaxed with the run of the place to herself, initially. He'd thought it best not to take the whole night off work too, to give them a chance to get settled in. Daisy needed to rest and enjoy the sea air for a few days, with just her children as much as possible. He smiled fondly, thinking of her tinkly laugh and the way she moved, quickly but with grace. Completely without the trappings of glamour that made most women look attractive, she had her own brand of natural beauty with her pert little face and slender body.

He smiled at the thought of the girls. Buying the buckets and spades had probably given him more pleasure than they'd had from receiving them. It was really important to him that they all had a good holiday. The weather had given them a warm welcome anyway, and he just couldn't wait to get back from work tonight to see them all again.

'I need more water for the moat,' announced Shirley, about to trail down to the sea with her bucket for the umpteenth time.

'Don't go out too far,' warned Daisy. 'You can't swim, remember. So stay at the edge.'

'Can me and Sherl learn to swim in the sea, Mum?' Belinda requested.

Her mother pondered the question. 'It might not be a bad idea to

179

give it a try while we're here,' she said, settled in a deck chair on the sand, watching her daughters play. Both girls were proudly sporting bright yellow swimsuits that Nora had bought them as holiday treats. Daisy was less daring in a rather shapeless cotton dress she'd bought years ago in Portobello market. 'The school will be taking you to the swimming baths for lessons when you're a bit older but the sooner you can swim the better so I'll give it some thought.'

'I love it here, Mum,' enthused Belinda, looking around at the golden sand that was only lightly sprinkled with people, the bay being uncommercialised and off the beaten track.

'So do I,' added Shirley. 'I want to stay here for ever.'

Those were Daisy's sentiments exactly. She'd felt she belonged here from the minute they'd arrived. Realistically, it was too soon to feel any significant change in her health but she fancied that the air agreed with her. Being in such a weak state, she had been exhausted by the journey but after just one afternoon in the fresh air she felt stronger and more energetic. The girls' pasty London complexions were already beginning to glow with colour too.

'It's certainly a lovely place,' she agreed with her daughters.

Thank you so much, June and Jack, for giving us all this, she said silently, raising her face to the sun, its warmth softened by a light summer breeze. She couldn't remember feeling this relaxed in a very long time.

Observing his visitor across the table, Lionel Rivers thought she had one of the friendliest faces he'd ever seen, with her sparkling blue eyes and warm, engaging smile. Initially she'd seemed rather odd to look at: bright, disorderly hair, tall gangling frame and freckled face that was so much smaller than the rest of her. But the instant she smiled, he stopped noticing anything else.

'I'm glad you agreed to let them issue me with a visiting order,' Nora explained in her deep husky voice. 'I didn't want you to be without visitors as the girls couldn't make it this time.'

'I've been looking forward to meeting you at last,' he said, and she saw genuine pleasure in his warm brown eyes. 'Though I feel as if I know you already because of your letters.'

'I feel like that about you too.'

He frowned. 'I hope there's nothing wrong with the girls to keep them away.'

'Quite the reverse,' she was pleased to be able to assure him. 'Daisy's away on holiday in Devon and June's tied up at work so we decided between us that it would be a good idea for me to meet my pen pal on my day off.'

'I really am very grateful to you for coming.' He cast a disapproving eye around the room. 'But I don't like the idea of you, or the girls,

180

having to come to such an awful place.'

'It doesn't worry me, dear,' Nora said, dismissing the subject by moving on, bringing him up to date with news of his daughters and telling him how Daisy's holiday had come about.

'I didn't even know she'd been ill,' Lionel said with concern.

'It happened only recently, and they'd have mentioned it next time they came to visit you, I expect,' she told him. 'Don't worry about Daisy. She'll be all right. She's tough. She's had to be, the amount of illness she's had in her life.'

'Really?'

She told him about Daisy's poor health. 'She's got stamina, though, that one. Never gives in. I've known her go to work when she's been half dead with bronchitis before now. She struggled on at work this time until they sent her home. She takes her responsibilities towards the girls very seriously.'

'Doesn't their father help her at all with their upkeep?' he wondered.

'No. Not on a regular basis,' Nora explained. 'He slips her a few bob now and again but that's about all.'

'Sounds as though you don't like him.'

'I don't. Because of the way he treats Daisy,' she admitted. 'The man's a complete dead loss. She knows he is too, in her heart, though she'd never admit it or give him up.' She shrugged, sighing. 'That's love for you.'

'It's weird to find out all these things about your own daughter at such a late stage,' Lionel told her.

'I'm sure it must be.'

'Finding them again is a dream come true, though.' He knew that Nora was fully in the picture about his family history. 'I thought I'd lost them for ever all those years ago. It was the worst moment of my life when I was told they were being taken into care. It was all so sudden. One minute I had a wife and family, the next I had no one. The girls were whisked out of the house sharpish, as soon as the police came. I wasn't even allowed to say goodbye to them before they carted me off to the nick.'

'It seems cruel but I suppose the authorities were acting in the children's best interests,' she said, her eyes moist with tears as she stared at this sad-eyed man whose face was lined beyond his years and who had a gentleness about him despite his tough appearance. The Rivers' story was one of the most poignant she'd ever heard. 'They would have needed to get the children away from the murder scene, and putting them into care was the only option they had with your wife dead, you in prison and no relatives willing to take them on.'

'They had no choice, I know that.' His eyes became glazed as he looked back. 'Losing my wife and being banged up for a murder I didn't do was bad enough, but losing my girls was the hardest blow of all. I thought they would think I'd abandoned them, which they did, of course.'

'It's all clear now as far as that's concerned, though,' Nora pointed out cheerfully.

'Yeah, thank God. Knowing that they don't think I stopped loving them has made me a happy man, and I'm so lucky to have them back in my life, even if that means only a brief visit now and then.'

'They're pleased to have found you too, and each other.' They'd been speaking in low voices but Nora lowered hers even more now against the prying ears of the warders. 'And although there's no movement at the moment, they are both still determined to clear your name and get you out of here.'

'It's good of them to want to do all that for me, but I'm not holding my breath.'

'That's very wise,' she said, nodding sagely. 'It was a long time ago and the people concerned could be anywhere by now. They might even be dead.'

'Which is what I told them,' he made clear. 'Anyway, I'm so used to prison life I'd probably be like a fish out of water if I ever did get out of here.'

'You'd be bound to feel strange at first, of course,' she told him. 'But now that you've got some family to help you, you'd soon adjust. You've got your daughters and granddaughters out there to welcome you.' She paused and gave him a shy grin. 'And me, of course. I'm part of the furniture.'

He smiled at her. 'Your letters mean a lot to me,' he said. 'They keep me going.'

'Good'. Nora paused thoughtfully, leaning towards him in a confidential manner. 'Look, even though it wouldn't be wise to bank on anything, you mustn't stop hoping. Just because nothing's happening at the moment, that doesn't mean it's been forgotten. The girls won't rest until they've found the Dodds. Daisy reckons they need just one break that'll set the whole thing in motion, and she's convinced that they'll get it sooner or later. That's Daisy for you – she always looks on the bright side and that's what you must do.'

Lionel nodded. 'You're sort of a mum to my daughters, then?' he assumed.

'Not to both of them. June and I are just friends because I haven't know her for so long. But I am like a mum to Daisy. She seems to want that. Daisy's strong but June has a tougher edge somehow. She isn't as open as Daisy so you can't get close to her.'

They were interrupted by the warder telling them that time was up.

'Thanks ever so much for coming,' Lionel said.

'It was a pleasure,' Nora smiled. 'I'll come again sometime if you'd like me to.'

'Yes, please.'

'I'll sort something out with the girls then, as you're only allowed a certain number of visits,' she told him.

He nodded in approval.

It was heartbreaking to see him being taken away, battered by the way life had treated him but retaining a proud stance, shoulders squared, chin up. She could see a lot of his younger daughter in him.

Nora's empathy for Lionel was strong because she'd had her share of loneliness; she knew what it was like to feel like an outsider. Until Daisy had come into her life she'd felt isolated from people because she was a spinster. It was the recognition of how true friendship had changed her life for the better that had inspired her to write to Lionel. She hoped she could give to him some of what his daughter had given her.

'Morning, madear,' the proprietor of the Gullscombe Bay village shop greeted Daisy in her rich Devonian accent. 'Another lovely day. You've certainly brought some good weather with you.'

'We seem to have – so far, anyway, Mrs Graham,' agreed Daisy. 'Let's hope it lasts.'

A plump-faced woman of middle years, with rosy cheeks and a fresh complexion, the shopkeeper turned her attention to Shirley and Belinda, to whom she'd taken a liking this past week. 'And how are my little maids today?' she asked.

'Very well, thank you, Mrs Graham,' they chanted politely, making their mother swell with pride at their lovely manners.

'That's good.' She turned to Daisy. 'Your usual this morning, madear?'

'Please.'

The other woman took a cottage loaf out of a basket, wrapped it in tissue paper and put it on the counter with a pint of milk. 'Anything else?'

'I think I'll take some apples and bananas too, please,' Daisy requested.

'Pick out what you want then, madear,' Mrs Graham instructed, 'and I'll weigh them up.'

While Daisy helped herself from the wooden trays and handed the fruit to the shopkeeper, Belinda asked in a proud tone, 'Do you know what I can do, Mrs Graham?'

'No, what's that, pet?' the woman smiled.

'I can swim.'

'Can you really?' Mrs Graham was most impressed. 'That's very good indeed.'

183

'She can't do it on her own yet.' Her sister's competitive streak went into top gear. 'She can only do it with the water wings on, same as me.'

'It's still swimming,' insisted Belinda.

'Not proper swimming until we can do it on our own,' argued Shirley. 'Uncle Jack says.'

Daisy gave Mrs Graham a wry grin. 'There's no shortage of sibling rivalry between these two.'

'No harm in a spot of healthy competition,' the shopkeeper pointed out.

'Jack's been helping me to teach them to swim,' Daisy told her. 'It would be good if they could do it before we go back. Once they've learned they've got it for ever.'

'If anyone can teach them, Jack will. He's got the patience of a saint, that man,' enthused Mrs Graham. 'You won't hear a bad word about him in this village.'

'Everyone seems to like him.'

'That's because he does so much for the people around here,' she confided. 'In the winter he clears the snow for the old folk; he even gets the coal in for them. And that's just two examples of the sort of man he is. Nothing's too much trouble.'

Jack was a local hero in these parts, Daisy had already gathered that. Gullscombe Bay was a small community, barely touched by tourism. There were no hotels or boarding houses. A few of the residents offered bed and breakfast in the summer but that was about it. Because Daisy and the girls were guests of the village hero, who had made it generally known that she was here to convalesce, they were being given the red-carpet treatment by the locals, many of whom had stories of courage and kindness to tell about Jack. Everything from rescuing a drowning man to lobbying the council to get more streetlights put up in the village.

'I've noticed that,' she agreed. 'It's very good of him to let us stay with him.'

'You're enjoying your holiday then.' It was a statement rather than a question since it would never occur to this local woman that any visitor to the area could do anything but enjoy themselves.

'I'll say we are,' enthused Daisy. 'We love it here. We won't want to go back when the time comes. Still, I won't think about that yet, as we've still got a week left.'

'Let's hope the weather stays fine.'

Daisy nodded, handing the woman some money. Daisy hadn't the means of knowing for sure but she believed that rain, shine, hail or storm, she would enjoy being in Gullscombe Bay.

'You're certainly looking a lot better than when you arrived,' observed the shopkeeper, handing Daisy her change. 'You looked quite poorly then.'

184

'I'm feeling heaps better now,' Daisy was pleased to be able to report.

After some more idle chat, she and the girls left the shop and walked across the village green and down the lane to the cottage. One of the highlights of the day for Daisy was walking to the shop every morning with the girls to get fresh bread and milk. She loved the smell of the sea in the morning air, the friendliness of the people she met and the fresh taste of the food when they got back to the cottage. The walk before breakfast gave them an appetite and they'd got into the habit of having just-baked bread and butter with fresh fruit or jam instead of the porridge and cornflakes they had in the mornings at home.

At the beginning Jack had offered quite insistently to do the morning trip to the shop but when Daisy explained how much she enjoyed it, he let her carry on while he had an extra half-hour in bed. There was a very relaxed atmosphere between them. Not once had he made her feel like a lodger in his house. Quite the opposite; he made her feel as though he was honoured to have her and the girls in the house.

So far, with such good weather, they'd been able to have breakfast in the garden looking out over the sea. It was the most wonderful start to the day. She could understand why Jack had settled here. It was the sort of place you never wanted to leave.

It was mid-afternoon and the residents of Seagull Cottage were all in the shallow waters of the sea. Even Daisy was wearing a swimsuit now, a flowery little one-piece she'd bought in Torquay when Jack had taken them in the car the other day for a look round. Because holidays away had been unknown to her until now, she hadn't owned such a thing before.

'Come on then, Shirley,' Jack instructed. 'Let's have some action here. Swim from your mum to me.'

The little girl looked doubtful. 'Not without the water wings,' she told him.

'You can do it on your own, I promise you,' he encouraged. 'That's why we took them off, so that you can try.'

'I'm scared to do it without them.'

'You've nothing to be scared of because you're ready to do it on your own now,' he promised her. 'Honestly, I wouldn't suggest you do it if I wasn't sure that you can. But I'm here to catch you if you can't manage.'

'Go on, love,' urged Daisy. 'Give it a try.'

Shirley tried and floundered, waving her arms in a panic.

'It's all right, I've got you,' said Jack, holding her firm until she was steady on her feet. Keen for her not to be put off by the failure, he suggested she should try again right away. 'Push yourself off from the bottom, come on, swim from Mummy to me.'

It worked. It was only a matter of a few yards but she did actually move through the water without artificial aid. By the end of the session she was swimming on her own and loving it, her sister almost ready to dispense with the water wings too.

Afterwards they got dried and had tea and scones in the garden. When they'd finished eating, the children went off to play on the sand where the adults could keep an eye on them.

'They can never have enough of the beach,' observed Daisy. 'Whenever it's time to go, it's too soon for them. I'm sure if we stayed till midnight I'd still have a battle to get them to come home.'

'That's all most kids want on holiday,' Jack remarked, 'sea, sand and sunshine.'

'They've never had it before,' she said. 'They are two happy little girls, thanks to you.'

'I do have an ulterior motive.'

She squinted at him, shielding her eyes from the sun with her hand. 'Yeah? What's that then?'

'I get to show off my little corner of the world,' he laughed.

'And understandably so,' she smiled. 'Gullscombe Bay has three more devoted fans now.'

'Good. Oh, and by the way,' he said, and Daisy sensed a sudden uneasiness in his manner, 'I'm not working tonight. I've got a night off.'

'Lovely,' she beamed. 'I'll cook for us.' She felt awkward suddenly and bit her lip. 'Sorry, I'm being presumptuous. You're probably going out – on a hot date or something.'

He looked at her, his heart melting at her smile and her shining eyes, her skin now suffused with a light tan, her brown hair bleached by the sun and blowing off her face in the light warm breeze. She'd even lost that raw skinniness she'd had when she first arrived. He'd made a point of studying her reaction to the news that he was going to be at home this evening, ever careful not to encroach upon her privacy. All week he'd given her the run of the cottage so she would feel completely at home without him around.

Now, halfway through the holiday, the time was right for him to get to know her better; before it was too late. He had nothing specific in mind for Daisy. He wasn't planning on making a move on her or anything because he knew she was involved with someone else. He just wanted to be with her because he was so smitten. There was no future in it but he couldn't help the way he felt.

'No hot date,' he informed her. 'Just a quiet night in . . . something good to eat and a bottle of wine, perhaps.'

'Wine, at home?' She looked surprised. 'I thought people only had wine at wedding receptions, or when they're staying at a posh hotel like the one where I work.' She gave him one of her delicious grins. 'But I'm forgetting, you being a restaurant manager you'd have more sophisticated tastes than me.'

'Don't be daft,' he said in a tone of light admonition. 'I just thought it would be a nice idea to make the meal a bit special, you being on holiday.'

'It's a lovely idea.'

'So if you tell me what you fancy to eat I'll pop into town on the bike and do some shopping.'

'You choose the food and I'll cook it,' she said, smiling into his eyes. 'Deal?'

'Deal,' he replied with a tender look.

That same evening June answered a knock at the door to find Nat Barker standing on the step. Naturally she was puzzled.

'Daisy's still away on holiday,' she reminded him.

'I know that,' he told her. 'I was just wondering if you'd heard from her.'

'No, not yet,' she replied. 'I expect we'll get a postcard in due course. I take it you haven't heard either.'

He shook his head, then enquired, 'Well, aren't you going to ask me in?'

She spread her hands, looking at him. 'Daisy isn't here so what would be the point?'

'So that we don't have to talk in full view of the neighbours is as good a reason as any,' he suggested. 'And also because I'm as good as your brother-in-law. I think that in itself warrants a cup of tea, don't you?'

'No,' was her frank reply. 'And you're about as likely to be my brother-in-law as the Duke of Edinburgh is.'

'Ooh,' he said, shaking his head disapprovingly and sucking in his breath, 'Daisy won't be pleased to hear that you kept me waiting on the doorstep, not pleased at all.'

He was right about that. June had promised Daisy that she'd be more sociable to Nat and she must keep that promise even though Daisy wasn't here. 'Come on in then,' she said with reluctance, ushering him into the living room.

'The sergeant major not about tonight then?' he said when she brought him a cup of tea a few minutes later.

'If you mean Nora, she's gone to her poetry group,' June informed him coolly. 'And I'd rather you didn't call her names, if you don't mind. The least she deserves is respect from you, considering she's been helping Daisy to raise your daughters for years with no assistance from you whatever.'

Nat shrugged indifferently. 'Poetry group, eh?' he said with a mocking grin.

'That's right,' she confirmed briskly. 'Nora likes that sort of thing. She's a very erudite woman.'

'That sounds like some sort of glue.'

'It means knowledgeable.'

'Yeah, well, books and stuff suit her,' he commented cynically. 'Both are as boring as hell.'

June didn't reply. She perched on the edge of an armchair opposite him, feeling intensely irritated and wondering again what Daisy saw in him. She supposed he was good-looking in a greasy sort of way but he had no dress sense whatever and, to her eyes, looked ridiculous with his quiffed hair, gaudy tie and royal-blue suit with a long jacket. It would be rude of her to leave him here on his own and she didn't want to give him any opportunity to make trouble between her and Daisy. But she didn't feel comfortable in the same room with him.

'Each to their own,' she said, keeping her temper, 'and Nora is very clever and well read.'

'She's a sad old bag.'

'Right, that's it.' This was justifiable grounds for eviction. 'I won't have my friends insulted in my own house. So get out. Go on, push off.'

'I haven't finished my tea yet.'

'Too bad. I want you out of here right now.'

'Look, I'm sorry,' he apologised, sounding unexpectedly contrite. 'I overstepped the mark.'

'It's no more than I've come to expect from you,' June said, 'as normal decent behaviour seems to be beyond you.'

'That's a bit strong,' he objected. 'Anyone would think I was some sort of ruffian to hear you talk.'

'I wonder why that is,' was her ironic retort.

Nat looked at her with a gleam in his eye. He hated the sight of the snooty cow and the way she looked down on him. He'd come here on impulse, as he'd been passing the end of the street, with no ulterior motive other than idling away a few minutes on his way to the pub. But with Daisy out of the way, he could see the perfect opportunity to bring her superior sister down a peg or two.

'Look, I know there's no love lost between us,' he said in a tone of fake conciliation, 'but can't we bury the hatchet for Daisy's sake? I know she would like us to get on better.'

June gave him a shrewd look. She didn't trust him an inch but if they could come to some understanding whereby they got along better, even if only in front of Daisy, it would make life easier for them all. If he was prepared to make an effort then so was she. 'OK. If you really mean it, I'm prepared to give it a try,' she told him.

'Good, I'm glad that's settled.' He looked at her innocently but was actually planning his next move. 'It's next Saturday Daisy gets back, isn't it?'

'That's right,' she confirmed. 'She's halfway through the holiday now. I hope she's enjoying herself. She's had a rough time and deserves a break.'

'Yeah, I hope she has a good time, an' all.' He fixed her with his dark, somnolent eyes. 'I know you don't think much of me but I do care about her, you know.'

'Don't make me laugh,' she said. 'You don't give a toss about her. There's only one person you care about and that's yourself.'

'Here, that's not very nice.' He looked peeved. 'I thought we'd agreed to call a truce.'

'Yes, we did,' she admitted, 'but if we're going to stay at peace we'd better steer clear of the subject of your feelings for Daisy.' She stood up. 'Anyway, I don't want to seem rude but I do have things to do.'

He drained his teacup and stood up.

She turned to lead him to the front door when she felt his arms slip around her from behind.

'What the hell do you think you're doing?' she gasped, turning to him and wrenching away.

'Come on, June, you know you want to,' he taunted.

'You must be off your head—'

'You don't like me but you do fancy me,' he interrupted. 'And don't deny it because I won't believe you.'

'You must be joking.'

'You women are all the same,' he persisted. 'You can't resist a bad boy.'

'Ugh!' She stared at him in disgust. 'I'd sooner be savaged by a mad Alsatian.'

'Don't give me that,' he persisted suggestively, coming towards her again. 'Why fight it when you know you won't win? What harm is there, eh? Daisy will never know.'

June whacked her hand across his face so hard it stung her. Caught unawares, he reeled back. 'You spiteful cow,' he muttered.

'Now get out,' she said, marching towards the door and opening it. 'Go on, get out – *now*.'

His eyes were simmering with rage. Such was his vanity, he'd planned only to get her interested, then make a fool of her by turning her down. The way she'd turned the tables on him was the ultimate humiliation. 'I'll get you for this,' he threatened. 'I can promise you that.'

'Just go,' she said, putting her hands on his chest and pushing him through the doorway.

'You'll pay for this, you bitch,' was his parting shot, and the haunting image she saw as she shut the door on him was his venomous eyes glaring at her.

Behind the closed door June was trembling, his threats making her shiver. How could someone as genuinely good-hearted as Daisy have got mixed up with such a brute? she wondered. Daisy really ought to have her eyes opened about the sort of man he was. But June knew that she could never hurt her sister by telling her what her beloved Nat had just done.

Chapter Twelve

'Thanks for helping us out with the wine, Paula. You're a pal.' Alan was talking to his friend in the Cliff Head reception, having just removed a dozen bottles of white wine from the boot of her car. 'We've usually got plenty in stock but our suppliers let us down at the last minute.' He tutted, giving her a wry grin. 'And, of course, Sod's law being as it is, everyone wants white wine tonight.'

'Isn't it always the way?'

'Yeah. Still, thanks to you we can stay in favour with the customers.' He put the cardboard box containing the wine down on the counter and looked at her, raising his eyes in a gesture of self-deprecation. 'A decent-class hotel without any white wine, I ask you.'

'These things happen in the most well-run establishments,' she reminded him. 'And I'm sure you'd help us out in similar circumstances.'

'Course we would.' He paused, looking at her. 'You should have let me come to get it, though, to save you driving over.'

'I was glad of the break,' she admitted. 'It's always so hectic on a Saturday night at our place.'

'Same here.' He glanced towards the wine. 'So, how much do we owe you?'

'I don't know off the top of my head,' she said casually. 'I'll find out the trade price and let you know.'

'OK.' Saturday night was in full swing at the Cliff Head and Alan needed to get back to work but he didn't want to be rude. 'Can I get you a drink?' he offered. 'It's the least I can do after you've gone to such trouble on our behalf.'

'Thanks, Alan, but no. I've had a breather but I mustn't stop to socialise.' She threw him a knowing look. 'And neither, I suspect, must you.'

'I am a bit pushed,' he was forced to admit. 'Jack's got the night off.'

Her brows rose. 'The restaurant manager off duty on a Saturday night at the height of the season?'

Alan made a face. 'I'm a soft touch to have agreed to it, I know, but he's got people staying with him,' he explained. 'My wife's sister and her two children, as a matter of fact.' He leaned towards her, becoming confidential. 'I think he's fallen for my sister-in-law, actually. I haven't been able to get a sensible word out of him since she's been here. It's Daisy this, Daisy that . . .'

'He must be smitten to ask for a Saturday night off at this time of the year.'

Alan nodded. 'I didn't make an issue of it, though, because he's such an asset to this place and he never pushes his luck about time off as a rule.'

Unexpectedly, he found himself noticing how attractive Paula looked in a pale blue summer suit with a pencil skirt and high-heeled court shoes. Since they'd cleared the air last Christmas, their friendship had blossomed and they met up for a meal or a drink on a regular basis. They had all the right ingredients for a friendship, being in the same line of business, having parents who were friends, and sharing a similar sense of humour.

But meeting her clear blue eyes now and feeling the stirrings of a physical response, he wondered if, perhaps, there could be something more for them. He and June were no longer at daggers drawn but she'd made it clear there was no future for them together. So maybe there could be one for him with Paula. Unlike Jack, Alan didn't enjoy the single life.

'How about dinner one evening soon?' he suggested. 'Once Jack's visitors have gone back to London and his mind is on the job again, I'll be able to get away, especially on a weekday evening.'

'That would be lovely, Alan,' she accepted graciously. 'I'd really like that.'

'I'll give you a ring soon to get something arranged then.'

'Sure.'

At that moment his mother sailed on to the scene from the direction of the restaurant. 'Alan, I've had to send— Oh, hello, Paula.' She looked from one to the other, beaming as she misread the situation. 'How nice to see you, dear. I didn't realise you were here.'

'I'm just on my way out,' Paula told her, making as though to leave. 'Nice to see you again, Mrs Masters. You're looking well. See you soon, Alan.'

'I'll ring you,' he said, smiling after her as she swung across the foyer in her high-heeled shoes.

His mother was looking very pleased with herself. 'You two seem to be getting along very well lately,' she observed.

'She came with the wine we needed, that's all,' Alan explained. 'It wasn't a social visit.'

'That doesn't alter the fact that the two of you seem to get on well now,' she persisted.

He shrugged and changed the subject. 'You wanted me for something?'

'Yes, so I did. I came to tell you that Chef isn't feeling well so I've sent him home. The sous-chef will have to take over.'

'Wonderful,' Alan said with irony. 'That's all we need.' He sighed. 'Oh, well, it's all in a night's work, I suppose.'

Daisy was feeling extremely happy and relaxed. The children were asleep in bed and she and Jack were having coffee in the living room at the cottage after dining on steak and salad, followed by chocolate eclairs, and all washed down with a bottle of wine.

Daisy had never talked to a man so much in her life – certainly not to Nat. There was something about Jack that made her want to confide. She was so much at ease she even told him about her background and her plans to get her father's name cleared. She told him everything.

Unlike Nat, Jack didn't react by immediately pouring scorn on the idea. But he was a little circumspect. 'Whilst I can understand your wanting to find this Morris Dodd and his wife, I think you should treat the whole thing with caution,' he told her. 'I mean, even if you do find him, he isn't going to put his hands up to the murder, is he? And he'll see you and your sister as a threat, turning up out of the blue after all these years. He could get nasty.'

'We've already thought of that and we'll be careful, of course,' she assured him. 'But it's his wife we're planning on dealing with, rather than him.'

'She isn't likely to admit to anything either.'

'Maybe not, but she holds the key to our father's freedom and the restoration of his good name,' Daisy pointed out. 'So I believe there must be some way to get her to admit that she lied under oath, and give us the evidence we need to get Dad's case reopened.'

Jack leaned back with his arms folded, considering the matter. 'The last thing I want to do is put you off because I can tell how much this means to you,' he began, 'but facts have to be faced. She's already committed perjury; she isn't going to change her story after all this time, is she? She'll be too scared of the consequences.'

'I know all that, Jack. But I'm still convinced that if we can only find the Dodds, we'll somehow be able to see that justice is done.' She shrugged, making a face. 'I admit we've come to a dead end at the moment but we're not going to give up because we *know* that the pair of them lied in court. That's got to give us a strong case for an appeal.'

'If you can get them to admit it, yes it will,' he said. 'And I agree with you that she's more likely to be persuaded to open up than he is. He was unfaithful to her, after all.'

'Exactly,' agreed Daisy. 'Look at this whole thing from Mrs Dodd's point of view: because of the murder the world knew that her husband had been cheating on her. That must have been extremely humiliating.

Being betrayed by your husband is painful enough, I should imagine. Having everyone know about it must have been excruciating.'

'No doubt about that.'

'Even though she lied for him, she must have felt resentful towards him. Any woman would,' Daisy went on. 'And the fact that she knew he wasn't at home with her at the time of the murder, as they both claimed, must have made her wonder if he did actually do it, whatever lies he told her about that. Over the years she might have become bitter about it and be ready to shop him – with a little encouragement.'

'Not at the expense of her own liberty.' Jack didn't want Daisy to fool herself about this.

'I know it's a long shot.'

'They might not even still be together,' he pointed out.

'We've thought of that too, and I know that when you consider all the drawbacks, our chances of success don't look good.' She pondered for a moment. 'But all I can say is, I've got a feeling about this whole thing.' Her voice rose with ardour. 'If it takes the rest of my life I'll see my father's name cleared.' She paused, guessing his thoughts. 'Even if it is posthumously.'

There was obviously no point in trying to talk her out of it so he wanted to be helpful. 'You say you've come to a dead end in your search for them?'

'Yeah,' she sighed. 'If we had any idea of the area to look it would help, but we haven't a flaming clue.' She told him what they'd done so far.

'Quite a task.'

'You can say that again. The trouble is, neither June nor I have much spare time. We both have demanding jobs and I've got the girls to consider. But, as I said, we'll get it sorted out. I don't know when but we'll do it.'

Infected by her optimism, Jack believed her suddenly. She was the sort of person who would do anything she set her mind to. 'Yes, I think you will too,' he said.

'Oh.' She sounded surprised because of the odds stacked against a successful outcome. 'It's encouraging to know that someone's got faith in me.'

She was wearing a white sleeveless top with a round neck and a full floral skirt, her hair shining in the light. She looked so pretty, he couldn't help telling her so.

'Thank you.' She smiled, blushing. 'Flattery will get you everywhere.' The way he looked at her made her feel different – sort of beautiful and special. Warmth flowed between them like a living thing. She couldn't remember feeling this good in a very long time, if ever. But compunction hovered, nudging her into making sure that Nat

194

didn't get forgotten. 'I'm not used to it because Nat isn't the complimentary type.'

'And talking of Nat,' he said, as though acknowledging the other man's place in her life, 'what does he think about these plans you have to help your father?'

'He doesn't approve.'

'Worried it might be risky for you, I suppose.'

'No, it isn't that,' she corrected with characteristic honesty. 'He just thinks it's a stupid idea that won't get a result.'

'You won't get any help from him then?'

Daisy puffed out her lips, shaking her head. 'Opposition is all I'll get from him,' she said with emphasis. 'Apart from anything else, he can't stand the sight of my sister so is against anything I do with her.'

'Tell me . . . are you actually engaged to him?' came Jack's tentative enquiry.

'Yeah, I suppose you could say that's what we are. I always think of us in that way.'

'You don't wear a ring, though.'

In the early days a ring had been promised but never materialised. But she just said, 'No. But we are seriously committed to each other.'

Jack nodded without comment.

'Poor old Nat is always in the doghouse with June and Nora over something or other,' she found herself saying without any prior intention. 'Neither of them likes him. They don't think he treats me right.'

'Really?' Jack said in a querying tone. 'And do they have a fair point?'

'He's not perfect, I'm the first to admit that,' she told him. 'He tends to be a bit too casual about things. But that's just his way. We can't all be steady and reliable, can we? It'd be a boring old world if we were.'

This Nat character sounded like a right cretin and obviously didn't value the prize he had in Daisy, thought Jack, finding himself angry about it. If the man had any sense or serious intentions he'd have married her years ago. But he spared her feelings and said, 'It certainly would.'

'Have you ever been married?' she asked conversationally.

'No.'

'Would you like to be?'

'Not especially, no. I'm quite happy as I am,' he informed her. 'I suppose I've got a bit selfish and set in my ways. You get used to pleasing yourself when you're on your own.'

'Yeah, I suppose you would.'

'Anyway,' he began, changing the subject, 'you're enjoying your stay in Gullscombe Bay?'

'I'll say. It's beautiful here. No wonder you made it your home. It's enough to tempt anyone. The idea of going back to Notting Hill isn't in the least appealing, I can tell you. The way I feel at the moment, I could happily stay away indefinitely.'

'Really?' He couldn't hide his enthusiasm.

'Yeah, really,' she confirmed with a wistful look. 'But I have to go back, of course.'

'Why?'

She threw him a puzzled look. 'I should have thought that was obvious,' she told him. 'My life is in London.'

'It doesn't have to be.'

'No, it doesn't have to be. But it is. I'm a Londoner, Jack.'

'So am I.'

'But it's where I belong. Everything I know is there,' she pointed out. 'Being here has made me understand why people move away from the city to places like this and I feel I'd like to do the same. But that's just the holiday atmosphere getting to me. Being realistic, it's just a holiday place, somewhere I'd love to come again for a visit. But not a place I could live in.'

'I've made it my home,' he reminded her.

'It's different for you,' she objected. 'You're a single man with only yourself to consider. Even apart from the fact that I couldn't leave Nat, I have the girls to support so I have to have steady work. And London is where the work is.'

He could hardly bear the thought of her leaving and wanted to beg her to stay. But he had no right. Her life was in London and she obviously thought the world of this Nat person. 'Yeah, of course it is,' he said in an understanding manner. 'It's just that . . . well, you seem to have taken the place so much to your heart and it obviously agrees with you. I suppose my enthusiasm for the area got a bit out of hand.'

'That's understandable.'

'It's true about the place being good for you, though,' he added. 'You're hardly recognisable from the pale, sickly woman I met off the train a week ago.'

'I feel different too.'

'You're very beautiful, Daisy,' he blurted out.

'Here, leave off,' she said, embarrassed to find herself on the receiving end of his admiration for the second time. 'I think you've had one too many to drink.'

'I haven't—'

'Well, I think I have,' she cut in quickly because she was enjoying the attention rather too much and needed to come down to earth. 'I think it's time I went to bed.' She gave him a wry grin. 'After we've done the dishes, naturally.'

'I'll see to that,' he offered. 'You cooked the meal so it's only fair that I do the washing up.'

'Are you sure?'

'Quite sure,' he confirmed. 'You go to bed.'

She stood up. 'I'll have to take you up on that,' she said, stifling a yawn, 'before I get too sleepy to get up the stairs. All this fresh air knocks me out. I'll see you in the morning.'

'Yeah.'

'Thanks for a lovely evening.'

'Thank *you*, Daisy.'

''Night, Jack.'

''Night, Daisy.'

Daisy slipped into bed, her head swimming with happy memories of today and excited thoughts of tomorrow. That was how it was since she'd been in Gullscombe Bay. Each new day was a fresh treat to be anticipated with pleasure. This must be why people are so keen to go away on holiday, she thought, because it's just one long round of fun and recreation. How could you not be happy in surroundings like these, going to sleep every night to the soothing sound of the sea and waking up to it every morning?

Who was she kidding? It wasn't just the environment that was making her feel so happy and alive. It was going to sleep at night knowing that she would see *him* the next morning. She wanted to go on doing it, to go on being with him and feeling like this. Refusing to spoil the moment by dwelling on the sobering thought that it would end all too soon, she lay back on the pillow and drifted into a peaceful sleep.

Downstairs Jack was humming softly to himself as he washed the dishes and put them to drain on the draining board. It was so good having Daisy here, he was literally dreading her departure. As he'd said to her, living alone had made him selfish and set in his ways. But he didn't feel selfish when he was with her. He wanted to put himself out for her benefit; enjoyed her appreciation of every little thing. Having the kids around was great fun too, their youthful exuberance filling the house with noise and laughter. Their energy and nonstop chatter was positively uplifting to him. Selfish he might be but he couldn't do enough for this little family. The trouble was, he wanted to go on doing it, and this time next week they'd be back in London.

The trio had breathed new life into him, and the cottage was never going to be the same after they'd gone. The thought of their departure was so depressing he blotted it out of his mind and looked forward to tomorrow and waking up knowing that Daisy and the girls were in the house.

The next morning the unthinkable happened. They awoke to find rain trickling down the windows and forming puddles in the garden. Jack insisted on going to the shop, which opened for a few hours on a Sunday morning, to get the milk and bread to save Daisy a drenching as she had recently been ill.

Breakfast was eaten indoors, but by the time they'd finished and done the dishes, the rain had stopped. It was still overcast, though, so Jack suggested a walk along the beach. He had to go to work a bit later on but had time to spare for a stroll.

So, with sweaters over their summer clothes, they set off around the bay, the girls stopping every so often to collect shells in their buckets, Daisy observing the patches of woodland that fringed the shore. Having spent most of the time on the beach up until now, they hadn't walked as far as this before so this bit of the landscape was new to her.

'Well, has the place lost some of its magic now that you've seen it in the rain?' asked Jack.

'Not on your life,' she assured him. 'The rain has freshened everything up and made it even better.'

'You won't say that if it rains every day for the rest of your holiday,' he grinned.

'You can bet I won't,' she admitted with a smile. 'But I'm sure I'll still love the place whatever the weather.'

'Let's hope the sun comes out so you're not put to the test,' he remarked casually.

They ambled on in comfortable silence. The girls were dragging behind, poking about in the rock pools.

'Wow! What a lovely house,' enthused Daisy as a large stone-faced property came into view through the trees. 'It's huge. Is it a private house or some sort of an institution?'

'It's a private house,' Jack informed her. 'I believe they call it a gentleman's residence. It's known as Gullscombe Manor.'

'It's beautiful,' she breathed, noticing a turreted roof and a veranda facing the sea.

'It used to be,' he corrected as they stared at the property, the rear of which was facing them. 'But it's been empty for ages and just left to rot.'

'Who owns it?'

'A wealthy businessman; retired now, though, and getting on a bit in years,' he told her. 'He's got pots of money.'

'You'd need it to maintain a place like that,' was Daisy's opinion.

'You're right there.'

'So what happened to the owner?'

'No one knows for sure. Rumour has it that he's gone to live with his married daughter in Exeter.'

'What, just moved out and left the place?'

Jack nodded. 'They say he went a bit soft in the head after his wife died,' he explained. 'They'd lived there all their married life and he just couldn't cope with being there after she'd gone. It's all a bit sad really.'

'Mm. But surely one of his family could make sure the place was looked after,' Daisy suggested. 'Either that or sell it rather than leave it to deteriorate.'

'You'd think so, wouldn't you?' he agreed. 'Maybe he can't bring himself to take the final step of selling it. And perhaps his daughter doesn't fancy living in such a remote spot.'

'It's probably something like that,' remarked Daisy. 'But it's a terrible shame for it to be so neglected.' She paused, squinting at the house. 'What's it like at the front?'

'We'll go and have a look if you like,' he said. 'There's no one around to object.'

Having called to the girls, and helped them on with their shoes, they climbed up a sloping path through the trees into the gardens, which were extensive and very overgrown. Making their way through the long wet grass to the front, they came to a gravel forecourt at the end of a driveway leading to the road.

The house entrance was imposing, with wide stone steps leading up to double doors on which the varnish was dull and faded. Daisy peered through one of the dirty windows to see a large room with dust sheets covering the furniture.

'I bet the spiders are having a whale of a time in there with all those cobwebs,' she said, shivering at the thought. 'It's creepy, as though it's got caught in a time warp, as though life suddenly stopped in there.'

'That is what happened when his wife died,' Jack told her. 'He just upped and left.'

'What will happen to it ultimately, I wonder?'

'I suppose eventually it'll be sold,' he suggested. 'Or the owner's daughter and her husband will take it over.'

'It certainly needs urgent attention, so let's hope something happens sooner rather than later,' she commented. 'Before it gets any worse.'

'Mm.' Noticing that the skies were darkening, Jack said, 'Anyway, I think it's about to chuck it down with rain so we'd better find some shelter.'

He was right. The heavens opened and they made a dash for the only protection they could find, the veranda at the back of the house. It was an attractive structure with mosaic tiles underfoot and intricate laced metalwork arched between the supporting pillars. There were glass doors leading into the house through which they could see a spacious room in which dust covers were a dominant presence.

'This is handy for us, and very pretty too,' observed Daisy as the downpour drenched the gardens and bounced on to some decrepit wooden garden furniture. She turned and peered through the glass doors. 'They must have really lived in style. The rooms are enormous.'

'You wouldn't buy a place like this unless you could afford to live in style, would you?' he mentioned.

'No, not unless you bought it for commercial use,' she remarked casually, 'to change into a nursing home or something.'

Jack nodded, looking at his watch.

'Oh dear. Are you going to be late for work?' Daisy looked worried.

'Not yet. But I do need to keep an eye on the time,' he told her. 'Alan's being very good about my having time off, but I don't want to upset him, especially as I want some time off next week.'

'Don't get into trouble at work on our account,' she advised him. 'You don't have to stay home from work because of us. The girls and I will be fine on our own.'

'I know that but I want to spend time with you,' he said, taking her hand and squeezing it in a sudden impulse. 'I enjoy your company.'

'The feeling's mutual,' she blurted out, instinctively moving closer to him. 'I just don't want you to put yourself out any more than you already have.'

The atmosphere changed from warm and friendly to vibrantly intimate but was shattered almost instantly by the two girls running out into the rain in sheer devilment.

'Come back in here, you two,' called Daisy. 'Your clothes will get soaked.'

Shirley raised her face to the rain. 'It feels lovely, Mum,' she called, lifting her arms. 'It's washing my face and making the garden smell nice.'

Belinda copied her sister, tilting her head back to let the rain soak her face and hair. 'It doesn't feel cold, does it, Sherl?'

'No. It feels smashing.'

Daisy could understand them being inspired to do this because she too was tempted to run out into the rain. She felt so alive she wanted to touch the elements. But the sensible, maternal side of her nature prevailed. 'I'm sure it's really good fun but come into the shelter just the same,' she said with as much authority as she could muster in her carefree mood. 'We're going in a minute, as soon as the rain eases off a bit.'

They did as she said, and stood dripping on the veranda, giggling at the sheer boldness of getting soaked through with their clothes on.

Jack smiled. 'What it's like to be a kid, eh?' he said. 'They make you remember, bring it all back.'

'Those two aren't concerned with practicalities like drying wet clothes or catching cold,' Daisy said. 'Kids just follow their instincts. And boring old Mum had to go and spoil it all by being sensible.' She sighed. 'Still, childhood is short enough. I want them to enjoy it to the full.'

The rain stopped quite suddenly and they headed back towards the cottage, the girls running on ahead, eager now to get changed into dry clothes.

'Oh, by the way,' Jack said as they walked along the beach and the cottage came into view, 'I've been thinking about your search for the Dodds and I've got a suggestion.'

'Oh, yeah?'

'You've been thinking in terms of finding a way of finding them, which, as you've indicated, is an impossible task when you've no idea at all where they might be, and both you and June have other commitments. Right?'

'Yes, that's right,' she confirmed. 'We can't afford a private detective.'

'Maybe you should change your strategy altogether and have them come to you,' he told her intriguingly.

'How on earth would we do that?'

'This is how . . .' he began.

The following week passed all too quickly. After the rain on Sunday, the sun reappeared on Monday, and Daisy and the girls returned to their glorious outdoor routine. They were joined by Jack whenever he could get away from the hotel and Daisy was aware of a tacit closeness growing between them.

He arranged to have the whole day off on Friday as it was their last day. In the morning he drove Daisy and the girls into Torquay to buy gifts to take home. They didn't have much money but, because Jack had refused to take anything for their food, they were able to afford a few modest presents.

The many gift shops were filled with novelty items and they had fun choosing what to buy. Daisy bought a jewellery box made of seashells for June to put on her dressing table, and a china cat with ginger fur and luminous green eyes for Nora because she was very fond of cats. For Nat she purchased a cigarette case.

Shirley bought her aunt and surrogate grannie each a comb in a leather case with 'Torquay' boldly displayed in gold letters. Belinda treated them each to a large, Cellophane-wrapped pink seashell filled with sweets that looked like pebbles.

They all had a good laugh in one of the shops at a hideous duck ornament that looked as though it had been thrown together. It had a bright yellow beak that was crooked and shaped in such a way as to give the impression that the bird was laughing.

'Honestly, some of the stuff they expect you to part with your money for,' disapproved Daisy, but she couldn't help but smile at the grinning artefact.

'You don't like it then?' said Jack.

'Of course I don't. How could anyone like such a shoddy piece of workmanship? Whoever made it must have been drunk when they put it together. The whole thing's lopsided.'

'This probably makes me the king of bad taste but it actually appeals to me,' he confessed, picking it up and examining it more closely. 'I like it.'

'You can't possibly like it,' said Daisy in disbelief. 'You're teasing us.'

'No. I'm not, honest. I really think he's great,' he told the amazed Daisy with a devilish grin. 'And at least you wouldn't be miserable with it in the house because it makes you laugh just to look at it.'

'You laugh with the sheer awfulness of it,' was Daisy's opinion.

'I gather you're not going to take it back to London as a souvenir of Torquay then?'

'Not on your life,' she replied without hesitation.

Because they were catching an early train back to London the next morning, Daisy needed to have all but the last-minute packing done before they went to bed that night. This created an air of gloom because it reminded them that their departure was imminent and meant they had to come off the beach earlier than usual.

Still at least Jack wasn't working, and as it was their last night he and Daisy agreed that the girls could stay up to eat with them. So while Daisy bathed the girls and did the bulk of the packing, Jack went to get fish and chips for them all from a shopping parade further up the coast that was just a few minutes away on his motorbike.

When he got back Daisy had laid the table and the girls were in a silly mood, giggling and spluttering behind their hands.

'Have you two got ants in your pants again?' he asked, making them laugh all the more.

When they all sat down at the table and he saw a package wrapped in fancy paper by the side of his plate, he began to understand.

'I've had the devil's own job keeping them quiet about it all afternoon,' Daisy explained.

'What's this?'

'Just a little something to say thank you for giving us such a wonderful holiday,' she told him.

He looked at her sternly and then the girls. 'You shouldn't have,' he said, looking delighted despite his protests. 'There's really no need. I've loved having you.'

'Open it then,' urged Shirley.

'Go on,' added Belinda, jumping up and down in her seat.

The removal of the wrapping revealed a book on the history of motorcycles. Jack was so touched by their thoughtfulness, he couldn't speak for a moment.

202

'Don't you like it?' Shirley looked anxious.

'I love it.' He got up and gave them each a hug. 'I really love it. It's so kind of you.'

'We think you deserve it for putting up with us for two weeks, don't we, girls?' said Daisy.

The girls nodded, still seeming a bit odd, he thought. There was still plenty of giggling going on.

'We did our secret shopping when you'd had enough of trailing around the shops and went for coffee and left us to it,' Daisy explained.

'I knew I shouldn't have let you loose on Torquay town on your own,' he joshed. 'But thank you all very much for the book. I shall treasure it, always.'

'Um, that isn't quite all,' said Daisy, looking at Shirley, who left the room and returned with another package.

'This is an extra thing that Mum thought you might like,' she said, handing it to him.

Curiously he tore off the wrapping paper. A roar of laughter went up as he held up the laughing duck ornament.

'Something to remember us by,' Daisy grinned. 'You might have awful taste in ornaments but you're a wonderful host.'

Now there were tears clearly visible in his eyes and they were not entirely from laughing.

'Thank you.' His gaze focused on Daisy and they both knew that this was her gift to him and it was an adult thing. Then he looked at the children and added, 'I shall put him on the kitchen windowsill to cheer me up when I'm washing the dishes. I shall think of you all every time I look at him.'

Even the girls picked up on the emotion in the air and were subdued.

'Come on then, everyone,' urged Daisy in a rousing tone to get things back to normal. 'Eat your fish and chips before they get cold.'

'The holiday's gone so quick, I can hardly believe it's over,' said Daisy to Jack later that evening after the children had gone to bed. 'This time tomorrow the girls will be in their own beds at home.'

He nodded gloomily. 'And you?' he said in a querying tone. 'Will you be seeing Nat?'

'Depends if he remembers we're coming home and comes round,' she told him.

'Will you go to his place if he doesn't turn up?'

'No.' She wasn't in the mood to go into much detail about the peculiar nature of her relationship with Nat, especially as she knew Jack would disapprove. 'I'm tied because of the girls so he always comes to me. It's a habit we've slipped into over the years.'

'I see.'

They were in the living room, having a last cup of coffee together, she on the sofa, he in an armchair. They'd been sitting here talking since the girls went to bed, the tension becoming unbearable for Daisy as the evening drew to a close.

'Well, I suppose I'd better be making my way towards bed as we've got to be up early in the morning,' she said, finishing her coffee and standing up.

He got up too, his blue eyes fiercely bright. 'I don't want you to go, Daisy,' he said quickly.

'I can't stay up all night,' she said.

'That isn't what I mean . . .'

She met his eyes. 'I know,' she said softly, 'and I don't want to leave tomorrow either.'

'Marry me, Daisy,' he blurted out.

'What!'

'I love you and I want to marry you.'

She stared at him, his words echoing in the silence. He was as shocked as she was by his proposal.

'Don't be daft, Jack,' she said at last. She was thrilled by what he'd said but it was too sudden, too impossible to be taken seriously. 'Don't mess about.'

He shook his head, as though in disbelief at this unexpected turn of events. 'I had no intention of proposing to you. It just sort of came out. But I'm serious,' he said, his eyes never leaving her face. 'I've fallen in love with you. And I think . . . well, I hope that you feel the same about me.'

She bit her lip, absently combing her hair back from her brow with her fingers. 'Maybe I do feel something but it'll be just a holiday thing.' She was afraid of the strength of her feelings. Here with Jack everything seemed possible but, as the mother of two children, she had to keep her feet planted firmly on the ground. 'All this sunshine and fresh air has gone to my head.'

'It's more than that and we both know it,' he contradicted ardently. 'Don't go back to London. Stay here with me.'

Overwhelmed, she tried to keep things light to hide how deeply she felt for him. 'If I were to stay here, the novelty would soon wear off for you, believe me, under the strain of everyday life and having two noisy kids under your feet.'

'Why not stay and give me the chance to prove you wrong?' he suggested.

She shook her head. 'I can't, Jack. It's all happened too fast. I can't be irresponsible, not with two kids relying on me.'

'Look, this might sound a bit sloppy but I felt something special for you when we first met back in the spring,' he confessed. 'I know we haven't known each other long but these past two weeks have been the most wonderful time of my life. And I know you well enough to know that I love you and I want to be with you . . . and the girls – for the rest of my life.'

Suddenly Daisy didn't want to protest. She didn't want to be sensible and think about the impossibility of a future for her and Jack. She didn't want to consider tomorrow and the parting she knew must come. No one had ever looked at her in the way Jack was looking at her now, as though she was the most important person on earth. All she could think of was what she could see in Jack's eyes, and knew she would never see again after tonight. The only thing that seemed to matter was her feelings for him at this moment.

'Come here,' she said, reaching out for him.

'No, Jack, no,' Daisy said, pulling away from him and dragging her blouse into place. 'I can't do this.'

'All right, don't panic,' he told her, drawing back quickly, his voice quivering slightly. 'I'm not going to force you into anything.'

'I shouldn't have led you on. I'm sorry,' she said, her hands trembling as she sat at the far end of the sofa, doing up her blouse. 'I got carried away.'

'Things got a bit out of hand, that's all,' he assured her. 'It wasn't your fault.'

'I hope you don't think I make a habit of leading men on.'

'Of course not. Why would I think that?'

'It's all right, it's just me being ultrasensitive,' she told him with a wry look. 'Being an unmarried mum brands you in the eyes of most people.'

'Not in mine,' he said. 'Things moved faster than we intended but it was only natural. We're a pair, you and me. We have a wonderful future ahead of us, you, me and the girls.'

Reality hit home like a physical blow. What was she doing allowing things to go this far? Had she lost her mind? 'No, Jack. Now is all there is,' she stated solemnly. 'I have to go home tomorrow.'

'Surely you're not going back to London as though nothing's changed.' He was distraught.

'Nothing's changed as far as my life there is concerned.' She was ignoring her heart and speaking from her mind because she knew she must be sensible. 'This . . . us, is lovely but it isn't the stuff of real life.'

'What we have is about as real as it gets,' he argued.

'I know it feels like that now but . . .' The sound of a child's voice calling to her from upstairs brought her even more firmly down to earth. When she came back downstairs, having given Shirley a drink of water, settled her and been reminded of her serious responsibilities, she was even more convinced that she must control these bewildering new feelings. 'There can't be a future for us and I shouldn't have let you think otherwise.'

Jack got up and paced around the room. 'You and I are right together,' he declared, standing still and looking down at her sitting stiffly on the sofa. 'Surely that's the most important thing.'

'In a sentimental love story it would be, but this isn't fiction and I'm not some teenager with no responsibilities. I have to go home tomorrow and get on with my life.'

'So, I mean nothing to you?'

'You know that isn't true. You mean the world to me,' she was quick to assure him. 'But nothing can come of it.'

'You're saying it's over between us then?'

'Oh, Jack, what is there to be over?' she said, spreading her hands in a gesture of helplessness. 'We've had two weeks together, that's all.'

'Don't trivialise something that means a lot to me,' he admonished sharply.

'It means a lot to me too,' Daisy made clear, 'but I'm a realist and I know that holiday romances rarely last.'

'This isn't just a holiday romance,' he insisted. 'We were drawn to each other when we met last spring. Now that we know each other better it's developed into something special. You must admit that's true.'

'I don't deny feeling something special for you, but I have commitments.'

'Nat, I suppose.'

'That's right,' she said, but there were many more confusing elements to it than that.

'You're not married to him,' he reminded her. 'You're not even officially engaged.'

'No, but he is the father of my children.'

'Are you in love with him?' he blurted out.

Once she would have said yes without hesitation. But she'd been disillusioned with Nat and much less besotted even before she'd met Jack, who was a better man than Nat would ever be. She still cared for Nat, despite all his faults, but she wasn't in love with him. Not now. But to marry her daughters' father was her long-held dream. There was a completeness in it somehow and she didn't feel able to let it go.

'I still feel something for him, yes.'

'That doesn't sound like a proclamation of love to me,' Jack said, his anger rising. 'It sounds more as though he's a habit you're afraid to break.'

'Don't get cross, please, Jack.' Daisy's eyes were full of regret. 'What you and I have shared this past two weeks has been wonderful, like nothing I have experienced before. And I'll never forget it. But that doesn't mean it will last.'

'I don't agree.' He was adamant. 'We have all the right ingredients to make it work.'

'There are too many complications . . .'

'Nothing that can't be resolved,' he told her. 'You'd be happy living here. I know it's right for you. The girls would love it and there's a school the other side of the village. It's a good place to bring children up. And think how healthy you've felt since you've been here. The air agrees with you. You've said so yourself.'

Daisy knew he was right and she wanted to stay more than anything. But her down-to-earth nature just wouldn't allow her to cut the ties with her other life. She'd never had any real stability and was afraid to leave her home and her job for a man she hardly knew and a relationship that could fizzle out under the strain of everyday life. Thinking she was in love with Jack wasn't enough to build a whole new life. She was a realist, used to hardship and disappointment. She couldn't believe that her life would change.

'And what would I do for money?' She was so accustomed to supporting herself and the girls, she couldn't imagine anything else. 'Move in here and sponge off you?'

'How can you sponge off me if you're my wife?' he wanted to know. 'I want to marry you, to look after you and support you . . . and the girls. So you wouldn't have to go out to work.'

'Oh . . .' She'd never imagined a man would ever be this caring to her. 'You're such a good man, Jack.'

'Of course, if you wanted to go out to work, I wouldn't try and stop you,' he added quickly. 'An experienced waitress is always in demand in Torquay. But you wouldn't have to work. The choice would be yours.'

'It's mostly seasonal work around here, I should imagine,' she commented. 'Anyway, as I'm not staying, that's neither here nor there.'

'Why do you have to go back to Nat?' He was fighting for her now so the truth must be told. 'If he was going to marry you he'd have done it years ago.'

'That is one way of looking at it.'

'Why keep fooling yourself then?'

She sighed. 'I suppose it's because Nat and I go back a long way and he's the girls' father,' she tried to explain, thinking it through as she spoke because she was still very confused.

'I can see that his being the girls' dad would create a bond between you and I would never want to come between a man and his children. But if he made you happy, this thing that's grown between us this past fortnight wouldn't be there, and we wouldn't be having this conversation.'

In a moment of clarity, she realised that happiness wasn't something she'd ever expected to have with Nat. It was the familiar pattern of her life that was drawing her back – a case of the devil she knew, perhaps. 'You can't just snatch what seems good in the moment and hope for the best for the future, not when you've got two kids.'

'You're entitled to grab the chance of happiness, though.'

'That isn't my way, Jack.'

He wasn't ready to give up. 'Would it make any difference if I was prepared to move to London to be with you?'

'No. London isn't the issue,' she told him. 'Anyway, you'd hate living there.'

'Yes, but I'd do it if it meant having you,' he stated gravely. 'That's how much you mean to me.'

Daisy was shocked by the depth of his feelings for her. No one had ever felt that much for her before and it was a huge responsibility. Marriage and a proper family life was all she'd ever wanted. Now she was being offered it and she wasn't in a position to take it. She wanted to seize the moment and accept Jack's proposal. He'd shown her what it felt like to be truly loved by a man. But she still felt bound to the father of her children.

'Jack, you're a great bloke and you'll always be very special to me but I'm going to stay with my old life,' she said. 'It's what I know; what I'm used to.'

Something about her tone must have finally convinced him that she wasn't going to change her mind because his manner became one of cool resignation. 'It's your decision, of course. But I think it's the wrong one.'

'I'm sorry.'

'Don't be,' he said coldly. 'I don't have the right to make you do anything you don't want to do.'

'Jack—'

'I have no claim on you.'

'No, but—'

'It's a simple misunderstanding.' His manner was piercingly abrupt and she knew how much she had hurt him. 'I really believed that you and I had something.'

'And we do,' she told him with emphasis. 'But it can't be permanent.'

'It could be if you wanted it,' he declared briskly. 'But you don't, so let's forget it.'

'Don't be like that, Jack, please.' She felt awful.

'Would you like a drink of something before you go to bed?' he offered, ever the gentleman.

'No, thanks,' Daisy said. 'But I would like you to stop behaving like the perfect host.'

It was as though he'd shut himself off from her. 'I'll go on up to bed if you don't want anything,' he said in a formal tone. 'See you in the morning.'

'Yeah,' she said dismally to his retreating back.

She stayed where she was for a while, too distressed to move. Eventually she made her way slowly up the stairs. Pausing outside his room, she reached for the door handle and almost touched it. But common sense finally prevailed and she moved on to the room she shared with her daughters and closed the door quietly behind her. She suspected that she'd just made the biggest mistake of her life but felt forced by circumstances to stand by her decision.

Chapter Thirteen

Daisy and the girls were out shopping with June and Nora in Portobello market. Weaving their way through the Saturday morning crowds, they purchased the weekend supply of fruit and vegetables, fresh flowers to brighten up the house, some fish and eggs, a joint of meat for Sunday dinner and a variety of other eatables.

They lingered at an antique stall where an oddly dressed man in a jauntily angled straw hat and a long black tailcoat was in the middle of an entertaining spiel on a rare item, a fine china cricket cage, which he claimed had been especially made for a rich oriental gentleman over two hundred years ago. According to the flamboyant trader's story, the man's servants would have collected the insects and put them into the cage where they would chirrup musically for the entertainment of their owner.

The crowd were taking a lively interest in what he was saying until the price of the unusual artefact was mentioned.

'Five quid for that piece o' junk? Don't make me laugh,' said someone.

'You'd have to pay me to take that lump o' rubbish off your hands,' added another.

'You want your head tested, mate, if you think anyone'll pay two bob for that, let alone five nicker,' came another disparaging utterance.

'Not very nice for the poor little crickets, being caged in,' was a typically soft-hearted reaction from Nora as the crowd began to disperse. 'Downright cruel, I reckon.'

'Have we finished then?' asked Daisy, as they were all weighed down with shopping bags.

Nora examined the list. 'Yes, that's about it for today,' she confirmed.

'I must just pop down to Notting Hill Gate to get my skirt from the dry-cleaner's,' June told them. 'I need it for work on Monday. You can start walking home if you like. I'll catch you up.'

'No. Let's all take a wander down there and have a cuppa coffee and a bun in the ABC,' suggested Daisy.

As the idea was greeted with approval, they left the market crowds behind and walked to the bustling shopping parade at Notting Hill Gate. While June went to Sketchleys, the others had a look round

Woolworth's. Moving on past the Gaumont Cinema on their way to the teashop, Daisy noticed a sign in the window of an antique dealer's which read, 'STREET WIDENING MEANS WE MUST MOVE – STOCK CLEARANCE SALE.'

There were similar announcements in several of the shops around here.

'We won't recognise the old place when they've finished knocking it about, will we?' remarked Daisy.

'I hope we still can.' Nora looked concerned. 'It could do with smartening up but I hope they don't change it beyond recognition when they do finally do it.'

' "When" being the operative word,' expressed Daisy, because the Notting Hill Gate road widening and redevelopment scheme had been on the cards for years. 'The council have been talking about it for long enough.'

'Have they really?' enquired June, who had met them outside Woolworth's.

'The idea goes back to the last century,' informed the knowledge-able Nora, who was a member of a local history society and took a keen interest in local affairs. 'But it wasn't finally approved until the nineteen thirties, then had to be postponed because of the outbreak of war. The latest news I've heard is that it's definitely scheduled to go ahead in the next year or two.'

'I'll believe that when I see it,' was Daisy's opinion.

'I think most people feel like that about it,' said Nora.

They reached the ABC – proudly declaring itself to be 'London's Popular Caterers' on the awning outside – and settled down at a table in the cafeteria with their elevenses.

'Just think, Daisy, a little over a week ago you were living it up by the seaside,' mentioned June conversationally, spreading a small pat of butter on her currant bun and trying, unsuccessfully, to make it reach the edges.

'I wouldn't call what we did "living it up" exactly,' said Daisy, sipping her coffee. 'It was all simple pleasure. But, yes, we were enjoying ourselves, weren't we, girls?'

'Cor, yeah,' enthused Shirley.

'I wish we were still there,' sighed Belinda.

'Are you telling us that you'd rather be at the seaside with Mummy than here at home with your Auntie June and me?' teased Nora.

'I'd rather we were all at Gullscombe Bay seaside than here,' the child clarified. 'You and Auntie June too.'

'So would I,' said her sister.

'Maybe the three of you can go again next year as you liked it so much,' suggested June, winking at the girls, then looking meaning-fully at Daisy.

'We'll see.' Daisy was noncommittal but she knew she wouldn't go again. It would be far too complicated.

June gave her a close look. 'You did enjoy yourself, didn't you, Daisy?'

'Yeah, of course I did. Why?'

'Because the girls haven't stopped talking about it since they got back,' June pointed out. 'But you've been noticeably quiet.'

'I've told you, I had a wonderful time.'

'You certainly look better for it, anyway,' approved Nora.

'Positively blooming,' agreed June. 'Back at work and ready to take the world on.'

'That's right,' confirmed Daisy.

'Why so quiet then?' persisted June.

'Probably an anticlimax,' suggested Nora.

'You got on all right with Jack, didn't you?' June was being persistent because she wanted to make sure there had been no problems with the holiday she'd arranged for her sister. 'And everything was all right with the accommodation?'

'Everything was perfect at the cottage, and Jack and I got on like a house on fire.' Daisy hadn't been able to stop thinking about him all week, his wide smile, his warm eyes. Anticlimax wasn't the word for how she'd felt this past week. Hell would be nearer to it, without Jack around. Knowing she'd made the right decision – or rather the only possible decision – didn't help much either.

Nat had picked up on her mood this past week. He'd accused her of being preoccupied and not paying enough attention to him, which he thought was a bit much as he'd agreed to her going away and had even shelled out some spending money. He hadn't seemed particularly pleased with the cigarette case she'd brought back for him either; he preferred to use fags straight from the packet, apparently. She'd been irritated by his ingratitude; had found herself comparing him to Jack. That was unfair and pointless, and would have to stop.

But now she found herself wondering what Jack would be doing at this moment. She looked at the big clock on the wall. It was eleven o'clock. He wouldn't have gone to work yet so he might have gone for a swim or be tinkering with that motorbike of his. Whatever he was doing, she wished she was still there with him.

June recalled her to the present, waving her hand in front of Daisy's eyes. 'Penny for them,' she said.

'I was just wondering,' she fibbed – because what had happened between her and Jack was too precious and delicate to talk about at the moment, and the subject she was about to raise needed discussion anyway – 'if you've thought any more about that idea I mentioned to you about finding the Dodds? The one that Jack came up with?'

'Yes, I've thought about it.' June pondered for a moment. 'And

213

although it's a bit of a long shot, I think we should do it. I don't know why we didn't think of it before.'

'Me neither.' Daisy turned to Nora. 'What do you think?'

'It's worth a try.'

'Good,' said Daisy. 'Let's have a proper discussion about it tonight when I get back from work.'

The two other women nodded in agreement.

'In the meantime, let's finish here and get the shopping home,' Daisy suggested. 'I'm on duty at four o'clock this afternoon to serve the teas so it would be useful to me if we could have our lunch a bit early, if that's all right with you.'

'Sure,' agreed June.

'Suits me,' added Nora.

They left the café soon after, chatting in a friendly manner. But Daisy wasn't paying attention to what was being said; her thoughts were lingering on a certain cottage by the sea.

Jack was thinking about Daisy at that time too. He was washing his hands at the kitchen sink after messing about with his motorbike when he noticed the laughing duck grinning at him from the windowsill.

He dried his hands and picked it up, remembering the moment he'd received it and feeling again the joy that had filled the house at that time. It brought Daisy so close to him he could hear her laugh, smell her hair, feel her skin. He put the ornament back on the windowsill, smiling despite the mood of melancholy that had settled over him since Daisy and the girls had left. He couldn't have Daisy and that broke his heart. But they'd had two wonderful weeks together and if that was all there was, it was better than nothing.

Grinning to himself as he recalled Daisy's disgust at his taste in ornaments, he made a cup of coffee and took it into the garden to read the newspaper in the sunshine until it was time to get ready for work.

One autumn morning in the back garden of a small house in a quiet Ruislip street, a thin, grey-haired woman wearing a floral apron over a dowdy grey jumper and skirt, was pegging the last of her washing on the line. She was hoping that her next-door neighbour – who was also in her garden doing the same thing – wouldn't try to engage her in conversation over the fence. It was a Monday morning so washing was flapping in the wind in rear gardens the length of the street.

Her hopes were dashed when the neighbour said, 'Good morning.'

'G'morning,' responded Eileen Dodd coolly.

'Looks like it's gonna be a good drying day,' commented the neighbour in a friendly manner.

'Mm.'

'And thank God for that too,' the woman went on. 'Nothing worse

214

than a wet Monday, is there? Wet washing all over the place, making everything steamy and damp. It always gives me the right hump.'

'Yeah.' Eileen kept her eyes down; she never looked at anyone when she spoke to them.

'There won't be many more nice days now that the summer is over,' the neighbour went on.

'I suppose not.' Eileen was moving towards the kitchen door as she spoke, in her eagerness to avoid any further dialogue. 'Ta-ta for now.'

'Ta-ta dear,' said the neighbour. 'See you again.'

Indoors Eileen made a sandwich with cold meat from yesterday's joint for her lunch, poured herself a cup of tea and went into the living room to eat it, her hand trembling slightly from the fright she had just had at being forced into conversation. That was what she had come down to: she was so introverted that just a few words with a next-door neighbour left her nerves in tatters. Any sort of social intercourse was difficult for Eileen, who was in her fifties and hadn't a friend in the world. It was just her and her husband, Morris, against the rest of the world.

Though that wasn't strictly true, she thought, slowly eating her sandwich. Morris wasn't with her against the world. He had a life of his own outside the house. As a representative for a fancy goods company, he met lots of people in the course of his work; he enjoyed a drink and a chat at the local, too. A gregarious man like Morris was never short of company.

Eileen hadn't always been a recluse. Years ago she'd had a normal life in Wembley with a happy marriage – or so she'd thought – and a social life.

Her life had changed so suddenly it was hardly believable in retrospect. One minute they'd been living an ordinary life in a quiet suburban street, the next they were the talk of the neighbourhood, her husband implicated in a murder case and his betrayal of his wife made public property by the newspapers. Immediately after the trial, they'd fled to an area where they weren't known. Morris would have been quite happy to stay put but she hadn't been able to cope with the shame, the gossip, the humiliation.

She'd known nothing of her husband's adultery with Rose Rivers until after the murder. The devastation she'd felt then still sent shock waves through her whenever it came into her mind. Rose had been a neighbour and friend. Suddenly she was Morris's dead lover. The whole terrible business had torn the heart out of Eileen; she'd never got over it.

The scandal of being associated with a murder investigation had never appeared to worry Morris. He'd even seemed to enjoy the notoriety. 'I've done nothing to be ashamed of, Eileen, except for being unfaithful to you, and that's nothing to do with anyone else,' he

215

would say to her as she became increasingly reclusive. 'Lionel Rivers killed his wife, not me, and he's doing time for it. So there's no need for either of us to hide away. Nobody around here knows about our past, anyway.'

It was as though he actually believed that neither of them had done anything wrong in lying under oath. He'd made a great performance of regret over the death of his lover and remorse at his adultery when giving evidence at Lionel Rivers' trial. After that he just carried on with his life as though nothing much had happened, as though having his wife commit perjury for him was no more than her duty.

At the time, he'd told her it would make things easier if she said he was at home with her when the murder had taken place. She was to tell the court that he'd come home early from the pub because he'd not been feeling well and had got home just after nine, having left the pub just before nine, as verified by the barman. He'd told her that he'd walked the streets for hours, after leaving the pub, working out how he was going to end his affair with Rose Rivers. But he couldn't prove where he'd been at that time and people might get the wrong idea. He was at pains to convince her that the only reason he'd asked her to say he'd been home at the earlier time instead of much later on, after she'd gone to bed, was not because he'd done the murder. Oh, no. It was just to prevent the police putting two and two together and making five.

In retrospect, she could see that she'd been extremely gullible to have believed him, and she didn't think she ever had, not in her heart. But telling herself what he said was true had been more acceptable than the alternative. It was hardly bearable for a woman to suspect that she was married to a murderer. As well as the horror, fear and revulsion, there were practical considerations. She was reliant on him to provide for her. If he'd gone to prison, her life would have been ruined as well as his because she would have had no means of support. Only the poorest or most exceptional married women had gone out to work back in those days before the war.

So she'd complied with his wishes, telling herself she was merely preventing complications and not protecting a murderer. Once the lies had been uttered in court, there had been no going back. She'd never forget the sheer terror of knowing that she had committed a criminal offence. She'd tried to blot out her crime and get on with life in an area where no one knew them. But compunction and fear had plagued her constantly, making her bitter and depressed. The Dodds' home had become a battleground for its occupants.

Then one night during an argument, Morris had confessed to the murder in a fit of temper. He'd even boasted about it. Even though he'd let it slip in a moment of reckless rage, he'd not been too concerned because he'd known his secret was safe with her. As he'd taken great pains to point out, she had too much to lose to open her mouth. If she went to the police she'd go down for a prison sentence for perjury.

So she'd remained silent, the past standing between them, a chilling and tangible presence. They coexisted with cold indifference and occasional violent arguments. She'd grown to hate him more with every passing day, loathing him for his arrogance, his unfaithfulness, his cruelty and cowardice in letting someone else pay the price for his crime. They slept in separate bedrooms and any sort of physical contact between them was carefully avoided apart from when he lost his temper and knocked her about. She guessed he made other arrangements in the sexual department. That didn't bother her. After the terrible things he'd done, continued adultery was nothing.

The only thing that kept them together was mutual fear. She was afraid of life without him as breadwinner; he feared she might put them both in jail if he wasn't on hand to remind her of the serious consequences for herself should she get tempted to unburden her guilty conscience.

Self-loathing for her weakness had made her withdraw into herself. Even when she was forced to work during the war, she'd not mixed with her workmates at the factory. The people around here knew nothing of her past but she still felt set apart from them, whilst at the same time longing for friendship. Her only outings were to the local shops, an occasional visit to the doctor and dentist and a rare trip to a hairdresser's for a perm. If she happened to meet a neighbour she couldn't avoid while she was out, she greeted them briefly then escaped into the security of her home. Fortunately, in this quiet suburban neighbourhood, people tended to keep to themselves anyway. The loneliness was terrible, though. It nagged away at her like a physical pain day after day.

But now she finished her lunch and picked up the newspaper, which they had delivered every day because Morris liked to read it in the evening. She always looked through it; it helped pass the time in her isolation.

Some film star called James Dean had been killed in a car crash at the age of just twenty-four, she noted. She'd read about him in the paper but not seen any of his films because she never went to the cinema. There was also an article about the new television programme called *Double Your Money* with Hughie Green. That was something she did have experience of, because Morris had done so well with sales recently, he'd bought a television set for the opening of commercial television, a week or so ago.

She flicked through the rest of the paper absently, thinking she must get on and wash the dishes, then give the kitchen a thoroughly good clean prior to the washing being dry enough to iron. Very much a slave to routine, she hated to deviate from her daily pattern. She was about to put the paper down on the coffee table ready for Morris to look at tonight, when something towards the back, in the personal column, leaped out at her. She blinked, thinking she must have imagined it. She stared hard at the print again, finding it difficult to focus because her hands were shaking so much.

'Would Eileen Dodd, last heard of at number three Laverstock Avenue, Wembley, in the 1930s please get in touch with Box No. 3350.'

Her initial reaction was a feeling of hope for escape from the prison she was in. One of her old friends from Wembley must want to get in touch with her for a reunion. It must be that. Who else would be trying to contact her? Warmth spread through her. How good it felt to have someone seeking her company, someone she'd have something in common with because she'd known them when her life had been normal. She'd had some good friends in Wembley at one time. But she hadn't been able to face them after what had happened so had cut herself off from them. When she and Morris had left the area they hadn't said goodbye to anyone or left a forwarding address.

But now someone was looking for her. On the heels of joy came disappointment. She couldn't respond to this. Anyone she knew from Wembley would know about her past. They didn't know the whole truth, of course, but they knew about Morris's public betrayal of her. She would be a laughing stock all over again and she simply couldn't face it.

But she looked longingly at the advertisement. Here was a chance to have company after all these years in the wilderness. To visit friends for tea, to go shopping with someone, all the ordinary everyday things other women took for granted. She stared at the words through a blur of tears as she accepted that she couldn't reply to it.

As a precaution, she carefully tore the advertisement out of the paper. If Morris spotted it he would force her to reply to it to see if there was anything of a financial nature in it for them, as was often the case when someone was being traced in this way. He would humiliate her all over again. She then screwed the piece of paper up and stuffed it in her apron pocket, collected her cup and plate and went to the kitchen to wash them.

'It doesn't look as though our plan is going to bear fruit, does it?' said Daisy gloomily, over a cup of bedtime cocoa one night in mid-October.

'It doesn't seem too hopeful,' agreed her sister, who was sitting on the sofa in her dressing gown with her legs curled under her. 'It's been two weeks since the advertisement went into the paper. If she was going to take the bait she'd have done so by now.'

'Not necessarily,' disagreed Nora. 'She could be busy and still

218

trying to find the time to get down to writing a letter. For all we know she might be out at work all day.'

'That's true,' said Daisy. 'We have no idea what her circumstances are. Or even if she's alive.'

'Maybe she smelled a rat,' suggested June. 'Or her husband saw the advertisement and he did. It could be that they're staying well clear, to be on the safe side.'

'I honestly don't think it's that,' was Daisy's opinion. 'As we agreed when we decided to give this a try, they wouldn't connect a notice in the personal column of a national newspaper with the murder. They'd think in terms of the police if anything had arisen about that. Anyway, it's such a long while ago she wouldn't expect anything to happen about it after all this time.'

'She'll think it's a friend or relative she's lost touch with, as we planned,' said Nora. 'That's the sort of thing personal columns are made up of. Unless, of course, they think someone's left them some money.'

'In which case they definitely would have got in touch,' reasoned Daisy.

'Maybe she just didn't see it,' was another idea of Nora's. 'It could be that she doesn't read that particular paper. I think if she did see it, she couldn't help but be intrigued. I mean, you would be, wouldn't you? That's just natural human curiosity.'

'Perhaps the second entry will bring us a result,' suggested Daisy hopefully. 'We got cheap rates for having it in twice so it isn't as if it cost us all that much more.'

'If it doesn't work we could think in terms of trying another one of the nationals,' said June.

There was a murmur of agreement from the others.

'It's going in on Friday this time instead of Monday,' mused Nora. 'Being a different day of the week might help. Some people have days when they don't have time to look at the paper and other days when they do.'

'Fingers crossed for Friday then,' said June.

'And in the meantime,' yawned Daisy, finishing her cocoa and standing up, 'my bed is calling.'

The others were of similar opinions so they took their cups into the kitchen, turned off the lights and went upstairs to bed.

June couldn't sleep but it wasn't thoughts of finding the Dodds that were keeping her awake. It was Alan. Every time she closed her eyes she could see his face, his warm eyes, his tender smile. The images just wouldn't go away. She wondered if she would ever stop missing him. Even now, more than a year since she'd left, she still wasn't over him.

Inevitably he would find someone else. Indeed, that was why she'd left, so that he could have a chance of a normal family life with a 'proper' woman. Maybe he was already seeing someone. She wouldn't blame him. The thought hurt even though she knew she was being unreasonable. Weary of tossing and turning, she got out of bed and made her way quietly downstairs, careful not to disturb anyone. She was in the kitchen waiting for the kettle to boil when her sister appeared.

'Another one who's tired of counting sheep, eh?' June surmised.

'That's right.'

'What's keeping you from your beauty sleep then?'

'Nothing in particular,' fibbed Daisy, because if she were to tell June the truth – that she'd been kept awake tonight and many other nights since her holiday by thoughts of Jack, whose marriage proposal she had turned down because she'd been afraid to let go of the past and move into a new, unfamiliar world – June would erupt into a fury of disapproval. Daisy had enough trouble coping with the decision herself; the last thing she needed was an argument about it. 'How about you?'

'I don't know what it is,' lied June, because she was dangerously close to confiding in her sister about the series of events that had led to her decision to leave Alan. She wanted to tell her everything she'd kept locked inside her for so many years. But to share the hideous secrets of her past in a weak moment would make her feel vulnerable and she knew she would regret it.

'Tea is supposed to keep you awake,' mentioned Daisy. 'But I'm going to have one anyway.'

'I'll risk it too,' said June.

They drank their tea at the kitchen table in a comfortable silence, each lost on her own thoughts. Then they made their way back upstairs to bed.

Alan was awake too that night, thinking first about June, then wondering what to do about Paula, whom he'd been seeing with increasing regularity since the late summer.

He cast his mind back to the previous evening. He and Paula had been out to a restaurant and he'd driven her home afterwards to the smart block of flats overlooking the sea where she lived. They'd sat in his car talking about business, as they so often did, and discussing the pros and cons of living on the job, which she preferred not to do. Although the conversation hadn't been of an intimate nature, he'd felt a change in the air and sensed that they'd been just a hair's breadth away from becoming lovers.

She'd invited him in for coffee. He'd wanted to accept but had politely declined because he'd known what would happen if he had, and wasn't sure if he wanted all the emotional upheaval that a change from friends to lovers would entail. He wasn't in love with Paula but he liked and respected her far too much to have an affair with her without commitment.

They were both on their own. He was lonely and so, he suspected, was she. His wife didn't want him. From the signals Paula was giving out lately she obviously wouldn't be adverse to a change in their relationship. So why not?

Looking at the question logically, he could see that Paula was the way forward for him. They would be good for each other. June wasn't going to change her mind, and he couldn't avoid a serious attachment for the rest of his life just because his marriage had failed.

One thing he did know for sure: he and Paula could no longer be just friends. It wouldn't work that way now that another element had made itself known. He sighed, sensing a certain inevitability about the situation.

'Oh no, not again,' complained Morris Dodd, staring through a large hole in the newspaper he was reading. 'I wish you wouldn't keep tearing great lumps out of the paper before I've had a chance to look at it, Eileen.'

'I didn't think it would matter as there was nothing of interest on the other side,' she told him. 'It was only an advert for cough mixture. I did check.'

'That isn't the point,' he grumbled. 'It makes the paper in such a mess and you know how I hate that.'

'Sorry.'

'It isn't as if it's the first time you've done it lately,' he went on irritably.

'I've said I'm sorry.'

'What was so important you had to tear it out, anyway?' he demanded.

'A recipe,' she lied.

'Oh really. Surely you could have left the paper intact until after I'd read it,' he admonished sternly. 'You could have torn your bloody stupid recipe out any time.'

'I can't see that it matters as there was nothing you'd want to see on the other side.'

'Well, it does matter to me,' he growled. 'You can do what you like with the bloody paper when I've looked at it but until then show a bit of respect, will you? As I pay the newsagent's bill I think I'm entitled to that much.'

'All right, there's no need to go on about it.'

He scowled at her, grunted and went back to the paper while Eileen stared absently at the wooden box in the corner. There was a serious play on the television and Morris didn't enjoy drama, apart from *Dixon of Dock Green*. Although the television set was still something of a novelty, Morris was selective in his viewing. He didn't like anything more demanding than sport, light comedy and variety shows.

Something seemed to have attracted his attention now, though, and he put the paper on his lap and stared at the screen. Eileen found herself observing him and thinking that he could still be considered an attractive man even though he was now in his fifties, and despite the fact that his dark hair was thinning and his figure gargantuan from his greedy appetite for food. He'd never been good-looking in the traditional sense – his dark eyes were too small, his nose too long. It was his personality that attracted women. He had a magnetism about him that was still very much in evidence, she guessed, even though it did nothing for her.

Eileen was having trouble concentrating on the television screen tonight, on account of what had really been on the bit she'd torn out of Morris's newspaper. Whoever it was who was looking for her must be serious about finding her to have put the notice in the paper again. Advertising in a national newspaper wasn't cheap. As well as being intriguing it was also rather worrying because if they put it in again and she missed it for some reason, Morris would spot it and take the matter out of her hands. The thought made her stomach churn.

But now he was bored with both the paper and the television apparently. 'I'm going out, down the pub,' he announced, getting up purposefully.

There was nothing new in that. It was Friday night and he always went out on Fridays. Whether he really went to the pub or had something of a more intimate nature lined up, she neither knew nor cared.

'All right,' she said indifferently.

'Don't wait up.'

'I won't.'

After the front door had closed behind him, she stayed where she was for a while, lost in thought. Eventually, she got up, went over to the sideboard and picked up her handbag. Hesitating for only a moment, she opened it and took out the crumpled piece of newspaper she'd removed earlier today and looked at it for a long time. Then, with her heart palpitating fit to burst, she took a writing pad out of the drawer, sat down at the table and began to write a letter, her hand trembling with a mixture of nervous apprehension and excitement.

Chapter Fourteen

Answering a knock at the front door one morning a week or so later, Eileen was confronted by two young women smiling at her on the doorstep.

'Yes?' she greeted in a cool, questioning manner.

'Good morning,' smiled the smarter of the two, who was tall, dark and slim, and carrying a small, brown attaché case.

'What do you want?' tutted Eileen, who wasn't about to indulge in doorstep small talk.

'We represent the Smithsons Vacuum Cleaner Company and we're in this area to tell people about the launch of our revolutionary new machine—'

'No thank you,' Eileen interrupted sharply. 'I already have a very good vacuum cleaner and I don't want another one.'

'But ours is no ordinary cleaner—'

'I never buy anything at the door.'

'And we don't sell at the door,' said the other woman, who was a tiny little thing, a bit on the shabby side, with big eyes and a shock of brown wind-blown hair.

'Why are you here then?'

The little woman moved closer to the door, which Eileen was about to close. 'Just for an informal chat.' She spread her hands. 'As you can see we have no cleaner with us to sell to you.'

'I don't care what sales pitch you're using,' the astute Eileen made clear. 'I said no and I mean it.'

'Would we be right in thinking that the man of the house isn't home at this time of the day?' the dark woman enquired.

'Of course he isn't at home,' was Eileen's sharp retort. 'He's out earning his living, like any other responsible man.'

'That's why we call on people during the day, initially. We like to speak to the lady of the house about our product,' said the little woman, her manner becoming chummy. 'As women, we all know that men haven't a clue about how housework is done so we prefer to speak to the people who actually do the job. A sensible idea, don't you think, Mrs, er . . .'

'Dodd,' she said without thinking. 'And yes, it is a good idea but

223

I'm still not going to buy a cleaner.'

'Look, I'll be straight with you.' The small woman moved her head forward and spoke to Eileen in a confiding manner. 'My colleague and I have to do a certain amount of preliminary presentations in the course of a working day, or we're in deep trouble back at the office. So . . .' she paused, smiling persuasively, 'I wonder if you could do us a favour and give us a few minutes of your time just so that we can put you down on our list of definite visits and stay sweet with the management.'

Eileen gave them full marks for persistence. She'd been married to a salesman for long enough to know that without tenacity you got nowhere in the job. Morris didn't sell door to door but the same principle applied to any form of selling. 'I'm too busy,' she said firmly. 'I'm sorry.'

'Ten minutes maximum,' the dark-haired woman requested insistently. 'Just let us come in to show you a few brochures, tell you how this new concept in cleaners works. Just so that we can put you down on our activity report for today.'

'And talk me into buying one of your cleaners at the same time,' was Eileen's cynical response.

'No, not at all,' denied the little one, who had a very pretty smile Eileen couldn't help noticing. 'Honestly, that isn't what we have in mind.'

'My husband has all the spending power in this house anyway, so you'd be on to a loser.'

'The men usually do,' the small woman agreed in an understanding manner. 'They earn the money so they say how it's going to be spent – that's the way it seems to work in most of the homes that we visit, anyway. So our policy is to tell the lady of the house about the cleaner and if they like what we have to say and are interested in seeing the cleaner, we come back in the evening when the husband is at home to do a demonstration for them both. In your case, of course, that won't happen because you've told us that you definitely don't want to buy one, and we respect that. So we'll just run through some brochures with you, fill in our time sheet and be on our way.'

'There wouldn't be any point in your coming back at another time with the cleaner because my husband won't buy from anyone selling door to door, anyway,' Eileen stated.

'That's perfectly understandable,' said the dark woman in a matey tone. 'Some of the door-to-door salespeople around give the rest of us a bad name by talking people into buying all sorts of rubbish. But we're not like that. Oh no. And in your case, all we want is your co-operation in keeping the boss off our backs. Just the chance to go through our brochures with you. You've nothing to lose except ten minutes of your time.'

224

Eileen looked from one to the other; she was beginning to weaken under the influence of their friendly enthusiasm. It was a refreshing change to have females selling at the door. Most of those working on the knocker were men who wouldn't take no for an answer until she slammed the door in their faces.

These two were persistent but nice with it, somehow. She thought of the lonely day ahead of her with not a soul to talk to. What harm could there be in letting them in for a few minutes to show her some brochures and tell her about their product? At least it would be human contact, and she'd made it clear that she wasn't going to buy from them.

'Ten minutes then,' she said, opening the door wider to let them in. 'When your time's up, you're out. Understand?'

'We understand,' said the small woman.

'Come on then, let's have a look at your brochures,' requested Eileen when she'd shown the two sales reps into the living room and offered them a seat.

The dark women opened her attaché case to reveal that it was empty. 'We don't have any brochures,' she said, turning the case upside down and shaking it to illustrate her point, her attitude now deadly serious.

'No brochures?' Eileen looked puzzled and somewhat annoyed. 'Why bother to talk me into letting you in then? How can you sell your cleaner without the product itself, or any sales literature?'

'We're not here to sell you a vacuum cleaner, Mrs Dodd,' said the little one.

'No?' Eileen was baffled. 'Then why—'

'We're here about this,' the dark woman told her, handing Eileen a newspaper cutting.

Eileen stared at it for a moment. 'You?' she said, looking from one to the other. 'You put that in the paper?'

'That's right,' the little one confirmed.

She gave them both a studious look, searching for some sort of recognition. 'I don't know you, so what was the advertisement all about?'

'We needed to find you urgently,' explained the dark-haired one. 'And now we have, thanks to your putting your address on your letter.'

'So it was all a trick to get into my house.' Eileen looked frightened now.

'Afraid so,' confirmed Daisy. Had they just knocked at her door and told her who they were, it would have been immediately slammed in their faces, which was why the rather elaborate subterfuge had been necessary.

'Who are you?' she demanded, her grey eyes darting from one to

225

the other. 'What do you want with me?'

'I'm Daisy Rivers and this is my sister, June.'

Eileen's eyes popped. Her face flushed momentarily, then became bloodless. She sat down heavily on the sofa as though her legs had buckled beneath her. 'Rose Rivers's daughters,' she gasped, her hand flying to her head. 'I would never have known you.'

'Well, you wouldn't do, would you?' June pointed out. 'Being that we were just little kids when you last saw us.'

'What,' Eileen began in a dry anxious voice, 'do you want with me after all this time?'

'Justice,' announced Daisy.

'Justice?' Eileen echoed fearfully, her eyes clouded with worry.

'That's right,' confirmed June. 'Our father has been in prison for over twenty years for the murder of our mother because you lied under oath to give your husband an alibi. And we intend to see to it that you put things right.'

The older woman sprang to her feet. She was visibly trembling. 'Get out,' she ordered in a quivering voice. 'Get out of my house this minute, before I call the police.'

Daisy gave her a hard look. 'We're not going anywhere until you've heard what we have to say,' she told her in a commanding tone. 'So sit down.'

'How dare you tell me what to do in my own house?'

'Sit down,' repeated Daisy.

'I could have you done for slander, saying I lied under oath,' protested Eileen weakly.

'You won't, though, will you? Because you know what we're saying is true.'

'I didn't do it,' Eileen insisted, sinking down on the sofa. 'I don't know what's made you think I did.'

'We don't just *think* you lied,' June amended evenly, 'we *know* you did.'

'Don't be ridiculous, you can't do.'

'We know that you were lying about your husband being at home with you at the time of our mother's murder because he was at the house where we lived,' Daisy informed her. 'And we know that because we saw him there.'

'Rubbish.'

'He saw us too,' June enlightened her. 'He threatened us with terrible things if we told anyone we'd seen him.'

From the look of sheer horror on Eileen's face it was obvious that Morris had told her nothing of his encounter with them that terrible night.

'He didn't tell you anything about that, did he?' surmised June.

'There was nothing to tell me,' she bluffed. 'Because he wasn't at

226

that house that night. As I told the court at the trial, he was at home with me.'

'Look,' began Daisy, stepping forward and looking down at her, 'all three of us know that isn't true so let's stop messing about.'

'Get out,' ordered Eileen again.

'It was your husband who murdered our mother and you damned well know it,' persisted Daisy. 'And it's time that terrible wrong was put right.'

'You've been imagining things,' claimed Eileen. 'You were just children back then. You couldn't possibly remember something that happened then, not after all this time.'

'We couldn't forget a thing like that,' June told her. 'Your husband put the fear of God into us in his anxiety to make sure we didn't spill the beans about his being there. We were too young to be questioned anyway so he was safe. As children we were powerless and no threat to him even though he was worried enough to terrorise us into keeping quiet. He made one fatal mistake, though. He didn't take into account the fact that one day we would grown up to be adults, and we would remember, and understand.'

'Childhood fantasies, nothing more,' Eileen taunted, becoming braver as she considered the flimsiness of their evidence. 'No one would believe a story like that.'

'Why did you commit perjury for such a man?' Daisy wanted to know. 'A man who had been unfaithful to you and humiliated you publicly, a man who killed his lover in a fit of rage. Was it because you were afraid of what he'd do to you if they didn't send him down for murder, was that it?'

'Or were you afraid of losing your breadwinner and your comfortable life?' added June.

The older woman didn't reply; she just sat there staring at her hands.

'If you were to make a confession to the police about what you've done and make it clear that your husband put pressure on you to lie for him, the courts might be lenient with you,' suggested Daisy hopefully.

Eileen clasped her head as though in pain. 'Stop it, stop saying these terrible things,' came her anguished cry. 'You tricked your way into my home and now you're behaving in a threatening manner. I could have the law on you.'

'You won't, though.' Daisy was confident about that. 'Because you wouldn't want to draw attention to yourself. You had enough of that in the past, when you lived in Wembley.'

'You've got nothing on me and my husband,' Eileen insisted, composing herself, 'so get out of my house.'

'We'll go,' complied Daisy. 'But just one thought before we leave, Mrs Dodd. For all these years you've thought you'd got away with

227

what you've done, believing it was just a matter between you and your conscience, that no one else knew. But you won't be able to rest easy any longer because you know that we know the truth, and one way or another we'll see that justice is done. You could make things easier for yourself by telling the police the truth because it's going to come out anyway, I promise you.'

'You're talking rubbish,' Eileen blustered. 'No one would take you seriously if you were to come out with your outlandish story.' She narrowed her eyes on Daisy. 'And you know that. Otherwise you'd have gone to the police already.'

She was right, of course, but Daisy wasn't going to admit it. 'What does it feel like to live with a murderer, knowing that you helped to put an innocent man behind bars, and robbed two little girls of their father?' she asked.

'I don't know what that feels like because I haven't experienced it.' Eileen was adamant. 'And if you stay here all day you won't get me to say different, so you might as well sling your hook.'

'We're going,' Daisy told her, moving towards the living-room door. 'But you haven't seen the last of us or heard the last of this matter, believe me.'

'We'll be back,' added June.

And they walked to the front door and let themselves out, leaving Eileen sitting on the sofa.

'You're bound to be disappointed that nothing more constructive came out of it,' said Nora that evening when, over cocoa, the three of them were doing a post-mortem on the incident. 'But we all knew she wouldn't admit to anything right away, didn't we? It was unrealistic to think that she would. It'll take time.'

'I suppose so, but it's such an anticlimax,' complained Daisy. 'I thought we were home and dry when we found out where the Dodds lived. But we're no further forward. Unless she admits she was lying we don't have a case. We got her rattled and we can do so again and again, but we can't make her confess.'

'What should our next move be, do you think?' wondered June.

'I honestly don't know,' confessed Daisy. 'It needs more thought. The one thing we mustn't do is give up now we've come this far.' She looked at June. 'Do you agree?'

'Absolutely.'

Daisy burst out laughing as she remembered something. 'I wonder what our chances are as vacuum cleaner sales reps,' she giggled.

'As you managed to get through the door without so much as a brochure between you, or a cleaner to demonstrate, you must have had some sort of a flair,' smiled Nora.

'We were pretty convincing,' boasted Daisy.

'All that stuff you gave her about us being in trouble at the office if she didn't let us in to do a presentation was nothing short of genius,' grinned June. 'I almost believed it myself.'

'I had to think on my feet when she seemed determined not to let us in.'

'It was brilliant,' complimented June.

Daisy's mood became grim again. 'Seriously, though, we have to think of a way to finish the job we've started. Now that we've come this close and found Eileen Dodd, there must be a way to get her to admit the truth.'

The other two women nodded in agreement but none of them knew the answer.

Nat came to the house late one night a few days later. He said he just happened to be passing and had called in to see Daisy.

'She isn't home from work yet,' June told him at the door.

'I'll come in and wait then,' he took it on himself to announce. 'She shouldn't be long.'

'Why don't you go and meet her?' suggested June, who didn't feel comfortable with him in the house after that disgusting incident in the summer when Daisy had been away on holiday. It hadn't been mentioned but she could tell by the way he looked at her sometimes that he hadn't forgiven her for rejecting him. 'She can't be further than the end of the street and she'll be thrilled to have you walk the rest of the way home with her.'

'Nah. It isn't worth it,' he said. 'She'll be here in a minute.'

Not wishing to be found quarrelling with him by her sister, June invited him in with reluctance, offered him a seat in the living room, and made herself scarce in the kitchen so that she didn't have to be alone with him. Nora was upstairs getting ready for bed and would probably come down in her dressing gown for a cup of cocoa later when Daisy got in.

June used the time to wash some cups from earlier and tidy the kitchen. She was drying her hands at the sink when the door opened and Nat swaggered in with a purposeful air.

'You after a cup of tea?' she asked. 'I thought you'd wait and have one with Daisy.'

'I don't want a cuppa tea.'

As his manner suggested that he'd come into the kitchen for some definite purpose, she said, 'What do you want then?'

'Isn't it obvious?'

'Not to me, no.'

'Surely you didn't think I'd forgotten what happened between us in the summer.'

'Nothing happened.'

229

'Exactly,' he said, coming towards her with a horrible smile on his face. 'And I aim to change that.'

'Daisy will be in any minute, so don't try anything.' She tried to sound firm but her voice was shaking.

'I'm not worried about Daisy.'

There was something very stage-managed about the way he was behaving that June found disconcerting.

'You touch me and I'll scream for Nora,' she warned. 'I mean it, so don't come any closer.'

But he moved so swiftly she didn't have a chance to do anything as he pushed her backwards against the sink, pressing his body against hers and clamping his hand over her mouth. Her heart sank as she distantly heard the sound of the front door opening and closing and Daisy's cheerful voice calling out, 'Hello, you lot, I'm home.'

June struggled but the element of surprise and his physical strength meant she didn't stand a chance. He dragged her arms around his neck and put his face to hers for a few horrible seconds, the smell of his sweat and stale cigarette smoke making her nauseous. She heard the kitchen door open and almost immediately he sprang away from her.

'Daisy,' he said, as though shocked to see her. 'Thank God you're back. She's been coming on to me for months . . . just wouldn't take no for an answer. Perhaps she'll stop now you've caught her at it.'

'Don't listen to him,' said June, observing with dismay the horror in her sister's eyes. 'He's lying because he wants to come between you and me. He knew you'd be home from work at any minute and he set this whole thing up.'

June reeled at the disgust exuding from Daisy as she looked from one to the other, then back at June, her eyes narrowed. 'Don't try and make any more of a fool of me than you already have,' she said to her sister icily.

'Daisy, no, it isn't what you think.'

'You're nothing but a tart, a filthy, rotten tart. I don't know why I ever trusted you.'

'It was him, please believe me . . .' June could feel her truthful words distorted to sound like lies by the damning appearance of the situation. 'He tried it on with me while you were away in Devon and he's done this to get back at me for turning him down then. He isn't interested in me. He just wants to hurt me by turning you against me.'

'I know now why you've never had a good word to say for him,' Daisy went on through gritted teeth. 'You wanted him for yourself so you tried to turn me against him and break us up, you scheming cow.'

'That just isn't true.' June's voice was ragged with emotion. 'Can't you see what he's up to?'

'I can see what's been going on under my nose. That was made very clear to me as soon as I opened this door.' She turned to Nat, who was looking triumphant. 'And as for you, I don't suppose you put up much of a fight against her. So get out of my sight. I never want to see you again.'

'What on earth's going on here?' asked Nora, appearing in her red dressing gown. 'You'll wake the children up in a minute with all this shouting.'

'Did you know about it?' asked Daisy.

'Know about what?'

'That these two have been at it like rabbits every time my back is turned,' she explained.

'Daisy, what are you saying?' was Nora's shocked response.

'You obviously didn't know. Well, they've been having an affair behind my back.'

'No!' gasped Nora.

'Yes. It's true, and I've just caught them at it.' She looked from Nat to June, her eyes full of hurt. 'You're welcome to each other and I want nothing more to do with either of you,' she said, and fled from the room.

Daisy sat on the edge of her bed, staring dismally at the floor. A grinding pain in the pit of her stomach was dragging her down, and she wasn't sure which hurt the most, Nat's betrayal or June's. She decided it was definitely the latter. She remembered that she herself has almost succumbed to temptation with Jack in the summer and knew how easily these things could happen. Nat had been unable to resist June's advances in the same way as Daisy had almost yielded to her passion for Jack.

Nobody was immune to this sort of thing. What cut so deep with Daisy was June's deceit in pretending to disapprove of Nat and trying to turn Daisy against him when all the time she fancied the pants off him herself.

There was a tap on the bedroom door.

'Go away.'

June came in anyway and stood tentatively just beside the closed door. 'I swear to God, Daisy, that it wasn't the way it seemed down there tonight,' she told her.

Her sister shrugged.

'Nat doesn't want me any more than I want him,' June went on to say, keeping her voice low because the girls were asleep in the next room. 'He hates the sight of me and I wouldn't have him if he came with the crown jewels as part of the package.'

'That's why you had your arms wrapped around him, is it?' said Daisy, looking up. 'God knows what I'd have seen if I'd been a few minutes later.'

'It was all a put-up job, can't you see that?' June tried to convince

231

her. 'This is his revenge on me for turning him down in the summer, and he only came on to me then to try and make a fool of me.'

'Don't make things worse by telling me a pack of lies.'

'I am not lying,' June told her. 'He knew exactly what time you'd be in from work tonight, and that you'd go straight to the kitchen if there was no one in the living room. You can't deny that's true. He came in and grabbed hold of me just seconds before you walked in so that you would see what he wanted you to see. He's trying to break us up, Daisy.'

'I know he isn't perfect but he isn't devious enough to come up with such a plan.'

'He is, Daisy, believe me.'

Daisy didn't respond; she sat staring at her feet, leaning forward slightly, her hands resting on her knees. 'I was so happy when you came back into my life, June,' she said sadly. 'After all those years, it was a dream come true for us to be together. The only thing that spoiled it was your disapproval of Nat, and you and I agreed to differ about that.' She looked up, her huge eyes heavy with disappointment. 'I'm not glamorous or sophisticated like you. There's only ever been one man in my life.' She paused, forced by her honest nature to correct this. 'Well, two actually. I got pretty close to Jack Saunders back in the summer.'

'Oh, really?' gasped June.

'You might find this hard to believe, but Jack asked me to marry him,' Daisy continued.

'Why on earth would I find that hard to believe?' June asked in astonishment.

'Because I'm not beautiful or refined.'

'Don't put yourself down,' admonished June angrily. 'You're very beautiful in a way that doesn't need make-up or smart clothes, as I do, and your manners are fine. This is what Nat's done to you. He's destroyed your sense of self-worth.'

'Maybe he has, I don't know. Anyway, that isn't the issue,' she went on. 'I was very tempted by Jack's offer, I admit. He's a really gorgeous bloke and I think the world of him. But in the end I chose the father of my children, the man I've been with for so long and who I believe does actually love me, despite what you think of him. And you have to wreck that for me.'

'Daisy, about tonight—'

'I feel sick to my stomach,' Daisy went on as though June hadn't spoken. 'To think that my sister, my own flesh and blood, could try to steal him from me.'

'I didn't—'

'Just leave it, will you?' Daisy cut in, putting her hands to her head wearily. 'I don't want to talk about it any more except to say that me

232

and the girls will be moving out of here as soon as I can find somewhere else.'

'Oh, Daisy, no, you can't . . .'

'Surely you can see that I can't stay here now,' Daisy told her. 'I don't want to share a roof with someone I can't trust.'

'You've got it all wrong.'

'Can you go now, please?' Daisy requested. 'Tell Nora I won't be down for cocoa tonight.'

Knowing it was useless to argue, a very dejected June left the room.

'You can cut the atmosphere in our place with a knife, the way those daughters of yours are carrying on, and I'm stuck in the middle of it,' Nora told Lionel, a week or so later. 'I think I'd be more comfortable sharing a cell with you than I am at home at the moment.'

He grinned. He enjoyed Nora's company and had grown to look forward to her visits. 'I very much doubt that. But what's the trouble at your place, then?'

She gave him a brief outline of what had happened. 'They're only speaking to each other when it can't be avoided and being polite in front of the children. It's breaking my heart to see them destroying something that means so much to them both. Finding each other after all those years apart was a gift. And now they're like two cats, wanting to scratch each other's eyes out the whole time.' She shook her head worriedly. 'Daisy's even looking for somewhere else to live.'

'Oh dear.' Lionel could see how concerned she was. 'Which one of them do you think is to blame?'

'Certainly not June. Daisy's being stubborn but it isn't really her fault either. Nat's the culprit here,' she had no hesitation in telling him. 'He obviously set the whole thing up, as June said, to break the sisters up. He's jealous of Daisy's relationship with June. June wouldn't be interested in him if he was the last man on earth. Neither she nor I can stand the sight of him. But Daisy can't see that. She's got a blind spot where he's concerned.'

'Have you tried talking to her?'

'I certainly have,' she told him. 'And she just accuses me of taking June's side because she knows I don't like Nat either. He's just using her and she can't see it – doesn't want to see it. I tell you, Lionel, it's given me no end of grief over the years, watching the way that man treats your daughter.'

'Daisy always strikes me as such a sensible sort of a girl too, not the type to be easily taken in,' he mentioned.

'Her feelings for Nat cut across her intellect, I think,' Nora explained. 'In every other area of her life she's full of common sense and she certainly doesn't let people trample on her. She's tough and independent, and has her eyes wide open about everything except this awful man she's got herself involved with.'

'I only wish I was in a position to do something to help.' He stroked his chin, looking worried. 'But I'm helpless being stuck in here . . .'

'You wouldn't be able to help even if you weren't stuck in here,' she pointed out. 'No one can help them on this one. The girls have to sort it out for themselves. And unless Daisy faces up to what Nat is really like, I can't see it having a happy conclusion. And if she can't see the truth about him after all these years, it isn't very likely to happen now.'

'What a shame.'

'It's an absolute tragedy.' Seeing how concerned he was she wondered if she'd done the right thing in telling him. 'Maybe I shouldn't have burdened you with it.'

'Don't be daft. I want news of my family, the bad as well as the good,' he assured her. 'I want to feel involved, even though I can't actually be there to help.'

Nora looked at him and saw hardship written all over that lined and craggy countenance. She so much wanted him to enjoy the pleasures of freedom again, to go out for a walk and feel the sun on his face. How good it would be if the girls were able to make this possible for him. They'd asked Nora not to tell him that they'd located the Dodds, partly because they didn't want to raise his hopes too high at this stage and also because he'd been so wary of them getting involved with Morris Dodd, it might worry him.

Anyway, with the girls being at loggerheads, Nora didn't know what would happen about their plans to help their father, except that they would continue, somehow, bad friends or not.

'You want to know about your family – I'll tell you what your granddaughters have been up to, then, shall I?' she suggested to cheer him up.

'Yes, please,' he said eagerly.

Ever since her falling out with June, Daisy had been studiously polite to her and very careful not to be rude to her in front of the children. So she was shocked to hear what Shirley had to say one morning at breakfast.

'Why are you and Auntie June always cross with each other now, Mummy?' she asked.

'What makes you think we're cross with each other?'

'You look cross and you don't seem to like each other much now,' she replied.

'We like each other,' said Daisy, exchanging a glance with her sister. 'Don't we, June?'

'Yes. Course we do.'

234

'Why are you being so horrid to one another then?' the child wanted to know.

'None of your business,' Daisy told her quickly. 'Now finish your breakfast, both of you. It's nearly time to go to school.'

'You're not supposed to be mean to people.' Shirley was determined to have her say. 'That's what you always tell me and Belinda when we have an argument. And that's what the nuns tell us at Sunday school.'

'Yeah, they do,' was Belinda's predictable contribution.

'Stop yapping, for goodness' sake, and finish your toast,' said Daisy, because she didn't want to have a lengthy discourse with a couple of children about something they weren't old enough to understand.

Daisy hated what was happening between her and June. It was tearing her apart. The barrier between them was more unbearable with every passing day. She wasn't an unforgiving woman; she wanted to put the whole thing behind them and carry on as before. But every time she thought of June and Nat together, anger flared towards June for destroying her trust. This battle was about Daisy and June rather than Daisy and Nat.

She'd valued the warmth of the burgeoning friendship with her sister and had looked forward to becoming closer in the future. All that had been swept away by June's betrayal. The last thing Daisy wanted was to move out of here, to drag the girls away from a home where they were happy to some awful little bedsit somewhere. But after what had happened, and the bitter resentment it had caused, she didn't think it would be fair to any of them to stay on. Every time she looked at June, she became angry and spiteful, and she didn't want to be like that.

Things had been going so well, too. Why had June had to destroy what they had? Was June to blame, though? she found herself wondering. Was it possible she could be telling the truth, after all? No, it couldn't be. Daisy had seen her and Nat together. You didn't have your arms wrapped around a man's neck if you were trying to fight him off. Anyway, Nat might be a bit of a bugger – and Daisy wasn't naïve enough to believe that he never flirted with other women – but he wasn't so lacking in principles that he'd go after her sister.

What about that story June had come out with about him setting the whole thing up with the deliberate intention of coming between the sisters to get back at June? No. It was too far-fetched to be true. Only a fool would believe such a story. Her racing thoughts stilled for a moment. Maybe that could work both ways; only a fool would make up such a story. And June certainly wasn't one of those.

Nat hadn't been near since the incident two weeks ago. Daisy knew him too well to think that he'd taken her literally when she'd told him she never wanted to see him again. He'd turn up eventually, like the

235

proverbial bad penny. He'd be waiting for her to cool down before he dared to show his face.

She decided suddenly that she wasn't prepared to wait for him, with resentment and suspicion eating away at her day after day. If he wouldn't come to her, she'd go to him and have this thing out once and for all. And the sooner the better.

Turning her mind to more immediate matters, she checked that the children had had enough to eat and got them ready for school, feeling slightly better for having made the decision to take some positive action.

Chapter Fifteen

Eileen was stirring gravy in a saucepan on the stove for the evening meal when there was a knock at the front door. She muttered a mild expletive because the liquid was at the crucial thickening stage and would go lumpy if left unstirred. Hearing Morris answer the door, however, she relaxed.

'The window cleaner wants paying,' he informed her, coming into the kitchen.

'Oh,' she said in surprise, continuing to stir. 'I didn't even realise he'd been.'

'He did the windows this morning, apparently,' he said, sounding bored. 'You must have been out shopping or something.'

She tutted. 'If I leave this now, to come to see to him, it'll be ruined.'

In a tone of mild irritation, Morris said, 'All right, tell me where the money is and I'll deal with it.' Domestic expenses such as window cleaning came out of Eileen's housekeeping money.

'You'll have to get it out of my purse,' she told him absently, her concentration focused on the contents of the saucepan. 'It's in my handbag on the sideboard, I think.'

'Right.' He headed off in search of the handbag.

She heard him talking to the window cleaner briefly before he shut the front door. A few minutes later, he marched into the kitchen seething with aggression, and waved a screwed-up scrap of newspaper under her nose.

'Perhaps you'd like to explain this,' he demanded, scowling at her. 'It fell out of your bag when I got your purse out.'

She was so startled, she dropped the wooden spoon on the floor and splashed gravy all over the cooker top, splattering her hand and staining the front of her apron. 'Junk has a habit of building up in my bag,' she said, blowing on her scalded hand and managing to recover sufficiently to looked unconcerned about his discovery. 'Stick it in the bin for me, would you?'

'This isn't just a bit of handbag junk,' he stated, his eyes narrowed on her accusingly. 'It's a newspaper cutting with your name on it.'

'Is it?' She turned the gas off under the saucepan and bent down to

237

pick the spoon up off the floor, trying to gather her wits and find a way out of this.

'You know perfectly well it is,' he snapped.

Morris was no fool and she'd been stupid to deny it. But she'd been caught unawares and panicked because she was terrified he would find out that the Rivers sisters had tracked them down because she'd responded to their advert and put her address on the letter. 'All right, so I know what it is,' she confessed. 'That isn't a crime, is it?'

'Who's looking for you?' He gave her a hard look. 'Have you been left some money or something?'

'Don't be ridiculous,' she protested. 'Who do I know with anything to leave?'

It was such a valid point he couldn't argue with it. 'What is it all about then and why did you say nothing to me about it?' he wanted to know.

'I don't know what it's all about because I didn't reply to it,' she continued to lie. 'And I didn't tell you because it didn't seem worth mentioning.'

He narrowed his eyes on her suspiciously. 'Your name in the paper, not worth mentioning? Don't take me for a mug, Eileen. You know damned well who's looking for you.'

'Why would I lie about it?'

'I don't know, but I intend to find out.'

'There's nothing to find out.'

'You're up to something, and I'll find out what it is one way or another,' he warned her. 'So you might as well make things easy for yourself and tell me.'

'I don't know who put that advertisement in the paper but it's obviously someone from the old days, wanting a get-together or something,' she tried to fob him off, a strong sense of self-preservation forcing the lies out of her. 'And because I don't want to see anyone from the past, I didn't bother to follow it up.'

'Why keep the advert hidden in your handbag, then?' Morris demanded.

'It wasn't hidden. It just happened to be in there.' She cursed herself for forgetting the advertisement was in her bag and telling Morris to look in there. If he discovered the truth he'd lose his temper and that meant bruises aplenty for her. 'I wouldn't have told you to go to my bag if I was hiding anything in there, would I?'

There was a brief hiatus while he pondered on this. 'I suppose not.' He was still doubtful, though. 'But you bothered to tear it out of the paper so you must have considered it important.'

'I was curious, naturally. Anyone would be, seeing their name in the newspaper.'

She didn't manage to convince him. 'You're keeping something from me,' he growled, gripping her arms so hard she cried out in pain. 'And I won't give up until you tell me what it is.'

'Morris, please . . . you're hurting me.'

'I think you did answer that advert.' He put his face close to hers. 'So tell me who's looking for you. Tell me, woman, before I break both your arms.'

'I don't know.'

Stars exploded in her head as he punched her face; she cowered back from him.

'There's plenty more where that came from if you don't tell me the truth,' he warned her.

'Don't hit me any more, please,' she begged.

'I'll stop when you tell me the truth.'

He hit her again, then took hold of her arms and held them so tight she could feel them bruising. 'There's nothing to tell.' Her voice was little more than a gasp.

'Do yourself a favour and tell me what's been going on,' he demanded, 'or I'll beat it out of you.'

Despite her dread of the brutality she knew from past experience he was capable of, she had a sudden unexpected surge of spirit, the misery of more than twenty years culminating in a blaze of fury. She knew she had no choice but to tell him the truth but she decided not to do so meekly, since he would punish her anyway. 'All right, I'll tell you,' she said, her voice rising with new courage. 'But you'll wish I hadn't.'

'Get on with it.'

'It was June and Daisy Rivers – the daughters of your dead lover,' she announced, her tone heavy with malice now. He'd been smug for too long. She wanted to see him suffer, and enjoyed seeing him struck with horror, eyes wide, mouth dropping open.

'Those little brats,' he gasped at last, letting go of Eileen in the shock of the moment. 'How did they find us?'

She told him. 'And they're not little brats now, Morris. Far from it,' she informed him with relish. 'They're women now. Intelligent women too.'

'What did they want with you?'

'Justice for their father.'

'What!'

'They know you killed their mother,' she told him with a note of triumph in her voice, the danger this posed to herself cast to one side in the pleasure of seeing the arrogant swine knocked off his perch. 'They saw you at the Rivers's house on the night of the murder so they know that we both lied under oath. They know, Morris.' Her voice rose, becoming shrill and hysterical as she recognised the gravity of the situation for them both. 'They know the truth.'

239

He couldn't hide his fear. 'They're bluffing,' he said. 'They must be.'

'You didn't tell me that someone besides Rose and Lionel Rivers knew you were at the house that night, did you?' she blurted out. 'You said no one could ever find out.'

'I didn't count a couple of little kids,' he was quick to point out. 'And I still don't. They can't possibly remember seeing me there after all this time.'

'They do.'

'Even if they do, who would believe them?' he scorned. 'Not a bloody soul, that's who. So I hope you haven't been opening your big mouth and admitting anything.'

'I'm not a complete idiot.'

'You were fool enough to put our address on your letter, though, weren't you?' he taunted.

'How was I to know they were behind the advert?'

'You should have been more careful.'

'I realise that now.'

'You've got as much to lose as I have in all this, remember,' he reminded her. 'If I go down, so do you.'

'As if I could ever forget.'

'And if it does happen it'll be because of your stupidity.'

Stress always inflamed Morris's temper. Rose Rivers had lost her life because of it and Eileen had sustained her share of injuries over the years. Now she took the full brunt as he looked at her with contempt, then pushed her hard against the wall and aimed one punishing blow after another at her face, her chest, her stomach.

'How dare you keep secrets from me?' he said, hitting her again and again. 'If those two come here again, I want to know about it. Understand? They can't prove anything so don't give them what they need by opening your mouth.'

She tried to get away but he dragged her back and hit her again in the stomach. 'I won't say anything, I promise,' she gasped at last, her hands raised to protect her head. 'But please stop hitting me . . . please.'

'You lied to your husband and that's wrong,' Another blow to the face.

'I'm sorry, I'm sorry . . .'

'You will be when I've finished with you.'

The violence continued until his anger finally abated and she was slumped on the floor, leaning against the wall, head down and sobbing quietly.

'You can stop snivelling and get my dinner,' he told her, walking to the door and turning, showing not a hint of remorse. 'I've been out working all day and I need a good meal when I get home. I don't expect to be kept waiting, either.'

The door closed after him. Slowly Eileen got up, her body racked with pain. She rinsed her face under the tap, wincing with the pain of a swollen eye and lip. The ruined gravy was poured down the sink and she got out the Bisto to make some more. She found herself with the chilling thought that one of these days her husband was going to go too far and she'd end up like Rose Rivers. In her dejected state, she didn't really care.

That same evening Daisy got the tube to Paddington and walked briskly along the main road towards Nat's place. It was typical November weather, bitterly cold, with a greyish mist shrouding everything. She was shivering despite the thick sweater she was wearing under her coat.

She couldn't afford to take the night off work but had decided that this was important enough to lose money for. Having made the decision to take action this morning, she wanted to get on with it, and there was no point in trying to find Nat at home during the day. Nora minded the children in the evenings anyway so that wasn't a problem.

The streets seemed even scruffier and more sinister around here than the ones Daisy was used to. Marauding yobs were out in force, looking for trouble, drunks staggered out of pubs, young couples were locked in clinches in shop doorways, and there were overflowing rubbish bins everywhere. Daisy had only ever been to Nat's place once or twice and that was years ago, but she was able to find the dilapidated flatlet house.

The front door wasn't locked so she went in and knocked on the door of the ground-floor flat where he lived. A blonde of about thirty opened the door with a small child clutching at her skirt.

'Yeah?' she said.

Daisy frowned, wondering who the woman was. 'Is Nat in, please?' she asked.

'Nat?'

'That's right. Is he at home at the moment?'

'Never 'eard of anyone called Nat.'

Wondering if she'd come to the wrong house, Daisy looked around her and was sure she hadn't. She looked back at the woman whose dark roots matched her black sweater and tight skirt. 'Nat Barker,' she said hopefully.

'Oh, Mr Barker, I know 'im,' the woman told her. 'He lived here before we moved in six months ago.'

'He's moved out?' Daisy couldn't believe he would change his address without telling her.

'Well, he certainly ain't dossing down here with us, dear,' the blonde said. 'We've hardly got enough room for ourselves, let alone having a lodger about the place.'

Daisy's throat was so constricted she could hardly swallow. 'Do you happen to know where he moved to?' she managed to utter at last.

'Over Queens Park way somewhere, as far as I remember. Dunno exactly where, though.'

'He didn't leave a forwarding address then?' muttered the shocked Daisy.

'No, nothing like that.' The woman thought for a moment. 'You could ask him in there,' she suggested, pointing at the door of the flat opposite. 'I think they were quite matey so he might have an address.'

Numb with shock, Daisy walked to the other flat and knocked on the door.

Afterwards Daisy couldn't remember getting to Queens Park that night. She was weak from the shock, and bitterly hurt to think that Nat would have done something as major as moving house without telling her, the woman in his life for more than seven years.

Admittedly she wasn't in the habit of visiting him, but she needed to know where he was in case of an emergency. He was the father of her children, for goodness' sake.

She'd forgiven him most things over the years but he'd have to have a damned good explanation for this, she thought, as she came out of the station and walked down a street of towering Victorian terraced houses converted into flats. The house she was looking for was smarter than Nat's previous address, she noticed with surprise. She pushed the front door open and knocked on the first door she came to because the neighbour from Nat's old address had only given her the house number.

A heavily pregnant young woman wearing a red maternity smock answered the door.

'Sorry to bother you but can you tell me which flat Nat Barker lives in, please?' enquired Daisy politely. 'I've been given this address but not the actual flat number.'

The woman, who had long black hair and dark eyes, fixed her with a steady gaze. 'What do you want him for?' she asked in a chilly manner.

Daisy bristled. She was having a terrible night. She'd just discovered that her long-standing boyfriend had moved house without telling her and now some stranger had the cheek to pry into her personal affairs. 'I think that's my business, don't you?' was her brisk reply. 'So can you please tell me where I can find him?'

There was silence for a moment as the woman considered the matter. 'Nat,' she shouted into the flat, 'come here. There's someone to see you.'

To Daisy's utter astonishment he appeared.

'Daisy . . .' He was clearly as shocked to see her as she was to see him. 'What are you doing here?'

242

'I might ask you the same thing,' came her sharp reply. 'How could you do such a thing – change your address without telling me?'

'I can explain—'

'Why should he tell you where he lives?' demanded the other woman, throwing Daisy a glare.

'You'd better ask him that,' she suggested.

'Who is she, Nat?' asked the woman, turning to him. 'And why should you explain anything to her?'

'Never mind who I am,' snapped Daisy, resenting the stranger's proprietary attitude towards Nat. 'Who are you? That's what I'd like to know.'

'That's easily sorted,' she replied, exuding confidence and pausing briefly before continuing as though to create the maximum effect. 'I'm Nat's wife.'

The hallway spun around her. Daisy gripped the stair banisters to steady herself, cold sweat suffusing her skin, her legs buckling.

'You can't be,' she muttered.

'I can and I am.'

'You're lying.'

'With him standing next to me?' she said in a mocking tone. 'Don't be such a silly cow.'

Daisy stared at her, still unable to take it in but knowing with sickening certainty that it was true.

'I don't understand,' she said numbly.

'Nothing complicated about it,' the woman went on breezily. 'He's my husband. We've been married for six months and have a baby due in a few weeks' time.'

'A baby.'

The woman patted her bump with both hands, looking at Daisy with a half-smile. 'Well, this ain't the result of too many doughnuts, mate,' she said.

'Oh, Nat,' gasped Daisy, looking at him with disbelief. 'How could you?'

And she turned and rushed out of the house.

'I couldn't just let you go like that, not after all the years we've been together,' said Nat, having chased after Daisy and persuaded her to go into the nearest pub with him so that he could explain.

'Won't you be in trouble with your ... with your ...' she could hardly bear to utter the title she had believed would belong to her one day, 'with your wife for chasing after me? You'll certainly have some explaining to do.'

'I can handle Marge, don't worry.'

Daisy emitted a humourless laugh. Her pain and humiliation went too deep for tears. 'All these years I thought that the only reason you wouldn't marry me was because you didn't want to marry anyone,' she said bitterly. 'And then you go and marry someone else. How's that for a punch in the throat?'

'I didn't want to get married and I didn't intend to marry Marge,' he informed her.

'But you went ahead and did it, just the same.'

'When she got pregnant I didn't have any choice in the matter,' he told her.

'I got pregnant, twice,' she reminded him. 'But you didn't feel obliged to do the decent thing by me, did you? And that hurts, Nat, that really hurts.'

'Marge has a very persistent father,' he explained.

'So if I'd had a dad to twist your arm, you'd have married me then, is that what you're saying?' she suggested.

'Not exactly, no.'

'Why did it work for her then?'

'Marge's dad is a powerful man around here,' he said. 'He owns several other houses besides the one we live in.'

'Ah, so that's it.' She gave him a knowing look. 'She has something I could never give you – money.'

'It isn't like that,' he denied somewhat unconvincingly.

'What then?'

'Her ol' man put on the pressure for me to marry her and he's the sort of bloke you don't defy if you value your health. He employs morons to deal with people who don't do what he wants. And they don't go in for small injuries, I can tell you.'

Daisy didn't believe a word of it. He'd married Marge because he saw something in it for himself. He was just using her as he'd used Daisy for so long. But at least Marge got to raise her child within the security of marriage. 'How blind can you get?' she said dully. 'All these years I thought I was the woman in your life when I was actually just your bit on the side.'

'No, Daisy, you were never that.' He looked suitably outraged at the suggestion.

'You must have been deceiving me for months,' she went on, her eyes narrowing in thought. 'No wonder you stayed away for weeks at a time. You had other fish to fry. God knows how many women there have been over the years, and I was too dim to suspect anything.' She paused, pondering, then added almost to herself, 'I suppose I knew in my heart there must be others but I didn't want to believe it so I deceived myself into thinking that I was the only one.'

He looked sheepish and didn't deny it.

'I don't suppose you ever loved me,' she went on. 'I was a fool to think you did.'

'I did love you, Daisy,' he claimed. 'I still do.'

244

'Don't make things worse by piling on the lies.' Her voice was hard. 'You've been found out so there's no point.'

He shrugged. 'I'm a bloke and we . . . well, these things just sort of happen,' he said lamely. 'It's different for men than it is for women. It's the way we're made.'

'Don't tar the whole of your gender with the same brush as yourself,' she admonished.

'You and me go back a long way, Daisy, and you are the only woman I've ever really loved.'

'How come you're married to Marge then?'

'I made a mistake and the choice was taken out of my hands, I told you.'

She took a large swallow of her gin and orange, looking at him. 'I don't think you're capable of loving anyone but yourself,' she told him. 'I don't suppose you even love your wife, the poor cow.'

He didn't say anything, just swigged his beer. 'You've every right to be upset,' he said after a while.

'You're not kidding.' She gave him a questioning look. 'One thing that does puzzle me: why bother to go on seeing me when you didn't want me?'

'I did want you.'

'But you had a wife, and a child on the way, a nice home and a rich father-in-law,' she pointed out. 'Why not be straight with me and tell me it was over?'

'I couldn't bring myself to end it, I suppose,' he told her. 'So I carried on seeing you.'

'In other words, you wanted to have your cake and eat it.'

'A woman would see it that way, I suppose.'

'Anyone with a scrap of decency in them would see it that way,' she amended.

With her perception altered by events, she saw him with a new and truthful eye. He was a flashily dressed man with greasy sideburns and a paunch around his middle, a chancer who cared for no one but himself. He wasn't even much to look at, if the truth be told. 'The reason I came looking for you tonight was because I was going to ask you to be honest with me about what happened between you and June,' she explained. 'Now that I know the sort of deception you are capable of, I don't suppose I need to.'

'I wanted to bring her down off her high horse,' he blurted out in a rare burst of honesty. 'I don't like her attitude. She thinks she's God's gift.'

'She's been telling the truth all along, hasn't she?'

He hesitated for only a second before nodding his head. Lying was like breathing to Nat, but even he could see that there was no point in continuing with the pretence now. 'I didn't fancy her,' he was keen to assure Daisy. 'The idea was to get her interested and then laugh in her face. I wanted to make her feel put down in the same way she always makes me feel, turning her nose up, the superior bitch. But she didn't want to know, turned me down flat. So I decided to get even with her by making trouble for her with you. That's why I set that scam up the other night.'

'Surely you've got better things to do with your time, now that you're a married man,' Daisy disapproved.

'My life and my feelings for you haven't ended just because I've married Marge, you know,' he informed her. 'I still have a life outside the home.'

'I bet you do,' she said harshly. 'If you hadn't been rumbled you'd have carried on seeing me, wouldn't you?'

He met her eyes. 'If I could have got away with it, yeah, I expect I would,' he admitted without shame.

'It's about time you grew up, Nat Barker,' she told him. 'My daughters have got more sense than you.'

'Our daughters,' he corrected.

'*My* daughters,' she countered, her voice rising. 'You've never wanted to be bothered with them, never been anything of a father to them.'

'Only because I'm no good with kids, you know that's the reason,' he defended.

'I know that you've never made any effort with them,' she said.

'Don't go on about it.'

'I'm not going to go on at you about anything ever again,' she made clear. 'I just hope you make a better job of fatherhood with your new baby than you ever did with Shirley and Belinda. Your poor wife doesn't know what she's letting herself in for with you. I wish her the best of luck.'

'Daisy, please, don't be so hard,' he urged her. 'It just isn't like you to be so nasty.'

'No, it isn't. And I should have been harder and nastier a long time ago as far as you were concerned. My biggest regret is that I didn't allow myself to see through you before,' she said, finishing her drink and standing up to go. 'You're a cheat and a liar and I never want to see you again.'

She left the pub with him in hot pursuit.

'Daisy, we can't part bad friends like this,' he said, taking her arm.

She pulled away from him and stared into his face. 'Don't you ever touch me again,' she ordered, her voice distorted with rage. 'Not ever!'

'But—'

'If you ever come near me or my girls again,' she said through gritted teeth, 'I'll go to the law and have a court order taken out against you.'

'Now you're just being bloody ridiculous,' he objected, moving back. 'You've got a wife at home waiting for you,' she reminded him tartly. 'So go to her and leave us alone. You're not fit to breathe the same air as my daughters or my sister or my dear friend Nora. So go away, you pathetic little man.'

'Don't worry,' he countered. 'I wouldn't want to come near you or your bastard brats again anyway.'

That was too much for even Daisy's patience. She clenched her fist and drove it hard into his face. 'That's for calling my daughters names,' she informed him, and walked away, leaving him looking after her with his handkerchief held to his bleeding nose.

When the parish priest went into the church to lock up he saw a woman sitting in the pew with her head bowed. He caught her eye and gave her a tentative smile.

'Are you waiting to lock up, Father?' she asked. It wasn't her local church so this priest was a stranger.

'When you're ready,' he said. 'No hurry.'

'I'll just be a few more minutes.'

'Take as long as you like.' He looked at her kindly. 'Is there anything I can do to help? I'm a good listener.'

'Thanks, Father. But not this time.'

He nodded and walked away, disappearing through the door to the vestry.

Daisy had never been able to define what the inside of a church meant to her. But she did know that part of it was a sense of belonging that dated back to the orphanage chapel. It was something familiar, something she'd grown up with. The atmosphere had comforted her as a child and still did today. She breathed in the lingering smell of incense and candlewax around her, finding it soothing.

She'd come in here on impulse tonight, passing the church on her way to the station after leaving Nat. Every nerve in her body had been stretched to the limit; she'd been full of disgust for him and humiliation for the years of self-delusion, believing that she and Nat had a future together.

But now, sitting here in tune with her spiritual self, she felt calmer and more able to clarify her thoughts. She'd been young and hungry for love when she'd fallen for Nat, dazzled by his confidence and colourful looks. She could see now that she'd clung on to what she'd thought they had, blinding herself to the truth even though the magic of that young love had gone long ago. She'd not allowed herself to move on from those immature feelings.

Looking back over the peculiar nature of their relationship and the fact that she had been excluded from so much of his life, it should have been obvious to her that there was more to him than she knew about. She could only assume that she hadn't wanted to face up to that so had told herself that it wasn't Nat's way to be bound by the normal rules of courtship because he was unconventional, a free spirit. He'd let her down so many times, she should have been tough in the face of this ultimate humiliation. But she wasn't and the pain was profound.

Somewhere at the back of her mind, though, she recognised something else which she couldn't quite identify but could feel growing. It was a lightness of heart that felt remarkably like relief and something beyond that too – a kind of strength. Only now could she fully accept that loving Nat, or thinking she loved him, had been a burden; it had held her back, stunted her emotional growth. It had made her lose a good man she could have had a future with, and caused a serious rift between herself and her sister.

She would never deny that there had been good times with Nat, and he had given her her greatest gift: her lovely daughters. But he had been a negative influence in her life for a long time. Now it was over. It was the end of an era. She had to get on with her life without him. And there was one thing she must do before anything else. Maybe it was too late to put things right with Jack. But not with June.

As she got up to leave, the priest appeared and came over to her.

'Feeling better?' he asked.

'Much better, thank you,' she was able to say truthfully. 'Good night, Father.'

'Good night.'

Facing the altar, she genuflected, then turned and walked to the back of the church, her footsteps echoing on the stone floor in the silent building. She pushed open the heavy door and walked out into the cold night air.

June and Nora were in the living room having their cocoa when Daisy finally got home. She came straight to the point.

'I've been a complete idiot,' she told them, sitting down and looking from one to the other. 'Can you ever forgive me?'

'I'll go and get you some cocoa,' offered Nora, with the idea of making a diplomatic exit.

'No, don't go, Nora,' Daisy requested. 'I want you to stay and hear what I have to say.'

Nora sat back down and listened while Daisy told them about the events of the evening.

'Daisy, love, I'm so sorry,' said Nora, removing her spectacles and rubbing the lens with the corner of her cardigan. 'I know I've sometimes upset you by speaking my mind about Nat but I wouldn't have had this happen to you for the world.'

'Nor me,' added June.

'I know you wouldn't and it's all right,' Daisy assured them. 'I feel OK about it now.'

'Are you sure?' asked Nora.

'Yeah. I'm very hurt, of course. It was one hell of a shock and I was shattered. But I think I needed something like this to make me face up to what I've known deep down all along and what the two of you have tried to make me see: that Nat doesn't live by the same rules as the rest of us.' Even now she couldn't bring herself to be unnecessarily hateful about him. 'I feel better now that it's finally over. It was never a proper relationship, even though I tried to tell myself it was.'

The two women looked at her in silence, a palpable sense of relief settling over the room.

'I'll go and get you that cup of cocoa now,' said Nora.

'Thanks, Nora.' Daisy managed a smile. 'And thanks, both of you, for not saying I told you so.'

Nora chortled. 'It's more than we dare do,' she told her. 'We're used to keeping quiet when it comes to Nat.'

'Not any more,' Daisy told them. 'That's all over and done with. From now on the shortcomings of Nat Barker are not unmentionable in this house.'

'Thank God for that,' said Nora, and disappeared into the kitchen to make Daisy some cocoa.

Hyped up by what had happened, Daisy didn't feel ready to go to bed when she'd finished her cocoa. June was upset on Daisy's behalf and feeling wakeful also, so they stayed up talking after Nora had gone to bed. Sitting either side of the dying embers of the fire, Daisy talked about Nat.

'I was young when I met him,' she said, in a reminiscent mood. 'Young and lonely and desperate for love, I suppose. I was very well looked after at St Clare's but there wasn't much love about.' She paused. 'So I fell for Nat in a big way.'

June gave her an understanding nod.

'Leaving the orphanage was worse than being there. Much worse. OK, so there are no home comforts in an institution but there was security and constant companionship. Coming into the outside world after all those years was a real shock to the system, I can tell you. I've never felt so alone as I did then.' Her eyes were glazed as she thought back on it. 'I had absolutely no one.'

'Didn't they do any sort of follow-up, to make sure you were all right?' enquired June.

'Oh, yeah, they did that. An aftercare officer used to visit me now and again to make sure I was surviving,' she explained. 'But they couldn't cure the grinding loneliness. Although I never felt loved at St Clare's, I never felt lonely either. But when I left there I felt as though

I'd lost everything because my security had gone. I was fifteen and on my own in the world, or that's what it felt like. I missed St Clare's dreadfully.' She looked at her sister. 'You weren't there for long enough to remember much about it, I suppose.'

'No. But I know all about feeling alone and unloved.'

June had indicated before that her childhood had somehow been lacking. But as she'd made it obvious that she didn't want to talk about it, Daisy didn't like to press her. 'Really?' she said.

Meeting her sister's sympathetic eyes, June felt comforted. She'd never told anyone the truth about her childhood, not even Alan. She couldn't bear to talk about it because to do so evoked the painful memories she'd spent the whole of her adult life trying to blot out. But now she sensed that the time had come to bring it all out into the open. Suddenly she knew that she needed to face the memories if she was ever to erase her fear of them. 'Contrary to what you might expect, my life was hell after I left St Clare's.'

'Why?'

'Downright wicked are the only words I can think of to describe the people who adopted me.'

'No!' Daisy was shocked. 'How can that be? I mean, surely if they wanted a child desperately enough to adopt one, they would love and cherish it.'

'Oh, they claimed to love me,' June said, bitterness creeping into her tone. 'When they were beating me, they told me it was for my own good, that it would make me into a better person, and I would thank them for it one day.'

'They beat you?'

'On a regular basis.' She looked grim. 'But the beatings I could take.'

'There were worse things?'

June cleared her throat, finding it difficult to say the words after keeping it all locked away for so long. 'Mental torture, and lots of it, though I didn't know that was what it was called at the time, of course,' she explained. 'They constantly told me that I was a useless human being and they wished they'd never taken me on. They used to lock me in my bedroom for hours on end, whole weekends sometimes, as a punishment for something as small as being a few minutes late back from school because I'd been chatting to the other kids on the way home. They got even stricter about that as I grew older.'

'That's terrible.'

'It was, I can tell you. I wasn't allowed to have any friends at all outside of school hours.' June gave Daisy a wry look. 'I don't suppose they'd have allowed me to go to school if it hadn't been against the law to keep me home.'

'Why didn't they want you to mix?'

'They didn't want me corrupted by the other kids, was what they said. I believed them; kids believe anything adults tell them, don't they? Later I realised it was because they saw outside influences as a threat to their control over me.'

'I can't understand why they went to the trouble of adopting a child, as they obviously weren't suited to parenthood.'

'That's often puzzled me too,' said June thoughtfully. 'I can only think it must have been because they wanted someone to control, to manipulate. They probably even convinced themselves they were doing the best thing for me. They must have convinced the authorities that they were good people. I imagine that couples wanting to adopt were vetted, even in those days when there were so many children in care.'

'You must have been relieved when you were old enough to leave home.'

'Phew, I'll say I was. I left when I was fifteen,' she explained. 'Like you I was alone and in lodgings at that tender age.'

'What happened? Did you reach a point at home when you'd had enough so just walked out?' Daisy enquired.

'No.' June turned very pale and Daisy could see that she was trembling. 'No, it wasn't like that. Something happened that made it impossible for me to stay there.'

'Oh . . .' Daisy didn't want to pry but she sensed that June needed to talk about whatever it was that still troubled her so deeply. She waited, hoping her sister would feel able to confide.

June stared at her shaking hands. 'I've never told a soul. I don't know if I can,' she began, looking up and biting her lip. 'It's just too awful to put into words. You'll be very shocked, Daisy.'

'Don't tell me if you'd rather not,' said her sister kindly. 'But it might help. And don't worry about shocking me. After tonight, I can face anything.'

There was a silence. June pushed her fingers distractedly through her hair. 'My adoptive father used to . . . to get fresh with me.' She paused, unable to continue. 'And then one time he raped me,' she finally managed to get out in a rush. 'And I got pregnant as a result.'

Daisy couldn't pretend not to be appalled. 'Oh, June, that's awful!' she gasped.

'That isn't all,' she went on, her skin paper-white but suffused with red blotches on her cheeks and neck. 'They made me have an abortion.'

The gasp emitted by Daisy filled the silent room.

'That's the bit I knew would upset you, you being a Catholic.' June was very distressed.

'I can't help it.'

'I had no choice in the matter,' June went on. 'I didn't know what

251

was going to happen when they took me to this woman's house. Not until she took me into a room and locked the door. By that time it was too late. I struggled but there were three strong adults against a fifteen-year-old girl. My parents held me down. Even though I didn't want to carry a baby of that monster's, I didn't want to do that, believe me.'

'You don't have to justify yourself to me,' Daisy assured her. 'I'm not going to judge you.'

'I had a miscarriage that night but I was very ill for days afterwards, terrible pains, floodings, a fever,' she continued. 'I thought I was going to die. I think they did too but they daren't call a doctor because questions would have been asked.'

'They ought to have been reported for breaking the law,' said the outraged Daisy. 'Was there nobody you could turn to?'

'Nobody at all because they'd never allowed me to have friends,' she explained. 'I wouldn't have said anything anyway because the shame was too great.'

'I can imagine.'

'Anyway, as soon as I was well enough after the abortion, I left,' she went on. 'I wasn't safe at home with him around. My mother wanted me out of the way by that time, too. She couldn't face up to what he was like and blamed me for the whole thing; she said I'd encouraged him. It was probably the only way she could bring herself to stay with him.'

'That's quite a story,' said Daisy.

'It's the reason why I left Alan,' June told her.

'Really?' Daisy was puzzled. 'Was it still haunting you and coming between you then?'

'It has always haunted me and always will do. But I was able to cope with it until Alan and I started to try for a baby and I couldn't get pregnant,' she explained. 'Obviously because of the damage caused by the abortion.'

'You don't know that for sure.'

'I can be pretty certain, though. I mean, what else could be stopping me from conceiving?'

'Any number of things.'

'With the abortion damage being the most likely.' June was in little doubt. 'Anyway, when Alan started talking about seeking medical advice, I knew it was time for me to leave. I couldn't risk having my past come out.'

'Surely, whatever the doctors discovered would have been confidential between you and them, wouldn't it?' suggested Daisy. 'I don't think it would be ethical for a doctor to discuss a patient's details with anyone else, even a husband.'

'But I would have had to lie to Alan about it,' she pointed out. 'And

I didn't want to do that. I lied to him about my reasons for leaving him but I had to do that so that he would get on with his life without me.'

'So he still doesn't know why you left?'

'Of course not. I could hardly tell him a thing like that, could I? It's better this way. With me out of the picture he can find a woman who can give him the child he wants. He deserves that. He's a really decent bloke. What right do I have to stop him having kids?'

'Sounds as though you still love him.'

'Desperately,' June admitted. 'I walked out on him because I love him and want the best for him.'

'Sounds like cockeyed logic to me,' Daisy disapproved. 'You could at least have given him the chance of an opinion on the matter.'

'I know what I did what was right for him.'

'I suppose that's the important thing,' sighed Daisy. 'When it comes down to it, you have to trust your own judgement about something as personal as that.'

'Mm.' June threw her a look. 'So what do you think of your smart sophisticated sister now you know the truth about her?'

'I think it's sad,' was Daisy's honest reply. 'Sad that you've had such a rotten life. And kids growing up in an orphanage are always thought of as the hard-done-by ones.'

'I'm glad I've told you.'

'I'm glad it's helped.'

Something happened to June at that moment, and she broke down, the stifled pain of the past finally culminating in a great outpouring of grief.

Daisy went over to her and held her while she sobbed. 'You're not on your own any more,' she said, stroking her hair. 'And neither am I. We've got each other now. We were given a gift when fate brought us together again. We nearly lost that when we fell out over Nat. We mustn't let anything come between us ever again.'

'Definitely not,' agreed June, in a muffled tone, but feeling better for having let go. 'Nothing will part us now.'

'And now that we're friends again, we have a job to finish,' Daisy reminded her.

June nodded, blowing her nose and composing herself. 'We need to work out our next move,' she said shakily. 'Not that we have many options.'

'I was wondering,' began Daisy, 'if perhaps we should give some more thought to the one lead we do have.'

'Go straight to the organ grinder, you mean?' suggested June, catching on.

'Exactly,' Daisy confirmed. 'It might be a bit risky but there will be two of us. And I really do think it's our only hope.'

'What exactly do you have in mind?'

'This is my plan . . .' began Daisy.

'Good evening, Mrs Dodd,' said Daisy, when Eileen answered the door.

She gasped and shrank back. 'Oh, no. Not you two again,' she complained. 'I thought I'd made it clear that I don't want to see you around here again.'

'You made it very clear,' confirmed June.

'Why are you here then?'

'We've come to see your husband,' explained Daisy. 'Is he at home this evening?'

Eileen looked guarded and very frightened. 'No, he isn't,' she said, and went to close the door.

'I don't believe you,' said Daisy, stepping forward and pushing her foot against it.

'Clear off.'

'We're going to pester the life out of you until we do see him, so you might as well get it over with,' Daisy told her.

'What do you want with him?' Eileen's wary eyes rested on them suspiciously. 'I made our position very clear the last time you were here.'

'Let us in and you can listen to what we have to say,' Daisy said in reply.

A booming voice came from inside the house: 'Who is it, Eileen?'

'Just a couple of Jehovah's Witnesses,' she lied.

'Tell them to bugger off,' Morris bellowed back at her. 'I'm waiting for my pudding.'

Daisy moved forward and shouted into the house, 'It isn't Jehovah's Witnesses, Mr Dodd. It's Daisy and June Rivers and we're not going to go away until we've seen you so you might as well let us in.'

In an instant he was at the door, his beady little eyes darting from one to the other in search of recognition, not quite able to hide his fear. 'My wife's already told you that you're not welcome here, so clear off.'

Daisy found it an eerie experience to see him again after all these years. He'd been a shadowy image in her mind, except for those evil eyes, which had remained vivid. She couldn't stop imagining what his plump, stubby hands had done to their mother. Anger imbued her, which she knew she must control or ruin their plan. 'You'll regret it if you don't listen to what we have to say,' she told him.

'You've got nothing on me,' he responded with an air of indifference that didn't quite come off.

'We wouldn't be here if we hadn't,' Daisy pointed out.

'Shush, all of you,' Eileen urged them, looking into the street and peering both ways. 'There's no need to let the whole neighbourhood know our business.'

'The whole world will know your business if you don't let us in,' said June.

'You'd better do what they say, Morris,' Eileen advised him nervously.

'Oh, all right,' he tutted, moving aside to let them in and leading them into the living room where he stood with his back to the fire. 'I won't offer you a seat because you won't be stopping. Just say what you have to say and get out.'

The sisters stood just inside the door 'How does it feel to see us again after all these years, Mr Dodd?' Daisy asked.

'It doesn't feel like anything in particular,' he replied with nonchalance that didn't ring true. 'You were nothing to me then and you're nothing now. Just the kids of a neighbour where we once lived, that's all.'

'Looking at you is like looking at the devil himself,' Daisy told him.

'For me too,' added June.

'My sister and I are the only people living who saw you at the house that night,' Daisy reminded him. 'Apart from our father, of course. And he's out of the picture for the moment.'

'Just temporarily,' June put in.

'I dunno what you're going on about,' Morris blustered. 'As I said just now, you've got nothing on me.'

'That's where you're wrong,' said Daisy, hoping to goad him into losing his temper which, from what they'd heard, shouldn't be too difficult.

'Very wrong,' June backed her up.

'We have something very incriminating,' Daisy went on. 'We have our own personal experience and the police will be interested to hear what we have to say about having seen you at our house on the night of our mother's murder.'

'You didn't see me there,' he denied. 'And if you think you did you're barmy.'

'We intend to leave no stone unturned to clear our father's name,' threatened Daisy. 'So be warned.'

'I knew there would be trouble.' Eileen was deathly white, her voice shaking. 'You shouldn't have done it, Morris.'

'Shut up, you stupid cow,' he bellowed at her. 'Keep your big mouth shut.'

'That's what you said to us that night,' Daisy reminded him.

'Rubbish!' he exclaimed. 'You were just a couple of snotty-nosed kids. You couldn't possibly remember anything as far back as that. This is just something you've dreamed up.'

'We wouldn't make a thing like that up.'

'There was only us and you in that hallway that night,' June reminded him. 'How could we know about it if we weren't actually there – that's the line the police will take.'

Daisy pointed to her head. 'It's all up here,' she informed him. 'And we intend to use it.'

'You know as well as I do that no one will believe such a story,' he challenged.

They did know that, which was why they needed Eileen to back them up and that was what they hoped to achieve with this visit. 'They'll have to look into what we have to say, whether they believe us or not,' Daisy bluffed. 'Especially as there are two of us.'

He narrowed his eyes on her. 'If you're so sure, why are you here bothering us?' he enquired. 'Why don't you just have done with it and go to the police?'

'It's only recently been possible but that's another story,' said June. 'We're here now because we wanted to see you, to see if you can look us in the eye after what you've done.'

'I've done nothing to be ashamed of.'

'I can believe that too, because you're the sort of man who wouldn't be ashamed of committing murder and letting someone else take the blame.' Daisy's tone was hard. 'We'll see you punished for it. No matter how long it takes, you'll pay for what you've done.'

'Do something, Morris,' cried Eileen in a panic. 'Do something or we'll both go down.'

His wife's fear seemed to enrage him and he replied with his fist, hard across her mouth, which immediately spurted with blood. 'I've told you to shut your big gob. Now perhaps you'll do what you're told,' he roared.

'Are you going to let him get away with that, Eileen?' challenged Daisy.

'He's murdered one woman,' put in June. 'You might be the next. He's certainly capable of it.'

'Stop them, Morris,' wailed Eileen, holding a handkerchief to her bleeding lip.

In reply he struck her across the face so hard she fell to the floor. He then lunged towards her with the idea of aiming more blows. But Daisy intervened.

'That's enough of that,' she said, dragging him away with June's help.

He swung round, his fists flying. 'Get out of my house, the pair of you,' he ordered, his voice shaking with rage. 'Your mother was scum anyway, leading me on, then turning cold. She deserved everything she got.'

'You admit you killed her then?' said Daisy.

'Yeah, I admit it.' He was shouting now, his face red with fury and his eyes wild; he'd obviously lost control as the sisters had hoped he would. 'And bloody good riddance to her too. She should never have played us off one against the other.'

Daisy was about to strike him but was pre-empted by him aiming a blow to her face that made her see stars.

'You animal.' She tried to push him away but he was too strong for her, especially as she was still dazed from the blow. 'Get off of me.'

'Leave her alone,' shouted June, trying to drag him off her sister and failing against his strength.

Suddenly help came from an unexpected source.

'Haven't you done enough damage to these women, you evil bugger?' said Eileen, struggling up from the floor and grabbing him by his other arm so that, between them, she and June were able to hold him back from Daisy. 'You robbed them of their parents when they were just little kids, and now you're trying to beat them up.'

'Shut up, Eileen.'

'No, I won't shut up,' she said, her voice distorted as she started to sob.

'You bloody well will.'

'You've ruined the childhood of these two women, and you've wrecked my life too,' she told him. 'But you've made my life a misery for long enough, I tell you. I'd sooner be in a prison cell than have to live another day with you.'

'Eileen,' he said in a warning tone, struggling to get free but failing because there were three women holding him now. 'What are you talking about?'

'I'm going to tell the police what you made me do, and get the case reopened so you will have to pay for your crime,' she said, her voice strong suddenly, despite the fact that she was crying.

'Don't make me laugh,' he scorned 'You won't have the bottle.'

'I will, you know. I'm going to tell the truth – that I lied under oath because you told me you hadn't done the murder,' she went on as though he hadn't spoken. 'I would never have lied if I'd known the truth. By the time I found out what you'd done I was caught in a trap that you'd put me in. Well, no more. Enough's enough.'

'You wouldn't dare.'

'Watch me.'

'You'll go down with me,' he warned.

'So what? I'm living in a prison now,' she told him. 'A real one can't be worse than the hell of a life I live with you.'

He made one last bid to get away and broke free, but Eileen landed him a blow to the face so hard he was stunned into immobility.

'Come on, girls,' she said to the astonished sisters. 'Let's go to the police station.'

While Morris was still gathering his wits from the shock of his wife's unprecedented violence, the three women fled from the house into the bitter night. They stopped only long enough for Daisy to grab a coat from the hallstand for Eileen.

257

Chapter Sixteen

Jack strode out along the beach, the cold January wind stinging his face, the tangy salt air filling his lungs and clearing his head. It was late Sunday morning and he didn't have to go on duty until this evening as they didn't open the restaurant for lunches in the winter. After a good hard walk, he'd have a sociable hour in the Gullscombe Arms, then go back to the cottage for a bite to eat followed by a leisurely browse through the Sunday papers by the fire until it was time to go to work. Smashing!

The sea breeze felt more like a gale this morning, the sky a great rolling dome of grey, the ocean rough and dark. The surf was so thunderous, each breaking wave seemed to shake the ground beneath his feet. Definitely not the sort of weather to attract the average person to the beach, but Jack had a curious fondness for it on wild winter days when the life force was so breathtakingly tangible. He found it invigorating and uplifting, especially as he was dressed for the elements, the hood of his duffel coat pulled right up over his ears.

There was hardly anyone about – just a man throwing sticks for a dog in the curve of the bay and a group of youngsters exploring the rock pools around the bottom of the cliffs, their high, youthful voices carried on the wind. Rock pools were like a magnet to kids, he thought, reminded of last summer and how Shirley and Belinda had loved poking about in them, looking for shells.

Of course, everything had been drenched in sunshine then: his life as well as the landscape, for that brief interlude when Daisy and her daughters had been a part of it. That was almost half a year ago, and nothing had been the same for him since. He didn't sit about feeling sorry for himself; that wasn't his way. He worked hard, went for long walks, tinkered with his motorbike and was his usual sociable self to anyone he encountered. He even dated women occasionally. But the dull ache of missing Daisy didn't go away.

He walked on with his head bent against the wind, passing Gullscombe Manor, more visible now than in summer because the trees were bare. Every time he passed this spot he thought of Daisy and how they'd sheltered from the rain on the veranda. He'd felt so close to her then; had really believed they had something worth nurturing.

259

But now, something attached to a post outside the house caught his eye and he halted in his step, peering at it. It looked like an estate agent's FOR SALE board but he couldn't see the details from this distance. Inspired by mild curiosity to take a closer look, he made his way up the sloping path through the trees.

It was an estate agent's board but with an auction notice pasted across it. He'd heard through the village grapevine that the owner had recently died. His descendants obviously wanted to dispose of the place as quickly as possible and it would go for a song at auction. There couldn't be much demand for a ruin like that, no matter how beautiful it had once been, because it would need such a huge injection of cash to return it to its former glory. So somebody would get a bargain.

A memory popped into his mind of a casual comment Daisy had made when they'd been here together, about the potential of the place for use as something other than a private house. He stood still, mulling a sudden idea over, then walked purposefully across the garden and down the slope to the beach. His step gathered momentum to such an extent that he was practically running back to the cottage in a fever of rising excitement. Stopping for only long enough to collect his crash helmet and goggles, he jumped on his motorbike and roared away towards town.

Alan and Jack were having a drink in a Torquay pub an hour or so later, Jack having turned up at Alan's flat in ebullient mood, saying he needed to speak to him urgently and in private away from the Cliff Head. When Alan heard what he had to say, his reaction was one of astonishment.

'You're saying that you want the two of us to go into partnership to buy Gullscombe Manor and turn it into a hotel that we will run together?' He was excited by the prospect, even though he wasn't in a position to consider such a proposition.

'That's exactly what I'm saying.' Jack was full of it. 'A great idea, isn't it?'

'But it's a wreck of a place,' Alan pointed out.

'Which is why it will go dirt cheap at auction.'

'It would need to go for practically nothing since it'll cost a fortune to restore,' was Alan's shrewd response. 'Even more to convert into a hotel.'

'If we got it at a low enough price, we should be able to manage it.' Jack's fervour was intense. 'Surely you can see how perfect the place would be as a hotel. The building and grounds, the location, everything.'

'Yeah, I can see the potential.' Alan would be a fool to deny it. 'I can also visualise the terrific amount of work it would take to renovate it and turn it into a hotel. And building work costs money, lots of it.'

'Just think, though, Alan, we could make it into a family hotel, the sort of place you've always dreamed of having,' Jack effused, his faith in the project causing him to ignore the obstacles Alan was putting in the way. 'It's the perfect setting, in extensive grounds with direct access to a safe beach. What could be better?'

'It's a good position but—'

'I know we could make a success of this,' Jack cut in excitedly. 'We could put in a swimming pool and a games room, all that sort of thing.'

'Just one minor point,' said Alan with irony. 'How are we supposed to fund this project?'

'By my selling my cottage and you could either raise money on your share in the Cliff Head or use your savings and get a bank loan if that isn't enough, based on the reputation you will have built up from running the Cliff Head.' He'd worked it all out on the way into town. 'I know when we were talking once you said that your savings wouldn't be anywhere near enough to get your own hotel, but as there would be the two of us sharing the cost, and we'd be starting something from scratch with no goodwill to pay for, you wouldn't need so much.'

'I can't believe you'd sell your cottage.' Alan shook his head slowly. 'You love that place.'

'I do. Very much. But it is only bricks and mortar when it comes down to it.'

'That isn't what you said when you were doing it up,' Alan reminded him.

'I know what I said, but when an opportunity like this comes up, you have to adapt, don't you?' Jack told him. 'Anyway, the thing I love most about the cottage is that it's on the seashore at Gullscombe Bay. If I moved to the manor I'd still be on the bay and in an even better position.'

Alan couldn't help but be infected by his friend's enthusiasm but he had to be realistic. 'It's a nice dream, mate,' he sighed wistfully.

'It's more than just a dream.' Jack was deadly serious. 'This is a sound business idea.'

'It is, I agree. But it will have to stay just a dream for me,' he said. 'I can't come in with you on it, Jack. I couldn't do that to my folks. As I told you before, if I ever left the Cliff Head I would give them my share. But I still wouldn't do it because I know they'd be devastated.'

'I thought that might be your reaction.' Jack couldn't hide his disappointment. 'And the last thing I want to do is interfere in a family matter.' He paused, sipping his beer. 'But I will say this. You were my first choice as a business partner for two reasons. Partly because I

261

believe we'd make a great team. And also because I know you're fed up and frustrated at the Cliff Head and need to do something in your own right, away from your parents. Well, mate, you'll never get a better chance than this.'

Because Alan wanted to seize this opportunity with both hands, he was beginning to delude himself into thinking it might be possible. 'Would it really be a viable proposition, do you think?' he asked.

'I'm as certain as I can be at such an early stage,' said Jack without hesitation. 'Obviously we'd have to find out what the reserve price is and work out some figures. But if we can get the finance side of things sorted, I don't see how the actual project can fail, not with us two at the helm, being both experienced in the hotel trade and having the same ideas for what we want in a hotel. Gullscombe Bay is a natural beauty spot badly in need of a hotel. Taking over the manor house would mean we could open one without spoiling the landscape. We'd keep everything as it is now as far as possible, with necessary changes inside done tastefully.' His enthusiasm was growing with every word. 'I could raise more money by selling my motorbike too, if necessary.'

'But that's your hobby – the love of your life,' said his amazed companion.

'It is, but I'd sell it to get this project off the ground,' Jack told him gravely. 'Harley-Davidsons fetch a good price, even old ones like mine.'

'I can't believe you'd be willing to sell your cottage *and* your bike.'

'That's how much I want to do this.'

'But you've never shown any interest in having your own hotel before,' mentioned Alan.

'I haven't thought about it until now, and I'm not interested in owning just any hotel,' he explained. 'But now that I've thought of this Gullscombe Manor thing, I can't let it go. The idea's too good.' He drank his beer, looking thoughtful. 'Anyway, I've been drifting for too long – going to work and coming home, messing about with the bike. I need a challenge in my life and I can't see a better one than this coming along – *ever*.'

'It's certainly got the makings.'

Jack put his pint glass down, looking at his friend closely. 'I want you to come in with me on this, Alan. But if you really don't feel able to, I'm still going to go ahead and bid for it at auction.'

'If things were different I'd jump at the chance of coming in with you on it.'

'I know you would, mate. But I'll have to find someone else as a partner.' Jack's thoughts were racing ahead. 'I won't be able to raise enough cash on my own. It's too big a project.'

Alan nodded.

'Still, I've got plenty of contacts in the hotel trade,' Jack continued.

'I should be able to arouse some interest.'

'I really wish it could be me.' Alan couldn't bring himself to let go of the idea completely. 'I'm long overdue a challenge.'

Jack looked at him. 'You wouldn't be going to the outback of Australia, you know,' he pointed out. 'You'd only be a few miles up the coast. You'd still be able to see your folks on a regular basis.'

'They wouldn't want to see me if I left their business,' Alan told him ruefully.

'*Their* being the operative word.' Jack didn't want to give up on Alan either. 'It's their business and not yours.'

'When they retire, things will be different. I'll be able to put my own stamp on the place then.'

'It'll still be a business they've built up,' persisted Jack.

'I'll just have to live with that.' Alan was resigned now. 'Because I just couldn't hurt them in that way.'

'We've been over this before and you know my feelings on the subject,' said Jack.

Alan sighed. 'It's easy for you to say but things aren't that simple when relatives are involved.'

'After leaving my family at the other side of the world, I think I know how difficult it is,' Jack reminded him. 'It's your decision, of course, but I wouldn't be a true mate if I didn't say that I think you're missing out on the chance of a lifetime. Not just because I'm certain that the two of us could make a go of it but also because I really do believe you need to break away from your parents' apron strings.'

'You're probably right,' agreed Alan. 'But it's actually doing it that's the problem.'

'I think you might be underestimating them, you know,' Jack went on sagely. 'They'll be upset at first, naturally, but they'd get used to it eventually. They might even be proud of you for having a go.'

'Sorry, mate, the answer still has to be no.'

Jack shrugged. 'OK. I've said my piece, I'll shut up about it now.'

'I hope it works out for you.'

'Me too.' His enthusiasm rose again. 'If it doesn't, it certainly won't be for the lack of trying. I've got a real good feeling about this one.'

'Keep me posted,' said Alan enviously.

'I'll do that,' said Jack.

During the winter months there was usually maintenance work of some sort in progress at the Cliff Head. General repairs, painting and decorating – bits of building work that couldn't be done when guests were around. It was Alan's sole responsibility to organise all of this. He decided what needed doing and when; he did the costings, found the tradesmen, did the hiring.

Or that was how it was supposed to work. But one morning a few

263

days after Jack's proposition, Alan was given cause seriously to question his authority when he arrived in reception to find an argument in progress. The altercation was between his parents and the proprietor of the small building firm Alan had hired to do various jobs around the hotel.

'You were supposed to be here by nine o'clock this morning and you roll in now at turned ten o'clock,' Alan's mother was admonishing the man. 'It really isn't good enough.'

'Sorry we were a bit late, missus.' He was a stockily built, square-jawed man who spoke with a rich Devon brogue. 'But I had a bit o' trouble with the van this morning. I just couldn't get her going – had to get a mechanic out to her in the end.'

'Excuses, excuses,' she said.

'It in't just an excuse,' he protested, looking miffed but staying patient. 'It's the God's honest truth.'

'You builders are all the same,' Irene went on rudely. 'Unreliable, the lot of you.'

'Look, I've said I'm sorry,' he said, less patiently. 'I can't do more. So if you'll excuse us, me and the lads have to get on with our work.'

'My wife's right.' Gerald wasn't going to be left out. 'We want this job finished before this summer season, not next. The way you're carrying on, it still won't be done this time next year.'

'We'll be finished by the completion date we gave you,' the man assured him. 'We'll be out of your way well before you open for Easter.'

'I should damned well think so too, the price you're charging us.' Alan's mother was in her element. There was nothing she enjoyed more than flaunting her power.

And to hell with the consequences, thought Alan, observing the builder's annoyance which was increasing, understandably. Good jobbing builders were hard to find. They could pick and choose the work they took on in this age of prosperity, with so many people having property renovated and extended. If Alan's mother's vicious tongue lost them this one they wouldn't get anyone to finish the work before the start of the season because all the reputable builders were booked up for months ahead.

'It's all right, Mother,' Alan said, winking surreptitiously at the builder, whose name was Bill. 'I'll take over now.'

But she was in the mood for a battle and there was no stopping her now she'd got the taste. 'You're nothing but a bunch of layabouts, the lot of you,' she accused the man, whose two employees were standing quietly beside him.

'Here, you wanna watch what you're saying,' Bill objected, his brown eyes hardening as his anger grew. 'That in't fair.'

'As I'm paying your wages, I'll decide what's fair,' she argued.

264

'You come and go when you please with no consideration for us at all. You can't deny that.'

'I certainly do deny it.'

'Do you think we're blind or something?' Gerald put in. 'Do you think we don't notice what time you turn up for work in the mornings?'

'You obviously don't pay attention to what time we finish at night or we wouldn't be having this conversation,' Bill pointed out. 'Anyway, I'm self-employed. I don't have to account to you about time-keeping. As long as the job is finished by the specified date, I'm within my rights.'

'As we're paying you, we have a right to some kind of reliability,' Irene argued.

Now she'd pushed the man too far. 'Right, that's it,' he retaliated. 'As you're obviously not happy with our way of working, we'll get out of your way. We've enough work to last us for a year ahead. We're not staying here to be insulted by the likes of you.'

'Now you're being ridiculous,' said Irene.

'You listen to me, missus,' said Bill, observing her coldly. 'We've plenty of customers waiting to have work done, people who appreciate us and treat us with respect. So you can pay us for what we've done so far and get some other mug to finish the job for you because we in't doing it.' He paused. 'If you can find anyone who'll put up with your attitude.'

'Don't be hasty, Bill,' intervened Alan worriedly. 'My mother doesn't mean what she says.'

'Oh yes I do,' she made plain, undermining her son's authority completely. 'Never mind you walking out on us, you're sacked, the lot of you.'

Alan was so angry he couldn't speak. Hiring and firing building staff was his job and she'd ignored him altogether; behaved as though he wasn't even there. This sort of thing wasn't unusual and he normally accepted it as an occupational hazard. But in a sudden moment of clarity he saw it with a fresh eye.

He could now see with absolute certainty how right Jack was when he said that Alan needed to break away from the family business. While he worked with his parents he would never amount to anything. He would always be twelve years old in their eyes, and he had had enough.

'Ignore my mother,' he said to Bill at last. 'I'm the one you deal with around here.'

'Really, Alan—' began Irene.

'Shut up, Mother,' he blasted.

'How dare you—' she began.

'Don't you dare speak to your mother like that,' added his father.

Had Alan not been so furious, he might have felt embarrassed at having to endure this public humiliation. But he was beyond that sort of sensitivity. He looked from one parent to the other. 'Fine, you deal with it then. I'll keep out of it altogether.' He turned to Bill. 'Sorry about this, mate,' he said.

Bill gave him a nod to let him know that he had no quarrel with him personally. He'd seen Alan humiliated by his parents too many times to bear a grudge.

'I'll leave you to it, then,' Alan announced to his parents, turning to go.

'There's no need for that,' said Irene, looking worried now. 'You can't just go off.'

'Watch me.' He paused, looking at them. 'And when you've finished with Bill, can you come up to my flat, please? I have something to say to you.'

And with that he headed for the lift.

'Your behaviour was utterly disgraceful, Alan,' reproached Irene, perched stiffly on the edge of an armchair in her son's flat a few minutes later. 'I was thoroughly ashamed.'

'I wasn't proud of your appalling behaviour, either,' was her son's unexpected response.

'What!' She wasn't used to having him answer her back and it shocked her. 'In what way did I behave badly?'

'Apart from being unnecessarily rude to the builders, you went over my head completely with them,' he told her. 'And it just isn't on.'

'I had to step in and deal with the situation because you're too damned soft with people who do work for us,' she said. 'You let them do exactly what they like.'

'You have to let them know who's boss,' added his father, standing with his back to the window, dominating the room. 'You can't let them make the rules. You can't allow them to win.'

'But they have won, haven't they?' Alan pointed out heatedly. 'You've sacked them and now there's no one to do the work we urgently need doing. So we're the losers, no doubt about that. They're not bothered because they've got plenty of jobs lined up, like all decent builders these days. About the only people who aren't booked up are cowboys, and there are plenty of those about.'

'You'll soon find someone reputable to finish the job,' was his mother's confident answer.

'Oh, no. Not me,' Alan put her straight. 'You took over from me, remember.'

'Only temporarily,' she told him.

'It's a permanent arrangement as far as I'm concerned,' he informed her. 'The job's all yours from now on. You've humiliated me once too often.' He shook his head. 'But never again.'

'Don't be ridiculous,' rebuked his father. 'It's your job to sort this out.'

'Not any more,' he said. 'I quit.'

They stared at him in bewilderment.

'You mean you're going to leave the job of finding another builder to us?' suggested Irene nervously, at last.

'I'm leaving everything to you from now on.' He forced himself to stay calm. 'I'm leaving the Cliff Head.'

Two pairs of eyes widened in horror.

'Now you really are being silly,' said his mother as though Alan was a recalcitrant child. 'Resigning just because you're in a temper because I paid the builder off.'

Alan looked from one to the other and when he spoke it was in a quiet, reasonable tone. 'That isn't the reason I'm leaving. That just forced me to take a close look at myself and my place in this business as well as my position as an adult human being. I'm not leaving the business in a fit of pique. I'm leaving because I need to do something on my own without the two of you looking over my shoulder the whole time.'

'We don't do that—' began his mother.

'With respect, you do, all the time,' Alan corrected firmly. 'Anyway, an interesting opportunity has come up for me and I've decided to take it.'

'You can't leave,' ordered Irene.

'I can and I will,' Alan told his parents in a definite tone. 'It's something I have to do. I need to prove myself.'

'And what are we supposed to do without you?' asked his mother aggressively.

'You won't have any trouble managing without me. You can run this place standing on your heads, as you've told me so often,' he reminded them. 'I wouldn't go if I wasn't absolutely certain of that.'

'You always have been selfish,' accused his father, hitting out unreasonably.

'I'm what you made me, which is one of the reasons why I have to get away,' Alan tried to explain. 'I'll never know what I'm really capable of if I stay here.'

'Rubbish,' said his mother.

'Absolutely,' supported his father.

'You'll be better off financially without me because I'm giving you my share of the business,' Alan went on to say. 'You can take on a manager to replace me and you won't have to pay him a share of the profits as you do me. I'll be moving out of the flat so you can offer the manager accommodation, too. It'll be an attractive opportunity and you shouldn't have any trouble finding someone suitable.'

267

'Moving out of your flat,' gasped Irene, realising at last that he was serious.

'I won't be far away, though,' he assured her. 'Just a few miles down the coast.'

'Where, exactly?'

He outlined his plans.

'I see.' Her eyes were as cold and hard as stones.

'What will you use for money?' his father enquired coolly.

'I'll use my savings and get a loan for the rest,' he explained. 'It's such a good proposition, I should be able to persuade the bank to lend me what I need.'

'And get yourself into debt with huge interest charges,' warned his father.

'If I have to, yes,' Alan confirmed.

'And if you don't get Gullscombe Manor at the auction, you'll want to stay on here, I suppose?' his mother mocked.

'Oh no. Whatever happens, I'm leaving the Cliff Head,' he made clear. 'It's something I now know I must do. If the Gullscombe Manor thing falls through I shall find something else. I'll find a way to use my experience.'

His mother burst into tears. 'I never thought my own son would be so uncaring of his parents,' she said through dramatic sobs. 'I thought we'd brought you up to respect family values.'

'You have,' he said in a softer tone, because he wasn't an unkind man and he did love his parents. 'My striking out on my own doesn't mean I don't still respect family values. I'll still be a good son to you, if you'll let me. The only thing that will change is that we won't be working together.'

'We gave you everything a child could possibly want . . .' she went on woefully.

'Yes, you did,' he agreed. 'But as an adult I need something else – independence.'

'I've always prided myself on being a good mother.' She just wouldn't let go.

'And you have been,' he assured her. 'I wouldn't dream of saying otherwise.'

'The Cliff Head has always been a family firm,' she rambled on tearfully. 'We've worked hard to make it into a good business for you to eventually inherit. As soon as you were old enough we made you a partner.'

'I know all that and I appreciate everything you've done for me. But I've worked hard too, and I think I've made a valuable contribution to the business,' he asserted. 'But I've gone as far as I can here now. I need a new challenge, my own space, and the chance to see if I can succeed or fail in my own right.'

'You can do that here,' came his mother's muffled suggestion. 'We won't stand in your way.'

He chewed his lip, looking at them. 'You will, without even realising it,' he said. 'The original idea was for you to gradually stand back and leave more of the responsibility to me. But it hasn't happened. This place is in your blood. You just can't let go and leave things to me, which is why we had that scene downstairs just now and why you won't consider any of my ideas for the place. This is *your* hotel with your plans and opinions. You're a part of the place and it's part of you because you built it and made it what it is. I want to do the same thing with a very different kind of hotel from this. So why not let me go with your blessing so that we can stay friends? Wish me well and take an interest. I'd really like that. I'm sure any advice you have to offer will be useful.'

But Irene's tone hardened even more and her tears stopped as suddenly as they'd started. 'We'll have the accountant work out a reasonable price for your share of the business and you'll be paid what you're owed,' she announced through tight lips.

'There's no need for that,' protested Alan. 'I've told you, I don't want any money from you. You can have my share of the Cliff Head and welcome.'

'You'll get what you're entitled to,' she said in an acerbic manner.

'I don't want it.'

'As you were so keen to point out,' she went on coldly, 'you've worked hard and made a contribution. I'm not having you say that we've done you out of anything – that we haven't been fair.'

'Surely you know me better than that.' He was very hurt. 'I would never say any such thing.'

'To eliminate any possibility of that, we will pay you for your share of the business,' she insisted. 'But there'll be no question of us staying friends. You want to leave, so go ahead. But you'll be paid off and all ties between us cut.'

'Mother!' He was shocked. He'd known they wouldn't be pleased but hadn't expected to be banished from their lives altogether. 'Now you're just being vindictive.'

'Steady on, Irene,' warned Gerald.

But she was far too engrossed in her own self-pity to take any notice of him. 'As you've just said, Alan, your father and I can run this place standing on our heads so there's no need for you to stay around for a minute longer,' she blasted at him, her tone increasing in speed with the swell of her temper. 'You can get out of here right away, and any contact we have in the future will be through a solicitor. If you let us have a forwarding address, the money you are owed for your share in the business will be sent to you when the amount has been decided. It will *not* be negotiable.'

Alan felt as though he'd been physically beaten. He looked at his father. 'Does that go for you too? Or are you going to stand up to her for once?'

Gerald looked at his wife. 'Don't you think you're being a bit harsh, dear?' he said in cautious admonition. 'They boy's entitled to a change.'

'You do what you like, Gerald,' she told him with a look that forbade disagreement. 'I've said my piece and I won't change my mind.'

'But, dear—'

'I've told you where I stand on this one, Gerald,' she confirmed. 'He's letting us down and I want no more to do with him. If you feel differently, that's up to you.'

Gerald studied his son's face, unable to hide a fleeting look of regret before saying, 'You heard what your mother said. We want you out of here right away.' His voice quivered slightly with emotion. 'So get yourself and your stuff out.'

Upset but not defeated, Alan said, 'OK. I'll go. I'm sure Jack will put me up at his cottage until something permanent can be sorted out.' He paused, looking at them. 'But aren't you just the tiniest bit proud of your son for finally having the courage to do something for himself?'

'You're no son of mine,' was his mother's parting shot before marching from the room, followed by his father.

For a long time Alan couldn't move; he just stood frozen in the centre of the room, so tense his limbs ached. He felt as though the heart had been ripped out of him; it was a terrible thing to happen between a man and his parents. But there was a new strength there too, a sense that he'd finally grown up. As much as he wanted to go after them, he knew he couldn't go back on what he'd said. To reverse his decision now would be the act of a coward.

Walking over to the window, he stared idly across the bay, the sea black and choppy on this winter's day, banks of low cloud obliterating the horizon altogether. But this view always soothed him, however bad the weather. Thinking back on what had been said, he decided not to refuse the money his mother insisted on paying him. It would make them feel better about cutting him out of their lives, he thought miserably, because they could fuel their grudge by telling themselves that they'd given him something to which he wasn't entitled. Anyway, if he was honest, he reckoned he'd earned it for all the hard work he'd put in over the years, as well as the humiliation they'd made him suffer.

June came into his mind as she often did at odd moments because she was never far from his thoughts. He knew instinctively that she would support him in his current plans and wished more strongly than ever that she was here to go forward with him.

He turned back into the room, sad at the thought of leaving here but strong in the belief that he'd done the right thing. A fresh start was long overdue. The excitement of the new project was clouded by the rift with his parents, though. The last thing he wanted was them out of his life.

Maybe they'd have a change of heart when they'd calmed down and thought the whole thing through, he found himself hoping. But being realistic, he doubted it. His mother could be very stubborn when she wanted her own way about something, and he couldn't give in to her over this, as tempting as that was. He emitted a long sigh, sadly accepting the fact that this really was a parting of the ways.

Chapter Seventeen

Things moved fast in the Lionel Rivers case after Eileen Dodd's confession. Morris's arrogance earned him an early arrest. He was far too conceited to believe that his wife would actually go through with her threat to shop him so made no attempt to escape and was arrested at home later that night.

The fact that Eileen had obviously punished herself over the years and had finally come forward and confessed went in her favour and she received only a suspended sentence for perjury and conspiring to pervert the course of justice.

As for Lionel – his release wasn't immediate because the formalities had to be adhered to and his appeal had to go through the normal channels. Despite his daughters constantly badgering the authorities to hurry things along, it was February before everything was finalised.

On a bitterly cold morning with heatless sun glinting on the frosty rooftops of West London, Daisy and June stood at the prison gates, both dressed in warm coats and fur-lined boots.

'We've waited a long time for this,' said June, her breath turning to steam as she spoke.

'Not nearly as long as Dad has,' her sister pointed out, stamping her feet because her toes were turning numb.

'That's true enough,' agreed June, hugging herself against the cold.

'I feel nervous,' Daisy confessed. 'Excited and happy but a bit scared too. It's such a traumatic thing for anyone to deal with. It'll take time for Dad to adjust to life on the outside.'

'I feel churned up too,' admitted June. 'I hope we don't have to wait much longer because the butterflies in my stomach are multiplying by the moment.'

Just then the small door in the heavy prison gates opened and Lionel Rivers stepped out into freedom. Wearing the smart suit and overcoat his daughters had brought him for this occasion, he stood looking around him with a bewildered expression as the door slammed shut behind him.

Both feeling oddly shy, his daughters walked slowly towards him.

Daisy was too choked up to say anything coherent and only managed a tearful, 'Hello, Dad.'

'Hi, Dad,' said June.

He didn't speak; just looked at them, his eyes brimming with tears. 'Thank you, girls,' he muttered thickly at last. 'Thank you for making this happen.'

That did it; the barriers were down and with one accord they threw their arms around him, all three of them weeping with joy and relief.

'Today is your day, Dad,' Daisy said when she'd recovered sufficiently to speak. 'You can do whatever you like. Get drunk, paint the town red, anything. You deserve it.'

'The only thing I want to do is go home to your place for a cup of tea and the chance to get to know you better,' he told them.

Moist-eyed but smiling, they walked away from the prison in the winter sunlight, a proud father and his two beloved daughters.

One Sunday lunchtime several months later, Daisy said, 'More apple pie, Dad? There's plenty.'

'Thank you, dear, but I couldn't manage another morsel,' he said, patting his stomach. 'It was lovely, though.'

'Nora made the pudding today,' Daisy informed him. 'June and I were in charge of the dinner.'

'You all did very well,' he complimented in his gracious way. 'The whole meal was delicious.'

'It's all down to teamwork,' she grinned. 'I enjoy making Sunday dinner into a family occasion now that we're all together again. I hate to miss it when I'm working Sunday lunchtime.'

'It's good of you to put up with me every Sunday,' said her father.

He was far too self-effacing, in Daisy's opinion, and it upset her. Prison seemed to have robbed him of all his self-esteem. 'We don't "put up" with you, Dad,' she corrected. 'We enjoy having you.'

'We do,' confirmed June.

'Very much so,' added Nora.

'The whole idea of your getting a place just around the corner from us was so that we could see plenty of you,' Daisy reminded him. 'And if you get lonely living on your own, you're welcome to come back here.'

'It's kind of you to offer but you don't have room.' His soft brown eyes had had a worried look about them since he'd been out of prison.

'I suppose not,' agreed June, because she didn't want to patronise him by denying the facts. 'But we managed when you first came out of prison.'

'I wouldn't have imposed on you then if I'd had anywhere else to go.'

'You weren't imposing,' Daisy was keen to make clear.

'Perhaps not. But you and June had to share a bedroom because you gave yours up for me,' he reminded her. 'That's all right in the short term but not as a permanent arrangement. Anyway, there's no need for it, thanks to my compensation money.'

'Just as long as you know that we always like to see you,' Daisy told him.

It was late summer and Morris Dodd was now serving a life sentence for the murder of Rose Rivers. Some people thought he'd got off too lightly, and should have been hanged as Ruth Ellis was last year for killing her lover. Daisy wasn't vindictive enough to wish that on him, or anyone. He was being punished and that was good enough for her.

As there had been no question about her father's wrongful imprisonment, his claim for compensation had been dealt with swiftly. He hadn't received a fortune, but enough to buy a small house in the next street. No amount of money could give him back what prison had taken from him, though: his confidence. He'd been shaky for ages after his release and was still finding it difficult to settle, though he didn't say much about it. Daisy thought it might help if he had a job more suited to him rather than the one in a factory he insisted on doing because there was nothing available in his own field.

Daisy, June and the girls made sure he never lacked for company, but it was Nora to whom he turned for friendship. Being such different types, Daisy didn't think they had much in common besides their age but they got on surprisingly well. Eager for him to be integrated back into the community, Nora had dragged Lionel off to various local associations, none of which he'd continued with except the gardening club, which he enjoyed, already having an interest because of the nature of his work before prison. Nora hadn't been a gardening enthusiast before but she went with him to keep him company and, typical of her, became keen. Between the two of them they kept his tiny garden and theirs a picture.

But now Daisy was recalled to the present by Nora, who was nudging her and saying, 'So what do you think, Daisy?'

'About what?' she asked, startled slightly.

'Cor, dear, oh dear, you're a dreamer today,' she said. 'I was just suggesting that we all go over the park after dinner as it's such a lovely afternoon.'

'Can we, Mum?' urged Shirley.

'Go on, Mum, say yes,' coaxed Belinda.

'OK,' agreed Daisy absently. 'I'm on duty later on, though, so I won't be able to stay for very long.'

June gave her a studious look. 'Are you all right?' she asked. 'You seem very distant.'

'I'm fine,' she nodded, but there was something on her mind apart from her father, and she just couldn't let it go.

However, the subject of the job Lionel had taken in a factory

275

because there were no vacancies in the council's parks department came up, and a discussion ensued on which she tried hard to concentrate. June pointed out that he didn't have to do that job. He could manage for a while on his compensation.

'I'm only fifty-two,' he reminded her. 'I'm not ready to be put out to grass yet. I need something definite to do, a proper purpose to the day.'

'But you hate it at the factory.'

'Yeah, but I'd sooner do that than be sitting on my arse at home all day.'

'You could afford to take some time to look for something more suitable,' June persisted. 'Isn't that right, Daisy? Daisy . . .?'

'What?'

'What *is* the matter with you?'

'Nothing, sorry. I'm listening now, honest.'

June repeated what she'd said and Daisy agreed. But she wasn't paying proper attention. Something about the shaft of sunlight pouring into the room through the window had set off a chain of memories about last summer and who had made that time, a year ago, so very special for her. Here the sun shining through the net curtains made dappled patterns on the wall. She recalled the effect of the same thing in Jack's cottage where there had been no need for net curtains. She remembered the feeling of fresh air and light and space, the prettiness of Gullscombe Bay. So vivid were her recollections, she could almost smell the air and taste the salt on her lips.

How ironic it had all turned out to be. She'd rejected Jack, only to have Nat betray her in the cruellest possible way. Dear Jack, just the thought of him made her feel warm inside. She must have been mad to turn him down.

She looked around the table at this cluster of loved ones, everyone interrupting each other in the way people do when they're close. It still gave her pleasure to see her father in their midst, her daughters sitting either side of the grandfather they'd taken to their hearts so readily. They all meant so much to her.

But there was something missing in her life, and it was that which dominated her thoughts all afternoon and right through her waitressing shift. By the time she got home from work that night, she had come to a decision. She asked June and Nora if they could do her rather a big favour this coming weekend . . .

The following Saturday her stomach churned throughout the train journey and she was visibly trembling in the taxi from Torquay station to Gullscombe Bay. What she was about to do was crazy; just to turn up at Jack's door without warning. It was a huge gamble but something she felt compelled to do. By arriving unannounced, she believed she would

276

get a genuine reaction and know if he still wanted her.

It was mid-afternoon. Sunshine bathed the landscape and gave her a feeling of *déjà vu* because it had been like this when Jack had driven her to Gullscombe Bay that first time with the girls. Now, seeing the bay through the trees at the top of the hill brought tears to her eyes. It was so good to be back.

Her heart was pounding, partly with excitement, partly with nerves when she paid the taxi driver and walked up the path to the cottage, carrying a small overnight bag. With a shaky hand, she lifted the heavy metal knocker and let it fall with a resounding thud on the front door.

In all her agonising about whether or not he would still want her, she had never imagined the possibility of being greeted at the door by anyone but him. So her spirits plummeted when she found herself staring into the sparkling brown eyes of a youngish woman with honey-blonde hair and smoothly tanned shoulders gleaming beneath a yellow sundress.

'Yes?' said the woman, smiling enquiringly at the little woman with the big worried eyes. 'Can I help you?'

Daisy cursed her impulsive behaviour. Not only had she off-loaded her responsibilities for the weekend, she was now about to cause trouble for Jack by turning up on his doorstep. Having an ex of her husband's on the doorstep with an overnight bag would be about as welcome to this woman as a smack in the mouth.

'I was looking for Jack, actually, Jack Saunders.' She wasn't about to get into deeper waters by lying about it but she felt extremely awkward.

Just then two small children appeared, a boy and a girl. 'How long till we can go down on the beach, Mummy?' asked the little boy. 'I'm dying to go in the sea.'

Mummy – Daisy's thoughts went into top gear. These children were about the same age as her own daughters, and it was only a year since she'd last seen Jack. Surely he wouldn't have . . .? No, she couldn't believe that he'd had a wife and kids he hadn't told her about. Not Jack.

'I'll only be a few minutes,' the woman told the children. 'Go and wait for me in the back garden. Don't get impatient and go without me down to the beach.'

The children hurried away and their mother gave Daisy a conspiratorial look. 'The beach here is very safe but I won't let them go down there by themselves. They're not quite big enough yet. They might wander into the sea and go too far out.'

Daisy nodded in an understanding manner which, knowing the beach so well, she could do truthfully.

'So you want to see Jack,' the woman went on, seeming unconcerned.

'If he's around . . .' Daisy felt terrible.

'He isn't, I'm afraid.'

'Oh well, it doesn't matter,' she told her, anxious to get away under the circumstances. 'I just thought I'd call on the off chance that he might be in.'

The woman looked at the overnight bag and gave Daisy a querying look.

'I thought I'd look him up but as he isn't in, it doesn't matter.' She felt really embarrassed now, as well as having a horrible ache in her heart.

'It isn't that he isn't in,' explained the woman. 'It's just that he doesn't live here any more.'

'What!' Daisy couldn't believe it.

'My husband and I bought the place from him earlier this year,' she said. 'We live in London. This is our holiday cottage, our little bolt hole. The children and I have been down here for most of the school summer holidays. My husband just comes down at the weekends.'

'Oh.' Daisy felt weak with relief. On the heels of this glorious feeling came concern for Jack. Something very dramatic must have happened for him to sell the cottage he loved so much.

'You seem surprised.'

'I'm absolutely shocked,' she confirmed. 'This place was his pride and joy. I can't imagine there could be anything bad enough to make him sell up and leave here.'

'It wasn't anything bad – quite the opposite, as far as I know.' She gave Daisy a close look. 'But you've obviously been travelling and must be feeling a bit weary. So why not come inside and I'll tell you exactly where you can find him over a cup of tea.'

'But your children are waiting to go to the beach.'

'It won't hurt them to wait a little longer,' she said, ushering Daisy into the cottage. 'They're not exactly deprived.'

'In that case, thank you very much indeed,' said Daisy politely, and followed the woman inside, eager to hear what she had to say.

'It doesn't look much like the beginnings of a swimming pool to me, mate,' said Jack, grinning at the leader of the team who were installing a swimming pool in the grounds of Gullscombe Manor. 'It looks more like something from the Battle of the Somme, as though you're digging in for trench warfare.'

'Give us a chance,' defended the man, who was bare-chested and wearing shorts. 'We've only just started the job. It'll be lovely when it's finished. Just like the pictures in the brochure.'

'Yeah, I know,' sighed Jack. 'I suppose I'm getting impatient for things to be finished.'

'I told you at the start the pool wouldn't be ready for this season,' the man reminded him.

'You did. I'm just over-anxious to have everything in place so that when we start promoting the hotel we can truthfully offer a full range of facilities,' said Jack. 'My partner and I have put all our money into this project and we have to make it work as a commercial proposition.'

'Just as well to get the pool done now,' the man chatted on with a strong Devon accent. 'While you're in a state of chaos, having a few more workmen around and a lump of the garden dug up won't make much difference.'

'You're right there.' Dressed in shorts and a T-shirt, his skin deeply tanned, Jack looked towards the house. It had scaffolding all around it. The whole place was crawling with workmen and had been for the past few months. Builders were repairing outside walls, knocking down internal ones, fitting en suite bathrooms, making one of the downstairs rooms into a bar and another into a restaurant. And to add to all that, work on the swimming pool had just begun.

'Sometimes when I look at it I feel as though it'll never be finished. The renovations seem to have been going on for ever.'

'You're bound to feel like that,' sympathised the man, speaking with a cigarette in the corner of his mouth. 'You're having a lot of work done all at the same time. You can't do that without inconvenience.'

'My partner and I won't know ourselves when we're not tripping over builders' rubble every time we move about inside.'

'Living in the middle of it doesn't help,' he commiserated.

'We've no choice,' Jack confided. 'As we're paying the mortgage on this place it would be financial suicide to pay out for other accommodation as well.'

'There are worse places to live than this, chaos or no chaos,' the man commented. 'It's a lovely spot you've got here.' He looked out across the bay, the sea shining in the sun.

'It is.'

'If I didn't live around here I'd come here for my holidays myself,' the man chortled.

'Let's hope lots of people from the towns and cities feel the same way as you and me,' agreed Jack, following the other man's gaze and looking out to sea, shading his eyes against the sun.

A movement on the edge of the wooded area caught his attention. Someone emerged from the trees and was heading for the gardens. A woman carrying a holdall. That was odd because this was private property. This time next year hotel guests would be trailing up and down the beach path all day but whoever that person was, she was trespassing.

He stared, squinting at the slight figure struggling up the slope. Even at this distance there was something achingly familiar about the way she moved. Now he really was getting delusions, he told himself,

279

imagining every woman he saw to be Daisy. But it really did look like her. She lifted her hand and waved and he knew that it was her. He didn't know how or why. *But it was her.* She'd come back. She really had come back to him.

Leaving the man staring after him, he tore across the garden to meet her, smiling fit to bust.

When Daisy saw him coming she dropped her bag on to the ground and ran to meet him, her laughter ringing out across the gardens. Everything she needed to know was there in his eyes. Words weren't necessary for either of them.

The swimming pool installer watched with interest as the couple clung to each other, making a romantic picture with the sea behind them. 'It's like something out of a bloomin' film,' he muttered to himself. 'Canoodling is all very well in its place but some of us have work to do.'

And he jumped down into the trench to talk to the men who were digging down there.

Alan was full of Jack's reunion with Daisy when he and Paula were dining in a Torquay restaurant that evening. 'Apparently she just turned up out of the blue, appeared on the beach path like a dream come true,' he told her excitedly. 'He thought he was seeing things at first. But no, it really was her. You should see him, Paula, he's like a ruddy teenager.'

She smiled. 'I can imagine. So what happens next?' she enquired conversationally. 'Will she leave London and come to live at Gullscombe Bay?'

'I don't know what their long-term plans are,' he told her. 'But he certainly can't up sticks and go to live in London now that we've taken on the manor, can he?'

'Not really, no.'

'So I suppose she will move to Devon,' he surmised. 'She's got to go back to London tomorrow, apparently, because of her two little girls. She's left them with her sister and her friend for the weekend, with her father helping out.'

'Her sister being your wife, of course?'

'Well, yes,' he confirmed, and went on to repeat what Daisy had told him about how they'd cleared their father's name.

'Quite a story.'

'Phew, I'll say. That's typical of June, though, to take on something like that,' he said in a tone of admiration. 'She's a very determined woman when she decides to do something.'

'Like when she decided to leave you,' Paula pointed out.

'Ouch, that's a bit harsh.'

'Yes, it was a bit bitchy,' she admitted, making a face. 'I'm sorry, Alan.'

He shrugged. 'That's all right,' he assured her. 'I'm the one who should apologise. I was going on about her, which is rude of me when I'm out with you for the evening, especially after what she did to me. I just didn't realise I was doing it.' He gave her a persuasive smile. 'Am I forgiven?'

'Sure.'

'Good.'

Breaking some bread to eat with her soup, she asked, 'Why are you so thrilled about Jack and Daisy getting back together?'

'Because he's crazy about her,' he explained. 'He's a good friend and I care about him.'

She gave him a shrewd look. 'It isn't because Daisy is your sister-in-law and her being together with Jack will give you contact with your wife, then?'

'Of course not,' he was rather too quick to deny.

Paula chewed her bread in thoughtful silence, then made an observation that took him aback. 'It isn't working out for us, is it, Alan?'

His soup spoon was poised in mid-air. 'Why . . . what makes you say that?'

'There's nothing there,' was her frank reply.

'I wouldn't say that.'

'As much as we both want it and as hard as we try, we just can't produce that magic ingredient.'

'That's just because we don't see enough of each other.' He was fighting against rejection even though he knew what she was saying was true. 'What with all the organisation for the manor and doing a job as well, I just never get any time as I only have the one night off a week.'

Both he and Jack still had jobs because they needed incomes until they opened the hotel for business next spring and got money that way. Jack had stayed on as restaurant manager at the Cliff Head since Alan's parents had no quarrel with him. Alan worked as a barman in a Torquay pub. It was quite a comedown after his previous position but it brought in enough cash for him to pay his way, and he actually rather enjoyed the job.

'It isn't just that, Alan, and we both know it,' came her candid opinion. 'I think if we'd been able to see more of each other we'd probably have ended our affair long before this.'

'Is that what you're leading up to, Paula?' he asked. 'You want to end it?'

She reached across the table and took his hand. 'I'm only doing what we both know is inevitable,' she told him in a tone of sad resignation. 'Let's finish it while we're still friends, which is what we should have stayed. Things were fine between us then.'

'And they still are.' He was reluctant to face facts because it would mean the awful loneliness of not having a female in his life again.

'No, they're not, Alan,' she disagreed, removing her hand and sipping a glass of wine.

'Is there someone else?' he enquired. 'Is that it?'

'Not for me,' was her cryptic reply.

'What's that supposed to mean?'

'You're the one with someone else.'

'I've not been seeing anyone else,' he denied hotly. 'I wouldn't do that to you.'

'I know. But you're still in love with your wife, Alan.' It was a categorical statement. 'That was what I meant.'

'June and I are finished, you know that.'

'You're still in love with her, though.'

'What makes you say that with such certainty?'

She gave a dry laugh. 'You should see yourself,' she told him. 'You light up when you mention her name.'

'Do I, really?' He hadn't realised his feelings were so obvious.

'Absolutely,' she confirmed. 'This probably isn't a conscious thing but I believe the reason you're so delighted about Jack's reconciliation with Daisy is because it brings June closer to you. Even if you don't see her, having Daisy around means you'll get news of her. It will give you contact with her again.'

'That isn't fair,' he protested. 'I am genuinely pleased for Jack's sake. You're making me sound selfish.'

'I don't mean to. And I'm not saying that your having a personal interest is intentional,' she explained. 'I know that you're pleased for Jack's sake. But I think that some of the pleasure comes from the reason I've mentioned, even if only subconsciously.'

He lowered his eyes for a moment because he couldn't honestly deny it. 'Even if it were true, it's only thoughts,' he pointed out. 'I'm not going to try and get her back or anything. June and I are history. I accepted that long ago.'

'You're not over her, though.'

'It isn't easy when you've been married to someone.'

'I accept that.' She looked at him over the small floral centrepiece of roses and sweet peas. 'Maybe there's a woman out there some-where who can make you light up in the same way as June does. But that woman isn't me.'

Alan wasn't going to insult her intelligence by denying it. 'I'm so sorry, Paula,' he said, looking sheepish. 'You're a lovely person and I'm very fond of you . . .' His voice tailed off.

'The feeling's mutual so let's part while we can still do it in a civilised manner,' she said, to avoid any further embarrassment. 'We'll see each other around, as we always have, and I'll follow the progress of Gullscombe Manor Hotel with interest. But let's not try to force something that's never going to happen.'

He sighed. 'What can I say?'

'Nothing,' she said. 'Just finish your soup before it gets cold. Then you can tell me how the renovations are coming along at the manor.'

They chatted amiably over the rest of the meal but the atmosphere wasn't relaxed. They were both deeply disappointed. Disappointed because they had failed to find something they both needed and had hoped for in each other.

Daisy was extremely impressed with Jack's plans for Gullscombe Manor. 'I think it's a wonderful idea. It'll be fabulous when it's finished,' she enthused.

'It had better be after all the chaos and expense,' he told her. 'Though it is sometimes hard to imagine the finished product with all this mess everywhere.'

They were sitting on the veranda, surrounded by scaffolding and builders' materials, including a cement mixer and a mechanical digger. Looking beyond the incipient swimming pool, they could see the lights coming on all around the bay, a necklace glowing in the dusk. 'I can visualise it already,' she said. 'It's in such a wonderful position.'

'I hope you realise that you're to blame for all of this,' he teased her.

'Why?'

'When I saw that the place was up for auction I remembered you saying something about the possibility of someone buying it for commercial reasons,' he explained. 'That was my inspiration.'

'Let's hope it'll be a success, then,' she said, 'or I'll be in dead trouble.'

'I'm that pleased to see you I can't imagine ever being angry with you about anything.'

'I feel the same.' She paused. 'But I nearly died when I found out you'd moved from the cottage.'

'You couldn't have been more amazed than I was when I saw you coming up the path,' Jack said. 'You still haven't told me what actually made you do it.'

'Well, we were all sitting around the table last Sunday dinner time and I suddenly wondered what I was doing there when I could be here with you,' she admitted. 'I couldn't get it off my mind all day so decided to make the necessary arrangements to turn up on your doorstep. That way, if you'd found someone else at least I'd have known.'

'No chance of that,' he assured her. 'I still want to marry you.'

'I'd have been very disappointed if you'd changed your mind,' she said softly.

'On a practical note, though,' he began, 'one of us is going to have to move.'

'I'll come here.' Her smile darkened into a frown. 'It'll be hard leaving the others and I'll miss them like mad but you can't have everything you want in life, and the girls and I belong with you.' She shrugged. 'You're obviously not in a position to move to London now, are you?'

'Well, no.' He waved his hand towards the house. 'Anyway, I want you to be a part of all this, to work in the new business with me. If you'd like that, of course,' he added, because Jack wasn't the type to take anything for granted.

'I'd love it,' she was quick to assure him. 'But how will Alan feel about it?'

'He'll be all for it, I should think. We're going to need plenty of willing hands, and who better to fill the breach than a member of the family with a special interest in the place.'

'Family,' she echoed. 'It sounds lovely.'

'Husband and wife working together. I hope you won't find that too much.'

'I could never have too much of you.'

'Time will tell.'

'If I say it myself, I'm a good waitress,' she mentioned, her thoughts moving on. 'Or wouldn't that be a fitting job for the wife of one of the proprietors?'

'Daisy,' he said, leaning forward and holding her hands, 'we are all going to have to muck in to make this place a success. We will be taking on staff but there'll be times when they're not around and we'll have to get on and do their work. I'll scrub the floors if I haven't got someone to do it. There'll be no standing on ceremony. We'll be part of a team.'

'Sounds great.' There was so much to think about and she did have to consider the girls' needs. 'Where will we live now that you've sold the cottage?'

'It'll have to be here at the manor somewhere. Even apart from the fact that I'll need to be on hand, I put all my money into this place so I can't afford to take on anything else.' He pondered for a moment. 'We're having the outhouses made into staff accommodation and making the attics into flats for management. Alan and I were going to have one of those each but that won't be suitable for us because of the girls.' He paused again, remembering something. 'There's an old gardener's cottage in the grounds that could be done up.'

'Sounds promising.'

'Leave it to me,' he assured her. 'I'll sort something nice out for us. The main thing is for us to set the date.'

'I can't wait.' She hesitated, looking worried suddenly. 'But I want to tell the others about it before I actually set the date, if you don't mind. I want to talk it over with them, you know. Obviously they'll be upset at the idea of me and the girls being so far away. I'm not happy about that aspect of it either. But I won't keep you waiting long because the sooner the better as far as I'm concerned.'

'Me too,' he enthused. 'I won't want you to go back to London tomorrow.'

'It won't be like when I left before, though, will it?' she pointed out tenderly. 'Because this time we both know that I'll be coming back.'

'So, what do you think of Daisy's news, then, Lionel?' asked Nora, a week or so later when they called in for a drink at the local pub after their weekly visit to the gardening club.

'I'm dead chuffed for her,' he enthused. 'This Jack sounds like a genuine sort of a bloke. I can't wait to meet him.'

'I'm looking forward to meeting him again too. I've only ever seen him once but he seemed like an absolute sweetheart when he came to the house before,' Nora told him, sipping a glass of stout. 'From what's been said, I get the idea that he's devoted to Daisy and the girls. You could tell they liked each other when he came to the house that time.'

'Sounds to me as though he's genuinely fond of her,' he said.

'I'm so pleased she's found someone decent at last,' Nora went on. 'She needs a bit of cherishing after the way that Nat fella treated her. As well as all the abuse she's had to endure as an unmarried mother.'

'Bad, was it?'

'Awful. It's disgusting the way people behave towards women in Daisy's position,' Nora declared. 'Even the midwife treated her like dirt when she had the girls. Wouldn't let her have anything to help with the pain because she wasn't married. I really gave her a mouthful over that.'

'I wish I'd been around at that time,' he said. 'I'd have given her what for.'

'Nat could have saved her from such a lot of pain by marrying her but he wouldn't do it.' She made a face. 'Still, it's just as well. He'd probably have been a lousy husband, anyway.'

'At least she's found someone nice now.'

'Mm. Although I'm pleased for her I'm devastated for myself,' Nora admitted, swallowing hard on a lump in her throat. 'She and the girls have been a part of my life for so long, their going away is bound to leave an awful gap. I've got so used to them being there, it never occurred to me that one day they wouldn't be.'

'We're all going to miss them and that's a fact,' Lionel agreed in a sympathetic manner. 'I feel as though I'm just getting to know Daisy and she's going away.' He paused. 'It's a weird feeling having to get to know your daughters from scratch when they're grown women. I haven't always known how to handle it, you know . . . being a bloke.'

'You're doing fine.'

'I feel as though I'm beginning to get there.' He shrugged. 'And now Daisy's off.'

'It's a shame,' Nora commiserated. 'I wouldn't dream of spoiling it for her by telling her but I'm absolutely dreading her going.'

'Still, we'll keep each other company,' he encouraged, patting her hand in a friendly manner.

'I know,' she said, rummaging in her pocket for her handkerchief and sniffing into it.

'And we'll have June.'

'Yes, of course we will. I've grown fond of June,' Nora told him. 'But we're not as close as Daisy and I are. Me and Daisy have been together a long time, since before she had the kids, even.' She raised her eyes in self-derision. 'But what must you think of me, worrying about myself when Daisy's got the chance of a better life? She deserves a break and I couldn't be more pleased for her. I just wish she wasn't going to be so far away.'

'You wouldn't be human if you didn't feel as you do. And I certainly don't think bad of you for being sad about it. I'm grateful to you for being so good to her over the years. I was certainly no help.'

'Don't start beating yourself up about something that wasn't your fault,' she admonished kindly.

He gave her a lopsided grin. 'You're a good friend, Nora,' he told her in a warm tone. 'As much as I love my daughters, I need someone of my own age to talk to.'

'Same here,' she enthused. 'I didn't realise just how much until you joined the family. However much we love the others, we are of a different generation and, as such, our ideas are different.' She paused thoughtfully. 'Of course, it doesn't always follow that you'll get on with someone just because you're in the same age group, but I felt comfortable with you right away, when I came to see you in prison that first time. Yet we're very different.'

'You're a lot brainier than I am, for a start.'

'Don't be daft,' she laughed. 'I'm curious about things so I take the trouble to find out more about them, that's all.'

'It isn't all down to that. You're an intelligent woman,' he insisted. 'But you don't shove it down my throat.'

'You'd soon tell me if I did.'

'Not half.'

A sudden commotion at the bar halted the conversation as a crowd of Teds came in and an argument erupted because the management were refusing to serve them with alcohol on the grounds that they were under age. The Teds denied it rowdily, even though the landlord was pointing out the undeniable fact that if they were eighteen they wouldn't have greased quiffs, long sideburns and a DA haircut but an army short back and sides.

'There's one good thing about Daisy going away,' Nora confided to Lionel as the Teds made a noisy exit. 'With all the trouble around here between the Teds and the immigrant community, with fights on the streets almost every night of the week, Daisy and the girls are better off out of it. At least she won't have to be out on her own late at night any more, travelling back from work.'

He nodded in agreement. 'You can feel the hostility simmering in the air, can't you?' he observed. 'As though violence is about to erupt at any minute.'

'I know what you mean.'

'Black and white don't mix around here, and from what I've heard, all the trouble isn't only down to the Teds,' he confided. 'The older generation aren't blameless. There are plenty of fascists stirring things up.'

'And the Teds jump at the chance of an excuse for a fight,' agreed Nora.

'Exactly. After doing a long stretch in the nick, I reckon I'm pretty tough, but even I don't like being out on the streets on my own of a night in this area,' he confessed. 'And I hate to think of Daisy doing that journey.'

'I've worried about it for years,' said Nora. 'Even before we had a racial problem around here, the streets were full of dodgy characters after dark.'

'Thank God that's coming to an end for Daisy. She'll have someone to look out for her from now on.'

'Daisy will do her whack in that hotel business, though. She's been independent for too long to sit back and let a man keep her.'

'It'll be a better life for her, though.'

'Definitely.' Nora finished her drink, looking at him. 'You must have found London a very different place after all those years locked away,' she remarked chattily.

'I still do,' Lionel told her. 'Especially as I wasn't from around here, and Wembley was a whole lot quieter.'

'You wouldn't want to go back to Wembley?'

He shook his head vigorously. 'No fear. Even apart from the bad memories, there's nothing for me there now,' he said. 'Whereas here, I do have people. I know Daisy's going away but there's still June . . .' He paused. 'And you.'

'We all need people nearby who care about us,' she said. 'I think one of the reasons Daisy and I got friendly so quickly was because neither of us had anyone else, unless you count that waste of space, Nat.'

He nodded.

'Sometimes it used to seem as though it was just Daisy and me against the rest of the world,' she went on. 'A spinster and an unmarried mum. Both outsiders.'

'And now you've got an ex-con in the gang as well,' he said with a grin.

She threw back her head and laughed. 'At least you can joke about it,' she chuckled.

'Just about.'

'Do you feel properly settled now?'

'No,' he replied without hesitation. 'I'm glad to be out of the nick, of course, and I value my freedom, naturally. But I still feel restless. I don't feel as though I belong.'

'Is that because you hate the job in the factory?'

'That doesn't help.'

'Can't you find something else?'

'No.'

'I thought there was supposed to be loads of jobs about.' She was puzzled. 'That's the impression I get from reading the paper, anyway.'

'There is plenty of work about but not in the parks department,' he informed her. 'There's nothing at all in that line at the moment. Still, beggars can't be choosers. So the factory will do me for the moment.'

'Hardly a beggar, Lionel, as you got your compensation,' she pointed out. 'Surely you've enough to live on until more suitable work comes up.'

'That money will soon fritter away if I sit on my backside all day doing nothing,' he said. 'I want to keep it in case of an emergency. One of the girls might suddenly need help, and if that happens, I want to be able to step in. Anyway, I want to give Daisy the best wedding ever. It's traditional for the bride's parents to shoulder most of the expense. Walking my daughter down the aisle is something I never thought I'd do. It'll be my proudest moment.'

'I can understand how you feel,' she remarked. 'But after all you've been through, you're entitled not to have to do work you loathe.'

'I'll be all right,' Lionel assured her perkily. 'Don't you worry about me. The important thing is being free, and all thanks to my lovely daughters.' He smiled at her. 'With backup support from you, as well.'

'I was just baby-sitter and general dogsbody,' she explained. 'They did it all. You can be very proud of those girls of yours. They're fighters, both of them.'

'You don't have to tell me,' he said, his eyes soft with affection for them.

'I wonder who they get it from?' she grinned knowingly.

'God knows,' he said in his usual modest way.

Attracted by a sudden clatter, she looked towards the door as a couple of the Teds burst back in and swaggered over to the bar, insisting to the landlord that they were over eighteen and deferred from army service.

'Drink up, Lionel. I think we'd better get out of here, sharpish,' Nora suggested. 'It looks as though there's going to be trouble.'

'It does, an' all,' he agreed, draining his glass and standing up to go.

They hurried to the door and went out on to the streets that had such a dangerous feel to them lately.

Chapter Eighteen

Daisy's wedding was everything she'd always dreamed of and thought she'd never have: a long dress, bridesmaids, church bells, a reception with a four-piece band – the works. Even the weather smiled on her. Being early December it was cold, but one of those glorious winter days with a dry crisp feel to it and sunshine glinting on everything.

'Happy?' asked Jack as they smooched around the dance floor at the wedding reception in the functions room of the Gullscombe Arms.

'Need you ask?' She was radiant in an ivory satin dress of a simple design with a fitted bodice, long sleeves and a high neckline suitable for a winter wedding. Her hair was taken back into a chignon and adorned with cream satin flowers attached to a billowing veil. 'Are you?'

'Are you a Catholic?' was his answer to that.

She laughed. 'It's been a great day, hasn't it?' she said. 'Thank you.'

'You're thanking *me*?'

'I certainly am. Not only for marrying me but also for doing it the way I wanted it, in a Catholic church, and all that that entails.' As a non-Catholic, it had been necessary for Jack to take some instruction from the priest beforehand, during which he had agreed to allow any children of the marriage to be raised in the faith; standard procedure in a mixed marriage.

'I'd have married you in a phone box if it was what you wanted, and could be arranged,' he smiled. 'And the other stuff wasn't a problem.'

They'd chosen to marry in Devon rather than the church in London where Daisy and the girls attended Mass because they had both wanted the reception to be in Gullscombe Bay, where they had fallen in love, and would be living. Fortunately the parish priest here hadn't had a problem with Daisy having two children out of wedlock, and had been happy to marry them. She wasn't divorced – that was the important thing as far as the Catholic Church was concerned. The Manor wasn't quite ready to host a wedding reception so they'd decided on the village pub instead.

Shirley and Belinda had been bridesmaids, June a matron of honour and Alan the best man. Because Jack was so popular in the village, the wedding had turned into something of a community event and many of Gullscombe Bay's residents were here this evening. It was surprising the amount of people you could get into a village pub.

'It's been such a smashing day, I don't want it to end,' she sighed.

'There'll be plenty more good days for us,' he told her. 'This is just the beginning.'

'I know it is and I'm really looking forward to our life together,' she assured him. 'But today is so special I feel as though I want to hang on to it.'

'That's understandable and I hate to bring you down to earth but it'll be time to get changed out of your wedding finery soon,' he reminded her. 'We don't want to be too late getting away.'

'I'll go and get changed after this dance.' They were staying overnight in a Torquay hotel before travelling to the Lake District tomorrow for a week. June, Nora and Lionel were all taking time off work and staying on here to look after the girls while they were away. They were staying at Gullscombe Manor and making a sort of holiday of it. 'I'm still a bit worried about going away and leaving the girls, you know,' she confessed.

'They'll have a whale of a time with June and Nora and your dad,' Jack said to reassure her. 'They're so used to them they won't even notice that we're not around. Especially as they'll get spoiled rotten.'

'I know I'm being soft,' she went on. 'But I've never left them for as long as that before.'

'It's only a week, and we'll make it up to them when we get back,' he promised her.

'You're so sweet to them.'

'It's no effort, I can assure you, because I think the world of them. You and I need a honeymoon, a little time away on our own. But after that, whenever we go away it'll be all of us together as a family.'

'I love you, Mr Saunders,' she chuckled.

'The feeling is mutual, Mrs Saunders,' he said, holding her very close.

One thing that was casting a dark shadow over Daisy's perfect day was the thought of living so far away from Nora and June and her father. She knew she couldn't have everything and that Jack and the girls must be her priority now, but the thought of them not being close by gave her a tight ache inside.

'Brings tears to your eyes to watch them, doesn't it?' June remarked to Alan as they sat together watching the newlyweds dancing. June and Alan were alone at the table; everyone else in their party had gone off – some to dance, others to mingle. Shirley and Belinda – resplendent in red velvet bridesmaids' dresses – were bopping with Nora and their grandfather close to the band; they'd been at it for ages and showed no sign of flagging. 'I've never seen a couple more right for each other than Daisy and Jack.'

'Just like us,' he said.

She forced a dry laugh to keep the tone light and hide the depth of her feelings for Alan, which were frightening in their intensity since seeing him again. Having been among the main participants in today's proceedings, they had been in each other's company for most of the time, albeit not on their own until now. 'Let's hope they don't end up the same way,' she said.

'It doesn't have to be like this, you know, June.'

'Alan, don't . . .'

'I still love you,' he burst out, unable to hold his feelings back.

She started visibly from the profound effect his sudden declaration had on her. But she daren't let a few sweet words allow her to lose track of the facts. 'Weddings have a romantic effect on people,' she said lightly, cheeks suffused with pink, folds of pale lemon satin so perfect with her dark colouring. 'They're known for it. It's got something to do with all the emotion floating about in the atmosphere.'

'I'd rather you didn't trivialise something that's so important to me,' he admonished.

'I didn't mean to trivialise it,' she explained. 'But this isn't the time to bring up our feelings for each other; not in a room full of people.'

'As far as I know, there is no special time to tell someone you love them,' was his simple answer to that.

It was what she wanted to hear so much, her good intentions weakened. 'Are you saying that even after the terrible thing I did to you, you'd still be willing to take me back?'

He met her eyes. 'Yes, that's exactly what I'm saying,' he affirmed. He had planned never to ask her back again but seeing her today, that resolution had disappeared.

'Alan, you don't understand—'

'Things are different now that I've made the break from the Cliff Head. I'm a different person, much more able to stand on my own two feet,' he cut in, having always suspected that his parents had been a contributing factor in June's decision to leave him, even though she'd denied it. 'It couldn't have been easy for you, working so close with my folks. I know my mother could be difficult at times.'

June felt like a different person too, since unburdening herself to Daisy about her past. The scars were still there but, bringing it out into the open had lessened the feeling of isolation and made her braver about her thoughts and memories. Being with Alan again was like being held in two loving arms and she wanted more of it, much more. That was all very well, she reminded herself, but nothing had changed as far as her reasons for leaving him were concerned.

Seeing the genuine warmth in his eyes, however, she felt a surge of hope and experienced a defining moment. There was only one way she and Alan stood a chance of happiness together and that entailed doing something that carried a huge risk. She decided to take that risk.

'Alan, we need to talk . . .'

'I'm all for that and the sooner the better—'

But at that crucial moment there was a noisy interruption.

'This is the best day ever, Auntie June,' announced Shirley, breathless from dancing, cheeks flushed with excitement. 'It's better than Christmas.'

'Mummy looks ever so pretty, doesn't she?' added Belinda. 'She looks like a film star.'

'I think so too,' agreed June.

'And you two look like little princesses,' said Alan, smiling at their shining faces, red velvet hair bands decorated with small white satin flowers adorning their heads. 'You're the prettiest bridesmaids I've ever seen.'

They beamed. This was their first taste of glamour.

'Come and dance,' urged Shirley, tugging at June's hand. 'And you, Uncle Alan.'

Nora and Lionel arrived back at the table just as the band struck up with 'Rock Around the Clock'.

'Phew, thank God for a sit-down,' said Nora, grinning at June and Alan. 'It's your turn now. Those kids will keep you at it until you're on your knees.'

June smiled at Alan and they allowed themselves to be led on to the floor to dance rock 'n' roll style. When they returned to the table the others were there so a private conversation wasn't possible. Anyway, Alan had to attend to his duties as best man, organising a send-off for the departing bride and groom.

Clouds of confetti showering the happy couple, they departed to cheers from the crowd gathered outside the pub. June stood beside Alan as they watched Jack's black Ford Anglia, with a 'Just Married' sign on the back, disappear out of sight. June was imbued with a mixture of emotions. She was happy for Daisy but sad that she was going to be living so far away. They would still see each other occasionally but it wouldn't be the same.

A hand holding hers recalled her to the present and she glanced down to see Shirley looking somewhat forlorn.

'What's the matter, poppet?' she asked.

'Nothing.' But she was brushing tears from her eyes with the back of her hand.

'They'll be back before you know it,' June comforted her, guessing what the problem was. 'And in the meantime, you and me and Nora and Granddad are all going to have such fun together.'

'Just because it's wintertime doesn't mean we can't go out and about,' Alan added. 'I'll take you all out in my car and you can help me show Nora and your granddad the area.'

'We have to go to school,' Belinda reminded him. Daisy had moved to Devon a couple of weeks ago so that she could be on hand for the wedding preparations. The girls had started at the village school right away. Daisy had wanted them to be settled in their new school before she went away on honeymoon.

'Yes, but we'll still have the rest of the weekend and the evenings,' June pointed out.

'Will you meet us from school?' enquired Shirley.

'Every day,' promised June, 'and I'll have Nora and Granddad with me.'

'And Uncle Alan?' asked Belinda hopefully.

'You'd better ask him,' suggested June, turning to him. 'But he does have to go to work.'

'I'm sure I can arrange things so that I can be at the school gate when you come out,' he told her.

This cheered both the children.

'Let's go and do some more dancing!' cried Shirley.

'Yeah!' added her echo.

And they all trooped back inside the hall.

'About that talk you were suggesting,' began Alan.

'That'll have to wait until they've all gone to bed tonight,' June whispered.

All the major structural work at Gullscombe Manor was done. Just the finishing touches were left to do before they opened for business at Easter: some of the decorating and the furnishings and fittings. June and her father and Nora were being accommodated in the rooms that were ready, albeit that the furnishings weren't complete.

What was to be the main visitors' lounge was more or less complete. It was a large, elegant room with huge bay windows, velvet curtains in a soft orange shade, wood-panelled walls, russet-patterned carpet and plenty of soft seating and subdued lighting. They'd had central heating installed throughout the building but had also had the original ironwork fireplace restored in the main lounge.

It was in this room, around midnight that same night, sitting either side of the dying embers of a log fire, that June told Alan everything.

'That was why I left,' she said in conclusion. 'Not because I didn't love you but because I didn't want to deprive you of the chance to have children. I just couldn't bring myself to tell you the truth. When you followed me to London, I had to pretend I didn't love you because I wanted you to give up all hope of my coming back so that you could get on with your life with someone else.'

He sat very still, his expression inscrutable. She felt physically ill with fear – sick and giddy – because she wanted him back so much, but only if he still wanted her, knowing the truth. It was expecting a lot of any man and she wouldn't blame him for not having her back after what she'd done. But it was the only way they could go forward together.

'I feel so hurt, June,' he said at last, looking at her with a grim expression.

'I'm sure you must do,' she said. 'I'm not proud of what happened. But I was just a young girl and I didn't have any power over the situation.'

'I'm not talking about that,' he was quick to amend with emphasis. 'I'm referring to the fact that you didn't trust me enough to confide in me about all the terrible things that had happened to you.' He looked at her sadly, shaking his head. 'To keep it all to yourself and then just go off like that, leaving me worried and wondering what I'd done wrong . . .'

'It was unforgivable, I know.' She bit her lip so hard it hurt. 'But I just couldn't tell you the truth, Alan, I was too ashamed to tell anyone. I kept it all locked up inside until it all came pouring out to Daisy one night.'

'You couldn't possibly know how I felt after you left.'

'I think I can because I was equally as devastated,' she told him. 'Looking back on it, it was crazy. But leaving seemed like the only decent thing to do at that time. You were pushing for us to take medical advice when I already knew the reason we couldn't have a child. Had I known before we got married that I wasn't going to be able to get pregnant I would never have married you. I didn't want to stop you having kids.'

'And it never occurred to you, I suppose, that I married you because you were the woman I loved, not because I wanted a baby-making machine.'

'Come on, Alan, you were dead keen for us to have a baby when we'd been married for a while,' she reminded him. 'You must admit that.'

'Yes, I did want us to have a family, I admit it. It's a natural thing and I'm not going to deny it,' was his candid reply. 'But I didn't want children more than I wanted you as my wife.'

'Are you speaking in the past tense?'

'No,' he said. 'The same thing still applies. If it isn't possible for us to have kids, I can accept that.'

She couldn't believe how lucky she was. 'Oh, Alan,' she said, smiling.

He gave her a sharp look. 'There is a condition, though,' he began sternly.

'Oh, dear,' she uttered nervously, waiting for him to go on.

'There are to be no more secrets between us.' He looked very grave.

'There won't be—'

'I'm serious about this, June,' he cut in grimly. 'I need to know that you'll tell me in future when there's a problem. I can't cope unless I can have your word on this.'

'I promise.'

'Good. Now that that's settled, can we be a couple again?' he asked with a hesitant smile. 'Will you move into Gullscombe Manor on a permanent basis, not just as a temporary guest?'

'Try stopping me,' she beamed.

'And as we're already married you can move in right away,' he suggested.

'I'll have to go back to London to clear up a few things, give my notice in at work and so on,' she said. 'But, yes, I can move in tonight, if you like.'

'Oh, yes,' he grinned, and as though of one mind they rose and moved towards each other.

'When you said you wanted me to tell you anything at all that's worrying me, did you mean everything?' she asked him later.

'Absolutely everything,' Alan confirmed.

'In that case, I have to tell you that there's one aspect of moving back to Devon that I'm not happy about.'

'What's that?'

'Being so far away from my father and Nora,' June explained. 'I don't want to leave Dad because I've only just found him and was enjoying getting to know him properly, and Nora because she's a true friend. She's already lost Daisy and the girls; with me gone as well she's going to be so lonely. I promised both her and Daisy that I would never leave them without a home so I'll have to work something out so that Nora's got somewhere to live.' She thought about this. 'I'll sell the house and get a flat or something for her because I won't leave her homeless.'

'And the fact that you're going to do the right thing by her doesn't make you feel any better?' he guessed.

'No, not really. The thought of leaving her and Dad makes me want to weep. We've all become so close, you see,' she told him. 'It's spoiling things for me a bit.'

He pondered the question for a while. 'Well, we can't have our reunion spoiled, can we? Not when the problem can be easily solved,' he said mysteriously.

Gullscombe Manor Hotel was ready to open in March. The rooms were all furnished, the cocktail bar fitted, an alcohol licence obtained and they were fully booked for Easter, following an extensive national advertising campaign.

Both Nora and Lionel had jumped at the chance of moving to Devon and joining the team at the hotel. Lionel was in his element looking after the grounds and doing any small maintenance jobs that didn't need an expert from outside. Nora's sharp brain made her a natural for the office, June was in reception and Daisy was in charge of the waiting staff. Jack and Alan were at the helm as joint managing directors. Versatility was of the essence here. They all worked as a team and helped out wherever they were needed in the hotel, regardless of job titles.

Daisy and Jack and the girls lived in the renovated gardener's cottage in the grounds, June and Alan were in an attic flat while Nora and Lionel both had rooms at the back of the house. The family atmosphere was strong among this group.

The children thrived in the healthy environment with so much space to run and play, and a more personal atmosphere at the village school than they'd been used to in London. Daisy was able to work flexible hours that fitted in with their routine and they always knew where to find her if she was on duty after school hours.

All ideas were discussed and suggestions welcomed. Daisy's brain wave of having a reception in the new bar of the hotel just prior to its opening, for local businessmen and other hoteliers in the area and the local press, was greeted with approval by them all. So the invitations went out and the acceptances came pouring in. They were planning a prestigious event and were all very excited.

When there was no response at all to one particular invitation, however, June decided to take action . . .

'You,' gasped Irene Masters one afternoon when she answered a knock at the door to find June standing on the step. Being out of season she'd guessed she'd find her mother-in-law at home. 'I didn't think you'd ever have the nerve to show your face here again. I suppose Alan sent you.'

'Not at all. He doesn't even know I'm here,' she informed her in an even tone.

'Why have you come then?' she demanded, looking at June with hostility.

'I need to talk to you and Gerald.'

'Well, we don't want to speak to you.'

'Look, it really is important or I wouldn't have come, so may I come in, please? It won't take long.' This was a much more confident June than the one who used to inwardly quiver in Irene's formidable presence. 'Just ten minutes or so . . .'

Irene tutted and sighed, then with seething irritation she ushered June into the living room, a lavishly appointed chamber with deep-pile carpet and lace-curtained bay windows overlooking the sea. Gerald was sitting in an armchair reading the newspaper.

'Well, well, you're quite a stranger,' he said, looking up in surprise as June entered the room; he was noticeably less hostile towards her than his wife.

She nodded. 'How have you been, Gerald?' she asked politely.

'Not so bad, thanks.' He squinted at her over the top of his spectacles. 'We heard that you and Alan were back together.'

'The local grapevine is still in good working order then.'

'That's enough chatter,' intervened Irene, throwing June an icy stare. 'Just say what you have to say and leave us in peace.'

June fixed her with a steady gaze. It felt so good not to be afraid of her. 'We have a mutual dislike of each other, and that's one thing we do agree on. Right?'

Irene nodded. Gerald made no comment.

'But we all care about Alan,' continued June. 'Well, I assume, as his parents, you must feel something for him even if you do have a funny way of showing it.'

This enraged Irene. 'How dare you?' she exploded. 'I won't be insulted in my own house.'

'I've come here to ask you to come to the reception we're having at Gullscombe Manor on Friday night,' she went on as though Irene hadn't spoken. 'You haven't replied to our invitation which probably means that you intend to hurt Alan by staying away.'

'Whether we go or not is our business,' snapped Irene. 'It has nothing to do with you.'

'I'm Alan's wife, which means it's everything to do with me,' June asserted. 'I'm not prepared to stand by and see him get hurt. Don't you think you've done enough of that already?'

'I think you'll find the boot's on the other foot there,' objected Irene. 'How do you think we felt when he told us he wanted to leave the family business?'

'Alan didn't do that to hurt you. He just needed to do something for himself and I admire him for it,' June replied.

'Yes, well, you're not a parent, are you? So you can't possibly know what it feels like to have your only son turn his back on you,' Irene went on.

'From what I've heard it was you who turned your back on him,' June corrected. 'You wanted to keep him at your beck and call indefinitely, and when he acted like a grown-up and showed some initiative, you were mean-spirited enough to cut him out of your life altogether.'

'We gave him what he was owed.'

'This isn't about money.' June was becoming heated. 'This is about Alan's right to make something of himself as a person as well as someone's son. It's a normal human desire. Anyway, you left him with

299

no choice. You wouldn't give him the respect he needed here so he had to break away.'

'I want you to leave—' Irene began.

'Not until you've heard me out.' June was adamant. 'Alan hasn't said as much to me but I know that your approval of our new venture would mean a lot to him and I suspect that you're going to deprive him of that. That's why we haven't had a reply. You didn't even have the decency to decline the invitation. You're just going to let him keep on hoping that you'll be there and spoil it for him by not turning up on the night.'

'You don't know that,' was Irene's sharp response.

'I'm willing to bet on it.'

'He does actually want us to be there, then?' Gerald seemed pleased at the idea.

'Of course he wants you to be there. You're his parents, for goodness' sake, and you're important to him.' June paused, looking from one to the other, then continuing in a more conciliatory manner, 'Look . . . his leaving the Cliff Head had nothing at all to do with his feelings for you.'

'You don't betray people you care about,' announced Irene.

'He didn't betray you.' Her voice rose with exasperation. 'I wasn't around at the time but I know Alan and I know that that would be the last thing he intended. From what I can gather he was really upset about the rift between you. He didn't want it and still doesn't. He'd give a lot to be on good terms with you again.'

'Do you think we're enjoying it?' demanded Irene cuttingly. 'He's our only son, for heaven's sake.'

'And a son to be proud of, too. He's worked so hard to make a success of Gullscombe Manor,' June went on, 'serving in a pub to bring in money and organising all the renovations for the hotel at the same time. Both he and Jack have worked their socks off this past year or so. Between the lot of us we are going to make a success of it.'

'You don't need us then, do you?' said Irene miserably.

'No, we don't need you,' was June's frank response. 'And your being at the reception on Friday night will make no difference to the success of the hotel because that's going to happen anyway. But it would make Alan so happy if you were there.' She paused, feeling an unexpected surge of pity for them. 'Look, you've made your own success with the Cliff Head, now it's Alan's turn to shine. So why not come along to the party and give him your support? It will mean so much to him, even if you just stay for an hour.' Another pause and she heard herself say, 'I'd like you to be there too.'

Gerald looked at Irene. 'What do you think?' he asked.

'I'll give it some thought,' she said, looking at June. 'That's all I'm prepared to say.'

'Fair enough,' agreed June, and allowed Gerald to show her to the door without further comment. She'd done what she could. It was up to them now. But she hoped they would find it in their hearts to be there because Alan's happiness was the most important thing in her life.

Daisy had never been to anything as posh as the reception before, and she was enjoying every moment. Having always, until recently, had clothes that were years old and from a market stall, it was fun being able to have nice things and she felt good in a turquoise figure-hugging cocktail dress with a boat-shaped neck, which she was wearing with high-heeled shoes. With the hotel still being in its infancy, they couldn't afford to be reckless with money but, as Jack's wife, the standard of living for her and her daughters had risen dramatically. And as she worked hard alongside him, she wasn't troubled by the independent spirit she'd developed after so many years on her own.

'If my waitress friends at the hotel where I used to work could see me now,' she said to June as they sipped champagne together in between mingling with the guests, 'they'd be green with envy.'

'Full of admiration, more like,' corrected June, who was much more used to this sort of thing than her sister. She thought Daisy had coped brilliantly with the new etiquette required of her in her position as the wife of one of the principles. Making the transition from waitress to management couldn't have been easy but she'd slipped into it as though born to it.

This evening they had brought in their newly appointed staff to look after the guests so that they were free to socialise.

'I could get used to this sort of thing,' Daisy told her sister.

'That's just as well because there'll be more of it in the future,' said June.

'We've all been working so hard to get the place ready, we haven't had the chance to be glamorous.'

'You've made up for that tonight, though,' complimented June, looking approvingly at her sister's radiant face glowing with a dusting of make-up, her hair worn loose and casual.

'You look nice too.'

June was wearing a red satin dress with a low neck and short sleeves and a gently flared skirt, her hair taken back into a pleat.

'Thanks, kid.' She looked around to see Nora and Lionel engaged in conversation with the landlord of the Gullscombe Arms and his wife. Nora had splashed out on a green dress and jacket, her hair cut shorter now and properly styled for the occasion while Lionel looked spruce in a suit. 'It all seems to be going very well. Everyone seems to be enjoying themselves.'

301

Daisy nodded. 'I still have to pinch myself to make sure that this is all really happening to me,' she said. 'It's such a different life from before. And the best part is that we're all here together. The thought of living so far away from you all was spoiling it for me when I got married.'

'I think we're all relieved about that.'

'You and Alan seem to be getting on well,' Daisy remarked casually.

'Better than ever now that everything's out in the open,' June told her. 'Alan's changed too, now that his parents aren't pulling his strings.'

Daisy sighed. 'Everything's so perfect, I keep thinking that it's too good to last.'

'That's what years of trouble and hardship have done to you. Fearing the worst becomes a habit, I suppose. But you'll get more confident in time. Nothing's going to go wrong, Daisy. This is your life now, yours and the girls', here in Gullscombe Bay with Jack and the rest of us.'

'Yeah, I know.'

Jack appeared at Daisy's side, looking dashing in a dark suit and crisp white shirt. 'Come on, you two, get mingling. That's enough of all this sisterly nattering,' he joshed. 'This might seem like a night off but you are actually working. Socialising with all the local business people. Putting Gullscombe Manor Hotel on the map so that if they ever need a function or a conference, they'll immediately think of us.'

'All right, slave driver,' smiled Daisy. 'We were just taking a little break.'

'Just kidding,' he grinned. 'You carry on chatting if it makes you happy.'

Noticing that June was looking around anxiously, Daisy asked her if anything was wrong.

'Some people I was hoping would turn up haven't done so, that's all,' she explained.

'There's bound to be a few who can't make it.'

June nodded.

'Anyway, enough of all this family rabbiting,' said Jack with a hearty grin. 'I must go and fly the flag for our hotel.'

Daisy watched him go, smiling affectionately after him. Nora and Lionel drifted over and the four of them talked about how well everything was going.

Jack appeared at June's side a little while later. 'Your missing guests have just turned up,' he informed her with a knowing look.

'Irene and Gerald?'

'The very ones,' he confirmed. 'Alan's talking to them in reception.'

'Thank goodness for that.' She shot him a look because she hadn't told anyone about her visit to Irene and Gerald. 'But how did you know it was them I was talking about? Have you added mind-reading to all your other talents?'

'Just a lucky guess. You and I have been friends a long time, remember,' he said, cocking his head and winking at her. 'I was hoping they'd turn up too, for Alan's sake. So now that they have, we can relax and enjoy ourselves.'

She nodded cheerfully.

'There's a couple of people over there looking a bit lost,' said Daisy, glancing across the room. 'I'll go over and make them feel welcome.'

'You're a natural for this sort of thing, a real asset,' was Jack's tender reply

Chapter Nineteen

Their first season surpassed all expectations and the hotel was fully booked right through until September. It was hectic, fulfilling and, at times, fraught with problems. Apart from the minor mishaps that arise in any business, a summer flu bug gave them a major staff shortage in the middle of high season, and a storm left them without electricity thus threatening to leave the guests without their evening meal. Fortunately, the power was restored at the eleventh hour and dinner was delayed rather than non-existent. But the experience was a salutary lesson and they had their own generator installed to avoid similar inconvenience in the future.

With a great deal of hard work, flexibility and an unflagging sense of humour on the part of the management team, they overcame these and other crises without the guests perceiving so much as a hint of the chaos that reigned behind the scenes.

Although they weren't planning to close for the winter, there were mixed opinions about Alan's idea of putting on a special Christmas programme. Mainly because they weren't sure if there would be sufficient bookings to make a party of it, Christmas being traditionally a time for hearth and home. In the end they decided to test the market by advertising, with the idea of not taking any bookings at all if there wasn't enough interest to make it financially viable and to create a festive atmosphere.

But the idea of a work-free Christmas with log fires, lashings of festive food, Santa Claus, a Boxing Day treasure hunt and various other social events appealed to a lot of people and the hotel was fully booked for Christmas and the New Year. Hosting the event was exhausting but enjoyable too, and a friendly atmosphere prevailed throughout the hotel.

In the quiet times during the winter they kept business ticking over by hosting conferences and seminars as well as keeping the restaurant open to non-residents all year. They also hosted special weekends for hobby societies and specialist groups. They had such enthusiasts as ballroom dancers, keep fitters, aspiring artists and writers, all of whom provided their own programme of events so only required food and accommodation. The introduction of the Gullscombe Manor Special

Cabaret Weekends with dinner dances and first-class entertainment proved to be enormously popular too.

The following year, as their second frantic summer season advanced towards its end, they were quietly confident that their hotel was becoming established.

'I reckon we'll all be ready for the pace to slow down a bit when the busy season finally ends,' Daisy said to Jack one morning in September.

'You're not kidding,' he agreed. 'We're all shattered.'

They were finishing breakfast in the kitchen of their cottage, a warm and cosy, oak-beamed room where the four of them ate their meals, talked things over and generally congregated. A shaft of autumn sunlight was shining through the window and lying cheerily across the corner of the solid wooden table that used to adorn the kitchen at Seagull Cottage. This house wasn't yet such a triumph to DIY as the other one because Jack hadn't had time to get busy on it. But it had had a certain amount of refurbishment and was comfortable enough and very pretty with stone-faced walls and leaded-light windows. At the moment Daisy and Jack were enjoying a quiet few minutes alone together because the girls had finished their breakfast and were upstairs getting ready for school.

'We won't have time to take it easy for long, though, will we? Because no sooner will things have slowed down after the summer season than it'll be time to organise the Christmas programme,' she pointed out.

He nodded. 'The hotel certainly doesn't give us time to get fat and lazy,' he observed.

'I don't mind, though,' she told him. 'I enjoy being busy.'

'No regrets then?'

'You're joking.' She was emphatic. 'This is the best thing that's ever happened to me. Even apart from loving every minute of being married to you, I enjoy being part of a business. After all those years slogging away as a waitress, actually helping to run a hotel is really exciting.'

'Hard work, though.'

'Not half,' she agreed. 'It's certainly destroyed all my illusions about management having it easy.'

As they were finishing their coffee they heard the clunk of the letter box as the morning paper came through the door and dropped on to the mat.

'I'll get it, love,' offered Daisy. 'I've finished my coffee anyway.'

When she came back into the room, she was looking somewhat distracted.

'Something the matter?' he asked.

She handed him the newspaper.

'Blimey,' was his shocked response as he took in the violent scenes

306

on the front page of race riots in the Notting Hill Gate region of London. 'Thank God you're out of that area.'

'I never thought things would get so bad,' she told him. 'I've noticed a few reports in the paper of racial attacks around there this past couple of weeks, but it seems to have escalated into a full-scale battle now.'

'This is shocking!' he exclaimed, reading on. 'They're fighting with anything they can lay their hands on. Cars have been torched, people knifed.'

'Let's have another look at the paper, please, Jack?' she asked with growing anxiety.

He handed it back to her and she read of a place she didn't recognise as the one she'd lived in for most of her adult life. This was a war zone, a place of petrol bombs, stabbings and fights with broken bottles, knives, sticks, iron bars and bicycle chains. Ordinary, decent people were confined to home because they were too afraid to leave their houses. In Paddington a house had been set on fire by a petrol bomb. 'It makes me want to weep,' Daisy said, her eyes fixed on the newsprint and pictures of policemen struggling with rioters. 'Who would have thought it would come to this, eh? I mean, trouble had been brewing for ages before I left there. Street fights between the Teds and the West Indians were par for the course around there. You couldn't not be aware of the racial tension if you lived there, even if you weren't involved, because it was all around you. But I didn't realise that feelings were running that high, probably because it was outside of my circle. Live and let live has always been my motto. And you only get to the heart of the culture of an area in so far as it affects yourself, don't you?'

'In a big crowded place like London that's probably true,' Jack agreed. 'Around here you only have to have a cross word with someone and the whole village knows about it.'

'Thinking about it, though,' she went on thoughtfully, 'the bad atmosphere was getting worse towards the end of my time there.'

'You must be glad you're away from it all.'

'I wouldn't want to still be living there, but I'll always be a Londoner at heart, wherever I live,' she told him. 'I have a special feeling for the place no matter how rough things get there. It has nothing to do with buildings or living conditions. It's an emotional thing. There's something about the place I can't shake off.'

'Oh.' He looked disappointed.

'Don't get all upset,' she said affectionately. 'Here is where I want to be. My home now is wherever you are.'

'That's all right then.' He seemed reassured.

'But I still miss London from time to time,' she continued. 'Don't you?'

'Yeah, course I do, sometimes. But not as much as you do, I suspect.' He gave a casual shrug. 'You know how attached I am to this part of the world.'

She raised her eyes, grinning. 'I couldn't fail to know that, and I'm very fond of it too,' she told him. 'But I think I'll always need to go back to London every so often to keep in touch with my roots, such as they are.'

'I can understand that.'

'And while we're on the subject of London,' she went on to say, remembering something, 'I've been meaning to tell you that June has asked me if I'll go with her when she goes to see the gynaecologist in Harley Street in a couple of months' time.'

'Has she got to go again?' He seemed surprised. 'Nothing wrong, is there?'

'Nothing new,' she told him. 'Still the same problem, the lack of a pregnancy.'

'I thought that was all in the lap of the gods now that she and Alan have both had tests and know that there's nothing wrong with either of them.'

'It is. There's no medical reason why June can't get pregnant. She's been given all sorts of advice about the right sort of diet, and told the most fertile times during her menstrual cycle and so on to increase her chances,' she informed him. 'This next appointment is just a follow-up.'

'I see.'

'I don't know if there's anything else they can do but if there is, June will jump at it. She'll do anything to have a baby, though she does try to accept that it might never happen.'

'Is Alan not going with her to the specialist this time?' queried Jack.

'He will if she wants him to,' Daisy replied. 'But she seems to want me to go with her instead. It's a woman thing, I think. She wants to make a shopping trip of it as it will be so near to Christmas.'

'She's still desperate to have a baby then?'

'God, yes. Everything's perfect except for that one thing. She and Alan are happy, the hotel's doing well and we're all here together. It's just that one thing that's spoiling it for her. And she knows that Alan would love a child, even though he keeps telling her not to worry about it.'

'Still, she's getting medical advice from someone who really knows their stuff.'

'Exactly. When she finally plucked up the courage to see a doctor, Alan insisted on the best, and this one is a specialist in fertility problems.' Daisy paused, looking at Jack. 'Anyway, love, do you mind if I go with her? You'll have to look after the girls but I'll only be away for a couple of days. And Nora will give you a hand.'

'Of course I don't mind,' he was quick to assure her. 'It'll be a nice break for you.' He paused, glancing towards the paper. 'As long as you keep away from Notting Hill Gate. It's too dangerous there at the moment.'

'We're not going until early December,' she told him. 'The trouble will be over long before then. The police have got it under control now, according to the paper.'

'Yeah, I expect you're right.'

'June suggested that we stay in the hotel where she used to work,' she went on. 'It's very central.'

'Good idea,' he approved. 'You go with my blessing and I hope you have a lovely time.'

'And in the meantime, I must take the girls to school.'

'I'd offer to take them for you but I know you enjoy going yourself.'

'You bet. One of the highlights of my day is that walk to the village school, especially on a glorious morning like this,' she said, glancing towards the window through which the sea could be seen beyond the hotel gardens. The cottage was tucked away at the far side of the tennis courts with just enough distance for its inhabitants to enjoy their privacy.

'On your way then, woman,' he joshed in the easy way they had with each other. 'Take your daughters to school and leave the old man to read the paper in peace.'

'You're gorgeous, do you know that?'

'You're only saying that because it's true,' he joked.

She brushed her lips against his hair then headed for the stairs. 'Time for school, you two,' she called up to the girls. 'So get yourselves down here sharpish.'

The West End of London was a seething mass of people when the Rivers sisters joined the crowds in Oxford Street one Friday afternoon in December. They'd got an early train from Devon and, as June's appointment wasn't until the next morning, they had the rest of today free for shopping, which they entered into with gusto.

'I don't know how we're going to get all this stuff back to Devon,' said June as they took a break for tea in Selfridges, piling their store bags on the floor beside them.

'We'll manage,' said Daisy, sinking her teeth into a buttered toasted teacake. 'Being in London at this time of the year is too good an opportunity to miss. I've certainly made inroads into my Christmas shopping list. I got some lovely things for the girls.'

'I've done well too,' said June, sipping her tea.

'That's a smashing wristwatch you got for Alan.'

'I think he'll be pleased.'

They fell into a comfortable silence. 'Aren't you going to eat your teacake?' Daisy enquired eventually as she made short work of hers.

'No, I'm not all that hungry,' June told her. 'I shouldn't have bought it.'

'It won't go to waste with me around,' grinned Daisy. 'But you ought to have something to keep your strength up if we're going to do some more shopping.'

June made a face. 'I hate to be a wet blanket but would you mind if I call it a day now?' she asked.

'Oh?' Daisy was surprised because they'd both been looking forward to doing their Christmas shopping. She squinted at her sister, noticing that she was looking rather pale. 'Are you OK?'

'I'm fine but I'm feeling a bit shattered after the early start this morning,' she explained. 'I'd like to go back to the hotel when I've finished my tea, if you don't mind. But you stay and do some more shopping if you like and I'll see you back at the hotel later.'

June hadn't been her usual self since they'd left home; she'd been quiet and preoccupied, Daisy thought. Probably had the doctor's appointment on her mind. 'I think I will wander around the shops for a little while longer,' she said. 'Though I won't be able to carry much more.'

'I'm sure you'll be able to manage a few more packages for those daughters of yours,' grinned June.

'Hello, Jack, it's Daisy.'

'Hello, love.' His voice was warm with pleasure and surprise to hear from her. 'Are you enjoying yourself?'

'I'm have a smashing time,' she told him. 'I'm just calling to find out if everything's OK.'

'Everything's fine.'

'The girls all right?'

'Good as gold,' he said. 'But you should be concentrating on enjoying yourself, not worrying about us.'

'I've got a few minutes to spare while June's in with the doctor so I thought I'd give you a call,' she explained. 'Just wanted to hear your voice.'

'It's lovely to hear yours. I've missed you.'

'I've missed you too,' she confessed. 'But I can't stay long because I'm in a phone box and the money I put in won't last long and I've no more change. I'll see you tonight.'

'I'll be at the station to meet you.'

'Can't wait.'

'Me neither.'

'Bye, then,' she said quickly as the coins were used and the line went dead.

She realised that she was smiling as she replaced the receiver. Just a few words with Jack was all it took to lift her spirits, she thought, as she crossed the road to the consultant's rooms. She'd been feeling a bit tense before the call. She hadn't wanted to worry Jack with it, but the trip had been rather a strain because June had been in such a strange mood. Her longing for a baby was really beginning to drag her down and Daisy was worried about her.

The waiting room was a far cry from the sort of doctor's waiting room Daisy was used to, she thought, as she went in and sat down on a sofa. Instead of hard chairs and well-thumbed, out-of-date magazines, here the seats were soft and the reading material new and of the thick glossy variety with photographs of beautiful homes and gardens.

She was immersed in a picture of a luxurious bedroom when the consultant's door opened and June came out. Oh Lord, she thought when she saw that her sister's face was wet with tears. She must have had bad news.

'June, love,' she said in concern, going towards her.

'Daisy, I've got the most amazing news,' she said shakily.

'Oh?' Daisy was wary.

'I'm pregnant.'

'What!'

'Isn't it wonderful?' She was smiling now and Daisy realised that the tears she'd seen were those of joy.

'But I thought . . .' The details could wait until later, she decided, hugging her sister, tears springing to her own eyes. 'That's the best news ever. Congratulations.'

Because their train didn't leave until late that afternoon, they had time to spare after lunch so decided on a nostalgia trip to Notting Hill Gate. Leaving their luggage at the hotel, they headed for Marble Arch tube station.

'I thought you'd seemed quiet ever since we left home,' remarked Daisy on the train, returning to the subject that was filling both their minds. 'I assumed you were fretting because you couldn't get pregnant when in actual fact you were preoccupied because you thought you might be. You're a dark horse.'

'I was dying to tell you but afraid that if I actually said the words out loud I would somehow be tempting providence. I know it's silly but I was scared to hope after waiting so long,' she explained. 'My periods have never been regular so being late is nothing new for me. I've been feeling a bit sick but that could have been anything.'

'I thought you were nervous about the doctor's appointment and that's why you didn't want much to eat.'

'That was part of it but I was feeling queasy too,' she said. 'Anyway, I told the consultant all this and he examined me and gave me the good news.' She shook her head, smiling. 'I still can't believe it.'

'You will do once you start expanding,' laughed Daisy, getting up as the train rumbled into Notting Hill Gate station.

It was a typical December afternoon: cold and still, a smoky haze hanging over everything. In contrast to the brightly lit West End shops and all the colourful Christmas decorations, the streets looked grey and dismal as they walked from the station to Larby Gardens, through run-down areas juxtaposed with pockets of affluence so characteristic of London. Passing through a shabby neighbourhood with the smell of poverty about it, it seemed to Daisy, who could now view the area from a broader perspective, having been away, that this bit of London had been forgotten by the affluent era.

In Larby Gardens, they stood outside their old house, staring at it like sightseers on their first trip to the capital. To Daisy's surprise she found the experience curiously unemotional, though they had had some good times there. Portobello market was as vibrantly vulgar as ever and evoked happy memories for them both. It also reminded Daisy of Nat, but she felt nothing more than a moment of sadness as she remembered the humiliating ending of a relationship that had once meant so much to her. He was her past, the same as this city. She would always want to come here to visit but she belonged in Devon now with Jack, and felt able to draw a line under her life here.

Thinking of her life in Gullscombe, a warm glow spread through her. As well as having her beloved Jack with her, she had all the other people who mattered most to her. The girls were thriving and her dad was happy and settled. She smiled, thinking of him and Nora, who were great pals and spent most of their spare time together. They sometimes reminded Daisy of an old married couple, the way they teased each other and joked around, but there had been no talk of anything other than friendship. It might change at some time in the future – who could say? And if it didn't they still had something really special.

On the way back to the station, snatches of jazz and calypso music drifted out of the drinking clubs. The pubs were closing after the lunchtime session and people were straggling out and talking in groups in the street. A gang of Teds were congregated outside a seedy-looking café with filthy net curtains at the windows.

'I wonder if they're plotting another riot,' said June.

'Now, June, we don't know for sure that the Teds started the riots,' Daisy pointed out in a tone of gentle admonition.

'I didn't think there was any doubt about it,' was June's answer. 'That's what we've been led to believe.'

'According to the papers they were to blame but Dad reckons the Teds were just convenient scapegoats,' Daisy told her. 'He used to listen to what was being said in the pubs when we lived there. They were at the centre of the riots, no one can deny that, but it might not

312

have been all their fault. Dad said they were used by the fascists to stir up racial trouble. The Teds jumped at the chance of a fight and got all the blame – that's Dad's theory, anyway.'

While they'd been talking some black youths had come out of a West Indian café and the atmosphere became threatening as the two gangs walked towards each other.

'Whatever the truth of it, the trouble obviously isn't over,' observed June. 'The riots have finished but the fighting hasn't.'

'You're right,' said Daisy, and they hurried away from a brawl in the making.

'It's quite frightening,' commented June. 'A relief to be away from there.'

'I'll say,' agreed Daisy. 'I'm glad to have got the girls out of that area before all the big trouble started. They love it in Gullscombe with Jack and me and the rest of the gang.'

'You only have to look at them to see that,' June remarked.

'Of course, your baby will know nothing of living in a place like this, will it?'

'Neither will it have to suffer any of the problems we had, Daisy.'

'No. Thank goodness.'

'Still, it turned out all right for us in the end, didn't it?' June reminded her cheerfully, linking arms with her sister. 'And the future is bright for us all.'

'Especially now that you've had such good news,' said Daisy.

'Yes,' June smiled, and they walked to the tube station, arm in arm, glad to be together and going home.